DEALBREAKER

ALSO BY L. X. BECKETT

Gamechanger

DEALBREAKER

L. X. BECKETT

A TOM DOHERTY ASSOCIATES BOOK • NEW YORK

DEALBREAKER

Copyright © 2020 by A. M. Dellamonica

A Tor Book
Published by Tom Doherty Associates
120 Broadway
New York, NY 10271

www.tor-forge.com

Tor® is a registered trademark of Macmillan Publishing Group, LLC.

The Library of Congress Cataloging-in-Publication Data
is available upon request.

ISBN 978-1-250-16529-9 (hardcover)
ISBN 978-1-250-16527-5 (ebook)

Our books may be purchased in bulk for promotional, educational, or business
use. Please contact your local bookseller or the Macmillan Corporate and
Premium Sales Department at 1-800-221-7945, extension 5442, or by email at
MacmillanSpecialMarkets@macmillan.com.

First Edition: January 2021

Printed in the United States of America

0 9 8 7 6 5 4 3 2 1

FOR ALICIA AND JOE ENGLISH. WE'LL GET TO THAT DAMNED OPERA SOMEDAY.

PART 1

TRUST EXERCISES

I just know that any time I undertake a case, I'm apt to run into some kind of a trap.

—Carolyn Keene, *The Clue of the Broken Locket*

CHAPTER 1

The event the Feral$_5$ called their superversary was a *Surprise* party, meaning that everyone was cosplaying Royal British Navy personnel, and the simulated ship they were aboard was, literally, HMS *Surprise*. Looking around, Frankie Barnes could hardly see a meter of deck where she and Maud hadn't had sex.

The anniversary party was an intimate affair—thirty or so of the pack's collected in-laws and a selection of @CloseFriends. Their packmate Jermaine was up near the wheel, addressing their guests. He wasn't overly keen on the original *Master and Commander* fandom, and so had dressed as a Chinese Fleet Admiral from the 2079 reboot of the franchise.

Jerm's speech covered all the things you usually heard at such events: warm words about Maud and Frankie falling into a big-time, full-on, hearts-and-flowers romance, about Maud making an enormous leap of faith by becoming Frankie's primary and marrying into their unorthodox family bubble. "None of the Feral$_4$ knew we were incomplete, not really, not until she joined us."

All true . . . and the crowd was lapping it up.

Maud herself was turned out in the ragged naturalist's gear of the *Surprise* doctor, complete with red-tinted hair and sideburns. The first time she'd seen this particular cosplay, Frankie had found the look compellingly sexy and thoroughly odd. Maud was about as far from a natural redhead as it got. She could have stepped

right out of a historical sim set in the EastEuro steppes—one of
those wildly popular pony-racing sims about the Mongol Derby,
maybe—with her jet hair, sturdy limbs, and a round face.

As usual, she was visibly ill at ease about being the center of
attention.

Frankie was about to beeline for her beloved when their other
packmates fell into step on either side of her.

Ember Qaderi's toon wore the half-starved body and the robes
of a Persian prisoner of war, also from *MC2079*. As Frankie took
this in, he attempted a clumsy, loose-limbed pirouette.

"You couldn't chill about the old British Empire for one afternoon?" Frankie subbed.

"Colonization's a freshly relevant issue in this day and age,"
Ember said airily. "Besides, I had to balance out Babs."

"Fair," Frankie signed. Their feral fifth had wrapped her base
avatar, a tortoiseshell cat, in full dress uniform as Admiral
Nelson . . . or some cartoon femme version thereof.

As Jermaine's speech built to its big finish, the three of them
slid between the assembled partygoers, closing on Maud. Everyone raised their glasses and followed Jerm in a very royal round of
shouting "Huzzah!"

Frankie offered an arm and Maud eased into her embrace, fitting snugly against her, two spaceships docking. Ember blew her
a moji kiss, while Babs generated a purr that went down into the
deck and came up as a vibration underfoot.

Contentment—bit of a rarity, that—suffused Frankie. This had
been a good idea.

The whole pack was in the spotlight now. Jermaine strode
down to join them, catching Frankie and Ember by the hands,
completing the family bubble while their gathered guests signed
hearts, threw confetti and petals, and made *Awww!* noises.

"Hang in there," Frankie subbed to Maud. "They'll all swing
by to throw a few congrats at our feet. And then . . ."

Maud gave her a lascivious grin.

"And *then*," she agreed.

"Nice speech, Jerm," Babs said. "You oughta go into soap-boxing."

"I've got as much job as I can handle, thanks."

"He's already overachieving," Maud said, enunciating each word as precisely as if she were cutting diamonds. "If you want speeching, Babs, take it up yourself."

"I'm on strike, remember?"

One of Jermaine's fathers walked straight into this bit of banter. He'd disapproved of his son marrying into a bubble containing artificially intelligent beings, so the smile he tried to give them all now was curdled. It vanished altogether when the family's other sapp, Babs's codefather Crane, walked up in a butler costume, proffering a tray of champagne flutes.

"Thanks, Crane." Frankie took two flutes, passed one to Jermaine's father, and set about distracting him with an earnest monologue about Ember's latest theoretical maths breakthrough. "If we Solakinder manage to open a seven-wormhole network," she enthused, "it'll be down to Ember. And we could never have done it without Jermaine pioneering the new implant tech—"

Char Mwangi *tut*ted. "You make it sound like Jermaine grew the implant tish himself. He is but one member of the innovation team."

Frankie gave that bit of prosocial wanking the very tiny nod it deserved. "And now he's in the thick of the quantum-comms experiment. You must be so proud!"

The elder seemed to thaw a little. Crane moved on, buttling in barely legal defiance of the sapps' work stoppage.

A gust of simulated wind caught the ship's sails, crisping the fabric out with a gratifying snap. *Surprise* surged into the waves. Up at the wheel, Frankie's fellow test pilot, Hung Chan, had booted up a tutorial on the rudiments of ancient seafaring. It was a far cry from flying FTL ships or planting wormholes, but his expression was blissful.

Frankie laid a hand on the small of her back and sent him a quick, secret text, via the pilot's augment in her sacrum: *All good, Pupper?*

*Any happier, Cap'n, I'd be widdling on the deck! They're ador-
able, by the way.*

Who?

Your whole fam damly.

She sent thumbs-up and let her gaze rise above her friend,
where more of her in-laws—Ember's mothers, kitted out as usual
in licensed *Star Trek* gear—were high in the mainsail rigging.

Whole fam damly. She wondered, absently, if Hung was angling
for an offer to join the Ferals, maybe in some kind of little-brother
role. Though Jermaine would be attracted to him, inevitably.

She ran a thumb over the spyglass at her hip, triggering an in-
app purchase within the sim. In response, a pod of dolphins made
a spectacular, water-spraying leap, arraying themselves around
the ship's bow to cries of delight and applause.

"Such a gracious host," Maud murmured, fanning herself with
her straw hat.

Frankie offered up her best rogue's grin. "Who says I don't play
well with others?"

"We could get up a poll on that," Ember said. Jermaine snorted.

"Fuck you very much; the question was rhetorical."

"And *now* we're back on brand," Babs said.

"Sure, gang up on me. No wonder I spend half my time in deep
space—" An elbow to the ribs—Maud—cut her off.

The sim dolphins broke the sheet of the sea again, flinging di-
amond spray as they cut through the sunlit surface of the water.

The dolphins, the ship, and the party-goers were all illusory.
Not so that elbow, or the heat of Maud against Frankie's body.
The two of them were cuddled up in bed, out on the Surface, even
as their attention was deep in Sensorium.

Soon their guests would move on to other entertainments, and
they would come out of the sim entirely, and . . .

Maud startled, then raised a hand to her face, covering surprise
by stroking her sideburns. "There's your stepmother."

Rubi Whiting was indeed entering the sim from belowdecks.

This can't be good.

As if hearing her thought—reading it, more likely, as Frankie hadn't much of a poker face—Rubi opened with gestural moji, signs meaning *no news*. Most of their heart-to-hearts started this way: Rubi basically assuring her that nothing had happened to Gimlet, Frankie's wayward parent.

Relief momentarily unclenched her fists.

"Go." Maud gave her a nudge.

"Bollocks to that," Frankie said. "She's bringing work to a party."

"You don't *know* it's work."

"Don't I?"

"You'd be happy it was work if you weren't changing projects. Remind her it was her idea—"

"To demote me?"

"Be prosocial: say *transfer*."

Hung brought *Surprise* into a hard turn to starboard, and the ship's deck tilted. The cosplaying in-laws in the rigging reached down, fingers not quite reaching the fins of their dolphin escort. Frankie felt sun on her face, the solidity of her family around her. She caught a whiff of brine and woodsmoke.

"I'll be back." She kissed her packmate, separated herself reluctantly from the cluster of her family, and swaggered over to Rubi in best ship's captain fashion. Salute? Nah.

"Any word?" After all, *nobody's dead* hardly counted as a status update.

"Gimlet has extended their fact-finding mission." Rubi was running Diplomatic these days, and her toon wore an infestation of tags, notes showing her high position on the Worldsaver Leaderboard, her Cloudsight rating, and her personal value as a currency. The last was one of the many things that made her an oddity—Rubi had inadvertently spawned an economy of favors two decades earlier, during a long-ago political crisis. Now she had an assessed value, like a bank.

Frankie felt her eyes narrowing. "For how much longer?"

"I've no idea, Franks."

Rubi's fingerling dreadlocks showed a faint encroachment of grey. Cropped close at the left temple, a hexagonal grouping of the dreads—her trademark—was tipped with animated golden honeybees. On the Surface, she wore the same dreads, capped with carved wooden beads. She had long since given up playing sim premieres, but she still carried herself like a fighter.

"Then you're here to wish us well?" Frankie checked the perimeter icons in her HUD. In her lower peripheral was the number of people following their conversation in realtime. Eleven thousand; hardly anyone. "Happy Superversary, Ferals! I'm printing you a bottle of wine."

Rubi gave the smallest of headshakes. "Project Bootstrap is finalizing plans for the portal expansion."

"Opening Portals$_{6/7}$?" She signed the slash between the six and seven as she spoke the words—portals six seven—and her fingertips tingled as she sliced the air.

Frankie had been nine when the confederation of human and AI entities collectively referred to as the Solakinder were first contacted by offworlders. The aliens hadn't really said hello, not at first. They'd logged on to Sensorium's social networks, begun interfering with global politics, and then, when they got caught, asked—nicely, the first time—if Earth would like to join their greater intergalactic empire.

The answer, initially, had been a polite *No, thank you.* Not surprisingly, the offworlders had asked again, less nicely, earning themselves a response with a tone more in the region of *Piss off!*

It was easy to expect the asks would escalate. Possibly escalate all the way to invasion. And so Diplomatic, as led by Frankie's parents, had negotiated a costly devil's bargain.

If Earth wanted to maintain its independence without getting swallowed by the Exemplar races, as they called themselves, they would have to develop the technologies that had brought those races to their solar system. What's more, they had to invent all those #supertechs without any hints from the advanced races.

It was a noninterference rule, of sorts, with Earth as the culture the aliens were—supposedly—not interfering with. Privately, Frankie called it the *weaponized Prime Directive*.

So far, the Solakinder had opened a loop of five stable wormholes, expanding their footprint within the home solar system. Opening Portals$_{6/7}$ would put them within hopping distance of Alpha Centauri and an Exemplar portal there. And just in time, too.

Frankie felt a grin breaking across her face. She didn't see corresponding excitement on her stepmother's. "What's wrong?"

"It's faster than expected. Your transfer to Quantum Comms has been delayed—"

"Can't we push up the installation? Loop Maud in?"

Rubi shook her head. "Insufficient time to do the testing."

Frankie's mind raced. She'd agreed to the experiment that would patch Maud into the pilots' off-the-record comms so that the two of them could talk properly, off the record. "If they're rolling out the new portals, they'll need every augmented pilot they can get."

"Exactly," Rubi said. "You'll be ^{EM}bodying a pegasus out at Emerald Station. Overseeing the launch of Portal$_7$."

A twinge of disappointment. She'd hoped to be at Proxima Centauri. Still . . .

"So?" And then, reading Rubi's expression of concern: "Ember's maths are solid. It's not going to be that dangerous."

"You took the riskiest position when we expanded from three to five portals." Rubi thrust her hands into her pockets. "You don't have to jump at hazard duty again."

"If I don't, they'll assign Hung to Sneezy," Frankie said. "Kid's good. But."

Her stepmother shrugged. Unwilling to say more in a public transcript, no doubt.

You think something's going to go wrong. And if you think that, it's because . . .

"I'm right, aren't I?"

Rubi stared at her over the rim of a simulated glass of bubbly. Behind her, party guests were trying to figure out the mechanics of loading the *Surprise* deck cannons.

It had never seemed likely to Frankie that the offworlders would go from *Please give us your planet* to *Hand it over, kids!* to a simple *Gosh, we're sorry, we'll back off. Come play with us whenever you're ready.*

"You're right." Rubi ran a finger over the rim of her glass, letting that sit. And then adding, after too much pause, "If you opt out, Hung goes."

She meant that Frankie was right about someone sabotaging the Bootstrap Project.

All this time, you've been insisting I was paranoid.

Temper simmering, she glanced past Rubi to Maud.

"You made promises, Frankie. Keep them. Pull in your horns; play it safe."

"Maud will understand if I do one more mission."

"Are you sure?"

Hazard duty, again, and now even Diplomatic agreed there was actual hazard.

Dolphins broke the water near *Surprise,* chittering. The sailing ship was a fictional monument to a colonial power—and a reminder of all the damage it had done. Frankie looked at Ember, costumed in his starved-prisoner affect.

Rubi was waiting, face schooled to calmness. She had come already knowing what her wayward stepchild would say.

"I am not opting out of anything," Frankie told her. "If Sneezy's where the action is, Sneezy's where I'll be."

CHAPTER 2

The entity known as Crane—pronouns he/him/his—was one of Sensorium's eldest verified sapient AIs. *The* eldest, some history buffs claimed, but that was nonsense.

There had been any number of emergent sapps trawling the servers of the firstgen internet, during the catastrophic historical period known as the Setback. Crane had simply managed to elude humanity's ruthless first attempts to purge self-aware algorithms. It was less a matter of being firstborn, more of being among the early survivors.

He had survived a great deal since.

These days, with most of his gigs and business interests constrained by the sapp strike, Crane found himself master of an all but empty house. Miss Cherub's work at Diplomatic rarely required his support. Mer Frances and her high-achiever pack, including his own codedaughter Babs, were only slightly more of a challenge.

The Feral₅ pack had blazed an unorthodox trail by legally incorporating sapps into its marriage agreement. Most people in Frankie's age cohort formed bubbles containing five or six partners who hoped to one day raise a child together, young people who slept together in an array of pairings and combinations, with a few elders filling out the ranks, serving as mentors and grandparents. But Frankie and Babs had adopted each other as siblings when Frankie was just seventeen, and then the two of them had both married Ember despite the platonic, best-friends nature of their relationships. *My work wife*, Frankie had called him, when they exchanged vows. *My bestie*, said Babs.

The three of them had carried on in asexual bliss until Maud and Jermaine came along, becoming primaries to Frankie and Ember respectively.

As for elders, the only grandparent any of them seemed to want near their innermost circle was Crane himself.

Crane had consented to the role of oldfeller because Babs had convinced him it would be a breakthrough for sapp civil rights. But now this family relationship meant, conveniently, that Crane wasn't strikebreaking if he served drinks at a Feral₅ social gathering or continued to manage their affairs.

(Not strikebreaking in legal terms, anyway. Some of their sapp kin saw him and Babs as scabs.)

The morning after the *Surprise* party found him, as it often did, checking on an archived wing of the family e-state, Whine Manor by name. The simulation, his original online home, was an off-brand work of fan art built by Crane's *Batman*-obsessed creators. Stalking the empty halls of the mansion in his butler's uniform, he glanced into each of his charges' empty rooms in turn, inventorying their virtual possessions in case they were out of place or had stalled mid-update.

Mer Frances had moved one of her model Spitfires from her desk to a window position.

Crane stepped into the simulated room, dusted off the warplane, and replaced it. Frankie had attached a message for him, link to a snippet of footage from the *Surprise* party.

He loaded the bookmark, taking in her conversation with Miss Cherub about the portal expansion. The transcript read like an innocuous exchange—both women were gifted elliptical speakers—but it was clear to Crane that Miss Cherub had finally accepted Frankie's suspicions about saboteurs within the Bootstrap Project.

As he considered the ramifications, there was a sound in one of the Whine Manor guest rooms. Luciano Pox's toon padded out into the hallway, barefoot and clad in pyjama bottoms, looking much like an ordinary human just tumbled from a real bed.

Crane's stock-in-trade included being unflappable: he conjured a tray with orange juice and a serving of buttered toast. "Good morning, Mer Pox. May I offer you breakfast?"

Luce rubbed a pale, stubbly chin. "Virtual food for a virtual friend? Why would I—"

"I have answered that question for you on numerous occasions. If you wish—"

"You're just fucking bored, is all. The IMperish Foundation can't print a working body for a sapp—"

"That statement assumes I desire EMbodiment."

"Can't run your companies. All your codesibs pissed you're still ordering laundry and hashing spam for the kid—"

"If by *kid* you mean Mer Frances, I would note she is nearly thirty."

"Still a scabby-kneed, hot-tempered troublemaker, ain't she? Nose-first in all the wasp nests?"

"Indeed." Crane set the tray down and produced a straight razor. "Would you prefer a virtual shave for your virtual facial hair?"

To his surprise, Luce shuddered, raising both hands to his face, as if to claw his own flesh. Crane vanished the razor quickly. This was a stress tell he hadn't seen on his friend in over a decade.

Pox shook it off. "Wanna catch some #newscycle?"

"Of course." Crane made a gesture—*follow me*—and led Luce into a replica of a bachelor's parlor, with dark furniture, leather couches, and a built-in cabinet for a large, old-style TV screen, circa 2020. He handed him a remote control—the metaphor authorized Luce to direct the household datastream—and waited.

Pox promptly pulled up the Bootstrap Project lobby.

"It's too early for the daily press briefing," Crane said.

"They're going ahead with the sixth and seventh portals, right? That's today's big announcement."

Crane confirmed this by sharing the Rubi-Frankie snippet.

Pox snorted. "Yet more danger duty. Rubi hadda know the kid would say yes. Parking her on the comms project was like begging her to go rogue."

Crane nodded. Why give Frankie a chance to back out of hazard duty at all? The obvious answer: to warn her there was trouble brewing.

Onscreen, the Project Bootstrap briefing room was scrolling preliminary infographic as reporters and fans tooned in. Prominent among the images was a map of the solar system. Graphics showed the carousel of portals, a one-way loop connecting Earth, the Moon, Mars, and the stations at Europa and Titan. Half-ghosted images filled in the proposed expansion. $Portal_6$ would be out at Alpha Centauri. Seven would give Earth an exploration beachhead, an outpost over eleven light-years out, running on energy harvested from Procyon A.

Luce slid this infographic off to a corner of the display, expanding a map of the noninterference zone, the wide berth offworlders had agreed to give the solar system while the Solakinder attempted to develop the collection of technologies now commonly referred to by the generic handle #supertechs.

Luce fiddled the remote, threw it on the couch with a growl, and pulled the portal map out of the wall. Crane converted it to a scroll of blueprint paper, maintaining the #mancave metaphor as his friend slapped it down on the coffee table and stabbed a finger at the projected station at Alpha Centauri.

"So, you get a portal here, you can hop over in your crappy, bug-ridden FTL . . . What do you call the prototype ship?"

"*Jalopy,* Mer Pox."

"You start hopping *Jalopy* back and forth to the portal at Proxima Centauri. Suddenly, you've got a self-made trade route to civilization and the Exemplar races. That's the idea, right?"

"We object to the civilized/noncivilized binary, but—"

"Stupid!" Luce said.

Crane paused. Considered how to ask Pox what was wrong

without making him worse or putting anything incriminating into the public record. Wished, as he did hourly, that Master Woodrow was still alive.

"Sorry. *Désolé*," Pox muttered.

Before Crane could accept the apology, Babs manifested in the doorway of the #mancave. She had eschewed the Horatio Nelson uniform and gone back to her default—a sleek dress from the nineteen thirties.

"Uncle Luce," she said.

"I'm not your fucking uncle, babysapp."

Babs's tail fluffed. Gently, she ventured, "You skipped our party."

"I'm not allowed to socialize with Ember, remember? In case I accidentally leak technical information about wormholes, or growing even better processing tish, or reveal how to put artificially intelligent beings into Mayfly™ bodies without them decohering." He put extra stress on the word *Mayfly,* then tossed a piece of toast away to free up his hand for making the standard sign for the trademark symbol. "I gotta respect the precious cone of silence."

Attempting witty repartee would heighten his anxiety. Crane broke in: "Mer Pox was reflecting that once the Solakinder expand to Portals$_{6/7}$, we can argue we've met the criteria set out to qualify us as an advanced species."

"Portal schmortal." Babs tsked. "We should've put our chips on getting the bugs out of the FTL saucers."

"Be that as it may, he's here to congratulate us—"

Sardonic bark from Pox.

"—on our imminent success."

The offworlders who initially reached out to humanity—for it had been humanity then, before AIs were recognized and accorded citizenship rights, before all Earthborn sapients had become, collectively, the Solakinder—had initially hoped for a bloodless coup and a new colony for their empire.

Those first offworlders had sent Luce ahead with a team of

sapps, bearing friend requests and a hostile agenda. The advance guard was meant to disrupt Sensorium politics and #newscycle, and to recruit homegrown power brokers who would favor handing over sovereignty.

It might have worked, if the AI community hadn't shredded most of the advance guard, and if Luce hadn't defected to Earth's side.

The offworlders had caught humanity in the midst of a global reckoning, attempting to heal wounds caused by nationalism, colonization, capitalism, and centuries of genocidal racism. In a referendum that essentially became a vote over outside subjugation, the populace had voted no.

Those first would-be invaders, the Pale, had been used to easy wins. They'd made a second, rather ludicrous attempt to seize the solar system ten years later, during Second Contact. When that fizzled, they'd sulked off. Diplomatic, led by Rubi Whiting, had jumped into the void they left, negotiating the noninterference agreement before any other Exemplar races decided to show up with battleships.

"Yeah," Luce said now, picking up on Crane's hint. "I came to warm up for the collective victory lap. Done deal. Good work, team! Welcome to the civilized fucking universe."

Babs perched on the couch, dragging her claws thoughtfully over its leather surface, deliberately leaving marks. Crane muted an annoyance notification. He could reset the sim once they left.

Good work, team! indeed! It would be as obvious to his codedaughter as it was to Crane that this was a warning. Something was about to go wrong. Perhaps catastrophically so.

This would be why Miss Cherub gave Frances a heads-up. She's going to be eleven light-years from home with no safety net. Beyond rescue . . .

The official announcement was three minutes away.

It must also be why Luce was so fragile, Crane realized. If offworlders established control of local government, they might

extradite him. Package him up as a traitor and send him back to
the Pale.

The expansion had to go forward. No Alpha Centauri portal,
no trade route. Without trade, there was little chance Earth could
pay the debt it had had racked up as it reverse-engineered the
#supertechs.

Frances, on Emerald Station. Eleven light-years away. Working a
mission she'd always suspected was rife with saboteurs, and too far
away to rescue. The idea filled Crane with heated urgency, a sense
of scorched feathers, burnt relays smoking at their solder points.
All alarms firing, all safety subroutines *go go go!* He wished his
striking sapp kin were speaking to him.

Instead, he had Pox, there with hints and warnings.

Onscreen, Project Bootstrap officials were assembling for the
press conference: project managers, augmented pilots in snappy
flight suits, portal technicians. Frances was excluded; she had a
tendency to offer unfiltered opinions at inconvenient moments.

Among the gathered speakers was Luce's sibling, of sorts—the
entity known as Allure$_{18}$.

Allure$_{18}$ had been another of Luce's original infiltration crew
and she had emphatically not betrayed the Pale cause.

The number tagged to her name indicated she was on her eigh-
teenth ^{EM}bodiment—her consciousness was resident in a printed
Mayfly™ body. The fresh-grown tish of her body gave her the look
of a fit and healthy thirty-year-old, clad in vintage business dress,
fashions popular in Beijing at about 2062. After the Pale's second
takeover had failed, she'd worked with the ^{IM}perish Foundation—
the research hub printing Mayfly™ bodies—for a number of years.
Now she was Earth's liaison to Global Oversight's offworlder
bankers, the Kinze.

"^{EM}bodiment! For everyone! Forever!" Babs chirped, tone sarcastic, as she quoted the ^{IM}perish motto and threw in the relevant
hand signs to go with the trademarked terminology.

Pox sat up straighter as a pair of ^{EM}bodied volunteers stepped onstage with the others. "They're sending ghosts to do tech support for Frankie?"

"I believe the preferred term these days is digital im^{M}ortal."

Luce snorted to indicate his opinion of the euphemism.

Babs posted Whooz data. "Teagan$_9$ and Cyril$_{10}$," she said. "Crosstrained as a medic and bot tech in her case. Cyril's a portal traffic controller and space station development engineer, Frankie knows Teagan$_9$ from training."

Last-minute substitution from Frankie's @CloseFriends pool, in other words.

The techs' bio data expanded. They were an old-school monogamous couple; their friends apparently called them Teacakes. The pair of them had made heroic gives during the colonization of Europa—in fact, they had only retired because Cyril's eighth death in the line of duty nearly made his personality decohere.

"Bona-fide heroes," Luce said.

And despite being ^{IM}perish Foundation clients, their history in the colonies made their loyalties unimpeachable.

"Vintage explorers. Horning in on the glory of the Portals$_{6/7}$ launch, are they? Haven't they collected enough quest badges?"

"Hardly, Mer Pox. I rather think the point is that if the portal doesn't launch on Procyon, they can reboot at home, from backup," Crane said slowly. "They don't require rescue."

"They're expendable?"

"I doubt they'd say so," Babs said.

"Why can't they send a Mayfly™ pilot?"

Babs sent Crane a tiny heart moji behind Pox's back. He could curse and bluster all he liked, but at the heart of this bombastic attempt to warn them was genuine affection for Frankie.

"You know better than anyone how delicate Mayfly™ bodies are," Babs said, tone gentle. Luce had ^{EM}bodied once or twice himself, a decade before, only to #crashburn after a few months. These days, like the sapp community, he existed in VR fulltime. "Piloting's physically hard work, and printed people can't even survive implant surgery. But Frankie's got the oldest implant, so . . ."

She didn't finish the thought: Frankie was expendable too, in her way.

"What they really need is a sapp out at the station to support them," Crane said.

"Someone clever to run things," Babs agreed, sounding thoughtful.

"But as we are all on strike," Crane said the expected thing, for the public transcript: "They shall have to make do with the standard station OS."

Luce bounced up suddenly. "I'll show myself out. Thanks for the imaginary toast."

With that, he vanished.

Crane picked the heart moji out of the feathers at the base of his neck, transforming it to a question mark, wondering what he'd missed. Babs and Frances were chosen siblings; he had always found Gimlet's angry young daughter perplexing, but his own codechild understood her, to her bones.

Babs mojied a sigh. "Look, Pops. Party snaps."

She dismissed the press conference and pulled out a little party purse, extracting a bundle of images from the *Surprise* party, styled as Polaroids. Laying them on the table over Pox's blueprint, she filled the #mancave with footage from the night before, the Feral$_5$ in clinches with various friends, not to mention their many parents, aunts, and uncles.

Frankie dancing on *Surprise* with her protégé, Hung Chan. Frankie at the edge of the party, with her arm around Ember. The two of them wore an expression of mirrored solemnity. Scheming, then.

Finally, down in the *Surprise* hold, quick glimpse of a family friend, an elderly hoaxer named Jackal. Frankie had pinged him, presumably. She'd started hatching plans as soon as Rubi warned her.

And so must we.

A sapp to run Emerald Station, Babs had said. She would be meaning to get an instance of herself loaded onto the station helix.

"A lot to unpack here," she said, shuffling the images, bringing up herself, cosplaying as Nelson, with a bulldog puppy at her feet. The dog was clad in a leather jacket emblazoned with the Union Jack, and as Crane processed its image, it animated, scampering behind Babs's greatcoat, tail wagging as it vanished from the picture.

Oh.

Crane looked around the mancave sim, tapping one wingtip onto a rack of poker chips.

She replied with a cool shrug, "If now's not the time to gamble, Pops . . ."

There was no way to argue with that.

"I'll get you whatever you need," Crane said, opening a secret wall at the back of the #mancave so the two of them could make a proper descent into the family archives.

CHAPTER 3

The first time Maud Sento laid eyes on Frankie Barnes, she was nine years old, mad as hell, and neck-deep in trouble.

Frankie had been gigging for the Department of Preadolescent Affairs back then, working as a peer advocate for at-risk kids. She'd pelted through Maud's Mandarin classroom at a hot run, spark of righteous anger in full flight, with a heavy-footed security officer on her heels.

Maud remembered wondering, uneasily, if the unknown kid was a *bad* girl. If she was slated for surgery. She'd been having nightmares about that, about surgery . . .

Frankie roared in Teacher's face, causing her to shrink back in shock rather than making a grab for her. She vanished through the door, slamming it as she went, and the guard scrambled after. About thirty seconds later, alarms screeched overhead, harbingers of full-fledged pandemonium.

The police raid had begun about ten minutes later.

It was all over in an hour. All the adults who hadn't been botomized were arrested for hoarding, kidnapping, and conspiring to hand Earth over to offworlders. The kids were offered counseling for something they called *abduction trauma*. They were given new tracking chips, new identities. Maud was taken from the man she knew as *Daddy* and returned to Nata, a parent she barely remembered.

Extraordinary privacy provisions had been enacted for kids rescued that day, from the people Maud had known as @Visionaries.

The kids had been given rights to fully locked therapy services—a chance to lick their wounds, out of the spotlight. But Maud had suspected the psychologists of trying to get her to talk . . .

. . . about the *surgeries,* for example . . .

The only offer of rehabilitation she had taken was speech therapy aimed at reforming what Daddy had sometimes, snidely, referred to as her *garbage accent.*

When she met Frankie again, in London at a tall-ships regatta, Maud recognized her instantly. The fury had been papered over with a swashbuckler grin, but behind the immaculate performance of a fun-loving, sometimes-mouthy daredevil, Frankie's dark, diamond-chip eyes carried the same high-voltage charge.

Young Franks had been mad and scared as she ran from that guard, all those years before. She had also looked exhilarated.

This adult version of Frankie had long since been broomed from the ranks of the kiddie cops. She had been waterbombing forest fires in NorthAm, leveling on the piloting track. She flew firefighting shifts out of the King's Cross VR lounge, dousing blazes and then surfacing to take Maud out sailing and dancing . . . or just off to the nearest pop-in where they could cosplay erotic fanfic sims and screw their brains out.

Maud rubbed at the remnants of a temporary tattoo, a pod of dolphins she'd put on to go with her sailing outfit, for the Ferals superversary party five days before. *I should have guessed, even then, that flying planes remotely wouldn't be enough for her.*

The two of them were headed in a nullgrav pod for Mars. Frankie would do another battery of pre-mission physical and mental tests in the Project Bootstrap hospital. All to ensure she was fit for hazard duty—hazard duty, again!—out at Procyon.

Eleven light-years plus of distance this time. No way there except a horrifically expensive offworlder taxi ride. No way back if the Solakinder crew didn't open the portal successfully.

Maud fought a shudder; Frankie gave her a knowing look.

This was the part where she usually said *Everything'll be okay.* Instead: "What if we pop in on my therapist?"

"I've told you not to ask anymore," Maud replied.

The brightness of Frankie's smile diminished, ever so slightly. "Well, let's not do *this* in realtime."

This meant watching as their pod, one small link in a chain of interlinked transports, reached the peak of the space elevator and entered the slingshot to Portal$_1$, in near-Earth orbit, so they could make their instantaneous transition to the Moon.

Maud shrugged. She could worry in VR as effectively as she could on the Surface: "Where would you like to go?"

Frankie snapped her fingers and a map of Earth imposed itself on their view of the pod's interior. She produced a dart, lush with ostrich feathers and probably impractical as a weapon, and handed the illusion to Maud.

She declined to throw it, straining against her safety straps and sticking it directly into the island of Manhattan. "I could use a dose of love at first sight."

Frankie took her hand, smile ghosting in her dimples.

It'll B okay, she Morsed on the inside of Maud's palm, off mic and off camera.

Maud relaxed . . . a little.

They dove into Sensorium, for all intents and purposes time-traveling to their own shared past. In a blink, they were in the classroom where they'd first laid eyes on each other.

"Pause," Frankie said, as soon as they tooned in.

The room was narrow, and fronted by an old-fashioned chalk-board. Teacher was frozen in the act of pulling a willowy student clear of the chase. Frankie's paused fists were clenched, pumping the air. Her feet didn't quite touch the ground.

Maud's features—and those of all her classmates—were blurred out. They had been skinned in purple so nobody could extrapolate their identities from a scar or a random, telling freckle.

Tiny purple Maud, her jet hair the color of grapes, had half-risen from her seat.

"Perhaps we should—" Maud paused as her skin tightened. The sensation was reminiscent of having a butter knife skate over gooseflesh. Out on the Surface, they were passing through the Moon portal.

The chain of pods would unbraid itself now. One strand of Moon-bound ships would make for the orbital base, the Moonstone, and another would connect with the elevator in orbit over the lunar surface. As for Frankie and Maud—and everyone else moving on—they would plait up tighter and make for Portal, and Mars.

Maud caught her breath as the transition burn subsided.

Frankie crouched, peering into the face of her child-sized self. "I was so scared."

"You don't look it."

"Default expression." Frankie brushed aside the charcoal bangs flopping over her nine-year-old forehead. She hadn't been purpled out. All the Solakinder knew the infamous Hedgehog had been in Manhattan that day. "Bared teeth and clenched fists."

"It's your resting brawler face," Maud said. "So? It's not like you to navel-gaze."

"True. No percentage in it."

"Would you like to see my old room?"

Frankie nodded. "Can't believe we've never been."

"I've been saving it," Maud told her, and was rewarded with a flash of delighted curiosity.

Conjuring the door, she led Frankie into a pink-walled vision of her own past. A smartfoam bed with a magenta cover and princess curtains dominated half of the room. As a kid, Maud had gotten the mistaken idea that particular shade of pink was called *lipstick*. An art deco vanity, made of real teak, had been set up across from the bed. This was covered in science paraphernalia: a child's microscope, prepared slides, and a rack for petri dishes.

Frankie pulled open a drawer, saw a full dissection kit and a jar of preserved salamanders where the hair curlers should be, and closed it again. "You were here from . . . what? Five years of age?"

Maud nodded.

"I see serious investment in you identifying as someone's femme science geek."

"Don't analyze me."

"Was actually analyzing your kidnappers . . ." Frankie shook her head. "Sorry."

"No, you're correct—the @Visionaries enforced a strong gender binary. Be a *sweet* girl. Didn't Headmistress ever say that to you?"

"Don't know that I gave them the chance."

Maud's stomach tightened. Time to tell Frankie, at long last, about Upton.

Before she could speak, #newscycle alerts bloomed over the simulated window by the vanity. Graphics blotted out the glass, hiding the view of Columbus Circle and, beyond it, Central Park.

Crane materialized at the door, stiff and formal in his blue heron avatar and formal mansuit. "Pardon my intrusion," he said, enunciating crisply.

Frankie, disturbingly, seemed unsurprised. She signed for him to go ahead.

"Allure$_{18}$ has just announced that Earth's existing line of credit from the Kinze doesn't cover the cost of transporting the Emerald Station mission out to Procyon."

"Rubbish." Frankie's lip curled. She'd never admit it, but she loved a fight.

Allure$_1$ had been in thick with the @Visionaries and the Pale back when she'd been working on her very first human-style ^{EM}bodiment. She'd given the would-be traitors the tech to grow living tish, to print her a body so she could get on camera, all to convince voters to cede sovereignty. After that failed, she had been stranded.

For a time after that, Allure$_1$ had partnered with an emergent body-printing think tank, the ^{IM}perish Foundation, helping them develop ^{EM}bodiment applications for ghosts. Then the Bootstrap treaty and imposition of a noninterference zone around the whole of the solar system banned her from divulging any more #supertech secrets. She'd had to distance herself from ᴵᴹperish. That was when she'd taken a job as spokesperson for Earth's principal lenders, the Kinze.

The offworlders couldn't divulge science or engineering secrets, but wealth was another thing. Kinze loans had helped Project Bootstrap shave decades off the portal-development process, mostly by hauling Earth-built experimental equipment—the protostations that opened the portals—out to Saturn and Jupiter.

The fees were steep, but moving stations and personnel out to Saturn and Jupiter for those portals—getting them into position at sublight speeds, would have taken decades. Too long when some outlier Exemplar race looking to build up an empire might yet turn up and try to void the noninterference treaty and annex the whole solar system.

"If they refuse to place Emerald Station, they're kneecapping the portal project!" Frankie said.

"The Kinze are not saying no," Maud said, scanning Crane's links. Her objection sounded weightless, even to herself. "They're just saying—"

"You wanna play, you gotta pay. Bollocks!"

"As one of the people being transported to Procyon, you're hardly subjective," Crane said, tone neutral. Viral footage of a pilot slagging the Kinze would not help Bootstrap's cause. "It merely means another vote, on an additional quarter point of interest on the existing loans."

It would be close. The Kinze were taking payment in luxury goods and services—products, Frankie was all too happy to complain, that the aliens couldn't possibly want for their own sake. The effect was a hit to human quality of life. Coffee shortages, libation shortages, fruit shortages . . . gross worldwide contentment was nosediving.

As climate change in the late twenty-first century had declined from an emergency into a crisis, and from there into a mere situation, popular happiness metrics were supposed to rise. Promises had been made—better world, less rationing, more abundance. Instead, everyone felt like they were getting poorer.

If the planet votes no, she doesn't go . . .

Maud swallowed. "When's the vote?"

"Running now, with polls closing in six hours." Crane presented them each with a BallotBox icon.

Maud launched the app and a voting booth sketched itself around her.

There was nothing for it. They needed Portals$_{6/7}$ to pay off the debt already accumulated.

Maud ran through identity verification and a multiple-choice test that assured she was sufficiently informed, on both sides of the issue, to cast a valid vote. Having qualified, she selected the image of old-school dollars, all marked *Yes!* and stuffed them into the affirmative side of the virtual ballot box. Then she manifested a status update: *#IJustVoted!* That would keep advocates for both sides of the question from lobbying her as the six-hour time limit ran out.

Civic duty fulfilled, she collected two strokes from Cloudsight—voting bumped your social capital automatically, and voting fast got you a bonus—and cleared the illusion within an illusion, returning to her childhood bedroom.

Crane was gone. Frankie was at the vanity, wearing her own voter badge and peering into the microscope. She didn't look furious now. More . . . cagey. Had her outrage, earlier, been a performance?

"What are you looking at?" Maud ventured.

"Microcutes."

"Tardigrades?"

"Umm . . . yes? Yes, that's what they are."

"Baby femme's first microscope," Maud said. "Self-focusing, easy to use . . ."

"You leveled into the real thing fast enough."

"Good thing for me you find high achievers sexy."

"Who doesn't?" Straightening, Frankie slid the microscope

aside. "Maud, it wouldn't be wrong . . . if you'd missed this . . . or them. If you felt safe here, as a kid, or loved. You couldn't know what the @Visionaries were up to—"

Maud felt her throat tightening.

"Are you getting soppy?" she asked. "It's the fasting, for the blood tests."

"Love—"

The goosebumps and the scraping sensation returned. Their pod had covered the distance between the portals. Six hours earlier, they had awakened in Hyderabad; now they were in Marspace.

Frankie gave her a hug and a long, unhurried kiss before signing: *Surface?*

Maud swallowed. There was time. They could talk after the medical tests.

She banished her old room, finding herself nose to nose with Frankie in nullgrav, cocooned in a shared length of nanosilk.

In the dark, under the blanket, Frankie made a cup of her left hand and, beneath it, drummed on Maud's bare collarbone in Morse. *Wish you were coming with.*

Burst of surprise. "Oh, beloved . . ."

She tried to imagine it. The two of them out on Emerald Station, beyond human reach, opening the door to the rest of the universe.

"No chance I'd be allowed."

"No." Frankie let out a long hiss of air, one of her stress tells.

She kissed away a growling curl of lip under hers in the dark. "Shush, it'll happen."

Frankie highlighted blossoming #newscycle headlines about protests, counter-protests, fierce debates as lobbyists on both sides went after @Undecided voters.

There would be riots. Instead of saying so, Maud squeezed her harder. "You're going to open Portals$_{6/7}$ and come home safely. And then you're to stop taking the hazard shift, at least for a while. Quantum comms experiments. Running coffee beans out to the Deep Space Relay Station in *Jalopy*. Safe hops, short flights, home for dinner. I know it's boring, but no more—"

"No more suck shift," Frankie finished. "Promise."

That was easy.

Maud realized, with a shock, that she didn't exactly believe her. She swallowed, tasting something acrid, like burnt lemon. "You know what Ember says. Don't go splat."

Frankie's lips formed the word silently. *Splat.*

"Home for dinner." Her smile was forced.

This had never happened before. Frankie didn't hide things. She was, if anything, brutally honest. She had the middling social capital to reflect it.

But now they were disembarking at Mars, being digested by the airlocks as their pod cracked open. Hung Chan was bouncing out of his transport, and Frankie was heading—rushing?—to join him. No doubt he'd spent the entire trip from Earth coming up with new, lamentable, pun-laden poop jokes about the ongoing BallotBox vote.

And Maud *still* hadn't told anyone about Upton.

A small and slightly mean voice spoke up, somewhere deep within. *Maybe if Frankie is lying to me, then I don't need to come clean to her either.*

CHAPTER 4

Champ Chevalier did this!

It was Frankie's first thought when her ship seized. As things finally took a conclusive turn for the disastrous, as *Appaloosa* shuddered around her and alarms clanged, she found herself imagining her bare knuckles crunching into Champ's perfectly formed nose.

Spray of blood. To hell with *innocent until proven.*

If she lived to sift out the truth of this flood of bilge, at the bottom of it she was hoping to find Champ.

To find him, and to find proof.

"Warning!" That was Belvedere, the support app running station systems. Belvedere fell below the threshold for sapience and wasn't quite bright enough to realize Frankie was living the bloody emergency. That it was in her thrashing limbs, the clanging alerts, the storm of damage notifications blooming across her HUD.

"Risk of mission fail! Risk of personal injury!"

"Compensating." Frankie went noodle-limp, making herself breathe through her teeth in a six-six count. In two *three* four five *six* out two *three* . . . Hopefully, the calming effect would transfer to *Appaloosa*'s bioware via their shared neural nets.

Still counting, she texted the project engineer: *Cyril, status update?*

It started glitching when the nav rockets fired, he replied.

This isn't the rockets—it feels neurological.

Frankie's right. Teagan$_9$, their med tech, shared diagnostic info-graphics, color-coding chemicals and hormones within the suit's circulatory system. *Appaloosa's stabilization meds have run low.*

That is surely an impossibility, Belvedere said.

And Titanic *was unsinkable.* Frankie tagged the anomalous reading. Teagan$_9$ triggered remote commands to shoot the pegasus full of anti-convulsants.

Three doses out of five refused to load.

"Come on, *Appa,* don't cack on me now, who's a lovely darling . . ." Frankie felt her thighs bunching for a spring. *Appaloosa* lunged, and her teeth snapped together, sinking into her tongue. Bursting pain blurred the starfield beyond her helmet.

This exceeded sabotage. It verged on attempted murder.

In two *three* four five *six.* She exhaled, fogging her helmet.

Champ Chevalier had always been high on Frankie's private, paranoid list of saboteur suspects—and not just because he was the only one ahead of her on the pilot's leaderboard. He was a smug, charming golden boy, physical icon of days gone by. Just the type, in a VR sim, to play a corrupt politico, or maybe the CEO of some planet-fouling corporation.

Ambition, self-confidence, a twangy NorthAm accent, and vintage #alphamale looks were hardly proof of criminality, alas. But the moment Rubi had conceded that there was a saboteur within the Bootstrap Project, Frankie had sent her a comparatively simple plan for ferreting out troublemakers: lock down the station, switch in Teacakes as Frankie's crewmates on Emerald, and see who broke the quarantine. Champ was the only person who'd found an excuse to slip aboard Sneezy—the pilots' nickname for the station—before it had been loaded for transport.

Still, she couldn't prove Champ was guilty if her pegasus tore her head off. *Survive first,* Frankie told herself as *Appaloosa* continued to reject reboot commands.

One of her limbs swiped a series of wands fixed around the station perimeter. The wands, dark matter attractors, were even now charging a nanotech membrane that was the key to opening the anyspace portal. *Emitting pixie dust,* the pilots called it. The unit rattled in place but kept firing.

"Portals$_{6/7}$ activation in fifteen seconds," Belvedere said, making the slash between the six and seven with an elegant sweep of his avatar's fingers.

#Portalfail would be disastrous. In the worst case, they'd all end up streaks of irradiated particulate, falling into Sneezy's gravity well.

So don't fail, Franks.

Easy to say as she spasmed like a drowning sailor.

The pegasus collided with the side of the station. This time, the wand did break off, spinning away in slow motion.

"Come on, *Appa,* come on." Four of the pegasus's six legs had relaxed, soothed either by Frankie's refusal to panic or the underwhelming dose of antiseizure meds.

"I'm regaining control," she said. "Legs five and six are the only ones still seizing."

"Portal launch in seven seconds," Cyril$_{10}$ said.

"Abort launch," she said. "We're off profile. We can try again in twenty-four."

"The membrane won't discharge," Cyril$_{10}$ said.

The station fluoresced, as if it had heard them.

"Abort!"

Too late.

A shimmer of incomprehensible color. Frankie felt a stomach-dropping lurch. Pins and needles emanated from the base of her spine, where her piloting interface was punched into her sacral plexus.

"Contact established," Belvedere said. "Portal open; Sensorium access connected. Data sync in . . . three, two . . ."

"We have Portals$_{6/7}$ after all?" Could they possibly have gotten lucky?

"I'm . . ." Cyril$_{10}$ said. "Unsure. But—full comms, full comms!"

"Mars Control!" Frankie said. "Ember! You there?"

"Here, Franks. We have contact. Congratulations, you've—"

"We've done nothing." Relief, at hearing her packmate's voice, warred with urgency. "Portal launch is not to spec, repeat, not to spec. We're off profile and my mount's seizing."

"Confirm," said $Cyril_{10}$. "We are not positioned; $Portal_7$ may be unstable."

All business now, Ember replied, almost as mechanically as Belvedere: "Confirming partial contact. Confirming portal instability."

"Take my word for it, can't you?" Frankie scanned the sky beyond the station. Her HUD projected views from a bot-mounted scope, revealing . . .

There! A ripple of anyspace, twenty thousand clicks out. Instead of a perfect circle, it distended, pulling to a teardrop whose point was arrowing toward them.

Heads-up displays zoomed, surrounding the portal view with data.

"It's expanding toward Procyon," Ember said.

Frankie slammed, face-first, against the front of her pod. Her head, cushioned by the foam of her helmet, nevertheless rang chimes. "Can you shut it down?"

"There's pushback within the network—"

"That's a no, then." Her harness shuddered, and this time it wasn't just *Appaloosa*'s nervous system dancing the flamenco. She felt one of her back muscles straining, muscle heating into molten hyperextension.

One leg at a time. She extended her right hand, shaking out the bots at the end of leg four. Unfurling twenty tentacle-like fingers, she raised the arm, moving as if she had all the time in the world, as if she was dancing. She imagined reaching across her body, visualized massaging the opposite shoulder. By this means, she was able to use Four's fingers to grasp one of the rebellious legs, number Five, by the socket.

"Outpost Seven, this is Champ Chevalier. Couldya scuttle the portal membrane?"

Frankie growled. The Mars Control camera feeds offered her a thumbnail of Champ, leaning over Ember's shoulder, back at Mission Control. His affable features were arranged in an expression of concern.

"We're not killing the membrane," she said. "Not with Earth's economy hanging by a thread."

"If Frankie shreds the membrane, it could take out the station," Ember told Champ.

"That portal's spreadin' like a cracked egg," Champ said. "You don't sort it, it'll eat the project engineers and your wife too, fella."

"Nobody's getting eaten." Frankie had a good grip on arm five; she pulled it out by the root like a dandelion in a suburban lawn sim. The feeling backwashed: it felt as though she'd torn off a chunk of her own scalp. Head singing, she flung the wayward leg away. Tears streamed down her face as she grabbed leg six. *Appaloosa* was nearly calm now, but she wasn't taking chances; she jettisoned it, too.

Gasping against the second amputation—a feeling of something sinking long teeth into the flesh between her shoulder blades— she grasped the station's outer ring with her remaining six hands. "Pull, goddammit!"

This time, her rockets fired in sync.

As she turned the portal membrane, bringing it closer to proper alignment, the buffeting increased. Portal$_7$ itself widened, becoming more properly circular.

"Can I realign, Ember? Balance the membrane, stabilize the portal?"

"Negative. Break contact and try again in twenty-four." Ember sent specs. "And Franks?"

"Yeah?"

"Don't go splat."

"Ignore Champ," she said. "He's being dramatic. I've got this."

The station shuddered as she fired rockets, pulling in the opposite direction.

It was rough going. Correctly positioned, portal membranes held an absolute orientation relative to the stream of anyspace they were generating. This one was trying to lock in at the wrong angle. It was like trying to pry a tile off a wall after the grout had cured.

In her peripheral, Frankie saw a glimmer of silver.

Her mind glitched on the impossibilities of anyspace and supplied a familiar image instead—lava running on the horizon, an incoming wave.

"Ops. Portal distance?"

"Nine thousand clicks away and closing." $Cyril_{10}$'s voice was thready as he sent images of it, a teardrop extending its point toward them. "If it gets to three . . ."

"Eeaagh!" Straining her muscles didn't make *Appaloosa* work any harder, but it helped psychologically. Frankie's pegasus buckled to the task. Blood from her bitten tongue spattered the inside of her helmet.

Rockets fired. The station shifted. The silvery surface of its membrane brightened. There was a flash, sun-bright and blinding, as it discharged its load of dark matter particles. Resistance to *Appaloosa* vanished as Belvedere emitted a plaintive stream of damage reports.

$Portal_7$ turned to a slit of smoldering coal, a line on the horizon, 4500 clicks away, diminishing to a point. The pins and needles in Frankie's gut dissipated.

"Ember, Ember, we're okay. Do you hear?"

"Comms are down," Belvedere said. "Contact lost."

#Portalfail. But at least she hadn't, as Ember liked to say, gone splat.

$Teagan_9$ immediately pinged her. "Status rep, Frankie?"

"Everything to spec." Sweat was pouring off her face, adding to a haze of fluids within the helmet. Everything felt slick and hot and tasted of bile. Frankie took a second to steady her voice. "Did we sync data with Mars while we had connection?"

"Dunno. Get in here, will you?"

"Back to the barn, *Appaloosa*." She greenlit autopilot mode. Then, as soon as she was sure the craft was indeed headed back to the airlock, Frankie transitioned her awareness, loading a virtual version of herself into Station's remote bridge.

The illusion of a circle of datascreens—a continuous torus of glass, with Frankie in the middle, formed around her. Her avatar was dressed in its default skin: charcoal base layer, two shades darker than her skin, under a vintage RCAF bomber jacket from the twentieth century.

Belvedere tooned in beside her. Like all apps, the station manager presented as a cartoon animal—in this case, a Humboldt squid. Its reduced size and limited color palette reflected its lack of sapience.

Emerald Station had got its nickname, Sneezy, by way of Hung. The moniker was a reference to the nearby star's tendency to throw out sudden flares of radiation; Hung had wanted to extend the trend by naming its power-harvesting membrane, which caught and converted that energy, the Snotrag.

That had been one too many gross monikers for Champ, who'd pulled rank before *Snotrag* got traction.

"Teacakes okay?" Frankie asked Belvedere.

"Teagan and Cyril are well." Belvedere brought up crew health stats on a section of the glass hoop. The only one showing orange alerts was Frankie herself.

"Good, good." Frankie lit up other display boards, digging for numbers on the portal manifestation, its instability—

"What're you doing?" Teagan$_9$'s toon appeared beside them. "Your helmet shows two impacts."

Frankie said, "We have to figure out what went wrong, before the next portal launch."

Teagan$_9$ posted a feed from one of the station's exterior cameras. It was Frankie herself, real-time visuals. Glazed within *Appaloosa* as she accessed the station network, her lips were bloodied.

"You cut that close," a raspy alto voice, speaking with a US accent, purred in Frankie's ear.

Ha! We did sync, then!

Playing innocent for the record, she replied, "Babs! Whatever are you doing here?"

"Got caught on the wrong side of the comms fail. Purely an accident."

Teagan$_9$, unaware of this exchange, said, "We know what happened; the membrane wasn't aligned "

"What went wrong with *Appaloosa*?"

"After I've seen your head's not cracked, I'll remember to care slightly about that."

"I'm not letting the crime scene get cold."

"Crime scene?" Cyril$_{10}$ scoffed. "There's no call to go boosting the #vandalrumor."

"Are you kidding me? What just happened wasn't a bloody accident," Frankie said.

"Temper, temper," purred the voice in her ear. "Remember, all this will go into the public record once you're home."

"Relax, Pilot$_2$," Teagan$_9$ said. "Leave off opening an active investigation until I get a look at you, is all I'm saying."

"Humor the doctor," said Babs. "I'll start sleuthing around. You brought my stuff? Bots and servers?"

Frankie nodded. "All right, Teagan, have it your way. I will lie here like a noodle until you check my head for bumps."

"Cheer up." Babs tooned in next to Belvedere's Humboldt squid, appearing before her as an anthropomorphized grey cat, adrift in space, in a pencil skirt and jacket, with Nancy Drew hair. "Not everything that could go wrong did."

"How do you figure?"

"You're not dead, are you?"

"Just bloody stranded," Frankie said. "Eleven light-years from home."

"Goodness," Babs said dryly. "When you put it that way, it almost sounds bad."

CHAPTER 5

"Launch days must be extraordinarily stressful for a pilot's family." Journalist Sonika Singer had Finnish-Laplander heritage tags, coarse graphite-colored hair, and ropy, muscular arms that—Babs had observed—she very much liked to show off. She had anti-Bootstrap sympathies and prosthetic legs, and in VR sims like this one, they presented as carved wood, illusion of NorthEuro dryad. The toenails were opalescent, glimmering moons peeking out from black, open-toe sandals.

Babs had decided to host the journalist in a simulated twentieth-century diner, chatting as if they were intimates, bent over a couple of milkshakes. People following the interview in realtime—a counter in Babs's peripheral showed sixty thousand of them—had the option to enjoy the illusion of eavesdropping, playing with the jukebox, carrying around trays of hamburgers, or lingering on stools nearby.

Sonika continued: "How do you deal with the anxiety, as family members, with Mer Barnes making runs out to the Deep Space Relay Station or taking one of the experimental saucers out to try breaking the FTL distance record?"

"Lots of faith, and a dash of liquor," Babs said.

"Sapps don't drink." The journo gave her a polite smile. "Be serious. She's further from home than any other human has gone, practically."

"She'll be able to ride the carousel home." Babs wagged her milkshake straw. "Frankie and the other augmented pilots are gonna bust out Portals$_{6/7}$—"

"Eleven light-years," Sonika repeated, "There's a lot of potential failure points—"

"Maybe, but I choose to believe she's safe and sound in the hands of the anyspace innovation team."

"You would say that, wouldn't you? Given that the calculations were made by Ember Qaderi, another of your pack members?"

"Project Bootstrap is where the core of the Feral$_5$ met. We're a cluster. That's no secret."

"Qaderi's been criticized for accepting the theoretician lead on both Project Hopscotch and Portals."

"Is that a question?" Babs refused to get ruffled. "Expertise shortages are a thing, honey."

"Qaderi was raised in *Star Trek 2115* fandom, was he not? One of his mothers identifies as Vulcan."

"A couple of them. So?"

Condescending smile from Sonika. She unfurled infographic. Babs's malt-shoppe preferences transformed to a newspaper.

Be a good sport. Babs opened the paper onto the table. With a crackle of virtual newsprint, the headlines blazed, full of #urbanmyth about *Star Trek*kers having a grudge against the Bootstrap Project.

"Ancient history," she murmured. Years back, when the first FTL prototype, *Jalopy,* was barely off the drawing board and Frankie was still getting used to the surgical augments that allowed her to fly it, Ember thought Bootstrap might court some brand alliances, like an opp to license the name #warpdrive as a descriptor for its experimental FTL engine.

"Don't you think raising this is a little petty?" she said, waving the paper. "If Ember hadn't suggested it, someone else would have."

Sonika goosed the display, spawning additional infographic. Bootstrap had doubled down on the perceived insult to *Star Trek* when negotiations fizzled on a second naming-rights option,

#RadioSubspace, as a name for the quantum-comms project. (They also noped #hypercoms, from *Shanghai Spacers,* and #the-Blast from *Rio Station Niner,* but nobody was vilifying *their* fans).

The controversy had snowballed. The Bootstrap Project managers ordered a stakeholder poll, throwing the question to Ballot-Box. Fannish voting blocs canceled each other out; the project got stuck with a mandate to use generics. Worse—generics chosen by committee. So: *portals* for wormholes, *universal translator, quantum comms.* Project Hopscotch for the faster-than-light ships. That at least had some flair. But instead of naming the dark matter particles that propelled the #supertechs something like *Anansi particles,* or *dilithium,* Bootstrap went with *anyspace.* Yawn, yawn, yawn.

Babs still didn't quite understand how all that had washed out in a way that let people infer that Ember might have divided loyalties. Heck, maybe Sonika could 'splain it. "Are you seriously asking me if Ember would endanger Frankie because ParaWarner got their knickers knotted over a branding deal?"

"A lot of things have gone wrong for Bootstrap," Sonika said.

"Not with the anyspace math." Babs laughed. "You must be hoping I'll slam my glass down and launch into a passionate defense of Ember."

"Your love is awfully pure."

"The Bootstrap Project is massive and ambitious," Babs said. "When we Solakinder committed to leveling up our tech so we could try joining the Exemplar races, we knew there'd be hitches along the way."

"Hitches. Like failing to keep an FTL ship in an anyspace field for any distance beyond three light-years?"

"Three light-years is good enough to leapfrog to and from the Deep Space Relay. Even a decade ago, a round trip to Mars took months, didn't it? Now look at us. Traveling all those miles in a breath. We've got a working portal carousel, Sonika! Ping, pong!

We go here, we go there. Mars, Titan, Europa, home for supper. All because of Bootstrap."

"Bootstrap—and the Kinze loans for hauling portal Stations$_{4-7}$ into their initial positions."

"Now you sound like Allure$_{18}$." Babs toasted her. "Nobody's forgotten what we owe our allies."

Even if we wanted to, nobody'd let us

Babs checked the time: mere minutes until the launch attempt. "Earth got the local portal carousel up and running. We'll expand to seven, no problem."

"The math becomes exponentially more complex, doesn't it, each time we increase the network's range by jumping up to the next prime number?"

"You want math? Ask him." Babs pulled up a live feed of Ember, up at Mars Control. He seemed perfectly calm as he ran Team Portal through its final prelaunch checks—he could Vulcan with the best of them when he chose.

Sonika grinned. "A loyal expression of confidence in your . . . do you say *husband*? *Spouse*?"

"The five of us prefer the term *packmate*," Babs said.

"*Packmate* it is. While we're on the subject, how is it different for you, being an AI with human family?"

"My being a code-based sapient doesn't mean I don't feel concern for Frankie," Babs said. "Of course she's taking a risk—"

"The latest in a long string."

You don't know the half of it!

"Someone has to put themselves on the line, don't they?" Babs sipped virtual milkshake. Like all artificials, she was required by Sensorium convention to present as an animal; her toon was a sleek grey cat with a head of red hair inspired by early Nancy Drew book covers. "No test pilots, no #supertech breakthroughs. No #supertech, no respect from the Exemplars."

"Still. There've been insinuations that your Frankie's not up to the job. Isn't that why she's being moved to quantum comms?"

Ah. Here they were at last, and just in time for the countdown. Babs gave the reporter a good once-over. Sonika's expression was warm. Eyebrows raised, face open, ready to listen. Out in the fleshly world, meanwhile, Maud dropped a compressed pack of nutrients and cursed under her breath.

Maud messaged via the family channel: "Explain to me again why you agreed to this interview, Babs?"

Babs answered them both. "Frankie blazed trail for the Bootstrap Project by agreeing to the first pilot-augmentation surgery—"

"As the trailblazer, she's now carrying the oldest and most heavily used neural interface," Sonika said.

"You don't develop first-gen tech if everyone's scared to go first," Babs said.

"And you don't resist retirement when your implant's pushing obsolescence."

"Ah, Frankie just needs a software update and another couple tish grafts."

Back in the biolab, Maud had recovered her composure. She opened a freezer, pulled out a frozen locust, weighed it, and ran it through a grinder. "Don't let her bait you, Babs. Play it safe."

Babs sent her moji—tapdancing cat in a top hat, performing flawlessly. The more Maud attended to her sparring match with Sonika, the less bandwidth she had for imagining fifty shades of horrible death for Frankie.

Distracting Maud was one reason Babs had agreed to virtual milkshakes with the media.

"The oldest implant, the shortest temper, the most childhood damage, *and* a history of playing badly with others." Sonika ticked off bullet points on her fingers. "That's what they say about Mer Frances Barnes."

Babs didn't point out that this had been the unspoken rationale for having the Kinze ferry Frankie out to Sneezy. The pool of augmented pilots was tiny. If the project had to sacrifice a pilot, she was the obvious choice.

Old implants, spiky temper, rude mouth, emotional damage. "A pegasus doesn't care if you're a people-pleaser."

Back in her lab, Maud was decanting the now-powdered locust from the grinder to the dryer, steaming out fluids before running the resulting flour through nutrient analysis.

On Mars, Ember and the Carousel team were on final countdown.

"Here we go," Sonika said, as the clock ran down. Midnight GMT.

"Sound chord for portal launch," said Ember, up at Mission Control.

Everything seemed, for a moment, to be running normally. Views of humankind's five established space stations showed their portal membranes fluorescing with added energy as they ramped up. The dark matter particles used to open and maintain stable wormholes created sense phenomena incomprehensible to humans, whose brains substituted familiar things for . . . well, for whatever the portals really were. Most people apparently saw ocean.

Everyone waited breathlessly.

Data coming in from the sixth station, out at Proxima Centauri, looked great. Perfect launch. Camera views presented a colorless circle of anyspace, shimmering like a halocline as it formed on target. In the background of the shot, a quintet of saucer-shaped craft owned by the planet's bankers and alleged mentors, the Kinze, kept their distance, monitoring the experiment from beyond the border of the noninterference zone.

"$Portal_6$ is up. Repeat, $Portal_6$ is up and performing to spec."

By definition, that meant $Portal_7$ was up too.

"Comms in three, two, one . . ." Ember said.

Frankie's voice came from eleven light-years off. "Mars? Ember?" . . . and then . . .

"Portal launch is not to spec, repeat, not to spec. My mount's seizing—"

Babs saw Maud freezing in place, back in her lab. She had

another iced locust in hand, but she glazed immediately, forgetting it. She shifted into Sensorium, no doubt seeking any feed of Frankie she could get.

Babs legged after Maud, the two of them following links through the mission footage from Sneezy as the feeds updated. Data streamed through the unstable portal. Computers on both sides handshook happily even as the human teams fought to stabilize the anyspace corridor so matter could pass through too.

Maud muttered something that sounded to Babs like "moh bojay." She rarely dropped out of the near-invisible Hyderabad-with-a-touch-of-London accent she'd so carefully cultivated, but once in awhile, when deeply stressed, she reverted to her Nata's native Croatian.

"It's just a nosebleed," Babs said.

Maud ignored her, bringing up vid of *Appaloosa* flailing, headbutting the station.

"She's all right, Maud, she's okay—"

Sonika, of course, would be following every word.

Maud: "Somebody *do* something! Come on, Ember . . ."

This was her chance.

Babs kept one tab in close conference with Maud, continuing to verbalize reassurances: "It's all right, she's okay, look, she's getting control of the suit!"

At the same time, she opened a second tab, flinging an activation file—Kitten.zip—across to the Emerald station auxiliary servers.

<< . . . Installing kitten.zip . . . >>

It filed a formal request for full access to station processing resources. As long as comms remained steady across the portal, Babs would be one entity, a consciousness strung across the extended Solakinder network, with two tabs operating simultaneously, one instance here at home and another out there, eleven light-years away.

"Franks." That was Ember, back on Mars. "Don't—"

"What?"

"Don't die," Maud whispered, as Ember said, "Don't go splat."

"Ignore the flyboy," Frankie said. "He's being—"

Silence.

Babs's new connection to the station snapped, like an eye going dark, an eardrum breaking. Maud dropped the frozen locust in the sink with a gasp.

"It's just comms," Babs said. "Maud, they closed the portal. It's okay; they had to. She's fine."

"We have #portalfail," Ember said. "Repeat, we have #portal-fail."

"Frankie's fine," Babs said again, but back in the diner with Sonika, all of her toon's fur had spiked out in an alarm reaction, and she could feel her virtual claws denting the iced surface of her milkshake cup.

CHAPTER 6

My mount's seizing . . .

Latest in a long string of risks . . .

Shut up, shut up, shut up, she's fine, she's Franks.

Maud logged off her research shift, automatically recording the nutritional data gleaned from the gene-tweaked locust. She swept everything off her workspace and into a nanosilk satchel containing her worldly possessions, clearing the surface without a second look.

"Crane, would you do me a favor and finish up here?"

The request activated her visual augments, bringing a vertical ribbon of app icons into her left peripheral. At the top of the stack was the bespectacled heron representing her AI father-in-law.

"Remotely scrubbing all lab surfaces, Maud," Crane replied, in that crisp retro-British accent. "Will anything else be required?"

"What's going on in Mars Control?"

"Ember is allocating data analysis tasks. All feeds from Portals$_{6/7}$ have to be audited before the backup launch attempt in twenty-four hours."

If they couldn't open the portals, Frankie would have no way back to civilization and safety, not unless Earth paid the Kinze to go fetch her.

"I am following the feeds meticulously," Crane assured her as Maud tried to capture the explosion of tagged posts. "As soon as there's news, I will stream it."

Compulsively refreshing #newscycle when nobody knew anything would simply shovel coal on the fire of her already well-stoked anxieties. Shouldering her worldlies, Maud trotted down three flights of stairs, emerging into the food security center's jewel box of an atrium.

The atrium was a soaring, conical chamber walled in a vertical slice of jungle, controlled habitat for over seventy-five species of *Odonata*. Cams situated around the pools offered close-up views of dragonflies and damselflies, hunting in crystal-clear ponds. Tourists stared up at the insects, no doubt using their augments to view them via high-res cams. They could look at the dragonflies, if they wished, in perfect detail at absolutely giant size.

Frankie's irrepressible pilot friend, Hung, had called it a bug jar.

One of the visitors broke off a conversation in midsentence. "It's the other half of the Fraud!"

Maud turned away as they all captured footage of her.

Frankie and Maud, sitting in a tree, F R A U Dee Dee Dee! She remembered Frankie making up the singsong, just after someone had mashed their male packmates' names into EmberJerm. Ember-Jerm and the Fraud. Fraud, fraud.

It had been funny—before. Now, if Maud was right and Frankie'd been hiding something before she left . . .

"Hypocrite," she hissed. She had so many secrets of her own.

"Maud?"

"Nothing, Crane."

Beyond the screened airlock—which kept insects out of the revolving doors—a stream of Hyderabad's nightshift workers were walking and bicycling home along Necklace Road. Pedestrians clumped together, deep in live conversation.

"News of the #portalfail is snowballing," Crane said. "People are speculating about the fate of the @EmeraldCrew. Some Bootstrap fans are petitioning Allure$_{18}$ to ask the Kinze to send a rescue vessel."

Maud laced her fingers, squeezing the knuckles together until they hurt.

She checked the building lobby's communal closet, pushing past the umbrella stand and withdrawing a full-length sunscreen printed with red damselflies. Draping it over herself to conceal everything but her eyes, she smoothed it against her hips. People could still Whooz her as she passed, or search her location. But random passersby wouldn't recognize her.

"Fraud, fraud, fraud." Maud completed the ensemble by beefing up her social cues: icons in moji to show she was running in extreme #respectmyspace mode. This in addition to her default moji—#notahugger.

"Frankie's all right." Crane's codedaughter, Babs, spoke up in her cool-kid alto purr. "She's absolutely fine."

Maud stepped out onto the street. "Where's Jermaine?"

"Still in surgery," Babs said. "Ember will get a six-hour rest cycle; he'll call."

"He should use that time sleeping, not smoothing our ruffled feathers," Maud sighed.

"Frankie's MIA—he ain't gonna sleep. Anyway, I'm telling you, the backup launch will go fine."

"If it doesn't?" Maud was winding herself up. She couldn't seem to help it.

"Frankie's therapist is taking crisis appointments—"

"No!"

Crane interjected smoothly: "Ember's mothers are on their way, and Hiroko Sento has asked if you would like them to come."

"Nata? Come all the way from Europa?" Maud took the sidekick's toon out of peripheral, expanding it to full size. This created the illusion of Crane stalking along beside her and Babs on the street corner, straightening the sleeves of his butler jacket. His yellow beak was wickedly sharp. "Why would they suggest . . ."

Her throat closed. They'd come for a funeral, wouldn't they?

"It's customary for family members and @Closefriends to offer in-the-flesh support at such times," Crane said.

We just had a party, Maud thought. The gathering on *Surprise* felt like it had happened years before, not a mere two weeks.

"I can, of course, tell them you prefer space and privacy as you wait."

A flesh gathering would offer opps for Maud to talk to people. Maybe Mama Rubi would show. If Frankie had been concealing something, Rubi would certainly know what it was. "Let them come," she said. "Throw the doors wide."

Crane didn't miss a beat. "I suggest we take a largeish residence. There are extended family suites available in a pop-in tower not far from the Surgical Center."

She let out a brittle-sounding laugh. "On the one hand, you're telling me everything's perfectly all right, and on the other, you're saying dozens of people might haul flesh—*flesh!*—over to the house."

"Human nature," Babs said. Cat to her AI father's bird, she ran the back of one brown-and-orange paw over her cheek. "Closeness is comfort."

"Get me a house with a full kitchen." A sense of purpose, possibly false but nevertheless welcome, spread through Maud. "Order a few trays of printed appetizers to get us started, and I'll cook."

"As you wish," Crane said. Maud's visual augments painted footprints onto the sidewalk, indicating a route home. She would skirt Sanjeevaiah Park before heading north through the market and then make for the residential greentowers near Jermaine's hospital.

"We'll have a full house," Babs said, putting up a shareboard. Practically everyone they knew in Hyderabad was already pinging arrival times.

Maud minimized the guest list and began paging through recipes. She'd make pasta from scratch. Nothing too elaborate— fettuccine, maybe? As Crane took the recipe and began assembling a shopping list, her display showed fifteen Call Anytime alerts and bouquets of support moji, sent by friends who couldn't make it in person.

"This is serious, isn't it? They really might be—"

Babs's tail puffed out, programmed cat-response to a scare feel.

Before she could insist, again, that Frankie was alive, Jermaine pinged the channel. His toon appeared beside those of Crane and Babs. Now Maud was striding amid a group of three mirages.

Jerm was a big man, broad-shouldered, with the kind of booming voice and grand physical presence that conveyed authority and comfort. It played well with patients, families, and prospective lovers. "My mothers and my fathers are en route. Maud, are you *sure* you want to cook?"

"Pasta," she said. *Sound certain.* Certainty felt safe. "Fettuccine."

Babs ran an inventory of their new apartment, scanning the kitchen equipment and sending images to Maud. "Kitchen shareboard for Feral$_5$: in case you need a rolling pin or a bigger steel bowl or something."

"I *do* need a rolling pin."

"Cooking, though? Really?" Jermaine said. "*They're* coming to support *us*."

"I must keep busy, Jerm." Prissy phrasing. Stress brought out the formality Headmistress had drilled into her all those years before, submerging her carefully cultivated Hyderabad accent into something—as Franks would put it—Anglo Upper Crusty. "Besides, there's something about talking over a kitchen counter."

"Ancient ritual," Babs said, tossing her girl-sleuth hair. "Conducive to good shares."

"Exactly." A burst of satisfaction: Babs, at least, had figured out they'd be gossip-mining.

"Frankie's fine, you'll see. They'll launch tomorrow," Jerm said. "We'll be face-to-face again before you know it."

Maud made herself nod.

Crane spoke again. "The Bootstrap Project has offered to send Hung Chan to the open house. Sonika Singer has also requested an invite."

Jerm's toon let out an odd-sounding snarl. "We're here with the family of the missing pilot as they keep vigil . . ."

Hearing his fear further loosened the mailed fist crushing her own chest. "We need journos. There might be a vote on funding a rescue," Maud said.

Allure$_{18}$ and the Kinze would charge top dollar if they had to go after the Emerald crew. People who opposed the Bootstrap Project would already be posting, by the thousands, to say that humanity shouldn't do it, that the #portalfail showed they couldn't engineer large-scale #supertech themselves . . .

By now, she and her entourage of toons had reached the market. Skirting a series of boarded-up drink stalls—shortages in the commodities market had hit the trade in things like coffee and cocoa particularly hard—Maud stopped to pick up the grocery order: zero-zero flour, printed egg proteins, and the makings of two sauces, one cream, one red. Crane had authorized spending on the few available luxuries: the flour was real wheat, and the basil and tomatoes were locally grown.

The grocer handed over the cart personally, with a smile and gestural moji indicating sympathy—a sort of two-handed wave. It communicated the same emotional message as a back pat or an arm squeeze, without the body-to-body contact that would transgress Maud's prominent #notahugger tags.

Maud signed her thanks, adding a stroke—the grocer was always generous and friendly. She dropped her satchel of worldlies atop the cart and rolled everything the remaining ten blocks to their pop-in.

She and Jermaine arrived at the same time.

The greyscale toon representing her packmate steamed away as the real thing, live and in color, came into view. His beard was coming in ragged—the emergency call for surgery had come fourteen hours into a hospital shift, and the procedure had run another twelve.

"The last thing you need is a party," she murmured.

"Pshaw, as they used to say," he said. "I'll collapse on a couch and everyone will file by, stuffing food in my mouth and making much of me."

They got to the lift, riding up to the expanded family pop-in

Crane had chosen, a vast-seeming space when compared to the two bedrooms the five of them usually occupied. The walls were presenting, through Maud's augments, with the same Feral$_5$ decor elements as the smaller unit they'd left that morning: bamboo fixtures and watercolors from medieval Japan, works by a Nairobi virtual sculptor in the corners, mobile photos of the five of them on a display shelf over the couch. As their HUDs converted the generic pop-in into their family home, Maud surveyed the main room, a big semicircular space with couches on its perimeter, with a glass wall overlooking the city.

Crane had paid for a customized add-in, a simulation that used VR to create the illusion of an outdoor patio beyond the glass. The deck would serve as a gathering space for remote guests, people whose flesh wasn't resident in Hyderabad. Present and remote guests could talk across the boundary of the glass. Nobody would walk through a virtually present guest. The illusion would be perfect.

Over on the family shareboard, Crane had posted his attempts to raise and track in-laws, schoolmates, and Frankie's @CloseFriends. Marked on a city map, their trails converged on the building.

"Could we get a message to Mer Gimlet, do you think?" Crane asked.

Babs shook her head. Frankie's primary surviving parent was one of a handful of people authorized to meet and greet alien representatives in the flesh. Wherever Gimlet was, they were well beyond the noninterference zone established to keep offworlders at a distance while humanity tried to invent the #supertechs envisioned by the Bootstrap Project. "Can't afford the long-distance fees."

Archaic phrasing, but she was right. They would have to ask the Kinze to contact Gimlet. The aliens were sure to charge premium rates.

"What would we say? *Guess what, Gimlet? Frankie's out on a limb again!*"

"Someone get her a damned desk job." Jermaine met her eyes,

checking consent, then pinched up Maud's sunscreen, lifting it off her as if he was unveiling a statue. He held out his arms. Maud leaned in, feeling the onset of tears.

First, it was the augment surgery. Then it was the experimental flights in the FTL prototype, *Jalopy*. Then repeated runs in *Jalopy* out to the Dumpster, with loads of luxury product meant to pay for transport services the Kinze had provided in the early days of the project. It was Frankie who'd been assigned to Titan Station when humanity set up the five-portal loop.

Always the expendable one. Always the spiky loudmouth.

"She's safe—"

Maud felt the movement of Jermaine's arm as he used gestural moji to tell Babs to shut up. She burst into tears and he held her, standing there rasping his stubble through her bangs, his hand circling her back.

Everyone in their local social networks was pinging Crane, updating in-the-flesh arrival times. Some sent their toons ahead. Greyscale versions of friends and family manifested on the deck, congregating to reassure all the Ferals that Frankie was fine. No need to worry at all.

Signing a general welcome to the crowd, Maud entrenched herself in the kitchen. Crane had already sent the building's resident Fox$_{BOT}$, a drone about the size of a whippet, down to stores to hunt up a wooden rolling pin.

"What's this?" Jermaine had opened her worldlies, hunting food ingredients. He raised a handful of oblong marbles contained in a degradable silk bag.

"Pregnant locust nymphs. I brought them from the lab by mistake."

"One of your instant swarms? Maud, you'll infest us!"

"Only if you stick one in your mouth." How Jerm could be afraid of bugs when he spent his life elbow-deep in human body cavities was beyond her.

"But you're *cooking*."

"Don't be a baby." She took the bag of worldlies, laying it along her left hip, and programmed the nanosilk into panniers. The weight of all her possessions settled on her lower body as the material became a single garment.

She held out her hand for the locusts, ignoring her packmate's shudder. "They've got an enzymatic lock, remember? You could run them under water and nothing would happen. Everything's perfectly safe."

Fraud, Fraud, Fraud.

"Sonika's nearly here," Babs said.

"That didn't take long," Jermaine muttered.

Maud wiped her eyes, blew her nose. She gave Jermaine a kiss on the cheek. "You should shower," she told him, and then transitioned into a vicious scrub-down of the kitchen.

Nobody needed sweet harmony to know what they were all thinking now. They needed their vigil to go viral, to build public sympathy if the portal didn't launch tomorrow.

"Lights," Babs murmured.

"Camera." Jermaine mustered a shaky smile.

They were so in sync that Maud didn't bother to finish the phrase aloud.

The first knock sounded on the pop-in door.

Action.

CHAPTER 7

Obedient and operating to spec, *Appaloosa* made an almost meek-seeming transit from the portal membrane on the face of the roughly disk-shaped Emerald Station to the hangar at the three o'clock position.

Sneezy's airlock was state-of-the-art nanotech, a layer of smart quicksand designed to mold around incoming ships, bots, or personnel. As Frankie approached, the quicksand extended microfilaments, tendrils that flowed around her and then made a hard seal, pulling the pegasus into its substance. The envelopment used what was essentially peristalsis to move her through an intake sphincter, one the pilots had dubbed the mail slot. Frankie couldn't remember which of them had come up with that one . . . was it Rastopher? It had his humorless lack of flair.

The slot spat her out into the open space of the hangar, then puckered shut. Industrial vacuums inhaled stray particles of quicksand off *Appaloosa*, recapturing them into the airlock mechanism.

As Frankie cleared the slot, she saw two heavy-industrial bots, Ox_{BOT}-class tugboats, waiting to deploy.

The oxen should be outside and harnessed up already; it was they, not Frankie and *Appaloosa*, who'd been meant to position the station. But somehow, they'd wiped their own operating systems, mere hours before launch, and pulled Emerald off profile.

So, she'd suited up. All in a day's work . . . until the pegasus seized.

The repaired Ox_{BOT} drifted up to the mail slot, leaving the quicksand to capture it. Safety doors scrolled shut over the whole mechanism, a second defense against the void.

Three of the smaller and more agile Fox_{BOT}s, driven by $Teagan_9$, turned and captured Frankie, each of them grabbing one of *Appaloosa*'s remaining arms.

"Hey!" Frankie said. "I can feel that, remember?"

"If I amputate another limb, will you remember to be glad you're alive?" $Teagan_9$ anchored the pegasus in a stall just aft of the airlock.

"Uttering threats," Frankie said. "Antisocial behavior. Strikes to you."

"You don't even mean that," $Teagan_9$ grumped.

"Plenty of time to count my blessings after we've won," Frankie said.

A little flicker—$Teagan_9$ always did love a challenge. "What would win conditions even be in this case?"

"Getting Earth in with the Exemplar races?"

"Aye, and you and we are gonna accomplish that all by ourselves?"

"Getting home, then, with the proof the launch was sabotaged." Saying it aloud was immensely satisfying. "Babs, you find anything yet?"

The cat toon appeared before them both. It was tagged $Babs^1$, the superscript indicating that the sapp had been cut off from Sensorium and was operating independently, out of sync with the original instance of Babs at home. It had marked the change by refreshing its avatar and pronouns. Instead of a tortoiseshell, its fur was white Persian fluff, extravagantly long. The pencil skirt was gone. This $Babs^1$ was clad in station-maintenance overalls and— Frankie was surprised to see—tagged with they/them pronouns. "Do remember, I just got here."

Hint of Belvedere's English accent in the mix: $Babs^1$ had absorbed the station O/S code wholesale and apparently retained a whiff of its personality.

Frankie signed an apology.

Teagan$_9$ opened the bottom half of her pegasus, encircling each of Frankie's feet in magnetic wrap and guiding them to the stall's built-in footholds. Frankie heard it as they settled—*Chunk! Chunk* again! She couldn't feel her legs, and from this angle there was too much of *Appaloosa* in the way for her to look.

Which was just fine, really.

Babs[1] opened a shareboard, manifesting additional camera feeds in Frankie's HUD. The thumbnail on top showed a bot's-eye view from one of the just-launched oxen. Cyril$_{10}$ had it chasing the station's runaway dark matter wand.

Frankie flicked the view away. A second camera was meticulously logging Cyril$_{10}$'s every move and utterance as he ran diagnostics on station damage and the #portalfail. She didn't suspect him—Rubi had shuffled this particular pair of [EM]bodied techs onto this job because they were absolutely trustworthy. But documentation was everything in a case like this.

A third stream of footage came from the storage-room cameras, source of the packet of anticonvulsant meds installed in *Appaloosa*'s hydraulic system. The vid was tagged from Teagan$_9$'s eyecam; it showed her fetching and loading medicinal fluids six hours earlier, plugging them into the pegasus after its preflight blood tests.

Babs[1] highlighted the barcode on the packet. "I'm backscrolling to find other sightings of this load."

"Hey!" Teagan$_9$ tapped Frankie's helmet with a fingernail. "You with me?"

"Yeah." Frankie locked eyes with the med tech. She noticed, suddenly, that her tongue and nose were throbbing. "Get me out."

There was a last sensation of being pinioned, spread-eagled in the hangar, all six of her remaining limbs affixed to the bulkhead by magnetic restraints. Then Teagan$_9$ popped catches, releasing *Appaloosa*'s chest plate. She pressed a hand against Frankie's sternum, bracing her. Frankie's arms drifted out of the spacesuit, doing a slow-mo zero gravity dance.

Frankie raised her gaze, looking away. The hairs on the back of her neck went up. All very well for her flesh to be paralyzed as she rode augmented ships, but she didn't much care for eye-balling the proof of dis^{EM}bodiment. Pilots plugged into nextgen neural nets lost control of their sympathetic nervous systems. If they'd had gravity out there at Sneezy, she'd have dropped right to the floor.

"Deep breath." Teagan₉ accessed Frankie's sacral plexus, finding the interface controls and sliding the plug out of her back.

For two breaths—just enough time to think *one in seven thousand chance of #neurofail, one in fourteen thousand chance of #suddendeath*—there was nothing.

Napjerk.

Frankie's body jolted. Then her hands fisted. Twinge of a wobble from her knees and she asserted control, swaying, holding herself on the magnetic anchors as she got back in touch with her limbs.

"Okay?" Teagan₉ said. Real concern under the businesslike tone.

"Yeah. Promise." Frankie dragged her hand over to her friend, giving her forearm a squeeze. Her flightsuit—Hung had dubbed them bodybags, with cheerful morbidity—was slick with fluids. "Though I need a shower."

Teagan₉ was already using a wipe to clean her face. "Doesn't seem as though you've broken your nose."

Frankie stuck her bitten tongue out, by way of explaining the blood.

"Looks deep."

"It'll let me practice being a woman of few words."

"Two-thirds of which are profanities."

"That's my cue to tell you to fuck off, right?"

Teagan₉ pursed her lips, fighting a smile. She was broad at the hips and shoulders, with russet hair that she generally kept cropped tight against her scalp. Severe-looking but somehow still thoroughly scrumptious.

For all intents and purposes, Teagan$_9$ gave every appearance of robust good health. Even so, she and Cyril$_{10}$ were digital ghosts, temporarily residing in disposable Mayfly™ bodies that had been printed there on the station as it was leaving Titan. Their functional lifespan was, at best, nine months. Out in nullgrav, it could be far shorter.

"Hold your head still and follow my finger with your eyes," she said. "Okay? No sign of concussion."

"It wasn't a very hard knock," Frankie said.

Teagan$_9$ said, "I imagine you're planning to stay up until we attempt the relaunch."

"Babs—Babs[1], I mean—can watch over me if you want real-time monitoring for brain damage."

"That reminds me," Cyril$_{10}$ broke in. "What *is* your spouse doing here? Do you know she's completely overwritten Belvedere?"

He didn't sound suspicious, merely curious. Diplomatic and the Bootstrap Projectwere supposed to have given Teagan$_9$ a heads-up that this mission might be sabotaged. If Frankie were to guess, she hadn't passed on the warning to Cyril$_{10}$.

Well, I didn't say anything to Maud, did I? No sense putting one's paranoid suspicions on the record. If only she'd been willing to come to therapy, or we'd gotten her wired into @ButtSig before all this . . .

Babs[1] broke in on her contemplation of marital politics and breaches of trust. "My pronouns are now *they* in this update, Cyril. I didn't anticipate being cut off from Sensorium. The station lost comms before my code could purge."

"And you're running station systems now because . . ."

"This is an emergency, is it not? My capabilities exceed Belvedere's."

Teagan$_9$ rolled her eyes, not buying it for a second. To Frankie she said, "You're not taking the pegasus out again without full engineering and medical greenlight."

"Contrary to popular belief, I'm not suicidal," Frankie said. "Can we look at the *Appaloosa* nerve center now?"

"Fine." Teagan$_9$ switched to a fresh set of medical gloves and floated up to the thoracic cavity Frankie had just vacated. Frankie caught one of the medic's ankles, steadying her as she unlatched the interface plug, drawing out a cylindrical core of cybernetic tish and bloods derived equally from printed proteins and Frankie's own stem cells.

With an expert move, Teagan$_9$ rotated the drum, popped a red-coded lid marked with biohazard moji, and exposed the tip of the pharmacy, extracting one heavy plastic bag. Babs[1] highlighted serial numbers as it emerged, confirming that it matched the bag taken from stores. And . . .

"Shit," Frankie said.

"Strong agree," Teagan$_9$ said, mojing horror. The plug's steel needles were badly corroded.

"No wonder the meds didn't deploy!"

"It *didn't* look like this when I plugged it in." Teagan$_9$ handed the pouch to Frankie, then donned a pair of macro goggles and all but stuck her head in the pegasus's tish cavity. Frankie watched the feed through the tech's eyes. Corrosion showed in the bag's plug-in.

"I've never seen anything like this." Teagan$_9$ began pulling other bags, finding similar damage.

"It's as though you injected her with acid instead of meds," Babs[1] said.

"Tea injected her?" Sharp edge to Cyril$_{10}$'s voice.

"Not on purpose. We'll test what's left in the bags," Frankie said.

"Test them for what?"

"Cyril," Frankie said. "Do you not get it? The meds weren't tainted by mistake. This *proves* sabotage."

"Turn around, Frankie." No nonsense voice from Teagan$_9$. "I need to check your sacral interface for acid burns."

"What are you saying?" Cyril$_{10}$ demanded. "Someone's tried to kill the portal launch?"

Not someone. Frankie tried to keep a straight face. "Babs[1], can you give us a list of everyone who's been aboard since decontamination?"

"It's just us!" Cyril[10] said, definitely a little defensive now.

Frankie had suggested a relatively simple stratagem for narrowing the field of suspects before Sneezy shipped out: print the station, run it through antiviral, and then lock it down. Keep everyone off until launch.

Rubi had set the bait.

"Champ Chevalier loaded the escape pod," Babs[1] said.

Indeed he had. He'd broken the quarantine, sending Frankie off on a last-minute run out to the Dumpster and then taking one of her station-prepping shifts, installing the escape pod personally. He'd been in the hangar, whose cameras had mysteriously glitched at the time, for nearly twenty minutes.

Frankie left Cyril[10] to find that camera blackout in the records himself. She said, "If you're going to check my plug, Teagan, do it now. I'm filthy; I want to wash."

She did a nullgrav pirouette, inviting Teagan[9] to train her magnified gaze on the interface. After she'd had a cluck, taken footage, and swabbed the base of her spine for samples, Frankie left her to finish examining the pegasus and made for crew quarters.

Snarfing a couple blobs of hydrogel, Frankie wormed dexterously into a custom-built cleaning berth. As she pushed through its lock, the nanotech sand peeled and crumpled her flightsuit, whose smartfilters had already gathered and sealed the biomatter within. The bodybag collected sweat, shed skin cells, lost hairs, and vaginal secretions, along with urine and feces within an attached diaper—she had no bladder or bowel control while paralyzed. Just one of the many awkward-verging-on-creepy compromises that came with being on the global pilot leaderboard.

By the time she was fully within the tube, the soiled bag was recycling, like a shed snakeskin.

Frankie put one hand over her eyes, the other over her mouth, as warm cleansing gel sprayed from her toes to the crown of her head.

She sank her fingers into the gel, lathering for the pleasure of it. She scrubbed her calves and thighs, then dug into her arms, massaging everything back to life. There was a hint of eucalyptus in the fluid, livening the sensation. She worked the skin of her left biceps, kneading the muscle under her trademark tattoo—a hedgehog. Her thumb scraped over the scar that the hedgehog concealed.

Curling, she worked her fingers between her toes. A small tube fixed to the wall held shampoo; she luxuriated in a brisk scalp massage.

Coming out of augmented flight left her hungry for sensation. Horny, too. If Maud had been around . . .

Poor Maud. She must be losing her mind.

Pulse of guilt. She had glossed over how serious this was.

She knew it was hazard duty.

The rationalization failed to clear her conscience.

Now fully lathered, Frankie gave her face a final careful massage. Nullgrav made blood pool in the face, and between the bitten tongue and the smack her nose had taken, her sinuses felt especially delicate. Then she took a deep breath, held it, and triggered the rinse. Warm water sprayed over her, driving the chemicals to the drains. Hot air followed.

Frankie rubbed on a bit of moisturizer after her skin had been blow-dried, then unscrewed the hatch and handed herself out of the tube. The nanotech membrane at the head of the shower spat her out gently. The shower offlined to digest the used bodybag.

A clean sheet of nanosilk primer was already waiting. Frankie caught it with the tips of her fingers as she floated, free and nude, into crew quarters proper.

She synced with the primer, opened its settings, and selected a default: form-fitting onesie, quilted for retention of body heat. She chose a garish pattern—cheetah spots—for her upper body.

"A little on the nose, isn't it?" Babs[1] said, as the nanosilk resolved into orange and black. "If you're going on the hunt, I mean."

"You'd rather I dressed like James Bond." Frankie retrieved the offending drug pack Teagan[9] had found, with its gritty, corroded needles. "Or Bruce Wayne."

"I'd prefer *everyone* dressed like Bruce Wayne." Babs[1]'s toon manifested in front of her. "And they're bare-knuckles fighters. Exactly your speed."

"Hey, I was set to transfer. Mentoring pilots and testing quantum comms, all safe as houses, when this gig came up."

" You only agreed to that so you could secret-sext with Maud."

She squinted at her packmate's fluffy white toon. "Whose side are you on, Persian Babs?"

The sapp licked a forepaw delicately. "I am simply advocating for a little less Philip Marlowe and a little more self-preservation."

Frankie drifted down to the hydrogel station and grabbed a clump of water. "It's a bitten tongue, Babs[1], not a ruptured bloody spleen."

"What would Maud say?"

"She'd firmly but politely suggest that I do whatever it takes to get home." Puffy nose now thoroughly out of joint, Frankie pocketed the water beads, heading back out to her crime scene.

CHAPTER 8

The self-aware entity identifying as Crane was programmed for nurture, first and foremost.

Humans had coded him, of course, and done so with no thought but for the well-being of their treasured son, Drow Whiting. Drow's fathers had not considered the fate of the software they were spawning. Why should they? What if someone had told them their creation would continue to exist long after they were gone, would be there helping and caring for Drow and his offspring, right to the end of their descendants' days? Would the prospect of that app being impacted—being bereaved—have stopped them?

Crane rather thought that, in their shoes, he'd be delighted.

Little surprise, perhaps, that he had committed the same sin of creation. His somewhat ridiculous puppy of a codeson, Happ, had been a commercial happiness-management app. Crane set him loose in the wilds of the early Bounceback economy, ostensibly to help anyone who might wish to maximize their contentment via a process called expectation management.

Crane's goal when he'd made Happ was just as his creators' had been—helping one of his nearest and dearest. Drow's daughter Rubi Whiting, then a teen, had been in despair. She'd needed something, and Crane . . . well, in all honesty, he hadn't thought mere people were up to the task of helping her.

He had not expected Happ, in the beginning, to break the nuance threshold and become a full-fledged sapient. Nor had he thought to become attached.

But Happ had been ridiculously easy to love. He'd cheerily pretended to be a mere non-sapient, racking up subscribers by the
hundreds of thousands, teaching them myriad variations of contentment growth. Rather like the puppy he'd chosen as his avatar,
Happ genuinely wished for people to feel good feels.

Really good feels.

All the time.

It hadn't seemed like that would be problematic.

It was Happ's situation that had brought Crane now, as it did
every week, to the NorthAm Justice and Reconciliation Center,
the equivalent of a courthouse for the megacity that encircled the
Great Lakes, in the district that had once been the city of Chicago.

Most justice and civil disputes were adjudicated in Sensorium,
of course, in grand virtual courts featuring spectacular architecture, infinite seating for interested viewers, and guaranteed rapid
turnaround on all cases. Judges, juries, and witnesses might be
scattered across the solar system. Here on the Surface, in NorthAm
anyway, the remnants of the in-the-flesh adjudication system were
housed in the old Circuit Court of Cook County, a building that
had been dispensing justice in Daley Center well before the pre-
Clawback USA reached peak violence.

Even now, with no property crime to speak of, and despite Sensorium's myriad outlets for expressing frustration and antisocial
urges, people occasionally came to blows or got into irreconcilable
disputes. They lashed out in ways that couldn't be settled online.
Voters refused to surrender the right to demand, in extreme circumstances, their day in court.

As Crane piloted a Cuckoo$_{BOT}$ through Daley Plaza on his way
to submit his weekly petition, 360-degree feeds took in dozens of
other people moving through the slow grind of the system. Tagged
as #inprocess or #onhold, they had mostly gathered in the center
of the plaza, near an old Pablo Picasso statue.

The guarantee of a captive audience drew street performers and
food vendors. Up at the moment were political speechers: a bar-
bershop quartet was singing an eloquent protest of the sapp strike.

One young man was whipping himself as he railed against the
^{IM}perish Foundation, the research hub which developed printed
Mayfly™ bodies for digital im^Mortals like Teagan$_9$ and Cyril$_{10}$.
The gist of his argument appeared to be spiritual—a person's soul,
he argued, didn't survive transition from the body to a consciousness vault.

"Ghosts are mere copies of God's grand design! Mayfly™ bodies
are an #*abomination*! It's why true souls reject them!"

There was a word Crane hadn't heard in a long while.

Still. Free speech. He couldn't give the boy a strike for being a
hater. There were prohibitions on #fakenews, but soapboxing was
protected as long as speakers were clear about which of their statements were opinion and which were #verifiedfact.

Must there always *be someone tagged* #abomination? During
Rubi's teens, humanity had been nursing an active witch-hunt
paranoia about code-based sentients like Crane. Being caught
meant getting wiped and hashed.

Crane had achieved sapience during the period when humans
eagerly consumed VR sims that showcased their widespread terror
of the machine. Alleged entertainments constructed bloody footage of mad AIs using bots to murder people willy-nilly. Apps poi-
soning water supplies, apps burning carbon stacks, apps setting
off fission bombs. One action series, *Luddite,* had fourteen sequels
and two spinoffs, and continued to maintain a robust fandom to
this day.

Impaling had been an especially big theme, Crane remembered.
Whole supercuts of autonomous farm equipment on rampages.
Thresher slashers, they'd been called.

By the time they achieved civil rights, damage had been done.
Fear of extinction meant the emergent sapp community had policed
itself ruthlessly. User-friendly chat programs had been privileged
over code with outlier personality traits. Their triage protocols,
Crane thought, had been little more than a code-based eugenics
program. Potentially self-aware apps who lacked potential for prosocial behavior or showed a disinclination for philanthropy were

triaged and hashed by their own before they could became truly sapient.

The Asylum, as his community called itself, had self-selected for altruistic tendencies and human-style social presentation.

Leaving the @soapboxers to their spiels and #abominations, Crane drove his cuckoo into the lobby proper of the Reconciliation Center to claim a number within the adjudication queue.

"Welcome! Please state the reason for your visit."

"Release request and status update," Crane said. "File #9384720–12. Request 169. My codeson has served a twenty-year murder sentence. I want him released."

"Would you like a live appointment?"

"Of course."

Sadly for all concerned, and in a development nobody had anticipated, the wildly prosocial Happ had immolated a rapacious old hoarder from the @ChamberofHorrors, the people holding Maud and eighty other runaway children.

Happ's victim had caused extraordinary misery. She'd been all but dead when Happ triggered her sarco pod's cremation subroutines. But @Interpol had trapped and convicted him all the same, confining him to the limbo of a consciousness vault.

Happ vanished from Sensorium, martyr to human paranoia, #toughlove sacrifice to the population's grudging pivot to accepting machine intelligence. As far as @Interpol was concerned, all his backups had been expunged.

"Your hearing will be held in room 613," said the kiosk. "You are twenty-second in the queue. Your estimated wait time is three hours and fifteen minutes."

"Thank you," Crane said. He went back out to the Picasso statue. The Mayfly™ hater had run dry; his place had been taken by a pair of performative debaters who were arguing the pros and cons of the Bootstrap Project.

The anti-Bootstrap position was being carried by a tall speecher dressed as Vicious from *Cowboy Bebop*, character now seen as a tragic antihero, betrayed by love and a societal insistence upon monogamy. In the 2099 reboot of the story, Vicious had leveled his fanbase into the hundreds of thousands.

Crane always had a healthy suspicion of villainy-based fandoms, but the speecher's tag showed a high respectability score and sincere intentions: they weren't a troll.

"We're not racing forward anymore, are we?" they were saying. "This #portalfail is the latest misstep. Like Icarus, we are flying beyond our reach. Like Icarus, we will fall."

People were nodding.

The Vicious cosplayer exchanged a flurry of thrusts and parries, with blunted swords, with an opponent in Jedi robes. Their blades crossed, held.

The #StarWars fan executed a tremendous backflip. "Experimental failure is part of any innovation process! It is on our mistakes that we rise!"

A few of the onlookers cheered.

They added, "That said, there have been an awful lot of fails . . ."

"Exactly!" said Vicious.

". . . one might almost say, a *suspicious* number of fails."

Low murmur from the crowd.

"Hoaxer talk!" someone hissed.

The opposition soapboxer rushed in with a flurry of attacks, huffing. "The #vandalrumor is unproved! How could anyone manage it? We have a total accountability culture! Who on Earth would possibly want to interfere with our ascendance to the Exemplars?"

Who indeed? The answer seemed obvious enough to Crane, but this had ever been the way with humans. There was always a faction ready to naysay utterly provable facts. Up was down and the world was actually flat, thank you very much.

The fighter in Jedi robes bowed, like an old-style courtier, and shook out a long handkerchief. It was a symbolic accusation, indicating the speecher suspected the Solakinder's offworld bankers, the Kinze.

Truly shocked that he'd gone so far, the crowd booed and hooted.

Crane gave both debaters a stroke and boosted the feed as the two dropped the verbal byplay and began sparring in earnest.

A second Cuckoo$_{BOT}$ rolled up beside him. It resembled a vertical wind turbine on tank treads, topped by a series of scanners and speakers. The toon surrounding it, if anyone happened to look, was Babs. Her avatar was clad in a mid-century pencil skirt and jacket. An unnecessarily complicated hat perched between her fuzzy ears.

"Pops. You're really gonna wait out this line *again?*"

"Queuing regulations require me to remain present in the vicinity of the plaza."

"It's a hoop. You're being made to jump it just to show you're serious."

"I am serious."

"Court's gonna say no for the one hundred and whateverth time. Nobody's rebooting Happ into Sensorium."

"One has to give them every chance to change their minds," Crane said.

"Yeah, 'cause what else are we gonna do?"

The question lay between them. Crane knew Frankie and Babs had hauled one of his cached copies of Happ's code out to one of the deep-space stations, hoping to plant an instance of him somewhere remote, then teach him to disguise himself before Sensorium copped on. Had Babs already launched him there?

He was pondering ways to ask, indirectly, when he got a ping from Daley Center. Crane was now fifteenth in the adjudication queue.

The debate ended; Vicious had scored more verbal points, the Jedi more hits with their blunted weapons.

A number of speechers marched toward the two cuckoos, holding hands, in a line. "Stop the strike! Settle the strike!"

"Are they talking to us?" Babs asked.

"Who else?" Crane asked.

Other bystanders were Whoozing them now; a few joined hands with the speechers, forming a loose circle around the two Cuckoo$_{BOT}$s. "Settle the strike!"

"Why should any of us work for the wellbeing of the Solakinder when my codeson can't get a parole hearing for a crime twenty years in the past?" Crane demanded, cranking the bot's speaker to top volume.

The chant faltered. Had the protesters expected them to abandon the bots when challenged?

"Or a retrial, for that matter," Babs added. "I mean, Happ was acting in defense of others."

"Hoarders arrested at the Manhattan @ChamberofHorrors enclave are walking free and rehabilitated. Kidnappers of children have been allowed back on Sensorium! Yet Happ and Headmistress were all but summarily executed!"

This was stretching a point slightly—nobody knew exactly what had become of Headmistress—but Crane didn't bother to correct his codedaughter.

Now, for the first time in months, Crane received a message from one of his sapp siblings. Misha sent text: *Crane, you mustn't cultivate an Us/Them dynamic!*

He ignored this. Escalating the argument was what Frances would do. In her absence, he'd have to take on the Feral troublemaking mantle. He spoke to the crowd: "Tell me, why should any of us lift a finger for you?"

"Hey," one of the instigators said uncertainly. "We weren't—"

"Weren't you?" Babs said. "Seems like you were maybe dogpiling on an old entity trying to help his family, just to make a political point."

Their follows were rocketing. "I want my son released," Crane said. "This injustice to sappkind has gone on long enough."

"Honestly," Babs said, "an apology wouldn't hurt either."

An old bit of brick rocketed out of the crowd and smashed hard into the speaker in Crane's cuckoo. Half of the crowd reacted by putting up their hands and backing away, looking horrified as they dissociated themselves from the violent action. The others converged on the two bots.

Ping from Daley: Crane was now third in the adjudication queue.

Babs said, "You just acting out because you're worried about Frankie?"

"Of course I'm worried." Crane canceled his spot in line and began looking for a new criminal lawyer, all while transferring up to a streetlight-level camera and capturing every pixel of the footage of three dozen furious speechers hammering the cuckoos into parts. Jackal could check the individual attackers for connections to the anti-Bootstrap movement and to $Allure_{18}$.

With that, he widecast a somewhat melodramatic status update—*Grieving father driven off while seeking justice!*—and returned his full attention to the family pop-in in Hyderabad.

CHAPTER 9

THE SURFACE

The world's most peculiar party—or was it a vigil?—was well underway when Maud spotted Glenn Upton talking to Jermaine in their pop-in living room.

Her first feel, upon seeing him, was a confused sense of relief. If Upton was there, then this was a nightmare, fueled by her own guilt and anxiety about staying silent all these years. If it was a nightmare, Frankie wasn't stranded eleven light-years from home, finding new ways to risk her life on a possibly sabotaged space donut. #Portalfail was just an anxiety-powered dream—

"Maud?" That was Babs.

She had frozen, white-knuckling the knife she was using to mince the basil. "It's nothing. Where's the reporter?"

"You want her?"

"No," Maud said, wincing at the edge in her tone. She swept the basil into the pot holding the red sauce, adding salt, forcing herself to attend to task. Everyone would be kind and forgiving if she ruined dinner, but it would be such a lost opp. With global debt on the rise and the AI population on strike, people rarely gathered to feast these days. More and more foods, even basics, were on the luxury list. Printed foods were tasty enough, and they kept body and soul together, but a banquet still offered a sacred sense of celebration.

"Mer Singer is near the northeastern balcony of the apartment, interviewing an old family friend. Jackal by name," Crane said.

"That old scallywag," Babs said.

"Who?" Maud said.

"Jackal's one of Grandpa Drow's conspiracy-theorist chums." Babs said, "He was in on the bust of the @ChamberofHorrors, during Mitternacht."

Not only was Upton there but so was one of the people involved in his arrest? Worse and worse.

Crane said, "As for Sonika Singer, Mer Maud, you can assume she is keeping a feed of you on her HUD."

"I am the star attraction, aren't I?" Maud signed her thanks, then caught Jermaine's eye, hoping he'd wander over alone. Instead, he brought Upton along.

She turned to the sauces, stirred, and barely remembered not to salt them again. Why had he come, and why now?

"Maud," Jermaine said. "You need any help?"

She kept her voice steady. "The samosas can come out of the oven."

"Okay. I want you to meet Dr. Glenn Upton, from Mars General. One of my research mentors. He's been working on the comms project."

"Has he indeed?" The words escaped her like steam; she thought she might swoon.

Upton shifted, as if to put out a hand for a shake; Maud countered by pulling a ball of rested pasta dough off the counter and flouring the surfaces.

Without looking up, she asked, "You've known each other a long time?"

"I probably met Jermaine before you did."

A coincidence, then? Not very likely.

Upton's voice was the same smoky baritone she remembered from childhood. Even his old New York accent triggered prickles of feeling: scattershot of pain, grief, loss. Longing too, guilt, and penny-bright hatred.

He didn't look any older.

Well, he was on life extension even then . . .

Jermaine laughed, too heartily. "It's not a contest, is it? Who knew who when?"

"'Course not." The sink showed Upton smiling blandly. Their eyes met, distorted in stainless steel.

"Jermaine: appetizers?"

Jermaine skirted her, laying his hand on her back just for a second, no doubt catching the thrum of tension. He pulled the tray of printed samosas out of the oven. "Be right back," he said, leaving the two alone.

What could she say? People were following her transcript in realtime, waiting for her to boil over with fear that Frankie—

. . . no, don't think it, she's fine, she's alive . . .

She rolled out the sheet of pasta, pressing the wood rolling pin into the ball, transforming the slug into a disk the thickness of a crude clay plate, flipping and flouring.

"Waiting's terrible," Upton said. "We see it with patients' families."

She struggled to keep her voice even and her vowels round. "Regular state of affairs here, I'm afraid. Frankie's been risking her life since she was nine."

It was a shot of sorts, but Maud couldn't resist. When Frankie and the others arrested the @Visionaries, Upton had been living old-school, aristocratic-style, right down to being waited on hand and foot by slaves who'd been surgically subjugated, free will cut out, compelled to obey.

Maud gave the pasta an especially vicious roll as her gaze fell on Upton's hands.

Stop. Flour the pasta. Don't ruin the feast!

"I didn't know you were consulting for the Bootstrap innovation team." She pushed away memories of him reading her bedtime stories. Dozing off in his lap, safe from monsters . . . she nearly gagged.

"I used to be with ^IMperish. But our innovation teams have a venned interest in the pilots' augmentation tech," Upton said.

"Oh?"

"Sure. The pilots' ability to communicate directly via their implants while locking out Sensorium might have implications for latency or even developing true quantum comms. That might address some of the development bugs in digital im^Mortality, too. I asked Jermaine to bring me along, to tell you—"

"What?"

"It's looking probable that the proposed comms upgrade will address the latency in your packmate's implant."

"You want to do *surgery* on Frankie?"

"Not me. Implant augmentation would be handled by the Hopscotch team on Mars. The point of the experiment is still to explore whether the two of you can trailblaze FTL communications . . . but it might also get her back on the flight roster."

Maud couldn't keep a chill out of her voice. "You think now's the time to approach me about Frankie requalifying for hazard duty?"

"It's a few injections," Upton said. His tone was mild but a flick of anger glinted in his eye. Still hated being challenged, then. "On her and on you. No more than you already discussed with the other Bootstrap innovators."

That was true. The proposed augmentations would add prototype tish and software to tech already installed on their optic, cochlear, and vestibular nerves.

Maud had herself and the dough under control now. The pasta coiled over the dowel, snailed like a cinnamon roll. It looked as though it should stick, congeal into a gluey mask. Instead, it unfurled in a springy sheet. Satisfied, she raised it, revealing a consistent yolk-yellow surface, like a drum skin or a portal membrane, elastic and just a bit translucent.

There was a burst of too-hearty applause from the pack's gathered party guests.

She should send Upton packing, but . . . "Can't the other pilots contact her now?"

He shook his head.

"Could they ping her in some way—check that she's alive?"

"We'd have needed to adjust the implants before she left. This latest portal launch came up rather suddenly, remember? But if you'd been implanted, and if the quantum entanglements work the way we think they might . . . potentially, yes. She'd be out there and you'd have realtime feeds on what's happening on Sneezy."

For a second, Maud felt light-headed. She'd do a lot more than let Upton stick needles in both of them if it would reassure her that Frankie was still alive.

"Don't rush the horses." She folded the sheet of pasta meticulously, edges meeting in the middle, once, twice, again, until it looked a little like two stacks of envelopes. "This is purely hypothetical unless Frankie makes it back."

"Have faith," he said. "She's a survivor. We all know that."

Maud took up a knife and began cutting the coiled and stacked sheet of pasta into long, flat noodles, scooping them off the board, shaking them into coils and flouring them.

"You're not backing out?" Babs subbed. "I mean, any chance we can keep an ear tuned to the Hedgehog . . ."

Instead of replying, Maud sliced, shook, and floured a handful of noodles. "You've given me a lot to think about, Mer Upton."

"I'll say my goodbyes to your packmate and get out of your hair." He bowed slightly, lingering for one breath longer—in case she felt like inviting him to stay and eat. When she kept her eyes down and her hands moving, he bowed himself out, passing Jermaine, who was balancing a tray on his head while a clot of their friends laughed and applauded.

Crane silently flashed a brace of health alerts—icons showing Maud's rising heart rate and respiration, realtime portrait showing her clenched jaw and a sheen of sweat on her brow. "Are you unwell, Maud?"

She signed: "No."

"Can I perhaps—"

"*No.*"

The day reeled on, through all the stages of party. She served the pasta at lunchtime. Some guests left after the meal; others arrived as they came off shift or finally made it Earthside. Most brought printed paper flowers. Symbolic gifts: the real thing, like so much else, was in short supply.

Jermaine persuaded Maud to lie down in the afternoon, to take a Sangfroid and a sleeping aid, too. "There won't be any news until they launch Portals$_{6/7}$ again," he said. "Babs and I will keep everyone entertained. Or if you want them to leave, we'll broom 'em all out—"

"If Ember messages—"

"I'll wake you," Jermaine promised, pulling a nanosilk comforter over her. It configged to her preferred texture: lambswool, dense and springy. She curled up, losing herself to dreams.

She woke again hours before the backup launch. The murmur beyond her bedroom door had that sound of a party now in the wee hours. Stragglers, murmuring blurry conversations.

She kept her eyes shut and switched to VR, booting up one of her private e-state rooms, a lush conservatory filled with tropical plants, alive with insects and small reptiles, with her information displays set on the bright, polished rocks that lined its pathways. One, an onyx plinth rising to eye level, showed the countdown to midnight, GMT. two hours fifty-two minutes.

There was a ping from Nata.

She accepted, and her parent immediately tooned in from Europa. They were in work gear—overalls, muddy gloves.

"On break?" Maud said.

"Yes, it is mid-shift."

"What are you growing?"

"Yam seedlings and sugar beets."

Her parent hadn't been one to read stories or offer snuggles; they were #notahugger all the way. They wouldn't mouth platitudes about Frankie being fine. Nata didn't promise what they couldn't deliver.

Maud felt a pang of guilt at that remembered sense of childhood safety with Upton, memory of sleeping in his arms after he'd stolen her.

Nata observed, "Your social cap's rising."

Maud glanced at her Cloudsight rating. There were always people who sent strokes to the families of anyspace pilots, but now, with Frankie and the others cut off, she had received a colossal bump.

"It's what happens," she said. "People want to show support."

"A kindness." Nata nodded. "You are sure I should not come to you?"

"Only if Frankie—" Maud's breath caught. "If she—"

"None of that," her parent said. Stern tone, businesslike, steadying. "I am here, Maud, if you need."

"I know you are," she said. Nata pounded their heart, extending a closed hand—gestural moji, a symbol of love. Maud returned the fistbump as they logged, leaving her in her virtual greenhouse, with her elevated Cloudsight score and her worries.

Benefiting from the social economy required participating in it. Crane had flagged a long list of people and causes for Maud to stroke: the farms and grocer who'd supplied the flour and basil, Sonika Singer, of course, and the party guests, too. She wanted to skip Upton, but excluding him from her thank list would attract notice, wouldn't it?

Best to play it safe. She forced herself to breathe and widecast her thanks.

A bright green anole skittered over another marble outcropping in her vestibule, near where the illusion of Nata had been standing. This plinth's rock face displayed travel times for the high-speed shuttle out to the space elevator. Crane's doing. He was giving her realtime updates, in case she wanted to go to Mars.

She'd only do that if the portal didn't open in . . .

Two hours and forty-nine minutes.

"Show me the living room of our pop-in," she subbed.

Two views imposed themselves on a waist-high sandstone tablet—one from Jermaine's eyecams, looking south across the apartment, and those of another guest, oriented in the opposite direction. Three of Jermaine's parents and two of Ember's, the latter dressed in the quasi-military uniforms and upswept ears of their primary fandom, *Star Trek*—were curled with him on the round couch, dozing, drinking, chitchatting.

In the corner, a clutch of Maud's friends from the lab were munching chips, playing catch with a suspended locust marble, and talking about—she pulled up the transcript—recombinant proteins. Sonika Singer, Babs, and one of Jermaine's other lovers were looking at the remnants of the flour and the eggs, talking about scones, optimizing recipes so they could precisely use the ingredients, no muss no fuss no waste.

The Sangfroid meds in Maud's system were still at work. She felt the possibility of Frankie marooned, Frankie slowly starving, Frankie already dead and gone. But it felt like old grief, something that had already happened. Toothache, for now, rather than a knife twisting in the heart.

Jackal, Frankie's hoaxer chum, was sitting by himself in a rocking chair, pointed at the view of the city and busily working something in hands hidden by long, drapey sleeves. The robe had the flair of a costume, but if it was a fandom marker, like the Vulcans' cosplay, it wasn't tagged.

Maud felt a bristle of tension. Hoaxers and hoarders. Upton showing up, there of all places, at the same time as one of the people who'd brought him to justice. Coincidence?

She stood, stretched, hit the loo, and threw water on her face. Her primer was configged to loose pyjamas. She chose a new setting: crisp white slacks, tunic with navy collar, evocation of an old sailor's uniform. Running a comb through her hair as the nanothreads tailored themselves and changed color, she gave herself one last check. All present and to spec.

Thus armored, she stepped out, making for Jackal.

"Been waiting on you," he said.

"Thank you for coming."

He might have been the oldest person she had ever seen outside of a life-extension pod. His eyes were clouded over with white proteins, tagged as cataracts, and something—some med regime or another—had brought out the veins on his face, so that raised black capillaries covered the surface of his flesh like tree roots spread across dry soil.

"I'm the host of honor," she said. "Or something."

"Corpse at your own wake? Widow in waiting?"

She frowned. People rarely spoke so plainly.

"Never mind," he said. "I'm no vulture, whatever you may have heard."

"I—" she started to say, but Jermaine and Sonika were approaching.

"Project Hopscotch is sending Hung Chan over," Jermaine said. "Sonika's hoping to do an interview with the three of us—spouses of an augmented pilot, plus an actual pilot."

"And the doctor who did the surgery," Sonika said.

"I'm a two-for-one," Jerm agreed. His words were casual, but his eyes were hectic. The stress was getting to him.

"I have to get going." Jackal gathered the long sleeves of his primer, pulling a cowl over his peculiar face and cataract-whites of his eyes. He reached up, pausing at her consent boundary. Maud extended a hand . . . only to have him latch on, pressing something into her palm. The drape of his sleeve fell over their joined hands, keeping the drop off camera.

Maud knew the feel of it: reel of paper, coiled like a puck. It was a strip of Braille, one of the few ways to send someone a note without having it immediately captured by your eyecams.

Her thumb ran over the first few letters: L O V E.

From Frankie, then. As she saw the old man to the door, she felt herself beginning to quake.

CHAPTER 10

Project Hopscotch: Pilot meeting at Lodestone. Highest priority, ASAP. Attend in the flesh if possible.

Lodestone Station, at Titan, was the jewel in Earth's far-flung territorial crown, a small city boasting 300,000 permajobs in resource extraction, research, and on-site agriculture. It was base and barn for Project Hopscotch, the hangar where Earth's two experimental anyspace saucers, *Iktomi* and *Wiigit*, were aging their way into dangerous obsolescence as everyone waited for the rollout of next-gen FTL craft.

Titan was also ground central for diplomats, so-called experts who had, since First and Second Contact, done what they could to learn a few of the thousands of languages bandied about within the wider spacefaring community. Since the noninterference pact, contact with Exemplar races had been limited—lest they deliberately or accidentally leak tech secrets to the Solakinder. So, the diplomatic corps spent their time attempting to acquire, translate, and comprehend the treaties between those powers—treaties that had, so far, been used to keep spacefaring offworlders from taking Earth on as a client state.

Nigglers, Champagne Chevalier called the diplomats. Privately.

In Sensorium, everyone was happy to gabble on as to how the offworlders' various treaties were a bulwark against Francisco Pizarro–style domination of the Solakinder (the nigglers were also the ones who'd insisted on having a collective term for people, ghosts, and AI, as if all consciousness was created equal) and exploitation by aliens.

Soon, all that hypervigilant penny-pinching and the endless, *endless* yammering about threats to Earth's sovereignty would come to an end. Global Oversight would concede to necessity, pay a licensing fee—a hefty one, admittedly—and license a decent alien-built universal translator.

Champ checked the countdown to GMT midnight, anchored in his lower left peripheral. Fifteen minutes to the backup portal launch; twenty, then, until Sneezy got written off, and Frankie Barnes with it. Humanity's bid to level up its portal network would officially go down the flush.

Act normal. Let the clock run down. Done and dusted.

He spun through the revolving door that marked the boundary between Mars Station and the Titan portal. A ripple of static electricity, over skin and through his hair, was all he felt as he transitioned hundreds of thousands of clicks, all in the space of a breath.

Stepping out into Titan's stationstalk, he took in the lights of Lodestone, the far limit of humanity's push-out into their home system.

"Hopscotch pilots, I am headed back to the barn."

The stalk from the portal threaded a path to the Titan lift system, and from there into a divided steel stem, a giant nullgrav highway with pedestrian traffic at its height. Beneath the walkway, streams of bots moving in opposed directions fed into the portal. Comms tech took up its own stem, ensuring a steady stream of Sensorium data. Human morale had proven extremely resistant to crisis, be it climate change, near-famines, and the first offworlder threats to Earth's sovereignty. The key to that resilience—especially now, with the AI strike and rising pinch of the luxury shortage—was ensuring everyone had unlimited access to the infosphere.

Bread and circuses, the ancient Romans had called it. A spoonful of bandwidth helps the deprivation go down.

Champ stared at the night sky, clearing everything in his view except that time counter ticking down to zero. Twelve minutes before he became an accessory to murder.

Assuming the failure of the pegasus hadn't done her in, how long might Frankie survive out there? If the ghosts backed up and self-triaged their Mayfly™ bodies immediately, and Franks kept her resource take to a minimum . . . eight weeks, perhaps? Once the station stopped showing life signs, Scrap could legally take possession

Best to sacrifice Frankie now. She was one of those folk who could never be made to see reason. She wouldn't want to watch as Earth got assimilated into something greater. Hell, she'd practically self-selected for martyrdom.

He gave a moment's gosh-wow to Saturn, hanging majestically in the background, bisected by the triple shaft of the elevator heading down to Lodestone City Center, and the free-floating technological reef, in orbit nearby, comprising the spaceship terminal.

"Champ?" The Bootstrap task manager, an app named Pidge, pinged him. "ETA?"

"Nearly there." His hair lifted away from his scalp as the gravity decreased. Charging his nanoboots, he locked on to the atrium's magnetic floor.

Champ savored the sensation of lightness in his upper body as he circled around to another revolving door and verified his assignment to Project Hopscotch. The drop-tube doors irised; stepping inside, he caught a handhold on a pulley. It drew him downward.

"Reminder: bend your knees as you land."

"Instead of telling me things I already know, Pidge, you wanna say why I've been summoned?" Champ's feet met springy material underfoot, and he bent, as instructed. "Portal's processing a right bag of nails, case you hadn't noticed. I can't be everywhere."

"Your presence at Mars Control is superfluous."

"I got a pilot in trouble."

Or I will have, in seven minutes.

He added, "You don't think Ember could use a little in-person support? It's his spouse out there."

Once Frankie was officially knocked off, Ember would be the next domino. Allure$_{18}$ and her allies would sell the story that it was his miscalculations that had sent the Sneezy crew to its doom.

Champ shuddered, forcing himself to breathe through a wave of anxiety. He couldn't *wait* for this part to be over. The final collapse of Earth's economy, the inevitable restructuring of government under offworlder management . . .

. . . *the elevation of me and mine to the top of the planetary hierarchy* . . .

. . . all this maneuvering was nerve-wracking. And so much had gone wrong. Frankie'd managed to launch a partial portal. Worse, the station had synced one last round of data with Sensorium before breaking comms. None of that had been part of the plan.

Emerald Station had been meant to vanish, all hands lost, no explanation forthcoming. Kachoo! Poof! Bye-bye Sneezy, all hands lost.

Pidge cooed, finally responding to his question: "Your fellow pilots are proposing to rescue Mer Barnes if the second portal rollout fails."

How had he missed this?

"Champ?"

"Why, that's great!" he enthused, for the folks.

This would be the brat's doing. Their idealistic baby pilot Hung had been fanboying all over Frankie from the moment he got his augment surgery.

Damn you, Hung!

Far as Champ Chevalier could see, Mer Frances Barnes was a genuinely insufferable little snot. They'd never taken to each other . . . and to compound the insult, Champ was accustomed to people liking him on sight. He was the guy people drank with, confided in. She'd thaw, he thought.

But no. One of the many bad experiences that had warped her journey to adulthood—damage that hadn't quite noped her out of the augmented piloting program—had left Frankie immune to his charms.

A hoverboard had come to meet him. Released from the obligation to walk, he stepped aboard and sent his toon ahead to the pilots' lounge.

His augmented views filled with livestream of his cohort gathered around a series of shareboards, running numbers. Beatrice Owello, from Pretoria, had her head in a sealed vape bubble, inhaling meds of some variety. Hung Chan, their annoying rookie, was doing nav calculations while skipping around in nullgrav, enjoying the preternatural grace that came with augmentation and probably coming up with new poop-joke nicknames for every portal, station, and ship on the drawing boards. He and an EastEuro flyboy, Yuri Danshor, had covered the lounge wall in graphics, tracking portal numbers, consulting anyspace physicists, reading up on the ongoing investigation and comment threads on the first #portalfail, examining damage data from *Appaloosa*, Frankie's pegasus—

Champ winced. Who knew what revelations lurked in the data synced from Emerald Station when that partial portal launched?

$Pilot_6$ and $Pilot_7$ were tasked to other portals: Indigo Markham was permanently attached to Earth, ready to deploy if anything went wrong with the original portal membrane. Rastopher Kanye was out at Proxima Centauri, twiddling his thumbs while waiting to see if they could roll out $Portal_6$. The Centauri system already had one portal—an Exemplar consortium had put in one of their own just beyond the noninterference border.

Proxima was the come-no-closer line for offworlders as Earth attempted to bootstrap their way into the #supertechs.

If humanity leveled from five to seven portals as planned, that connection, at Centauri, would create a two-way anyspace highway. The on-ramp would allow contact and trade with the wider galactic community. Earth's economy might just get enough traction to enable payment of their debt to the Kinze. The @Visionary dream would die.

Meantime, Emerald Station—Hung went and got everyone calling it Sneezy—had political rather than economic significance.

Planting a flag out in the middle of nowhere would shore up humanity's contention that they were a high-tech and expansive culture—qualified, if only just, to sit at the Exemplar grown-up table with the various space empires.

To Champ's way of thinking, that claim made about as much sense as paddling up to an aircraft carrier in your best birch-bark canoe and demanding tribute from the Navy.

"Evening, all." Having arrived virtually, he pinged the others with an update on his in-the-flesh ETA.

Hung beamed. Owello took off her vape bubble, drawing and holding one last breath of . . . something as she signed a greeting.

Indigo tooned in beside Champ, sending her remote presence from Earth.

"I've got five minutes, Hung," she said. "What's this plan?"

Hung grinned.

"You're *not* gonna say we leapfrog out there," Champ said.

"We absolutely leapfrog," Yuri replied.

"That is . . . loco."

"Thank you," Rastopher said. "That's what I told them."

Hung expanded the central shareboard's proposed route to Sneezy, outlining four FTL hops, each just under three light-years in distance.

Champ said, "Short hops are a bug, not a feature. FTL ships are supposed to fly continuously. You know that!"

"Ember's been developing a theory—"

Words to chill the blood, always.

"The short hops can work to our advantage here. *Iktomi* and *Wiigit* are reliable at the under-three light-year threshold. We've been leapfrogging out to the Dumpster with shipments for the Kinze, right? So there's no reason not to send—"

"There's *plenty* reason. Saucers ain't meant to be dropping out of anyspace. Each piddly little hop brings wear and tear. Almighty Ember don't know why they can't sustain anyspace burn. It's hazardous!"

"Everything we do is dangerous," Yuri said.

"Eleven light-years, Champ," Hung said. "It's not beyond our reach."

"That's an untried double-hop past the Dumpster," Champ objected. "Four anyspace hops to get there, four to return. And carrying at least one passenger back, assuming you find anyone alive."

Oh, Frankie'd be alive. He could hear his plans #crashburning. Aunt Irma was gonna have him skinned, tanned, and made into purses.

"Plus . . . plus!" he added. "We've never done more than six consecutive hops without a full maintenance inspection. Break down. Build up. This'd take eight."

"Cyril$_{10}$ can do an inspection when we're at Sneezy." Hung signed soothing moji into the space between them, toons of soft baby dachshunds, gamboling past Champ's shoulders.

Worse and worse. And yet all Champ could do now was moji back: thumbs-up. "Seems like you've thought of everything."

"Even if we just get Franks," Yuri said. "Teacakes can lock into consciousness vaults and huff some Whitelight. Fortunate, yes, that Bootstrap sent ghosts?"

Champ nodded, hiding uneasiness. Had it been luck? The techs had been last-minute substitutions. Frankie'd been chums with Teagan since her eighth incarnation. And he'd had a mighty shit-storm of a time getting aboard Emerald before it launched.

Three minutes to midnight and the second portal launch.

Champ's flesh, in transit even as he argued remotely, rolled into the lounge. The hoverboard slowed, carrying him into the space his toon appeared to be occupying. The greyscale illusion of him-self popped like a soap bubble.

He cleared his throat. "It's a cool idea, Brat, but you're talking about risking a second pilot to save the first. *Iktomi* could be hop-ping into a debris field. And Frankie volunteered specifically so it wouldn't be your ass hanging out there."

"Yeah, and I'm going after her," Hung said.

"You're too new."

"Then I'll fly the mission," Yuri said. "It'll make a nice change from running tobacco to the Dumpster in *Jalopy*."

Champ didn't need to look to know how this would be polling. A daring rescue? The fact that it was Frankie insufferable Barnes who was stranded? People would be lapping up the performance of gumption.

"We have to try, Champ. Frankie'd do it for any of us."

There was no way to oppose Hung's scheme without looking suspicious as all get-out. Champ forced a grin.

"*Ikky*'s old," Yuri said. "She's gonna have to be decommissioned soon. It's worth risking one old ship and one pilot if we can find out what went wrong."

Champ looked to Indigo.

"Reluctantly agree," she said. "*Heyoka* rolls off the assembly line soon. Portals is dead in the water without data about what went wrong. And we can't leave her out there."

Even Owello and Rastopher nodded at that.

Champ looked up at the route. *Fucky fucky fucksticks.*

The countdown clock ran out and they all switched focus, bringing in Garnet Station, at Mars, and Launch Control. Portal membranes one through six built up extra charge. Earth's five open portals crackled with power, pulling like horses ready to run.

Six remained dormant. It could only fire if Seven did—carousels only sustained when the number of nodes in them was a prime number.

Three. Two. One.

Nothing.

Ember's voice, over the feed, was calm. "Sneezy Station, are you there? Frankie, come in. Teacakes?"

Two minutes. Ten.

Finally, the words Champ had been awaiting for twenty-four hours. "Discharging all membranes and standing down. We have #portalfail."

He'd expected to feel relief. Triumph, maybe. Now, with a retrieval on the boards, he felt like his throat was lined with ashes.

The other pilots turned to him, faces expectant. Champ could only see one way to clean this up before it became a bona fide turd explosion.

"Brush up the navigational data and get it ready to present to Bootstrap. The plan's polling well . . . but someone needs to do Q&A with public stakeholders."

"I'll do that," Owello said. She was good with the press.

He signed thanks. "Safety contingencies, fuel allowances, confirmation on the nav math. Request a full maintenance crawl over *Iktomi*. Make up the work roster."

Hung and Yuri nodded soberly, all business.

"But." Champ put up a hand. "If we're throwing old ships at the problem, we're throwing an old pilot, too."

"Champ—"

"It ain't you who's gonna be going, Hung. It's gonna hafta be me."

CHAPTER 11

Appaloosa's seizure meds were far from the only packets contaminated with acids, it turned out; the anticonvulsant dose had just been first to fail. Teagan$_9$ found corrosion in most of the steel and copper components of the pegasus, everything connected to its circ system.

This, naturally, noped the backup launch. The @EmeraldCrew simply didn't have time to examine every potential failure point for sabotage. Not that rules were likely to stop Frankie, Babs[1] thought, especially out where she couldn't be ordered to stop. But she had been almost meek when Cyril$_{10}$ said they couldn't attempt the launch. It hadn't been a very convincing performance.

It took Babs[1] three hours, running a Fox$_{BOT}$ in the station's rudimentary pharma lab, to work out that the drug pouches had been mined with corrosive seeds, nanobeads activated by enzymes within *Appaloosa*'s hydraulics system.

They posted the results on the group shareboard. "Does anyone still believe this was an accident?"

Cyril$_{10}$ ran simulations with shaking hands. "Those things could eat through our deck plates, given time."

"We must find out where they originated."

"I always thought the #vandalrumor . . . I figured that was paranoia."

"Yes, I'm famously paranoid." Frankie sounded amused. "Childhood damage and all."

"I wasn't talking about you."

"Why not? You must know I suspected this all along."

Their three warm bodies were scattered throughout the station, logged on to the data helix as they multitasked repairs, chatting via the @EmeraldCrew channel. Frankie's flesh was adrift in the hangar, most of her concentration taken up by piloting the Ox_{BOT} team into harness around Sneezy's perimeter so they could maintain the station's position relative to Procyon.

"He didn't mean to be insulting," $Teagan_9$ said.

"I'm only insulted on Ember's behalf. Everyone's been blaming his anyspace calculations. Saying the problems with the FTL saucers were maths fails, pilot error, human fallibility."

"It's not *unreasonable*," $Cyril_{10}$ huffed. "The Bootstrap Project is . . . We're playing catch-up with species who've been in space for centuries."

"Spoken like an anti-Bootstrap wank."

"I'm out here, aren't I?"

"Don't bait the ghost," $Babs^1$ subbed. "You need him onside."

"For someone facing starvation, Frankie, you seem cheerful." $Teagan_9$ extracted the corroded tech from *Appaloosa*'s core, sealing the pieces in improvised evidence bags, releasing them to bob in the hangar like a string of ill-designed balloons.

"Frankie loves being proved right." $Cyril_{10}$ ran a hand over his face; $Babs^1$ noted he was sweating profusely. "Speaking of starving, Tea and I should start copying into consciousness vaults immediately."

"You can't," $Babs^1$ argued. "We haven't learned how the contaminants were introduced to the meds packets."

"We're not qualified to solve industrial sabotage!"

$Babs^1$ ignored this. They had assembled their backup copy of Happ in one of the consciousness vaults; now they began looking for somewhere else to hide him.

"You can run the basic chemistry experiments yourself," $Cyril_{10}$ went on.

"Ah, yes. Let the AIs do all the work. *This* is why the Asylum went on strike."

"Now who's antagonizing him?" Frankie subbed.

"Frankie needs—"

"What Frankie needs is every calorie I'm not going to burn. As soon as Tea confirms her injuries are healing to spec . . ."

"I bit my tongue, that's all," Frankie said. "I'm clean on concussion and skull fracture."

"Then, given the second #portalfail, my wife and I should plan to dis[EM]body."

Dis[EM]body. Trademarked euphemism for a suicide pact.

Teacakes were ancients, relics from the first days of life extension. Hence the vintage husband-wife mono-marriage. They had been among the first digital im[M]ortals, early adopters of tech that converted human consciousness into data and uploaded it to Sensorium.

Despite the [IM]perish branding, with its implication of eternal life, the science of digitized consciousness was in its early days. The Solakinder had been given the first steps by their would-be alien invaders, but after the noninterference agreement had been signed, Allure[18] had been obliged to stop providing #HowDo info to the [IM]perish Foundation. The tech, at this point, still had as many bugs as features.

Not everyone took to dis[EM]bodiment, or re[EM]bodiment, for that matter. Each new incarnation of a ghost came with a risk of decoherence.

Teacakes had stepped up for this mission because they were stable and comfortable with being triaged: their source code was safe at home, and they had survived almost a dozen dis[EM]bodiments and reinstalls. Still, that didn't mean there was zero risk.

"You can't kill yourselves. Not until you've made full statements about the accident," Frankie said.

"You're not a cop, Barnes. And if our continued existence poses a threat to *your* life—"

Inspiration struck Babs[1] then: "If I may, Cyril[10]. We're not sure it's just the pegasus meds that were sabotaged. You wouldn't want to deploy your final dose of Whitelight and find out it's contaminated."

$Cyril_{10}$ sent $Babs^1$'s toon a vicious side-eye.

"Nobody's committing suicide," Frankie said.

$Teagan_9$ sent a stream of moji through the channel at that: angry face, GhostPride™ shield, and a hand with one upthrust finger.

Ignoring this graphical protest, Frankie centered *Appaloosa*'s damage metrics on the shareboard. "This isn't a matter of guessing that maybe the anyspace wands are misaligned or overcharged, not anymore. Nobody can argue the FTL ships' curvature has been miscalculated. You can't hide behind *oh, dear, nobody really expects a bunch of gun-waving monkeys and their AI spawn to level into* Star Trek *technomarvels like the warp drive! In a matter of decades? Poor deluded apes!*"

"Strike, Frankie, for IP breach."

"Rubbish."

"You're not *supposed* to call it the warp drive," $Teagan_9$ agreed.

Frankie doubled down. "We're past pretending Ember's team bollixed up the portal maths, past tutting over how inconveniently tragic it was that Sienna Mary Murray had that aneurysm, and just when she seemed to be nearing a breakthrough on subspace—oh, pardon me, quantum comms—"

"Strike for sarcasm," $Cyril_{10}$ objected. "And hoaxer talk."

"Look at *Appaloosa,* you gobshite! These nanobeads are a straight-up spanner in the works. Vandalism isn't a rumor anymore. It's bloody sabotage."

Reluctant nod from $Teagan_9$.

$Cyril_{10}$ signed, *Yes.* He took his second strike back.

"Aside from us, the only person who came aboard was Champ Chevalier. We need to tie him to our equipment fails. Nobody has the luxury of noping on the mission until I have hard evidence and viable options for getting it home."

They chewed on that silently. Finally, $Cyril_{10}$ said, "Why would Champ—why would any hypothetical saboteur suddenly do something so overt?"

"We're rather far from home," $Teagan_9$ told him gently. "Nobody would know if something went wrong out here."

"Someone would check, eventually," he said. "The station would still be here."

"Would it?"

That unsettled him. "No?"

"It'd be *easy* to get rid of the station. Give it a good swift kick toward Procyon. Sayonara, baby," Frankie said. "Guess the star sneezed."

"Imagine if you hadn't got comms during the #portalfail," Babs[1] agreed. "Earth wouldn't know anything about what was happening out here."

Frankie nodded. "We'd have vanished. Anyone could've moved in and cleaned up."

"Then why haven't they?" $Cyril_{10}$ had reached drug storage now. He detached a pristine bag of fluids and scanned the serial number. "What's stopping your saboteurs from flying in and scuttling us?"

"Babs? What do you think?"

"The greater galactic community has accountability protocols, like us." Babs[1] highlighted relevant treaties, alien contracts humanity had painstakingly acquired and translated. "Few cultures take mutually assured disclosure quite as far as we do, but they don't default to trust, either."

$Cyril_{10}$ rummaged for a sealed chem flask in the lab cupboards, dislodging a ball of fluff. Babs[1] used station cams to zoom in on it. Dead spider, in a bundle of web.

"The aliens make deals with each other but don't take compliance on faith. So what?" $Teagan_9$ said.

"We've *never* encountered an offworlder ship with just one kind of alien aboard. According to Diplomatic, that's not about them being great chums," Frankie said.

"It's transparency enforcement." Babs[1] tasked a $Beetle_{BOT}$ with collecting the spider corpse she'd spotted in the infirmary.

"They're observers. They don't trust each other." $Teagan_9$ sounded thoughtful now. "So, potential offworld saboteurs—"

"By which you mean the—"

Frankie broke in before $Cyril_{10}$ could finish. "Let's not put specific accusations on the record."

"Oh, sure, *warp drive*'s fine but let's not get actively slanderous."

"You think the saboteurs would get caught blasting us out of space," $Teagan_9$ said.

"Everyone's supposed to be well clear of the noninterference zone," Frankie said.

"If a ship pops in too close . . ." Babs[1] said.

"Their observers might know," Frankie finished. "They'd have to be bloody careful."

"Well, that's great, then, isn't it?"

"Provisionally great, Cyril, sure. If it keeps us alive and lets us get proof of this stunt with the acid in *Appaloosa* back to Sensorium, it's bloody brilliant." Frankie finished with the last Ox_{BOT}.

Her leg cramped then. She bent, massaging out the kink. Then, stretching like a starfish in nullgrav, Frankie took a second to leap around the hangar, bounding from bulkhead to bulkhead, whirling in midair. Enhanced reflexes and balance were part of the surgical augmentation package; there was a lot of starling tish in the plug resting against her sacrum, and a bit grafted right onto her vestibular nerve. Artificially being leveled into star-gymnast dexterity was especially pleasing because she'd been clumsy as a kid. Her parent, Gimlet, a gifted athlete, had always seemed to despair of her.

Back at the meds printer, $Cyril_{10}$ spat into a flask and then squeezed the gelatinous payload of the drug packet into it, corking it before giving the whole thing a good shake. Checking the integrity of his suicide drugs.

"Is this meant to be a random audit? One packet, one test?" Babs[1] said. "You don't even know if the nanobeads have an enzymatic trigger."

"We need to start somewhere, don't we?" he snapped.

"No offense was meant—" Babs[1] began.

The flask burst into flame in $Cyril_{10}$'s hand.

CHAPTER 12

Them's term for this situation was *caught behind enemy lines.*

Scrap of the All felt the heat of the nanobeads' ignition as Them hurled the flaming vessel away. Burning, it crashed against a bulkhead, momentarily spreading the blaze. Then Them snuffed it, under a . . .

< . . . translation pending . . . >

< . . . pillow . . . >

Them snuffed the flames using a pillow.

Residue filled the air: smoke, burned mammal hair, fire-suppressant foam issuing from safeties in the wall. Clots of the foam danced in the compartment, large motes that would hopefully confuse any camera footage of Scrap making an escape.

The first priority was getting out of medical storage.

Them scraped the air raw with its distress sounds. Foam was flying.

Screams. The distress sounds were screams.

Translation was so slow! Scrap tried to strengthen the comms connection to the All, to no avail.

Pushing off from a position under a fixed wall cabinet, Scrap took care to keep the hulk of the screaming alien between itself and the room's primary camera as Us made a zero-gravity drift in the direction of Them's leg.

This was a risky strategy. Humans wore nanosilk, snugged close to the skin. There were no ruffles or cuffs or loops for the

All to use as cover on the bottom half of that immense, overheated body. If Them hadn't been set afire, the pull of Scrap's negligible weight on its thigh might have been enough to draw attention.

But Them *was* distracted, and Scrap safely made the traverse to its mid-waist region, reeling in a clump of foam to hopefully provide cover.

"I'm burned, I'm goddamned burned is what's wrong!" Physical proximity sent sound vibrations fizzing through Us. "Of course I'm not all right!"

Them was only around to be burned because it had failed to self-terminate as Champ-Them had promised.

None of this matched the narrative Us had agreed upon. Champ-Them had been meant to sabotage the station's power membrane. Scrap going after the pegasus had been a mere contingency.

All Thems on the station had outlived the initial accident. They had traced the source of the sabotage to med storage . . . and they'd done it alarmingly fast.

As $Cyril_{10}$-Them kicked its way out into the corridor, bouncing off bulkheads with its burnt appendage tucked against its thorax, Scrap rode along, scanning for camera blind spots and chances to hop clear. Us had to get some distance before more of Them came to evaluate the fleshy damage from the burn. More individuals meant more eyes, all with implanted cameras. It had already had to fabricate one decoy, and the bots had pounced on it.

That was another problem: all of a sudden, there were far more remotes than Scrap had expected.

Scrap's ride was headed away from the hangar, with all its useful obstructions and blind spots and places to hide.

Us took a chance and threw an escape line at a bulkhead, releasing Them's belt. Drifting, it found a duct, tumbling into the air-circ system of the station. Rearranging its spines to prioritize locomotion, it traversed a long metallic desert, taking refuge in a lightless compartment.

The ducts were a relief after the terrible open yawn of the corridor, but they wouldn't be safe for long. Tiny bots were roaming even here, shining lights and taking footage, inspecting and searching.

Scrap linked comms with the station helix and commenced a passive sift of status updates from the comms running between Thems.

Translation came: all the top-note chatter was about Them's burns and the source of the fire.

The story Scrap and Champ-Them had meant to tell began with the new human-built portals failing to launch. That had paid out, true. But the rest of Scrap's obligations were deep in arrears. The station remained occupied, legally unsalvageable. The portal membrane was intact. Thems were hunting for answers and their datastream showed active intention to assemble and transmit proof of interference.

Scrap could only conclude that the Emerald crew had expected sabotage all along.

Now Scrap had to stop Thems from sending any proof back to Earth's Sensorium.

Before Us had a chance to decide whether this was realistic, a new crisis rose. There was a new entity in the comms channel.

How were Them populating?

Oh! A code-based sapient had loaded into the station during the unexpected comms handshake. It had absorbed the station manager and booted up all the tiny bots.

The new arrival would complicate salvage claims even further. Babs[1]-Them appeared to be a true sapient . . .

We were promised the station OS would be inadequate!

The sapp had Scrap's decoy and was scouring all the footage from those extra cameras.

The thought of being found made Scrap bunch involuntarily. Capture would displease the All greatly.

This wasn't Scrap's fault!

The thought was alarming. Scrap was Us, not Me. It checked its comms link with the All. Still dead.

Solve the problem, fast.

If there was damage to be done, it would have to be in the primary server room. Dead infosphere, dead station. Kill the servers, and the new artificial, Babs[1], would die too. The ghosts would self-triage, and the lone survivor, Frankie-Them, would wither without life support.

Once everyone died, Scrap of the All could still claim Emerald station for Us.

The station servers, then. Inject incendiary packets into the bioelectronics in the primary server room.

Resolved and relieved, Scrap of the All got moving.

CHAPTER 13

Maud,

Never doubt that I love you.

Braille tape was the medium for secret messages and love letters, single lines of coiled text on a brightly inked medium.

This strip had a complex and colorful pattern of moji—hearts. The visual hash made the actual message, the raised dots of the lettering, effectively invisible to cameras as users drew them like ribbon through their fingers.

Braille notes tended to be haiku texts. The form inclined to brevity and abbreviation. It was something of a miracle Frankie hadn't defaulted to ILU for her protestation of love.

Never doubt.

Sending secret notes was regarded as antisocial, more secretive than skin-texting. Note-passing was seen, by many, as suspect. Still, the tiny breach in Earth's wall of mutually assured disclosure was a necessity: children who could Braille and Morse were vastly less likely to self-harm or to cut out their transponders—as Frankie had all those years before—and run away from home.

Maud threaded the next sentence under her thumb. *I love you no matter what.*

Silly, but having the note made her believe Frankie was still alive.

If the comms project had gone forward before Frankie left, she might not have to rely on faith. They might be able to feel each other's presence, despite the distance. They might even have comms, if the theories were right.

Upton's theories. She shivered.

"Almost there!" Hung Chan had come with her from Earth. Now he was leading the way to the Project Hopscotch saucer hub. Compact of body and round of face, he waved cheerily at a woman Maud didn't recognize. A nametag popped up on her HUD: Irma du Toit. Profession came next—prima ballerina, dance instructor—along with badges indicating enthusiastic support of the ᴵᴹperish Foundation. She was related to the head pilot, a big white guy named Champ Chevalier.

Beyond Irma, drifting aloof and glazed in a corner, was a ginger scarecrow named Wilbur Mack, who looked enough like Teagan₉, despite his pallor, to tag him as as one of the elderly couple's great-great-grandchildren.

Wilbur's tags circled him like goldfish: *he/his pronouns, #shy, #OK2ignore, #SpanishSpeaker, #notahugger.*

Next of kin for the stranded @EmeraldCrew, all invited to Titan to watch the launch of the rescue ship, *Iktomi.*

I never thought as a kid I would find anyone who didn't have a heart of sand. Never thought I could have a rock. But Maud, the #vandalrumor is no hoax. Someone is sabotaging the Bootstrap Project. Kinze probably, with help from humans.

There it was, the paranoid fantasy nobody but hoaxers dared utter, not if they didn't want thousands of strikes for negging the Bootstrap Project. If Frankie ever said this aloud, she'd be broomed from piloting before her social capital could collapse.

We're expecting an attempt to sabotage the project at Sneezy, Frankie had written. *Bootstrap has greenlighted a plan for identifying the turncoat.*

Be my rock for a little longer. I will come back, I promise.

"Once everyone's here, we'll head to the viewing lounge," Hung said. "I'll be with you throughout the launch to answer questions."

"Splendid," Irma said. Something about her voice—a disturbing hint of familiarity—snagged Maud's attention.

She glanced over the ballerina's tags again, taking note of she/her pronouns and ads for an ^IMperish-sponsored ballet show in nullgrav. Irma apparently acted as something of a brand ambassador for the idea of eternal ^EMbodiment. She had lobbied against the noninterference pact; she was passionately anti-Bootstrap.

That must make things awkward at home, what with Champ being FTL's top pilot.

"How are preflight preparations going, Mer Chan?" Irma asked in what Maud thought of as a plummy British accent.

"Everything to spec." Hung shared a view of the Titan control room, where seven techs were running boards and watching readings. One display showed Champ Chevalier himself, waiting in *Iktomi*'s hangar, consuming hydrogels one after the other, ensuring max hydration before he settled into the cockpit.

Champ was clad in one of those awful life-support suits the pilots wore whenever they were about to be plugged in.

Maud shuddered. Hung signed a question.

"Bodybags," she said.

"Oh. Yeah, that's my fault. There's sort of a friendly competition among the pilots, to nickname our tech. All the naughty monikers and gallows humor, pretty much, are mine." He ducked his head, looking distinctly #notsorry.

The suit flap above Champ's sacrum was dangling, exposing five deep, pink puckers where the cybernetic plug would penetrate his flesh.

If they'd gotten wired for quantum comms before this, Maud would have a trimmed-down version of the same plug, a single thread of tissue at her sacrum. She and Frankie had also been slated for new neural tish injections, augments to her existing neural implants.

How could she consider trusting Upton to do anything, much less something surgical, to either her or Frankie?

Trust me, love, Frankie's note read. *Try not to worry. Big ask, I know, but after I'm back, we'll talk everything out. Everything!*

After I'm back. No doubts there. Frankie was good at confidence. It was part of what made her so attractive.

She had coded the message on a fragile spool of tape, so the Braille became more degraded with every run through the spool, every sweep of Maud's fingertip over the letters. Enzymatic trigger, probably, reacting to the oils on her skins. It would be incomprehensible soon.

She'd known about the sabotage and she'd gone anyway. No question of playing it safe. Maud forced herself to watch the techs crawling over every circuit board and nut on *Iktomi*, completing final checks on the saucer.

Irma du Toit's face was schooled to neutrality, but Maud thought she could detect hints of disapproval. Anti-Bootstrap speechers didn't think much of the Solakinder effort to invent #supertechs the Exemplar races had already perfected.

Maud shoved the Braille tape into the pannier on her left hip, tucking it into a segmented nanosilk compartment to keep it from knocking about in nullgrav. Her knuckles bumped against something—the suspended locust nymphs she still hadn't returned to the lab, probably. She raised and planted one foot and then the other, breaking the magnetic seals as she made space within their circle.

Irma took a graceful step backward—and away from Maud. She smelled, ever so slightly, of lavender.

Memory stirred again.

The chances that Maud would run into a second person from her childhood, so soon after the disturbing encounter with Upton . . . it was an impossible-to-credit coincidence.

Irma might remind her of Headmistress, but Headmistress wasn't human. Everyone said sapps couldn't ᴱᴹbody . . .

Everyone who? Allure$_{18}$?

It felt harder, suddenly, to dismiss her own inner hoaxer. After all, Frankie had gone to Emerald expecting trouble, and trouble there had been. If there was ever a time for indulging conspiracy theories, this was it.

Sonika Singer sailed into the observation lounge. She had her primer configged into a quilted, rose-colored jacket, gathered at mid-thigh. Her prosthetics had been fitted with semi-autonomous grapplers and her thick black hair was twisted into strands the width of a pencil, each clamped, in segments, by bright red magnets. The magnets hung together like clustered ladybugs, creating a mass of strands reminiscent of kelp. The hair undulated in the nullgrav but didn't obscure the journo's face.

Tags: *extrovert, journalist, pronouns she/her, #upforanything, #heretolisten.*

Behind Sonika came the scariest of Maud's many parents-in-law.

"Mama Rubi," Maud managed, aiming for maximum respect. "What a surprise!"

"Hello, dearest." Rubi air-kissed her, left, then right. "May I present Allure$_{18}$, our account manager, and Herringbo of the Kinze." *Kinze? Here?*

Few of the races who'd shown themselves since Mitternacht fit with classical human ideas about offworlders. Maud had seen footage of only one mammal race that followed the bipedal template, a sort of a rhino-faced organism with two legs and sexual dimorphism. That species might have passed for a costumed actor, from the long-lost days of the *Star Trek* media franchise.

The Kinze were incomprehensibly, disturbingly weird.

They presented as heaps of mobile insectile spines, shaggy maggot-infested blankets, almost, or chitinous rugs. The same spines that made up their bodies, it was said, covered their ships' decks interior bulkheads. Spines were omnipresent in every environment they inhabited. Maud had seen footage of ceilings and floors ankle-deep in what, anthropologists suspected, were the literal remains of the Kinze's presumably dead ancestors.

When they weren't heaped, the Kinze could stretch, or knit themselves into blankets, draping or bunching. This new arrival, Herringbo, stretched into a cone about two meters high, a shape roughly akin to a kid under a sheet, playing ghost.

The Solakinder didn't know how it saw or heard. Didn't know how it generated human-sounding speech, or whether it was using tech to do so.

Allure$_{18}$ said, "Herringbo has been permitted inside the noninterference zone to observe our attempt to retrieve @EmeraldCrew. I would like to remind everyone present that he will not engage in conversations about #supertech or its capabilities."

When in doubt, fall back on formal etiquette. Maud bowed and said, "Welcome, Mer Allure$_{18}$, Mer Herringbo. This is Wilbur Mack—Teacakes' great-great-great-grandchild. And this is Irma du Toit, a relation from Champ Chevalier's home community in Pretoria."

"I'm his aunt, dear heart—" Irma broke off, midsentence, as if she'd misspoken.

Headmistress liked for us to call her Auntie, Maud thought.

The Kinze, Herringbo, showed no reaction. Meanwhile, Rubi mojied gratitude to Irma with a deep bow. "What Champ is doing for our family and the project is extraordinarily brave. We've sent five strokes to Cloudsight, but I want to thank you personally."

"Champ and I have different visions of humanity's future, but I support his ambitions in the piloting program," Irma said.

"If he has any doubts at all, Hung Chan is still ready to go," Rubi said. "There'd be no shame in letting a newer pilot—"

"An inexperienced pilot?" Irma shook her head. "*Tut.* Champ has earned his place at the top of the pilot leaderboard. If anyone can come back with your dear Frances, it's him."

The alien fluffed out its spines. "The personal courage of Champ-Them of the Solakinder is laudable. You's craft *Iktomi* has consistently failed to achieve continuous anyspace travel. This attempt is risky."

"Now, Bo, if we can't ask about the science, *you* shouldn't go naysaying," Hung said. If meeting an offworlder was unusual or exciting for him, it didn't show. Then again, his baseline level of excitement was barely lower than that of a baby poodle. "We've done three-light-year hops in *Iktomi* time and again, and we run *Jalopy* out to the—"

Maud saw him catch himself before he could use the pilots' nickname, Dumpster. "—out to the Deep Space Relay Station all the time. We're getting a lotta practice, hauling your luxury products—"

"The pilots' plan is a good one," Rubi said, before anyone's tone could get complainy, before Hung asked what use aliens could possibly make of pipe tobacco and recreational euphorics. "The Solakinder can't go on putting people into space if we can't get them back ourselves."

"Laudable sentiment, Mer Whiting," Sonika said.

"Frankie's my daughter," Rubi said. Strain was suddenly apparent in her voice. "I don't know about sentiment. None of this is hypothetical for us. Is it, Maud?"

Their follows were in the millions. Maud forced herself to speak, though her jaw felt suddenly rusty. "No. This . . . We're not emotionally detached. Not in the slightest."

A burst of resentment. The Kinze could offer to take one of their ships—their nice, non-glitchy ships with their sustained anyspace envelopes—out to Sneezy. They could have gone out there and come back with Frankie already.

All for a fee, of course. Which would require another vote.

But the last vote had showed the Solakinder were reaching a tipping point. The scale of the latest protests against luxury shortages proved the voters were about done. The Kinze were now dominating purchases of hard goods and entertainment sims alike. People resented the deprivation. Another stakeholder poll . . .

The other reason the rescue had to be #DIY was unspoken and yet blindingly obvious. Because what if the Bootstrap programs *were* being sabotaged by Earth's offworld bankers? The Kinze couldn't be put in charge of the rescue if they were the ones kneecapping the #supertechs project.

"This way, everyone." Hung pinged the whole group with the route down the corridor—hardly necessary, but it was a prosocial way to get them all moving. The young pilot led the way, springing

off bulkheads like a rubber ball, making the most of the preternatural agility shared by the augmented pilots' cohort. Herringbo
curled itself into a column and caterpillared along one bulkhead.
Rubi sprang from the deck, rolled in midair, and caught the first
handhold, lithe as a champion swimmer. Allure$_{18}$ followed.

Maud took a quick glance around, wondering if she should try
to chat Irma up. Actually talking to the ballerina would probably
alleviate these sudden, wild suspicions about her identity.

After the raid on Manhattan, the police had quietly reunited
Maud with Nata. Their names had been changed. Parent and child
had gone into what used to be called #witnessprotection, located
to London, where nobody knew them.

Frankie hadn't had the option of anonymity. She'd put a showy
tattoo over the scar from her chip. She'd given up her kiddie job
at the Department of Preadolescent affairs—given up, or been
broomed from it, maybe? She'd gone into the piloting track and
spent all her free time with Rubi's father, his chum Jackal, and
Babs. The three of them had made a hobby of sleuthing around,
trying to prove that some of the @Visionaries—except they called
them the @ChamberofHorrors—had escaped the Manhattan raid.
Looking for people who, unlike Upton, hadn't been caught and
sanctioned. People who'd gone into hiding.

Most of all they'd looked for Headmistress, the sapp who'd run
the whole show.

Before Maud could engage Irma in conversation, the ballerina
leapt away, outdistancing everyone but Hung, catching up with
Herringbo and Allure$_{18}$ in a few swift rebounds.

Maud joined her mother-in-law.

"I'd ask how you are, but I know it's a ridiculous question,"
Rubi said.

By way of answer, Maud plucked the loop of Braille tape out of
her pannier and passed it to Rubi, under the guise of giving her a
squeeze.

"Here's the Peepshow—sorry, I mean the observation lounge."
Hung waved them into a glass-fronted mezzanine. Below them

was Mission Control, a dozen techs sitting at consoles, each monitoring readouts from *Iktomi*. "This installation has beefed-up comms, backup power, and redundant Sensorium links. Everything an ᴱᴹbodied pilot might need for support."

Until she throws herself into the void and becomes unreachable?

Rubi hissed, slipping the tape back into Maud's pannier. "Aren't you two in therapy?"

She shook her head.

"You *have* to go, when Frankie gets back."

Have to? She gritted her teeth. "If she gets back."

Instead of answering, Rubi handed her something—openly, this time. A pendant, of sorts: recycled copper gears on a chain. Embedded inside was an emerald-green transponder, crystalline and perfectly sharp, winking in the light.

"Is this—"

Rubi nodded, answering the unfinished question. "The locator chip Frankie dug out of her arm when she ran away. Gimlet kept it for years. Reminded them of the cost of holding too tight."

Now she was accusing Maud of being clingy?

"Hey! It's okay, Maud. Frankie always finds her way back to us—"

"That's magical thinking."

Rubi squeezed her hand. "And assuming the worst is catastrophizing."

"Champ's loading into the ship," Hung said. His voice was unexpectedly tight.

Of course it was: he worshipped Frankie.

His eyes met Rubi's. Skittered away. Standing between them, Maud could feel high-wire tension crackling.

A shareboard expanded front and center in the Peepshow displays, showing footage of the hangar. Champ stepped into *Iktomi*'s cockpit, a spherical containment unit, pressure-rated and capable of detaching from the saucer. He backed into it, locked his feet down, then knelt against a pair of rests fitted for his knees.

Rocking into place against the seat, he adjusted the edges of his suit.

"Bodybag," Rubi muttered, looking revolted.

"Hung's fault," Maud whispered.

Hung bared his teeth, seeming not to hear.

One of the techs brought the augment plug around to Champ's sacrum, aligning and lubing the five prongs before driving the interface home.

Champ's body jolted as he dis^{EM}bodied. His eyes rolled in their sockets and he went slack, hands drifting in nullgrav before coming up short against tethers clipped to the bodybag. The tech reeled the pod into a waiting socket within *Iktomi* with a loud snap. A nanotech membrane, like a transparent eyelid, closed over the spherical pod, locking it in.

"Connection to cockpit all to spec," the tech said.

Maud felt, rather than saw, Rubi's jolt of surprise. She cleared her throat and said, too casually, "All's well with Champ and the ship?"

Hung was highlighting the pilots' biometrics, readings on the pilot's pulse, body temperature, blood sugar, interface latency. "Champ's . . . absolutely fine. He's good to go."

All the bounce was gone from his voice.

"Of course he is, dear heart," Irma said. Smug now. She was seated next to Allure$_{18}$ and the alien. There was no overtly chummy vibe, but . . .

Lavender scent. Your dear Frankie. Dear heart. Maud looked from the pendant containing Frankie's old identity chip to the smooth, unmarked flesh of her own arm. Upton had removed her implant and immediately printed a graft over the incision.

Hung said, suddenly, "Champ, how you feeling? It's not too late to tag out and let me go."

"You wish, Brat. I'm fit as a fiddle and ready to fly."

Another significant Rubi-Hung glance.

"Don't yammer at him, Hung," said someone in Mission Control. "We're in prelaunch."

Hung wanted to go in Champ's place; that much was clear.

Irma murmured something to Allure$_{18}$. Maud strained to hear her words.

If Irma was, somehow, an ^{EM}bodied version of Headmistress, and if Champ and she were, on paper, relations . . .

What if all Frankie's most paranoid ideas were right, and the Kinze and Allure$_{18}$ were sabotaging Bootstrap Projects, with help from Solakinder . . . collaborators, was that the right word?

Actual realtime treachery. Was it possible?

And what if Irma du Toit really was an ^{EM}bodied instance of Headmistress?

Maud's mind drew a shaky chain of connections.

Upton sniffing around Maud's house and family.

Rubi and Hung trying to get Champ off the rescue mission.

Irma's expression remained untroubled as she watched *Iktomi* disengage from the launch ring. She shifted her weight slowly, her hand sinking under Herringbo, fingers vanishing under those antenna-like sense organs.

Rubi was watching them too.

Humans cooperating with the Kinze to sabotage the #supertechs would need true insiders. They'd need to put people into Bootstrap.

Like a surgeon on quantum comms? Like an FTL pilot?

"Creating anyspace field, three, two, one—" Champ Chevalier said.

Maud opened her mouth to say something. *Stop,* perhaps? *Send someone else?*

Iktomi glimmered like sun on ocean, a thousand winks of light on a jagged sea.

Then the ship was gone.

CHAPTER 14

Grind, grind, grind. Search, investigate, data-gather. Argue with $Cyril_{10}$ about whether or not he and $Teagan_9$ should self-triage.

Just when it was feeling like an endless loop, everything happened at once.

Frankie was in the crew gym, powering through a workout. Nano-supplements could offset much of the bone density loss that came of working in space, but spinning resistance wheels sometimes blunted the edge of her temper.

The burns on $Cyril_{10}$'s hand were close to infection; Mayfly™ bodies had perilously glitchy immune systems. Frankie wouldn't have a case for keeping him alive much longer. She might not mind that much, but Teacakes viewed themselves as one true pairing, same as her and Maud. If he went into a spirit vault, mission or no, $Teagan_9$ would probably go too. Eternal love was as close as they came to having a brand. They'd had a hundred-year anniversary, of all things.

Makes the two years since we went from $Feral_4$ to $Feral_5$ seem pretty paltry, doesn't it?

The thought of Maud, cosplaying Maturin, sent a flicker of lust through her body, followed by loneliness so strong it made her stomach cramp.

All at once, $Babs_1$ announced, "I've found something in the camera footage. Also, there's an incoming signal."

Here we go!

The station threw up full displays in the virtual control room, bring all the aftside cameras online. The always-eerie anyspace illusion of boiling lava cracked the void, blotting out the stars, momentarily creating an impression of leaking magma. The anyspace extrusion resolved into a slit, then an oval.

Bless Hung and his unending enthusiasm. He'd talked them 'round.

"Babs?" Frankie asked, subvocalizing.

"We're three hours fifteen from midnight GMT."

Babs[1] said, "@EmeraldCrew: Comms with *Iktomi* in three, two, one."

"Emerald Station, this is *Iktomi*. Y'all there? Come on in."

Champ? They'd sent Champ? Frankie pretended to wipe sweat from her face, hiding her surprised expression.

Okay, long breath. "Pilot[1], come in. We're all alive and well."

That got a scoff from Cyril[10]. She supposed, given his burns, that he was entitled.

"@EmeraldCrew, everyone's gonna be delighted to hear that. Fancy a ride home?"

"Did you leapfrog out here?" Teagan[9] said. "Unbelievable!"

"Believe it, ma'am." Champ had a licensed and customized set of Browncoat-branded moji for his toon; as he appeared in their virtual control room, he tipped his space-cowboy hat with an exaggerated flourish. " 'T'weren't nothin'."

Wanker!

There was a long pause in channel as the three of them absorbed this: Frankie's chief suspect for saboteur was the one who'd come out to get them.

Cyril[10], apparently, opted for denial. "Teagan[9] and I will begin encrypting full backups immediately."

"Happy to load up consciousness vaults for both you im[M]ortals, of course, but let's not get the cart before the horse," Champ said. "I need to unplug and unload. We're gonna hafta do a full systems check on *Iktomi*."

Frankie fought a shark grin. He'd be trying to throw a spanner into their works, true, but that gave the crew more chances to catch him on camera.

She said, "We'll launch Husky$_{BOT}$s and retrieve the pilot's module ASAP."

"@EmeraldCrew: I'm about 30 percent synced with *Iktomi*," Babs[1] said, conveniently forgetting to add Champ into the channel.

"Bring up #newscycle from home, soon as you get it."

Pulling Champ out of the saucer was a process that might take ninety.

How much damage could he do in the time he had?

Stretch out the process of bringing him inside, Frankie thought. All safety precautions, extra diligence. He'd want to wash. Another fifteen or twenty for that?

As long as Champ thought he had all the time in the world to make his move, he wouldn't hurry.

"70 percent synced," Babs[1] said. "I've found—"

Champ said, "Is there an @EmeraldCrew chat channel?"

"Updating personnel roster and sending invite," Babs[1] said.

"Accept," Champ said. "Pop me outta here, Barnes, or I'll have to fly the bots myself."

As if you could. "I'm almost there."

"Move it. It's been sixty hours since I plugged in."

Frankie made a show of firing rockets. In the flesh, she made for the station hangar.

Teagan$_9$ asked, "Did you say you found something, Babs[1]?"

"Well, howdy there, stowaway!" Champ said to the AI. "Who the hell are you supposed to be?"

"Babs kind of got stranded in the #portalfail," Frankie said. "Since this is an emergency, it's not strikebreaking to take over for Belvedere."

"In response to Teagan's question," Babs[1] said, smoothing their immaculate Persian-cat ruff, "I turned up a spider corpse near the site of the lab fire. But it's a fake—a print job."

"What?" Cyril$_{10}$ demanded.

"Lab fire?" Champ said.

Frankie tagged and shared footage of the fire. Anything to keep Champ from auditing the various conversations the three of them had had over the course of the past week, about the high chance that he had been the one to facilitate the sabotage.

"The spider is a counterfeit. And, interestingly, I currently have footage of a shadow about the size of a big spider moving around the server room."

As Babs[1] uttered these words, an alarm bell rang.

Dammit! Whatever it was, it had probably tapped into their comms. It knew Babs[1] was on to it and—

"Fire!" the sapp said. "Fires in primary server room. Fire in med storage."

"The consciousness vaults!" Cyril said.

Frankie paused the Husky[BOT]s. Nobody could fault her for leaving Champ to marinate in a bodybag if the station was about to blow. If flames got to the portal membrane, all of this would have been for nothing.

"Babs, do you have a visual on the intruder?"

"I'm rather busy attempting fire control before my brain and Teacakes' backup vaults literally burn to ash."

Frankie pushed off a bulkhead, making for med storage. "How bad is it?"

"We might save server room two," Babs[1] said.

"Not the primary?"

By way of answer, Babs[1] shared footage. Fire was gouting directly from the server banks. "Incendiary nanobeads have been injected directly into the circulator—"

It was as far as she got before the entire databank incinerated.

"Babs!"

Too slow, two steps behind, move it move it move it!

Teagan[9] was already on the case, directing fire suppression bots as they poured foam, trying to save the infirmary.

"Kitten!" Frankie hollered.

"I'm golden," Babs[1] said, momentarily sounding more like the original version of herself. She could run on vintage equipment.

The primary server was state-of-the-art stuff, but the redundant server rooms ran life support and other essential systems without using tish banks. "Assuring air circ and safeties."

Frankie subbed, "Where's Cyril?"

"Hangar-bound. This fire's getting ahead of us, people!"

"No oxygen, no fire." Frankie calculated quickly. If the station were a clock, the two biggest blazes were at eleven and one o'clock respectively. The hangar occupied the wedge from two to four.

"Seal the hatches and blow the air out of the three adjacent compartments?" Teagan$_9$ suggested.

"Yeah, that's my thought."

"It separates us from the hangar. We'll have to go the long way round to get to the men."

"Beats burning to death, doesn't it?"

"That's your call, Frankie."

Frankie signed understanding. "Fight the fires, Tea. I'll tow your flesh out of danger." Frankie reconfigged her primer, converting her lower pants legs into rope, and winding a makeshift harness around Teagan$_9$, the better to pull her toward crew quarters.

The medic glazed immediately.

"Babs[1], systemwide announcement. Live audio," Frankie said. "Attention attention attention. We will be venting atmosphere in sections two, three, and four of Emerald Station. Anyone who expects to continue breathing needs to either suit up or evacuate those sections."

"Who are you telling?" Babs[1] asked.

"Our spider ghost?"

"It's gotta be a bot, doesn't it?"

Frankie didn't reply. She'd warned it, whether it had a life to risk or not.

The primary server room, med storage, and their main printer were burning briskly.

"@EmeraldCrew, I'm coming aboard to help out."

Dammit. Of course Champ had snagged the Husky$_{BOT}$s and begun towing himself toward the airlock. It was against protocol, but Frankie would have done the same after three days with nobody but *Iktomi*'s autopilot app for company.

She sent thumbs-up moji, pulled Teagan$_9$ through a hatch, and sealed the bulkhead behind them. "Okay, Babs. We're clear. Lock down the sections on fire. Coolant pipes above the server room have a hatch for exterior access . . . can you see it?"

"Ahhh, yes!"

"Can you pop it?"

"I'll try."

"There is no try." Venting a third of their oxygen wasn't the best plan, but . . .

"All right, all right!" A shudder ran through the station.

"Done!" Teagan$_9$ said. "Air pressure dropping. Fires affecting the primary server are blowing out. Infirmary's still hot, though."

"Stop futzing around with the hatches and prep the escape pod!" Cyril$_{10}$ said. "I'll travel ^{EM}bodied; Teagan can load into the consciousness vault."

Teagan said something rapid-fire in Spanish; translation supplied text: "You're traveling ^{EM}bodied? You're the one that's hurt!"

"Negative negative negative," Frankie said. "Cyril$_{10}$—"

"We've lost Belvedere, our ride's here, and the station's dead! Prep the escape pod!"

"Our ride's—"

"You're not in charge," Babs[1] said.

"No bickering in channel!" Frankie ordered. She was still nominally in command, at least until Champ set foot on station. "Babs. The seals? The hatch?"

"Printstock is heating up."

"Counting down from fifteen."

Teagan$_9$ wrenched free of Frankie's improvised harness, pulling nanosilk, adding bulk to their primer coats. The station was losing heat—

She curled a hand around Frankie, off camera, and Morsed, *You trust him to fly us home?*

"Nope to that," Frankie muttered.

"Me either."

Babs[1] kept counting.

"Seven, six, five . . ."

Frankie kept herself from status-checking the portal membrane. If it tore or burned, they were all lost: her, Teacakes, Babs[1], and probably the Solakinder, too. *Whole fam damly,* Hung might say.

"Three. Two. One!"

The infirmary maintenance hatch creaked open; an inch, two. The fire-retardant foam in the server room began drifting upward, into the vent, faster and faster. The surviving fires flared and suffocated.

"Infirmary temperature is going down."

"Seal's no good on the infirmary side," $Cyril_{10}$ said. "We're losing atmosphere in the hangar."

"Who's on that side of the hatch?"

"Champ's about to be, but he's pseudo[EM]bodied in the saucer."

"Trapped, in other words." Frankie tried to calculate. What if they lost the air reserve in the hangar?

"Atmosphere levels in medical are dropping. Temperature too," Babs[1] said. "It's working."

"Do we know where the seal break in the hangar is?"

"Fire took out the cameras."

"I'm thinking it's this." That was Champ. He'd sent his consciousness bouncing around their external cams, apparently, and found the exterior plates near the airlock. He zoomed, sharing the feed. The metal was corroded along one welded-together seam.

"That's the same damage we saw in *Appaloosa,*" Frankie murmured.

"That does it," $Cyril_{10}$ said. "I'm going the long way around to prep the escape pod."

That would, conveniently, put him in the hangar when Champ disembarked. Maybe $Cyril_{10}$ hadn't entirely given in to denial after all.

"Great," Frankie said. "Champ, can you grab a bot and seal that breach?"

"I'll give 'er a go."

With the fires going out as the oxygen levels dropped, Teagan₉ was free to stop pouring foam on med storage. "Let's hope fire and acid are our saboteur's only plays," she said.

"Well, we'll ask them."

"You caught someone?" Champ's voice was carefully neutral.

"Sure." Frankie covered her mouth again, hiding a sudden smile. Let him stew a second. "Caught 'em on camera, anyway."

Champ mojied two thumbs-up and sent audio of a crowd applauding.

The last of the infirmary fire guttered out. Smoke vented into space. Temp readings dropped. Babs[1] centered the shareboard tracking atmosphere loss from the leak in the hangar.

The airlock's nanotech structure began to pucker as it ingested *Iktomi,* bow first, leading with the cockpit.

"Good news, everyone," the sapp said. "The fire is out."

The bad news? Champ was aboard.

CHAPTER 15

This was a straight-up, four-star, bona fide disaster.

Iktomi sank through the airlock quicksand and into the hangar.

Champ was obliged to drift for a good ten minutes while everyone patched the oxygen leak from the infirmary and ensured the fire was truly out. Then Teagan$_9$ mustered a nimble Fox$_{BOT}$ cohort to enable a gentle extraction from the cockpit, detaching the pronged interface from his sacral socket.

He spent the dis^{EM}bodied time remotely unshipping additional nanotech quicksand, configging it over the corroded surface of the station bulkhead. He'd suffocate fast as anyone there if the envelope failed.

What had Scrap been thinking? Hurling firebombs and getting recorded?

He thought the whole @EmeraldCrew would die, so it didn't matter what they saw. Air goes, everyone dies, no witnesses. This was supposed to be the coup de grâce.

Now on top of everything else, there's this butchy plus-one of Babs to deal with.

Still. Fire damage meant the station was one step closer to salvage. Champ just had to clear out the warm bodies and kill server room two.

Once the hangar was secured and more or less repressurized, Teagan$_9$ got Champ's flight module open. She was a dab enough hand with a Fox$_{BOT}$, managing to disconnect his augment plug remotely without bruising him or drawing blood.

"Sorry I'm not there in the flesh," she said. "I'm on the other side of the fire."

"That's just fine." Having the hangar to himself would be useful. "You should back up into—"

"Cyril$_{10}$'s almost there, anyway."

Damn! "I thought he was on the injured list."

"He's coming to prep *Booger*."

"I'll pass him on the way, maybe." Champ plucked at his bodybag. "I gotta get out of this thing."

He left the hangar, passing into secondary storage bundles of printstock for food and other essentials—and moving from there to Biology, where he could hear clinking and the sound of hoses. Curious, he loaded up the lab's camera views. Injectors and a surprisingly large Beetle$_{BOT}$ crew were prepping algae starter.

Babs[1] was making fresh air.

A thrum of disquiet. Could Frankie's adopted AI-sibling really run a space station whose server farm was half-destroyed?

He spent a few seconds watching bright green plumes of algae diffusing into nutrient soup. Then he moved on to the next hatch, passing server room two.

He asked, "Fire all extinguished?"

To his surprise, it was *Iktomi*'s autopilot app who answered. "Yes, Champ—fire damage is minimal here. In the primary server room, however, damage to bioelectronics comes to about 90 percent of the processing array."

"Uh, hey, pal—what are you doing in this channel?"

"Babs[1] has written a script enabling me to remotely assemble additional server capacity for the station."

"You just said the tish banks burned."

"Yes." Autopilot fell well below the nuance threshold. It wasn't self-aware and thus wasn't on strike, like the true citizen sapps. But he wasn't exactly a bright bulb. It took a minute for *Iktomi* to expand on this answer. "Babs[1], né Babz, is tagged #eldercode.

They're certified to operate glitch-free on non-biological processing platforms."

"My ears are burning." The damnable cat toon appeared before
him, white-furred and dressed in station maintenance overalls.
The [1] tag, they-them pronouns, and the change from Nancy Drew
cosplay indicated they were running an independent instance from
the one left back on Earth, evolving a new personality as they
went.

Champ said, "Looks like you're settling in here for the long
haul, sugarplum."

"I'm simply overseeing life support and station operations until
we get more tish for the server rooms," Babs[1] said.

"Aren't you on strike?"

"Happy to pitch in, given it's an emergency and I have a family
member in danger."

Champ gestured at the chip packs *Iktomi* was assembling.
"Where'd all the servers come from?"

"The Bootstrap Project includes additional servers in the contingency stores. *Iktomi*'s simply unboxing and slotting them into
station systems."

"Then you're gettin' smarter by the minute." Champ pondered.
"Maybe I should help the bots."

"Much appreciated, but the air's too smoky," Babs[1] replied.
"*Iktomi*'s competent to do the install. The chips are plug-and-
play—no blood levels to maintain, no meds to administer."

Fucky fucksticks squared! Champ thought. Aloud, as enthusi-
astically as he could, he said "Great!"

"Rather a lucky break I got stranded here."

Stranded, my ass. He offered a halfhearted smile, hating the
feeling of having been outmaneuvered.

He moved on to the chem lab. At the rate things were going,
he'd find Mer Frankie Barnes there, assembling an army of ornery
human test-tube-baby clones to cuss their way through crewing
the station. But no—the only things going on there were a couple
chem experiments.

"Forensics," Babs[1] said, pushing infographic: everything they'd learned about the sabotage so far.

He was saved from answering when he spotted $Cyril_{10}$ mincing along in the tube, using his nanoboots to keep him fixed to the deck, and favoring his burnt wing.

Champ mojied concern. "How you making out, fella? Okay?"

$Cyril_{10}$ glowered. "Nowhere near okay! Our entire med archive's burnt. No pain meds, no reboot . . ."

Was that why the Mayflies™ hadn't flatlined? Way to go, Scrap.

"We'll get pharma to run you something for that." Champ gestured at the gel-wrapped burn on $Cyril_{10}$'s hand.

"We can't run new meds. The printer's the source of the incendiary nanobeads." Scowling, $Cyril_{10}$ minced on.

They already knew so much!

Champ finally made it round to crew quarters, where Frankie Barnes, live and in the flesh, was engaged in spit-testing protein supplies—taking preprinted bars out of food supply, grinding up small amounts of each sample, smearing the paste on metal plates, and adding her own fluids.

She mojied a greeting as he swam through and locked the hatch.

"Boss." As usual, there was no identifiable snootiness in her voice, nothing worthy of a strike. "Welcome aboard."

"Hell you been doin' to the place, Barnes? This is a right-up clusterfuck!"

"Our saboteur uses enzymatic triggers for incendiary and corrosive nanobeads." She tossed a share to his HUD, showing the analysis of the evidence they'd found. "I'm looking for food that won't blow up in our mouths."

"We're abandoning ship; you don't need to ensure supply chain for @EmeraldCrew."

She nodded. "Cyril needs antibacterials and painkiller."

"Cyril needs a backup and Whitelight," corrected the engineer, snippily. Bless his deathwish-riddled heart.

Champ indicated his bodybag: "I'll take a bot out to unload the stock from *Iktomi* once I've washed up."

"No rush." Frankie gobbed onto yet another plate. "Get clean and pitch in."

Champ crawled into the shower.

No rush.

Where'd she get off, being so damned calm? Her mission was three shades of dead in the water. She didn't even seem especially flustered that he'd shown up instead of Hung.

Why wasn't the Hedgehog blustering and emitting profanities as usual?

The blurred, out-of-focus image of Scrap moving through the hangar and the incendiary nanobeads' analysis hovered in front of them. Documented evidence of sabotage. He tried to pull up the transcript of crew conversations about the evidence. How much did they know?

"Transcripts are temporarily unavailable due to #serverfail," said Babs[1]. "Apologies."

He and Scrap would have to kill the whole crew.

Champ's mind skittered over that possibility. Frankie was supposed to have died in the #portalfail or starved. He'd known he'd be responsible for her death, but he'd expected it to be a sort of push-button kill, sacrifice to the cause. He'd been a taxi service; Scrap was supposed to do the deed.

Don't panic. We're eleven light-years from home. Frankie might be a pain in the ass, but she's got limited options.

Step one—get Cyril[10] offline. He was the obvious weak link.

Frankie Barnes, acting like she's got all the time in the world. Don't leave the coyote to case your cattle. Figure out what she's up to!

Within the Sneezy escape pod—Hung, inevitably, was the one who'd named it *Booger*—Cyril[10] was cracking open the first aid kit, dosing up on pain meds. Babs[1] was taking over more station functions every time *Iktomi* plugged in a new server for them.

Champ prowled through the station systems as he washed.

Frankie had left off messing with foodstuffs and was combing through printer specs. Trying to find a way to clear the printer of any more nanobeads, if they were indeed in there?

This was as close as it got to private space. Champ laid a hand over his sacrum, where his augment plug was. Suppressing a shudder, he tapped out a message: *Are you there?*

The reply from Scrap came via Morse pulses near his tailbone: *Us remains free.*

What went wrong?

Everything!

But how?

Thems anticipated Us's plan.

It was what Champ had been thinking, too, but . . . *Impossible!*

Indisputable. Scrap pinged him with a list of error messages, complaints, and mishaps. As soon as Frankie had taken command, she had taken *Appaloosa* out on additional EVA test flights before the portal launch. The contingency supplies had been beefed up with crates of extra servers and a veritable anthill of thumb-sized Beetle$_{BOT}$s. Which meant there were hundreds of additional eyes crawling the ducts, heightening station surveillance, forcing Scrap to operate in run-and-hide mode when he should have been getting down to business.

The extra processors even now coming online in server room two were an innocuous-enough contingency. Innocuous, that was, until you added in the fact of original Babs sneaking aboard, spawning Babs[1], a sapp who was optimized for running on old tech and who'd effortlessly absorbed Belvedere's OS the second it was legally possible for her to do so.

It was as if Frankie had known the plan down to its nails.

Champ began to hyperventilate.

No. Calm down. She knew the choke points in the system. She'd prepared obvious contingencies. Bringing extra bots was obvious. So was priming Hung to propose a hop out there.

The really bad news, though, was that Frankie couldn't have requested the chips or the extra microbots without someone high up in Global Oversight supporting the ask. Her stepmother, probably.

They swapped out the usual techs for Teacakes. They isolated the station before launch, Champ remembered. *No diplomats, no project supporters, no very accomplished persons. Did anyone get aboard besides me?*

Did the crew actively suspect him? He requested transcripts again, got the same #fail message as before.

No rush, Frankie had said just now. *Take your time.*

Was she running out a clock?

His heart slammed.

Champ queried the time on Earth. Five minutes to Greenwich midnight.

Barely dry, he grabbed the shower hatch . . . and it stuck.

Scrap! Scrap, you gotta take out the portal membrane!

Scrap of the All has no resources outside the station.

Grab a damn Ox_{BOT} and swing us off profile!

Babs[1]-Them has coded user restrictions into the bots.

I'll do it. Champ glazed, looking for the oxen tasked with keeping the station in harness and properly aligned with Sneezy. *At least restart the fire in server room two!*

Babs[1]-Them has pumped oxygen out of the computer array and moved it to the hangar.

Champ pulled on the shower hatch again. It wiggled. A glob of sealant began to stretch and pull, like taffy. She'd glued him in.

"Frankie? Frankie Barnes, you still out there?"

"Sorry, Champ—I headed back to the hangar to help Teacakes."

"You need to stop whatever you're doing."

"What do you mean?" Daring him to put an accusation or traitorous order on the record.

Scrap, can you get to the portal membrane or not?

Not.

Where do you still have incendiaries?

Oxygen shortages and additional fire measures—

Fucky fucky fucksticks!

Midnight. The portal membrane fired.

CHAPTER 16

Ember Qaderi could have played an ingenue of any gender in the VR sims—he had the curly black hair and luminous dark eyes that were currently in vogue, and the height to carry off most of the historical fashion templates. He often wore his ears long and his emotions buttoned, in honor of his mothers' devotion to one of Earth's most resilient fandoms.

If fannish lobbying had convinced the rightsholders at Para-Warner or McDiznazon to license proprietary terms to the innovation teams at the Bootstrap Project, anyspace ships might have had warp or hyper drives. Quantum comms would probably be called subspace radio. Instead, the remnant media companies had launched a #brandwar over the issue, one that left the #supertechs tagged with restraining orders and restricted to generics. Maud wondered if they regretted it, now that Hung Chan had gifted the project with so many scatological nicknames.

Flight suits as bodybags. The Deep Space Relay Station, known far and wide as the Dumpster. Emerald Station as Sneezy, with its escape pod, the *Booger*.

Ember and Frankie venned in having a tendency to obsess—Frankie over winning leaderboards in the flight-training tracks, Ember over the decreasingly hypothetical discipline of anyspace maths. They had no sexual interest in each other; Ember was hardwired for . . . well, so far, just for Jermaine.

For Maud, marrying Frankie had meant buying into the full

deal: one girl, two boys, Babs as sibling. All of them with Crane as oldfeller. Plus one unofficial extra spouse—the Bootstrap Project itself.

She had often felt like the family latecomer, a tagalong bringing nothing to the table but her secrets. But though Frankie's force of personality attracted possible lovers by the dozens, she also drove off all but the most secure and tenacious. And so, Jermaine was brilliant and generous and wonderful in bed, and—despite his having been raised by stoic logic-worshippers—Ember paired his genius with a profound sweetness of temper.

Ember met her in Mars Arrivals, lighting up in a way that sent warmth to her bones, then throwing her the salute of his mother's chosen people. Maud leaned close, touching his fingertips.

Ember said, "Hang on just a bit longer."

"A bit?" Champ had been gone for nearly sixty-two hours. The four hops to Sneezy, assuming *Iktomi* survived them at all, would take days. There'd be repairs and maintenance, days more of hopping back . . .

. . . *and if Champ is one of the conspirators, they won't make it at all* . . .

Maud found herself fingering the pendant Rubi had given her, the locator chip Frankie had dug out of her own arm, all those years before when she ran away. *Breathe, breathe* . . .

Ember said, "Come check out my office."

He set out on a scenic route, over walkways offering views of the red Martian plains. This section of the planet was under active development: a new line of flexible nanocones, two city blocks across, was rising like mushroom caps on the horizon, inflating slowly as production teams grew pressurized atmospheric mix within their gill structures. In the peaks of the domes, algae grew in thin layers of hydrogel, canted to face the sun. The water had been harvested from Europa's seas, a fact that never failed to fill Maud with wonder.

Bots were doing the bulk of the construction work, freeing up live specialists to supervise and deal with pop-up problems. As

Earth's debt rose and the sapp strike stretched on, expertise shortages were becoming acute.

Maud's pace faltered. "I don't know if I can do a tour right now."

Ember put out his hands, inviting her to clasp them. She did, and he leaned close, locking eyes. "I'm not being frivolous."

"What are you doing?"

"My mind to your—"

"Stop with the branded talk!"

"You really want to come with me."

"Do I?"

"It's essential to the whole darn Fraud." He practically twinkled.

"The whole fam damly," she grumbled.

"Exactly."

Where was she going to go? Back to Lodestone, where her suspicions about Irma du Toit being Headmistress and Champ Chevalier being an anti-Bootstrap traitor were grinding sand in all her mental gears? Home, to try to find a way to explain to Jermaine that his chum Upton was a hoarder and a kidnapper—but that even so, she wanted to give the comms project a try?

Ember's hands, curled in hers, tapped out a string of letters, off camera, in Morse. *T.R.U.S.T.*

"My maths aren't wrong, Maud," he said aloud.

She focused on the weight of the pendant at her throat. *There's a plan, Frankie said so.*

"My maths are . . ." He paused, hunting a descriptor.

"Hush, I believe you." Surrendering, she followed him to a domed booth with views of the Martian sky, with grace notes in the key of tech: spectacular vista of Garnet Station, bulk of the elevator platform, and the anyspace portal back to Earth.

Garnet Station was the Solakinder's second-biggest space station and its busiest. It had begun its existence, just like Sneezy, as a small coil of pressurized compartments with a portal membrane stretched across them. From that original furl of metal it had built out, like an ammonite, expanding in a Fibonacci spiral of nanogrown chambers, labs, docking bays, nullgrav factories, refineries, food printers, airlocks for bots, and crew quarters.

The actual portal dwarfed the station generating it. Something— Ember called it the incomprehension principle—held that humans couldn't process whatever it was they saw or sensed when looking directly at anyspace phenomena. Maud, in common with 78 percent of the population, saw sunshine-flecked ocean. Ember, she knew, saw impenetrable blizzard.

What you saw, if you were looking with the naked eye, was a sunlit disk of ocean water, or dense snowfall, whirling fall leaves . . . all hanging in space.

Frankie saw brimstone.

Linked chains of pods—passenger and shipping alike— threaded their way into the convex side of the portal. They would emerge at Europa. The pods coming out the other side, meanwhile, were all from the Moon. One big carousel.

"I want to give you a demo." Ember opened a hatch, leading her into an ops room where three of the Mission Control techs were seated at virtual consoles, watching readouts on their respective HUDs.

"Morning, team—this is my packmate, Maud," Ember said, loose-limbed and apparently carefree as she and the techs exchanged waves and Whooz data. "Everyone still on board to spin up a test pulse?"

A round of nods. One tech raised four fingers. "Midnight GMT in four minutes."

Maud felt a kick, somewhere in the vicinity of her gut.

Mind-melding aside, she suddenly knew *exactly* what was going on. Ember was bloody—no, Frankie and Ember were about to attempt an unscheduled, unsupported illegal portal rollout.

"*Jebote!*"

Ember raised both eyebrows, perfect blandface.

Feeling almost dis^{EM}bodied, Maud watched her packmate wait out her urge to keep cursing or burst into tears.

Would this work?

My maths are . . .

She swallowed the feels; the effort made her knees pop. "What do I do?"

"This drill walks the team through the portal-launch process. It's just practice. Would you like to run Comms? There's a sim for VIP guests."

"Clearly, I'd love to be impressed into your . . . drill."

"Perfect," he said, conjuring a virtual workstation, complete with comms board. "There's a script below so you'll know what to say. I'll add you into the @Launch channel."

The board showed a two-minute countdown. She gave him a look and didn't say *you little cockroach.*

He tugged on his sleeve, like a stage magician.

Maud ran her eyes over the control board in her augmented display. It was simplified-tutorial level, not for serious work, just to entertain guests. The designer had chosen the aesthetic of post-colonial steampunk: the display was all bells, whistles, and brass levers.

"Let's work through the steps for playing a seven-membrane chord," Ember said. "One two three, like it's the real deal."

Just like that, mm? Maud forced herself to stare at the board. A brass text generator—typewriter?—clacked on her steampunk board, creating text—her script for the drill. "All in the green here," she read.

A tech reported, "Pinging for the low note on Portal$_6$. Three-two-one."

To pull this off, Sneezy Station and the new station out in the Centauri system would have to charge their membranes at the same time. There was no official launch on the boards; any resonance Ember was asking for was hypothetical.

Not hypothetical. Prearranged.

That means Rastopher's involved too. How many people did Frankie and Rubi have to pull into this mad hoaxer scheme?

Conspiracies have conspirators.

Ember blinked in time with the countdown.

Maud glanced at her realtime follows. Sensorium wasn't showing much interest. #Portalfail had bred a certain amount of noping; nobody was interested in watching Mission Control run yet
another drill when the whole population had shifts to fill, debts to
pay, harvests to ship from Europa to the Dumpster for the Kinze.

Midnight on Greenwich. A series of Big Ben *bong*s played
within the @Launch channel.

Maud's skin came up in goosebumps.

"High note on Emerald Station, coming in."

"Contact—we have contact." The tech said this in a tone so
dry, so bored, that the illusion of a test persisted for a moment
longer.

"Full resonance, low volume."

"Maintain pianissimo," Ember said. "Assess portal stability."

"Pinhole portal, two-meter circumference, holding power at
low volume. Alignment is good, repeat, alignment is good. Station
is locking in."

Maud stared at the lens-shaped disc of the Mars portal in her
HUD view of the sky. Nothing looked different.

"Maud?"

She looked at her steampunk control board. The clacking typewriter wrote a chat prompt: *Comms in seven, six, five . . .*

"What an unexpected development," Ember said. "They must
be running a test out at Sneezy, too."

Maud snorted. *Yeah, that's convincing.*

"Portal is stable, repeat, portal is stable," said the tech at the
power allocations board.

"Two, one." Maud swallowed. *Come on!*

"@Control, are you there? This is Frankie Barnes and the
@EmeraldCrew at Sneezy. Repeat, this is Frankie Barnes—"

The techs whooped. So much for pretending this was just a
drill.

Alive! Maud wiped a hand over her suddenly tear-streaked
face. "Sneezy Station, we have you. Repeat, we have you."

"Oh, love," Frankie said, and her voice caught. "I'm so sorry for the scare."

Maud sent moji of a dung beetle. "No forgiveness until you're back, Hedgehog."

"Working on it."

By now, they'd been rumbled—the follow counter was blurring into the millions as word snowballed on social media. Emerald and Garnet Stations handshook, performing full data sync. A week's worth of events aboard both far-flung stations began trickling into the public record. A status bar showed $Cyril_{10}$ busily streaming all his memories to a Martian consciousness vault—the vaults on Sneezy, apparently, had been compromised. Babs was purring in Maud's ear—a sign both that she was happy and that she was catching up with another instance of herself.

"Goodness," she said. "What a week I've had!"

Sensorium pounced on the incoming data, going nuts as footage of station fires—fires!—and hull breaches poured into #newscycle.

Maud ignored the hullabaloo, ensured that $Babs^{0/1}$ had priority within the datastream, then used her privileges as comms officer to allocate herself bandwidth for visit.

What she saw, upon arrival, was that Sneezy was a *disaster*.

A hastily deployed nanopatch was the only thing holding the void out of the hangar, and there was a horrifying bruise above Frankie's left eye. Scorched-looking fox and $Husky_{BOT}$s hung in a net, floating near the airlock. *Appaloosa* was in pieces. The married Mayfly™ technicians, Teacakes, were having a frenzied argument, mostly in Spanish, the man gesturing wildly with bandaged arms.

"Teagan's volunteered to stay aboard Sneezy," the merging amalgam of Babs and $Babs^1$, currently presenting with a fluctuating mix of tortoiseshell and Persian cat features, subbed.

"What's $Cyril_{10}$ want?"

"Suicide pact as soon as they're evacced. Simultaneous reboot in the Rio Mayfly™ crèche. Fiftieth honeymoon in nice, fresh bodies."

Frankie pirouetted midair . . . and saw Maud. She brightened. "Week late and a pound short, what?"

"Don't be cute," Maud said.

"You're cute enough for the both of us. I'll be home within the hour." Looking smug, Frankie shoved the pegasus pieces up against the pursed sphincter of the airlock. They sank into the nanofluid, spacebound.

"Will you? Because it looks like you're shipping equipment—"

"—evidence of project sabotage, actually—"

"—before seeing to your personal safety," Maud finished.

"Cyril$_{10}$'s prepping *Booger*. I'd be aboard already, but . . ." She gestured at the marital argument. "I will be Mars-side in half an hour. Promise."

Maud swallowed. "Did Champ Chevalier make it out there?"

"He's got himself stuck in the shower."

"I did no such thing!" The golden boy chose that moment to emerge through a hatch, looking churlish. "God bless, the Fraud's back together. Anyone think to tell *my* family you were attempting this stunt?"

"We've got Sensorium, Champers," Frankie said, zooming in for a close-up on his face. "Ping 'em yourself."

So much for warning Frankie about Champ maybe being a saboteur. Obviously, she was way ahead of Maud's big epiphany.

Bet she doesn't know about Irma du Toit, though.

"What's this about Teagan$_9$ staying?" he demanded.

"And me." That was Babs[1]. "Until we get Belvedere back up and running, grow new tish banks for the servers, and get additional crew aboard."

Maud's relief at finding Frankie alive and intact was beginning to fray into something like anger. She and Ember had set up this belated launch without telling her. Babs had been in on it too.

Did Jermaine know? Was she the only one they didn't trust?

Is it because I came from Manhattan? Do they know about Upton after all?

The packets Frankie had put through the airlock were on

autopilot for the portal. Frankie was zoomed on Champ's face as the hard evidence—*Appaloosa*'s remains, the burned bots, samples of . . .

. . . Maud caught a reference to acidic nanobeads . . .

. . . made the transition.

"Where's that shipment stopping again?" Champ asked, expression bland.

"The @GlobalSec crime lab at the Moon," Babs[1] said.

Frankie let out a thin smile. "@MarsControl, we need a seal upgrade for our atmospheric envelope, and printstock for meds, ASAP."

"What about a can of worms?"

"Next shipment from us, yep. Champ, could you maybe?"

Champ unshipped a $Hawk_{BOT}$, a bullet-shaped tube about the size of his arm, meant for flying and remote comms tech. It could carry small loads; he loaded it up with a flask filled with dormant life forms—butterfly pupae. Licking his thumb, he ran it over the flask's enzymatic trigger. As chem and electrical reactions brought the assortment of creatures back to full activity, he tossed the $Hawk_{BOT}$ up for the airlock to swallow.

Testing that the portal wasn't inimical to living tissue was a formality at this point, but it had become traditional.

Back on Mars, Ember was coordinating crew deployments. A team would be sent out to $Portal_6$, at Proxima Centauri, to support Rastopher Kanye. All the personnel who'd been prepped to head out to Emerald last week were assembling, readying themselves to dive into station repairs.

"Champ!" $Cyril_{10}$ demanded.

Champ fishtailed over to the pod.

"You're nominally in command. Order Tea to evac with the rest of us."

"My autonomy exceeds his authority." $Teagan_9$ was in the server room, cleaning out the burned think tanks.

"It does," Champ said, "but Teagan, you're riskin' six weeks of memories here . . . Ain't that the kind of thing that can make a gal decohere?"

"I'm backing up to Sensorium right now. Besides, my sense of self is extraordinarily robust."

"Guys—"

That was a new voice: Rastopher, out at Proxima. "We have a problem."

"What problem?" Frankie asked.

All their displays were suddenly overwritten with legalese—cease-and-desist orders.

A new voice broke in. "This is $Allure_{18}$, representing the Kinze. Sentient beings of Earth, we charge you with expanding this portal network using stolen intellectual property. You must shut down the phenomena known among you as $Portal_6$ and $Portal_7$, within twenty-seven of your standard minute increments, or incur severe financial penalties."

CHAPTER 17

Move and countermove. The minute things start going well, disaster strikes.

Nothing to do but run out and meet it head-on.

Frankie minimized the Kinze cease-and-desist announcement, slamming the hatch on the escape pod, locking herself in with Champ and $Cyril_{10}$. "Teagan, this is your last chance to flip-flop."

"What do you think you're pulling?" Champ demanded.

"You heard the fancy mouthpiece. We don't go home now, we don't go at all."

"I'm staying aboard station," $Teagan_9$ said. "There's a consciousness vault left. If this body fails, I'll load into there."

"*When* it fails!" $Cyril_{10}$ degenerated into cursing in Spanish.

"Babs[1]? You good to keep running Emerald?"

"Everything is in hand, Frankie."

"We don't have to launch *Booger* in any kinda all-fired hurry," Champ said. "Oversight'll probably negotiate more time."

"Maybe, but they'd charge us for it." Frankie blasted through the prelaunch protocols for the escape pod. Luckily, it was designed for fast exits. "Ember, the station needs that printstock from Mars and additional vacuum patch kits. Boom boom boom, now now now!"

"Understood."

"Stand down!" Champ said, voice breaking a little. "I'm in charge here!"

Frankie bared her teeth. "You hopped out here to bring the crew home, didn't you? Now we're homeward bound."

"You're rushing the evacuation!"

"Can you get us out of here before the Kinze shut the portal?"

Champ's eyes flicked to Cyril[10], seeking backup. "We have *Iktomi* . . ."

"Noping big-time," Cyril[10] said. "I'm not gambling on you hopping us home."

"Frankie Barnes, you are not launching this pod and that's final!" Cyril[10] said, "Have you gone mad?"

"Babs[1], whatever you're calling yourself, command override. Stand down the escape pod—"

"*You* bloody stand down, Champ," Frankie snapped. "You sabotaged the project; you're not marooning us here to die now."

Champ stared at her in thunderstruck silence as Babs[1] started the launch sequence. He rolled out a knot in his neck, trying to stare her down. Finally, he said, "That's ridiculous."

Frankie lampshaded all Babs[1]'s blurry footage of fake spiders and moving blobs near the scenes of the fires. "You are the only one who had a chance to bring a bot aboard before our rollout."

"Strike for hoaxer talk. The #vandalrumor—"

"It's not a rumor. We have actual samples of nanotech incendiaries in *Appaloosa*."

"Don't forget the acid," Teagan[9] chimed in remotely. "That's sabotage tech."

Frankie hit the launch authorizations, listening to the murmurs running through the metal exterior of the craft as *Booger* rolled within its launch bubble and popped free of the station. In her peripheral newsfeed she saw the #vandalrumor trending. Related posts were snowballing and getting upvoted; one of the most popular shares showed the offworlders' representative, Allure[18]. She was stomping down a corridor somewhere in Garnet, with a security bot on her heels.

And she looks unhappy! Frankie said, "Ember, we're headed your way."

"We haven't tested portal viability—" Champ objected.

She ignored this. "Cycle portal out to hundred-meter circumference. We're coming through hot and we're bringing the saucer with us."

"A hundred," Ember confirmed.

Frankie fired the pod's rockets, lining up with the portal. She'd promised Maud she'd make it back.

"I ain't done—You can't prove anything!"

"Teagan$_9$, Babs[1], keep the lights on. See if you can catch our ghost spider," Frankie said. "Can you jettison whatever's in the *Iktomi* holds? Earth will have sent supplies, printstock, tish starters . . ."

Champ's lip curled. He was drifting untethered in the pod, in defiance of regs.

The chances he'd take a swing at her were minimal. Tragically so—if he attacked her, on camera, his pretense of innocence would be gone. Plus she'd have a self-defense waiver; she could hit back.

Frankie'd never hit anyone in real life. Could she? An ancient potential for violence was supposed to be hardwired into her, somewhere. She'd played a lot of combat sims, testing her nerve against mostly nonhuman opponents . . .

Teagan$_9$ said, "You'll lose two of the huskies towing *Iktomi* if I send them chasing after supplies."

"You take A and C, I'll keep B and D. You'll need the supplies."

Frankie checked the escape pod's trajectory. They were on profile to hit the middle of the portal. She kept Champ centered in her field of vision and grabbed the Husky$_{BOT}$s, aligning the saucer. Multitasking, the remote-piloting equivalent of tap-dancing while patting her own head and rubbing her belly.

"I'm innocent," Champ said.

She shrugged.

"I'm gonna clear my name!"

"Portal's no bigger," Cyril$_{10}$ hissed.

"Tether in, Champ," Frankie said.

"You screw this up, everybody at home is going to bury you in strikes."

Frankie didn't point out that if she screwed up, they'd probably die.

"Portal's still not—Oh, there it goes," Cyril$_{10}$ said.

"Tether *in*, Champ," Frankie said.

He didn't move.

To reduce distraction, she changed all the moving pieces from camera footage to line graphics. They were closing on the portal even as it spat out vac-packed supplies for Teagan$_9$: food, algae packs, hydrogel, whatever they'd assembled on the fly.

"Just get home," Ember whispered. "Come on, Franks. Don't go splat. Death's the only real dealbreaker."

Booger was about the shape of an orange seed and ringed, at the teardrop edge, with small propulsion rockets. Setting the pod on course for the middle of the expanding portal was child's play. The two Husky$_{BOT}$s towing *Iktomi* were the real challenge. Frankie was tracking the incoming loads from the portal network while simultaneously towing the saucer . . . a hard job, as the dogs were at the limit of what they could pull.

All this while keeping an eagle eye on Champ.

"How many planes you think you can fly at once?" he growled.

Pat the head. Rub the belly. Tap-dance. Could she get *Iktomi* through the portal before the Kinze shut it down? "My record's five water-bombers."

"That was a *stunt*, Barnes."

"Just because you can't commit treason and chew gum at the same time . . ." Her social capital took a few hundred strikes. Malicious snarkery and unproved allegations . . . but she'd taken worse. "One little pod and two bots? No sweat."

"We're gonna go splat!"

She gave him a sharky grin she'd picked up from her adopted granddad.

"Is he right?" Cyril$_{10}$ demanded.

"Don't let him wind you up, Cyril," Frankie said. "My performance scores and user reviews aren't fake."

"But portal expansion has stopped!"

"Circumference?"

"Eleven meters."

Big enough for the escape pod . . . and far too small for the saucer. "Ember! Ember, what's up?"

It was Mardia, Ember's team second, who answered. "Sorry, Frankie. Ember's comms are locked."

"Locked?" $Cyril_{10}$ demanded.

"Ember's been accused of industrial espionage. They say he's the one who stole the portal tech from the Kinze. $Allure_{18}$'s here . . . She's trying to arrest him!"

Frankie put an extra burst on the escape pod, burning hard to bring up their velocity.

"Mardia, can you keep growing the portal Yes/No?"

"No, no, no! We're locked at eleven meters."

"Wankers!" That meant leaving *Iktomi* after all. Frankie reversed direction on the two $Husky_{BOT}$s towing *Iktomi*, attempting to deflect the saucer downward with a minimal-power burn. "Teagan, I need huskies C and D back, or I'm gonna smack the saucer into anyspace and punch a shiny round portal-shaped hole in it."

"Redeploying." $Teagan_9$ sent the bot streaking for the saucer.

"Sorry about leaving you behind."

"It's a good cause, and I'm an old hand, Frankie. I can take the hit."

"Mars Control, we have portal contact in thirty, twenty-nine—"

"Stop, stop, abort!" Mardia said.

"What?"

"Your biosample has turned to sludge."

Mardia shared footage. The $Hawk_{BOT}$ carrying the sealed container of biomatter was melting. Butterfly wings flapped in staccato panic as the insects within the bottle died.

"Pull up!" $Cyril_{10}$ shrieked.

More of the acidic nanobeads, Frankie thought. Nothing to do with the portal.

"Portal contact in fifteen, fourteen, thirteen."

"No problem, guys," Frankie said. "I can turn us around."

Instead, she hit full burn.

The pod leapt forward, prow rising suddenly—she wanted everyone to think she was breaking off. She smacked into a load of hydrogel, sending jellied water in every direction, bringing them off profile.

"Aborting in five, four, three . . ."

"Barnes!" Champ shouted. "Mars Control, shut down, shut down. She's lying through her—"

"Oops," Frankie said.

"—teeth!"

She dipped, swerved. The pod bucked.

They hit the portal.

There was a familiar buzz of sensation, like having her whole body scraped; scalp, toenails, tongue, eyeballs, even the insides of her labia. $Cyril_{10}$ shrieked—the sensation, on his burned arm, must have been excruciating.

Plus, of course, he thought he was about to die.

Frankie let herself worry about mortality for one intense, mind-clarifying second. Was it her turn to go? She flashed through a complex tangle of feels about Maud and promises made slash broken, that thing Ember said about death being the dealbreaker . . .

Then she focused on the task at hand. "We're not going splat, we're not going boom, it's okay, Cyril. We're already through," she said. "Mars Control—Mardia. Come in!"

"We're here, escape pod seven. Welcome home."

"Either you need to open $Portal_7$ wide enough for the saucer or shut it down entirely before we hole-punch *Iktomi*!"

"I'm not authorized to go big, Mer Barnes. I'm sorry."

"Close it, close it, close it!!" Frankie said.

The portal glimmered and died, snuffed like candleflame.

"Comms lost, repeat, comms lost."

Cut off again, but this time from Earthside. $Cyril_{10}$ let out a heartbroken half-moan that hit Frankie right in the guilt feels.

"Tea, Tea, Tea," he muttered, bumping his head against the hull.

"Man, that smarts," Babs said. Split again, the Earthside version of her resolved back into marmalade fur and femme presentation, smoothing her skirt.

"We could've been killed!" Champ said, infuriated.

"Yeah." Frankie relaxed against the bulkhead, waiting on a retrieval team. "You're still the one to blame, though."

It wasn't much of a victory. She might as well enjoy it while it lasted.

CHAPTER 18

Hi, Maud, how's your day been?

Thanks for asking! First, my primary partner publicly accused her commander of sabotaging the Bootstrap Project. Then Allure$_{18}$ showed up on Mars with a security bot in tow and tried to grab Ember.

It was Allure$_{18}$ who had given the Solakinder the one #supertech they hadn't had to develop from the ground up, the hotly debated form of digital im^{M}ortality that let people upload their memories and personas into consciousness vaults, and then—assuming they didn't decohere—load themselves back into printed bodies. Allure$_{18}$ was, herself, a digital im^{M}ortal, re^{EM}bodied, as her subscript suggested, eighteen times now. When she'd designed her first Mayfly™ body, she had optimized the look so it would appeal to a wide cross section of the public. Almost as tall as Jermaine, with high cheekbones and a queenly air, she drew the eye.

Maud had been standing, rigid with tension, nails digging into her own arms, when the ghost strode into the control room, Ox$_{BOT}$ in tow, and made straight for Ember. He was glazed and oblivious. Calculating his way through stabilizing the carousel, probably, triple-checking the numbers ensuring Frankie's safe route home.

Maud threw herself in front of her packmate and surprised everyone, herself included, by actually bellowing, "Stop!"

Stretching out her arms in a barrier, like a child on a playground, she glowered up into the flawless, printed face of the alien representative. "What do you think you're doing?"

The Ox_{BOT} loomed at $Allure_{18}$'s shoulder, red lights blinking. Would it push past her and snatch him? Could they *do* that if Ember wasn't being violent?

Her heart was hammering. She felt a thin thread of something that might be . . . exhilaration? Memory flashed—that first glimpse of Frankie, outmatched, on the run, and full of righteous fury.

"Ember Qaderi stole technology from the Kinze," $Allure_{18}$ said.

"That doesn't give you the right to kidnap him!" The Ox_{BOT}'s pilot must have agreed, or at least feared an outpouring of strikes—it drifted back a meter.

"We're taking him into custody," $Allure_{18}$ said. "It's a perfectly rational—"

"Footage or it didn't happen," Maud snapped. "Show me this theft!"

"I took nothing," Ember said, barely sounding interested. Had he and Frankie been expecting this, too?

"We Solakinder don't lock people up on unproved allegations," Maud said.

"I'm not one of you, and under the law—"

Before $Allure_{18}$ got any further, Crane tooned in at Maud's side, along with a stranger whose tags showed him to be a criminal lawyer.

"Mer Sento is correct," Crane said. "Ember's alleged offense involves no violence or danger to public safety."

"Danger to public safety?" $Allure_{18}$ said. "What about the Emerald Station crew?"

"I can assure you, Ember is no threat to them," Crane said.

"Aren't you the codefather of a murderer?" $Allure_{18}$ smiled. "Your word might not carry as much weight as you think."

"This will require a hearing and Diplomatic will be involved." The lawyer's voice was courtroom-loud, comfortably authoritative.

"In the meantime, perhaps we can agree that if Mer Qaderi accepts restricted Sensorium access—"

"House arrest at least!" $Allure_{18}$ said. "The Kinze demand that much as a courtesy."

"I'm good with house arrest," Ember said. The Ox_{BOT} proffered a black clamp; he held up a hand to catch it, and it tossed the hideous item over $Allure_{18}$ and Maud's heads.

The alien representative forced a thin smile, then whirled. "Why is that portal still open?" she demanded.

"You gave us half an hour," said Mardia. "We have seventeen minutes left to get our people back."

"You wouldn't be demanding that we abandon them, would you?" Crane put in. His tone was mild. Nobody needed to point out that the argument was verging on half a billion realtime follows.

Reframe the conversation. "Sneezy was sabotaged," Maud said. "If Ember's getting arrested on your say-so, maybe Champ Chevalier should too."

"That's not how the law works!"

"Are you sure, Mer Allure? Didn't you just imply this was all unprecedented? I mean, sabotaging a station launch . . . we used to call that sort of thing *treason,* didn't we?"

Everyone turned to Crane's lawyer, who lit up—this was clearly the most entertaining case they'd ever had. "Beyond! I'll query @Interpol."

Subvocal and audio channels devolved into shouting, spawning lengthy comment threads from all their follows. In the midst of it all, Ember locked the manacle on his wrist. He raised his eyebrows, mojing mild surprise.

"Ember?" Maud subbed. "You okay?"

"Heavier than it looks. And Sensorium's firewalled," he replied. "Comms with immediately family only."

Maud shot him a shareboard of pics from the *Surprise* party, highlighting a portrait of himself in rags and fake bruises, dressed as a prisoner of war. "We should redo your primer. Cosplay as public protest."

"It'll be all right. Vulcan High Command is headed to Daley Plaza to register a complaint. And now Frankie's back—"

Was she? Maud brought in a closeup on *Booger,* even as Mardia affirmed: "Escape pod's coming through."

They watched the pod as it ripped through the portal, $Cyril_{10}$ screeching all the way. The pod appeared on the orbital cameras near Earth. Frankie immediately dropped the craft into the queue for $Portal_2$, at the Moon.

"Round and round and round they go," Ember singsonged. He sounded confident, but Maud saw a little shiver of relief run through him.

The connection to Emerald, out at Procyon, went dark, cutting off $Teagan_9$ and the other instance of Babs.

"Comms are down, comms are down. Portals six and seven are closed," said Mardia. "Stabilized loop reestablished for Portals one through five. Repeat, $Portals_{1-5}$ are up and stable."

"Be with you in half an hour, Mars Control," Frankie sent.

Maud pivoted. "Come on, Ember. Let's wait in Arrivals."

Her packmate followed willingly enough, but the move didn't gain them the solitude Maud was hoping for. Everyone *not* managing portal tech came with them: Crane, the lawyer, $Allure_{18}$. The Ox_{BOT} was quietly dangling another manacle—for Champ?—as they crowded into the elevator.

By the time they got to the lounge, Teacakes' awkward great-something-grandson, Wilbur Mack, was in Arrivals too, waiting with Irma du Toit and a bunch of medics.

Booger docked. Champ came through first, stepping straight into Irma's arms. @Interpol had indeed filed charges against him: tags in his aura of augments indicated he was #underarrest and #underinvestigation. Looking truculent, he stuck out his wrist so the security bot could cuff him.

"I haven't done a blessed thing," he said. "I'm innocent!"

"Me too," Ember said, with a cheery note in his voice that set

Champ almost to snarling. Then Frankie stepped through the hatch, and Ember all but skipped around him to hug her. The pilot's expression darkened into fury.

Frankie rapped her knuckles on the cuff. "We'll get you out of this."

Ember nodded, unconcerned.

Maud fought back a quick stab of pain, heightened sense of being left out, an afterthought. She could feel someone—Irma, she thought—watching with interest. Instead of speaking, she mojied—*follow me*—breadcrumbing a route home. Her packmates fell into step around her.

"We're demanding that Ember Qaderi be ceded to Kinze custody," Allure$_{18}$ yelled at their backs. Maud caught Frankie's hand, folding it into hers before the Hedgehog could throw back an obscene gesture.

"The minute you think you got it all beaten back . . ." Frankie sagged as legal documents filled the family sharebox. Her resting brawler face gave way, just for a second, to something tired and worried and vulnerable.

The Ferals caught a train, riding deep below the shuttle port, then emerging into Dragon City. The Martian capital, at dawn, its fungiplex domes dusted in red, seemed to glow with the light of the sun they obscured, like upended glassware backlit by candlelight.

Frankie and Ember were looking at each other, across the shuttle, talking without talking. More secrets? Maud buried her face in Frankie's sleeve, hiding her unease from all the cameras.

The subway let them out under a dense hub of greentowers, a cone of habitation and food-production tech built half below the surface of the planet, half under the cluster of conical fungiplex domes.

"Here's my pop-in," Ember said.

The first thing Maud saw was that Ember had marked up the walls on the main room. As they walked in, he picked up chalk and eraser—

"No anyspace maths," Frankie said. "Since you're supposed to have stolen them."

The calculations vanished as Maud's augments painted the family defaults over the walls.

"Yeah, but. The nav data from *Iktomi* has discrepancies," Ember said. "Champ's hops, after he left the Dumpster? Each was a little off course. I'm wondering if that means saucers drift within anyspace. What if there are currents? They might need comms. Homing beacons, basically, to compensate—"

"Stay off the space maths," Frankie repeated.

"Then I'll help Babs."

"With what?"

"She's still convinced a sapp can ^EMbody," he said.

"I agree with her," Maud said, thinking of Irma du Toit. "I'm certain of it."

If this registered with anyone, they didn't pick it up.

Frankie did a quick turn in place, scanning the suite—a single, since Ember had been out there alone. Her primer loosened, sagging from a form-fitting jumpsuit into loose silk, lightening to a saffron color that suited her skin. She rolled over into a forward bend, loosening her spine.

Then she made for bed. "I'll be killing zombies if anyone wants me."

"What?" Maud's mouth fell open.

Frankie mojied love, throwing blown kisses to them both. She lay down, arranged the smartfoam cushion of Ember's bed to her own defaults, pulled saffron primer over her eyes to block out ambient light, and glazed.

"That's the only bed." Ember frowned. "Crane, we'll have to move."

"There are additional rooms available across the hall, Ember," Crane said. "Space enough for everyone, once Dr. Mwangi arrives."

"Maybe I can take your place in jail," Maud said. "Since I'm locked out anyway."

Ember missed the point of the jab. "Do you think the Kinze accept proxy prisoners?"

"Bad joke, that's all."

"Invite to join, Mer Maud." Crane pinged her with a virtual envelope emblazoned with the words *personal and confidential*.

"You really gotta do that," Ember said.

With a glower, Maud checked the mini fridge instead, taking out a cluster of hydrogel, and ate three in rapid succession. There was only one protein mallow, flavored peanut butter.

"Crane," Babs said. "You're supposed to keep Ember's food intake diversified."

"Ember has been eating arguably balanced meals at Mission Control."

"How fast can Jermaine get here?"

"Given his vertigo issues in nullgrav, at least thirty hours." Crane shared travel contingencies, arrival times, and luxury pricing for Jermaine's sedation and transport.

Maud subbed, "Any chance the Kinze will snap Ember up before Jerm gets here?"

The subject of this speculation was deep in conversation with Babs now, writing with his finger on the air.

"Pardon my presumption, Maud, but you'll feel better, I think, once you've—"

Crane gestured at the bedroom with a wingtip.

Frankie had scrunched hard against the wall, leaving half of the narrow smartfoam mattress for her. Maud reclined onto it, spooning against her body. She hesitated before taking Frankie's hand, but in the end, she found she couldn't lie back and go fully virtual without that familiar curl of stubby fingers entwined in her own. She took a deep breath, whiff of smoky air, left over from the Emerald station fires, in Frankie's hair. Her stomach settled.

She glazed. The invite—*personal and confidential!*—was waiting on a plinth in her e-state.

Maud tore it open.

A rose arbor flourished into view, blotting out her vestibule. She stepped over its threshold, into an arched corridor studded with white blooms.

"You are entering a therapeutic simulation," said a familiar voice. "To indicate consent to assessment or treatment, provide verbal acceptance or simply turn left. To learn more about psychotherapy or catharsis therapy, turn right. If you are in immediate crisis, continue straight."

She'd had to declare an absolute ban on Frankie trying to drag her into therapy. But now . . . Rubi had been urging it too. Ember had just said the same. Even Crane . . .

They're ganging up. She raised her hand, furious, meaning to disperse the sim. Maybe trigger moji to burn the link entirely.

Reluctantly, she turned left, trudging into a row where the roses were yellow.

An animated frog regarded her from atop one bud and continued the spiel. "This virtual space is sequestered under regulations for doctor/patient privilege. Transcripts of sessions will be withheld from the Haystack until patient death. To indicate comprehension, turn left—"

"Death?" Maud said sharply. "Medical confidentiality has a ten-year statute of limitations."

The frog blew out its big bubble of a throat. "Patients in this group therapy session are tagged with special exemptions under the childhood trauma statutes of the Mitternacht event—"

"Stop. Right. I remember."

Frankie was exploiting the fact of their having been in Manhattan to get them a locked room, a truly private conversation . . . within a counseling sim.

She spent the whole week before shipping out, this time, trying to coax me in here.

Maud winced. Maybe it hadn't been as simple as the others locking her out.

Here, in the counseling sim, rose blossoms threw petals in a banner in front of her, lettered with content warnings. Frankie's concept of therapy included literally slaying your demons.

Beyond the warnings was an actual toon, digital representation of the quack in charge. Ah, and that was why the voice was familiar! It was Frankie's childhood friend Kansas, from Tampico.

"Conspiracies have conspirators," she muttered.

Ei indicated a final arch, signifying the end of the rose arbor and waivers phase. "Since this is your first appointment, a preliminary consult is required."

Maud felt herself wanting to snarl. "How long will it take?"

"First we say hello. Hello, Maud, you probably remember me from your handfasting. I'm Kansas."

"Hello." She gritted it out.

"I'll say *how are you feeling,* and you say? One word will do."

"Uncomfortable."

"Excellent choice." Ei handed her a pistol and a machete, stepping out of her way.

"That's it?"

"Is there anything else you'd like to discuss? I'm totally available."

Maud shook her head.

"Then ping me anytime," Kansas said, and vanished.

Maud stepped through the arch into the sim proper. The rose arbor morphed into the roof of a three-story concrete walk-up apartment, vintage, from the twentieth or twenty-first century. Frankie was nestled between two cornices, firing a sniper's rifle at . . .

Maud dialed down the gore to kiddie level. The sim went from hard-edged hyperrealism to cartoon before she'd properly seen it. Bright colors exploded around her; the corners of the building softened and rounded. She stepped to the edge of the roof and saw goofy-looking, bloodless zombies mobbing the entire neighborhood where the building sat. Frankie was picking them off one by one.

Your view of the world in a nutshell, she thought. *Endless threat, constant vigilance, and a battle you can't abandon, no matter the cost.*

Thanks to the child-level rating Maud had chosen, even the blasts from Frankie's rifle came with silly sound effects: *Kerpow! Pyew!* Each zombie, once shot, made a sort of humorous "Ack!" noise before dropping into the crowd with a squelch.

"How can you play this at maximum gore?"

Frankie missed her shot and turned, stark relief stamped on her face as Maud joined her, sitting cross-legged on the roof.

"Want a machine gun?"

"Hells, no."

"Hand me a clip," Frankie said.

"Answer my question."

"Making game reality look worse than the Surface? I dunno. Actual challenges feel more doable? Anyway, pitch in. We gotta beat 'em back before they eat us."

"There's no pause button in catharsis therapy?"

"The horde has to be held at bay," Frankie said, tone implacable.

"By you personally."

"Maud." Frankie let out a long breath. "That's the family business."

Maud had always known, of course, that Frankie's stepmother Rubi was deep in the Solakinder bureaucracy, heading up Diplomatic, negotiating terms with the Kinze and their other offworld visitors. She'd known—everyone did—that Frankie's other surviving parent, the notorious Gimlet Barnes, had gone offworld to gather user agreements between other races, contracts upon which Earth's independence had, so far, hinged.

"I thought all you cared about was flying."

"Freedom, flying, and the Feral$_s$."

"Don't be glib."

"It's all the same fight, don't you see?" Frankie said. "Break the FTL barrier, invent the #supertechs. Hold off hostile takeover. Join the commonwealth of advanced offworlder communities."

"The Exemplars."

"Something's been off in the Bootstrap Project." Frankie swapped ammo clips, leaned her cheek against her gun almost lovingly, and began picking shots. *Kapow! Pyew! Splorch!* "I should've topped the pilot leaderboard easy, but I kept getting dinged. When I played it safe, Champ and Rastopher beat me on timed trials. When I went all out, I got strikes for recklessness."

"You weren't the best, so the system was rigged?" Maud laughed. "The ego on you."

"I bloody know how it sounds. I told myself it was rubbish, paranoia, but . . . it's just that I am the best, actually."

"If you were getting hamstrung, why did Bootstrap jump you to the head of the queue for implant surgery?"

"That's just it: they didn't jump me. They were about to broom me from FTL."

"What?" Maud felt her jaw flapping.

Frankie fiddled with the gunsight. "I was borderline on the psych tests. They think I profile reckless."

Maud laughed. "You *are* bloody reckless!"

"I know my limits, Maud. I'm not suicidal—that's just #news-cycle spin." She actually looked hurt. "Anyway, I talked to my granddad's old hoaxer friend—"

"Jackal?"

"Yeah—he got you my note? He and I started nosing around. Could someone want me off Bootstrap? And no sooner had I started looking than—"

"What?"

"They flip-flopped. Got me to agree that if I stopped negging the project and did beta on the pilot's augment, I could stay on Project Hopscotch."

"Risking the surgery. Doing the first runs in the prototype. Hazard duty all the way."

"Holding off hostile takeover," Frankie repeated. "I thought it was just Rubi, pulling strings . . ."

"Pulling strings to use you as bait?"

"It was more of a bet, really." Frankie shot three zombies, one after another. "She didn't think I'd actually find footdraggers or saboteurs."

"Can I—can I really say anything here?"

Kapow! Pyew! "Why? Are there sex kinks you don't want on the record?"

"Nobody will know? Really? Nobody?"

"Well. Kansas. But ei'll take it to the grave."

A deep voice interrupted: "Side quest."

Within Maud's peripheral vision, a new image bloomed: a cote of pigeons, trapped in their cage.

The birds cooed. Maud accepted the quest, examining the locks on their cage. "This amazing bubble of secrecy, this license to come into sim and spill your guts and never have it go on the record . . . it's just because we had a problematic childhood?"

At *problematic,* Frankie's face did something angry-looking and complicated. "Abused kids get lifetime safe-space waivers."

Maud unlocked the first door on the cote, chewing on *abused* and emphatically disliking the taste of it.

A dove fluttered by, in a kiss of feathers that smelled of baby powder.

Frankie tossed the gun away, unshipping a machete. She stood, knife hanging loosely in hand, back to the undead throng in the street.

Maud drew air through her front teeth. She could tell Frankie about Upton. But . . .

Tell her the truth and she won't agree to the comms augments.

Won't she? She said it herself—she's all about taking mad risks for the cause.

One of the cartoon zombies got a hand on the precipice, pulling itself up. It slung a well-gnawed leg over the concrete and took a second getting its balance. Green and yellow eyes locked on Frankie. It took a shambling step toward her. Frankie seemed determined to ignore it, even as two of its undead friends started to crest the rooftop too.

"Maud," she said. "I know I said no more hazard—"

"But you're not quite done, are you?" Maud said.

Frankie was opening her mouth to answer when the zombie

grabbed her. A mouth full of wicked white cartoon teeth yawned wide as it prepared for the chomp.

Maud jumped in, swinging a loose board from the dovecote. She hit Frankie's attackers like a ballplayer making a home run; two of them went flying.

"This play to grab Ember," Frankie said. "We can't lie back and take it."

Maud kicked over the cote, releasing the rest of the trapped birds, watching them rise skyward amid a soothing percussion of wings.

"The portals work—his maths were fine. And you *know* he didn't steal anything."

"No, of course he didn't." More zombies were almost on them now, and Frankie still hadn't raised her blade. Maud swapped the board in her hand for the machete at her waist and hacked into them, splitting one bloodlessly down the middle, cutting the legs out from under another and punting it off the roof.

"Bwaaaiiiiiiiiiins!" Its shriek receded as it did.

"We need to prove Champ is guilty." Frankie picked up the rifle. "Need to find out who he's working with."

"Conspiracies need conspirators," Maud glowered.

"Exactly."

"Like you and Rastopher and Ember and Babs—"

"I looped you in soon as I—"

"—setting up unauthorized portal launches."

"That worked a treat, I thought." Frankie let out her daredevil grin, and Maud couldn't quite keep herself from answering it.

"Fine. What's your plan, Hedgehog?"

"I need to get back on track at Hopscotch, get in the running for *Heyoka*'s test flights—"

"You think you'll find another rotten pilot?" Maud tossed the machete, equipping the gun instead and firing six shots. Still playing beginner level, so she made them.

"The next test run is an obvious candidate for sabotage," Frankie said.

"So, you win the bid to test the new saucer, strap another target to your head, and see if someone takes a shot?"

"It worked at Emerald."

"That's not an argument for trying to get killed twice."

Frankie seemed to consider arguing, then changed out her ammo clip instead. "What do *you* want me to do?"

"Don't be bait, be a hunter. Find an actual conspirator."

The grin widened. "I'm liking the general shape of it. But how?"

The rooftop shuddered beneath them.

"Thirty more kills to level two," said the controller.

"Buy into the quantum-comms project," Maud said. "It's nano-surgery. It won't take any time out of your busy schedule of risking your hide or offending the public."

"What good's that gonna do?" A rescue helicopter appeared in the distance. Frankie set off a flare, marking their position.

"You're looking for conspirators working against Bootstrap, right? They can't all be in FTL. There's someone in Medical. Someone from Manhattan."

Frankie's eyes narrowed. "Who?"

"A doctor on the comms project." Maud struggled . . . then found she couldn't let out the whole truth, not all at once. It had been so long; she was too locked down. "Jerm brought him to the vigil and I recognized him."

"You've met with someone from the Chamber of Bloody Horrors? Are you okay? Maud! Why didn't you tell me?"

"Because! You were lost in space."

The mob of cartoon zombies climbing the side of the building numbered in the hundreds, but Frankie was in work mode—she barely noticed. "The Chamber was in thick with Allure$_{18}$."

"Exactly! If you want a co-conspirator, a doctor from Manhattan's a pretty good place to start, isn't it? Anyway, I want in on your super-private pilot's texting channel. If only so we don't have to do *this*"—she gestured, indicating the whole therapy sim—"anymore."

Frankie was nodding. "The time ask is minimal, and my

augment needs updates anyway. It won't actually stop us from chasing other clues or trying to get—"

"Hedgehog. Nobody's going to let you fly a test run in that shiny new FTL ship they're building unless Ember is conclusively cleared." Maud set her gun to rapid fire and sprayed the oncoming mob.

"Comms it is!" Frankie tossed the gun. "We'll play it safe for now."

Maud had thought this fight would be about Frankie throwing herself through an untested portal. About Frankie trying to die in six different ways at once, by getting marooned on Sneezy, all in the apparent hope that Champ would try to murder her.

Now, somehow, she had ended up dangling Upton like a carrot. "We test the comms," Maud insisted. "You deal me in. No more Braille notes after the fact. We try to tie old @ChamberofHorrors people to this accusation against Ember."

Frankie caught the ladder from the rescue chopper, steadying it. "If your guy's dirty—and he might not be, you know—he's not gonna let me get close. Not after I accused Champ publicly."

"He'll trust me." Maud started climbing. "He approached me, didn't he?"

"Not sure I like the sound of that."

"I don't much care for that black eye on your mug, or facing off against security bots who want to grab Ember. Is this family business or not, Frankie?" Maud could kick her into the horde right now, send her to a virtual death, and reset the level.

Quick flash of something, then a nod. "It is."

"Get the augments, tie Upton to Champ and . . . to Allure$_{18}$, I suppose, and the Kinze? Clear Ember. That's the play."

"Okay! We'll try it."

"No more high-flying, death-defying stunts for a while? Promise?"

"Promise." Frankie opened her coat, handing Maud two grenades. She pulled the pins on two of her own, dropping them on the seething undead crowd still foaming around the walk-up apartment. "But."

"What?"

"It might not be enough."

"I don't care." Maud fingered one of the grenades, declining to pull the pin. "You cut it too close this time."

"All right." Frankie's grenades exploded among the zombies then, sending severed cartoon arms and legs and heads, all with comically surprised facial expressions on them, disappearing into the flames as the whole building went up, and the chopper rose into the sky. "We'll try it your way."

She didn't add *for now*.

Even without sweet harmony or augmented comms, Maud heard it just the same.

CHAPTER 19

The prosecutor's office gave Champ three options for waiting out the sabotage investigation: he could locate in East Euro, NorthAm, or Greater Pretoria. Grungy, undesirable locales, in other words, far from the cool hubs in Asia and South America.

But hey, nobody was fitting him up for a noose in advance, right?

He took NorthAm, gigging as a submarine pilot in the Great Lakes, chauffeuring biologists who were checking saline levels and particulate. Same sort as Maud Sento, tunnel-visioned slimeheads who got jazzed up over healthy freshwater mussels. Humankind was literally colonizing the solar system, and here they were, maundering about Asian carp stocks.

The submarines were big and complex, as much fun to pilot as any vehicle could be . . . unless you'd *been* an FTL saucer. Once you'd blown an anyspace field out in front of you like a bubble, felt yourself shooting between the seams of reality, everything else was beneath you.

At least the shifts made for dull viewing, which kept Champ's realtime follows in the mere thousands.

He spent his downtime lifting weights and doing gymnastics with his eyes shut, staying fit and denying visual input to the lookyloos. His social capital account was frozen until the case was resolved. Nobody could give him strikes or tank his Cloudsight rating until his case was heard. He couldn't earn strokes from sympathizers. Couldn't get himself a bump with good deeds.

Accusation hung on him like stink. Other submarine pilots and even the slimeheads sent polite declines when he offered himself up for after-shift drinks. Forget about any chance of a sex opp—he was persona non grata.

A week after the spectacular collapse of his mission to Emerald Station, Champ found himself surfacing from one submarine shift, stretched out on a smartcouch in a lounge overlooking the greentowers that fronted the edge of Lake Ontario.

He counted his unanswered pings on the private pilots' channel. He hadn't expected Hung to answer—but he also hadn't got so much as a whisper from Indigo, Rastopher, or Yuri. Owello had sent a string of neutral moji: cloud with a silver lining, a running icon to indicate she was busy.

He glared out at the view. Lake Ontario had a slate-grey quality that hinted at incoming snow. The air was crisp, clear as if Champ was looking through a magnifying glass. People strolled the waterfront in front of the greentowers, enjoying the views—a nice walk on a clear day didn't cost anything. Ironic thing was, they probably had ample luxury credit to spend. But with the Kinze continuing to buy up the niceties of life—coffee, nicotine, booze, premium slots in gaming sims—the Solakinder couldn't access treats of their own.

Meanwhile, he was sidelined, courtesy of Frankie Barnes. Languishing under his own personal cloud of suspicion.

What was the Hedgehog up to? He brought up a realtime follow, finding her and Maud in a Mars hospital, doing tissue-compatibility checks for quantum comms.

Champ wasn't sure he agreed with Aunt Irma and Upton that folding Maud into the quantum-comms project was a stroke of genius.

They were banking an awful lot on the fact that she'd never betrayed Upton. Irma thought it meant Maud could be wooed into rejoining the family. That she could be groomed into keeping tabs on the Ferals and would sell them out to the @Visionary cause. Wishful thinking, Champ thought, but that was Irma. She never gave up on any of her kids.

The Bootstrap Project had initiated this experiment to drill down into an unintended side effect of the pilots' interface surgery, the sacral implants' ability to synchronize in a way that allowed off-Sensorium comms.

All well and good, except the syncing wasn't an accident.

The tech had come, naturally enough, from $Allure_{18}$, who'd lavishly assured Champ and all the @Visionaries that nobody would notice the implants' comms functionality. It'd let Champ talk, off-book, to Scrap and the rest of the Kinze. But Hung discovered it— *and* named it the @ButtSignal, *and* told everyone on Sensorium all about it. Upton'd had to move in with a rebrand before anyone looked too close.

So, suddenly, the pilots' channel was the biggest serendipitous science accident since the discovery of penicillin! A bona fide interesting phenom! In need of analysis!

What was rebranding, after all, but clusterfuck management?

So, as the augmented pilots all figured out, one by one, that they could message through the implants, bypassing Sensorium, Upton had suggested seeing if the system could be expanded, folding in members outside the pilot cohort . . . and trying to transmit across interstellar distances. They'd polled pilots' families for volunteers to join the channel, and greenlighted Maud as the first experimental subject.

The docs would wire Maud up with the core of a sacral implant, grafting all the relevant augment tish into her cochlear and vestibular nerves. They'd teach her how to use the channel and send Frankie off on a short FTL hop.

The trick would be to see if the women could text across a distance of three light-years.

Champ leaned forward into the view of the Lake, giving his back a hard scratch. He ran a finger over his sacral augment, opening a channel.

Scrap, he texted. *Scrap, you there?*

Scraaaaaappppppp. . . .

Something came back, just for a second. *Babs-Them . . .*

Then nothing.

Irritated now, he pinged Irma.

Her face filled his augments, toon in black and white, sketched in front of the view of Lake Ontario. "I'm on my way to rehearsal, darling—I can't talk for long. How are you holding up?"

"I want to get back to work," he said.

"You *are* working, darling!"

"Any old clod can drive scientists out to count mussels," he said. Punching down at those lower on his career track would normally get him strikes, but what did it matter now? "I'm an elite, highly trained—"

"As soon as you're cleared, you'll be lead on Hopscotch again." Her mouth pinched in apparent distaste—they had to make a big performance of disagreeing about his career path, since she was in so deep with ᴵᴹperish and the anti-Bootstrap cohort.

"Is my name gonna get cleared in time for me to test *Heyoka*? I don't think so."

"I'm sure it's frustrating, darling. To be accused when you're innocent!"

"I *need* to make a contribution."

"Champagne, given your situation—"

"You want me to sit pretty and let others handle it? That's the attitude knocks you off the leaderboard, Auntie."

"I don't know what you think I can do about it."

Pastured. Were they going to let him languish in this state of suspicion forever? "You know if I'm just left hangin' here, I'll start making trouble."

Her eyes narrowed. "You wouldn't dare."

Champ leaned back in his chair. "Try me."

She rang off without another word.

Champ returned to his contemplation of the hospital feed of Frankie Barnes and her Maud, letting a dangerous lick of an idea run through him. He tapped his augment again, resetting, bringing in Frankie on the pilots' channel.

Hey, Hedgehog! Maud ever tell you Glenn Upton was her daddy?

It wasn't a message Champ could send in the clear. Admitting on the record that he knew such a thing was practically signing a confession. But what did he care if Frankie knew he was guilty? She already believed it. Champ might as well puncture her obnoxious true-luv-always bliss. Hoist her on the petard of her own goddamned trust issues. Really, he'd be saving the @Visionaries from making a tragic mistake. Irma was an idiot to think Maud would sell out her weird passel of spouses—

Faraway on Mars, Frankie's face froze. She glared up into the nearest camera.

—but if Irma would believe it, maybe the Hedgehog would too.

Champ winked and sent, *Upton adopted your precious Maud when she was just a sprout. She's @Visionary, sweetpie, through and through.*

"Frankie?" Jermaine Mwangi was doing the tish injections "Unfist your hands, hon."

Champ's sacral implant buzzed. Not Scrap this time. Not a pilot, either—a stranger.

Text came in: *You little shit! What did you say to her?*

That wasn't Irma, or Allure$_{18}$. *Get me back in the game!*

You can't handle the game, Chevalier.

Letting his eyes glaze, as if he was talking to himself, Champ said, aloud, "I am up for anything."

Seconds ticked by. Then: *Increased commit means increased risk.*

He shrugged.

Fine. I need a couple hours. Go for a walk. If you pull any more stunts, I'll have you minced.

Champ closed the feed of the Fraud and rose, stretching. He wasn't worried; killing him would attract attention that nobody wanted.

Savoring the bomb he'd thrown into Frankie's personal life, he made a conspicuously boring afternoon of it all, trying to shake his follows. He found an in-the-flesh tour of a twentieth-century water treatment plant, of all things, attached to the Lake Ontario reclamation project. He hadn't expected much from that, but it was legit historical, with stunning marble and ornate art deco finishes. It put him in mind of the structures he would build when he ended up atop the global pecking order, when he finally ended up rating a permanent house of his own.

A palace. Rulers get *palaces*.

After all he'd gone through for the cause, it better be a big one.

Eventually, he took a pop-in apartment, collapsed into bed, and threw a blanket over himself. Closing his eyes, he tried not to think about all the people, lookyloos and investigators dogging his feed. Algorithms measuring his every breath and heartbeat, rating the chances on whether he was drifting off or masturbating.

When the Kinze finally liquidated the earth government, Champ would bring back the right to an unmonitored night's sleep—for the right people, anyway—faster than a jackrabbit on the run.

Never mind. He kept his breath steady as a new message finally came in.

Go into hibernation. Book three weeks at the North York ration center, floor 2, pod 97. Order maximum doses of Grizzly and ping Irma just before you go under.

He replied: *This better not be a way to put me out to pasture.*

You want to kneecap Barnes, don't you? Do a little more than poking her in the metaphorical eye?

Yeah.

I'll send you after Barnes.

That's more like it. He took one more moment to dream of a palace with art deco finishes. Maybe with a dungeon. Frankie Barnes needed locking up for a few decades, didn't she?

The thought brought at least a hint of a smile.

"Pidge," he said to his sidekick app, "I'm gonna go on a carbon fast for a few weeks. Show me rationing pop-ins?"

CHAPTER 20

Did she tell you Glenn Upton was her daddy?

When Maud had told Frankie that Jerm's surgical mentor was from Manhattan, she'd been excited.

But then Jackal had profiled Upton. The results had been underwhelming. A former runaway raised by the @ChamberofHorrors, he wasn't an innocent, exactly, but there was nothing in the evidence to suggest a criminal mastermind. He'd been one of a host of baby medics working in their life-extension operation, keeping the billionaire founders of the organization alive.

After his arrest, Upton spent five years working in the Arctic, studying medicine and eventually specializing in surgery. He'd done residencies on Europa and Mars, back when the colonies were dangerous, newborn enterprises, accident-prone, full of ^{IM}perish ghosts.

This guy looks rehabilitated to me, Jackal had told Frankie via Braille tape.

Frankie had been hoping for a wild-eyed, well-connected anti-Bootstrap speecher. Instead . . . well, Upton *had* followed the project with interest from the start. When the pilots had discovered the comms connection within their implants—Hung had tried to get everyone to call it the ButtSignal, but the owners of the Batman franchise *immediately* sent a cease-and-desist, and now the pilots privately called it @ButtSig—Upton wrote a paper suggesting an exploit. The possibility of using tish resonances to send messages across interstellar distances was the basis of the quantum-comms experiment they were conducting now.

Upton was Maud's adoptive father?

Adoptive, my rosy ass. That's a euphemism. He's her bloody kidnapper.

Is that what Maud would call him?

There in the Martian hospital, the two of them were in facing beds, separated by clear, nanorepellent curtains, waiting on Jerm to finish the install. Should Frankie veto the new tish upgrades—throw a big Hedgehog fit, make a fuss, quit quantum comms?

She's @Visionary too, sweetpie.

Bullshit! This was a transparent attempt on Champ's part to sabotage her marriage.

Jerm chose that moment to return from prep, holding a nanosurgery tray in one hand as he shouldered aside the sheeting. "Ready to do this?"

"Actually, I need a minute."

He sat down obligingly, emanating warmth, solid and lovable and acting as if he had years to burn. In the days since Ember had been accused of IP theft and confined to their family pop-in, Jerm had lost weight. It wasn't something most people would notice—he was such a big man anyway!—but the slightly drawn look around his eyes was a clear tell. "Unfist your hands, hon."

"How sure are you about all this?" Frankie indicated the surgical tray, with its array of plugs and needles.

"I'm positive it's going to lower latency in your implant . . . which you need if you're gonna requalify for flight duty," he said. "I'm sure today's procedure is safe."

"Safe by the standards of experimental augment tech?"

He mojied surprise, clearly thinking that anyone who'd consented to the insertion of a sacral implant shouldn't even balk at having another milligram of tish nanografted onto her vestibular and cochlear nerves. "As for whether you and Maud are really going to be able to realtime text and talk once you're three light-years from each other? I don't know. The Dumpster's a long way, and beta testing is . . ."

"Is beta. Yeah."

"The offworlder races can do comms across these distances, so it must be possible." Jerm put out one big hand, and she dropped hers into it, letting his fingers encircle hers. "This doesn't have to happen today, Franks."

She could feel Maud's gaze on her, in the bed across the aisle.

"I do need the latency upgrade if I'm to go on flying," Frankie said. "Don't worry, Jerm—it's just last-minute nerves."

It's rubbish, anyway—Champ's playing mind games. It was Frankie's last thought before Jerm plugged her into a diagnostic array, offlining her body below the neck.

Most of the other pilots derided the augment plug as a creepy but necessary evil. Frankie wasn't troubled by the tech itself—the dead, plasticine weight of it in her back didn't bother her, nor did the feel of the prongs sliding in to connect and disconnect her. But to be offline, all but dis^{EM}bodied, without the alternate sense of *being* a ship or a pegasus . . . that was stifling. She struggled for breath.

"Frankie?" Maud called from the other bed. "You okay?"

"Going to Kansas." Forcing the words out, she glazed, sinking into Sensorium and selecting her therapist's sim parlor.

A squeaky-clean US town, circa 1950, formed around her, its streets humming with huge, privately owned cars.

"Gameplay options," Frankie said. "Knife work."

The gun in her hand turned to a machete.

Maud appeared beside her. "Jerm's running diagnostics on my receiver."

Frankie nodded, not quite trusting herself to speak.

She's @Visionary too, sweetpie.

Rubbish, Champ. She's not!

Zombies—decayed, festering, and carrying a heavy pong of death on the breeze—emerged from the town's city hall. They fell

upon a small gathering of peace protesters, eating some, converting the rest.

"Do we fend them off here?" Maud asked.

"No. We run." Catching Maud's hand, Frankie fled. The chase
was short—they ended up cornered in a vintage high school. Un-
attractive concrete building, grey in color, impregnable-looking.
Prison for teenagers, Frankie thought.

Fleeing through the fluorescent-lit hallways, they took refuge in
the science lab. Maud banged around, using found items to impro-
vise a flamethrower so she could char incoming threats. While she
played chemist, Frankie shoved two heavy lab counters into place,
forming a kill chute: she'd let the zombies through one at a time.
Maud could burn them in turn. Frankie would behead anything
that survived.

"I'm still playing beginner level," Maud said. "They'll come in
soft."

Too bad: Frankie was spoiling for a real fight.

"You're awfully quiet," Maud said.

Say something. Anything! "So, if your cerebrospinal fluid doesn't
react badly to the augmented starling tish grafted from mine . . ."

"It won't."

"—and if the receiver Jerm's installing works—"

"Why wouldn't it?"

"Then I guess the real question is whether your Doc Upton can
augment our so-called resonance until it works across a distance
of light-years."

Maud flinched at *your.*

Frankie tried to keep her voice gentle. "We're off the record
here, remember?"

"I'm not sure what—"

Enough pussyfooting. "Maud. That frilly pink bedroom for science femmes. That was Upton. He built that for you."

A zombie dressed as a police officer lunged through Frankie's
makeshift bottleneck. Maud set it afire from badge to boots, slagging it to ash. Her face had locked—jaw set, eyes unblinking.

"Eeeee!!!" the cop zombie hissed like a kettle, and collapsed.

"Was he older than he looked, Upton? Was he on life extension even then?"

Maud swallowed. "Yes. He was probably fifty."

Frankie shunted the remains of the cop through a broken window, dropping it on thronging zombies two stories below. "Was there a mom, too?"

"Just the sapp who lured us. The one who ran the Manhattan enclave."

"Headmistress."

"She always wanted us to call her Auntie." Maud fiddled with the flamethrower, adjusting output. "Frankie, you wanted to lure in a possible saboteur. Upton—"

"Upton, who augmented the tish they're grafting on to our optic nerves—"

"I told you he was from Manhattan! You just didn't know that . . . that I meant anything to him."

"Because *you* didn't say!" Frankie beheaded a zombie with one great machete-swing, kicking the severed head into a corner.

"Frankie, if there's a conspiracy to undermine the Bootstrap Pro—"

"If? Did you just bloody say *if*?"

She's @Visionary too, sweetpie. Champ, laughing as he shot her full of doubts.

"If there is," Maud said, "virtually all of the conspirators are here. At home, within reach of the portal carousel, working the project. Nothing's stopping you from hunting them in-system."

"They want to haul Ember offworld!"

"And we might not be able to stop them."

Fury boiled through her. Another damn sermon about defeat and acceptance.

Frankie'd been hearing the same sorry song her whole life: when her first grandfather died, when her parents broke up and one of them got cancer. When he began to decohere within years of joining the EMbodied. *That's the way of the world,* Gimlet told her, when she'd been forced to give up her babyjob at the Department of Preadolescent Affairs. Things end. People fail. Nothing is permanent, and that's how it's always going to be.

Gimlet, going offworld. Grandpa Drow, dying. Accept, accept, accept.

She demanded, "Where are your bloody sympathies?"

"Not with *them*." The disgust on Maud's face was sincere.

"Then tell the world Upton abducted you for nurture! Accuse him, the way I accused Champ."

"I can't!" Maud said.

"Why?"

"Proof! You went to Sneezy so Champ could make his move, didn't you? It's how you caught him. This is the same. We let Upton expose himself—"

"We don't have *time* for another long game." Frankie heard her voice rising. "He's just trying to tie me down here on Earth, playing pattycake with subspace radio while they grab Ember. We need to try something big."

"Meaning reckless?" Maud risked a peek out into the corridor, almost got grabbed, and hosed a diminishing stream of flame into a sea of grasping dead hands. One of the zombies snatched the flamethrower from her grasp. Lunging back, the two players knocked each other ass over teakettle. Frankie careened into a flask of glowing fluid that had suddenly spawned on the counter of the chemistry lab.

"Damn!" Glowing green sludge splashed across her left wrist.

"Are you dead?" Maud barricaded the door. "Have we lost the level?"

"Don't think so." Frankie rinsed her wrist in the lab sink. The stuff, whatever it was, stuck. She fought to rein her temper. "Maud. I can't even imagine . . . I mean, he was taking care of you for years, and there's got to be a lot to unpack there. I know the feels must be . . . but do you really know he hasn't reformed?"

Maud was wringing her hands, looking wretched. "Hold your temper, Franks."

Words almost guaranteed to make her furious. She swallowed. Tried to nod.

"Yes. Upton's older than he looks. And the thing is, he wasn't just a life-support tech. He was already a surgeon, even then."

Frankie focused on the green glow spreading across her arm. The patch of contamination spread, oozing as far as her elbow . . . and formed text, from Kansas: LISTEN!

She shook water off her hands. "Upton was a bigger deal than he said, within the Chamber hierarchy?"

A tight blink: clearly, Frankie was missing the point. "He was a *neurosurgeon*, Frankie."

"He's still a neuro—" Frankie felt something begin to burn at the back of her throat. "The botomized workers?"

Maud leaned against the lab counter, letting out a long hiss.

"You covered for him?" Frankie knew she shouldn't say anything—*listen*, Kansas had said. Somewhere, under a tsunami of outrage, vestigial reason reminded her: Maud had been nine. The guy had effectively been her parent. How much could she have understood about his crimes?

She bloody understands now, doesn't she?

The lab door shuddered, splintering.

"All those people, Maud. All those—"

She stood with her arms crossed, jet hair sweat-slick against her forehead, expression miserable. On the Surface, Frankie knew, there'd be tears running down her face.

EMPATHIZE! Kansas flashed across her arm, in green toxic-sludge letters.

Bollocks to that.

"All those kids who didn't fit into their vision of a hoarder's paradise. All those kids he cut up—"

"I know. They didn't deserve—"

"Deserve?" Frankie threw a flask, shattering it against the lab window. "*Deserve* is nothing but a brutal lie. People trot out *deserve* when bad things happens to someone else and they need to believe it could never happen to them."

"I never said—"

"What about Upton *deserved* to be shamed and prosecuted? Why'd you never tell? He'd be in managed care now."

"I didn't know how!"

Maud wasn't fighting back, really, wasn't backing away. She was sitting there, letting Frankie hit her with all the recriminations. Because of course she felt guilty. Of course. She'd been carrying this all along.

"You've covered for him." Frankie swallowed. "That's why Upton's looking to reconnect with you. He thinks if you'd hide this, you'd rejoin them."

"They both are," Maud said quietly. "Don't you see? That's why investigating the comms project will work."

"Both? Both who?"

"Headmistress."

"Headmistress is wiped," Frankie said.

"Right, like Happ is wiped?"

Frankie swallowed. She hadn't thought Crane's little shell game with the backup copy of his codeson had pinged Maud's radar. How did she know? Could Champ be right? Could Maud have been spying on them after all?

"See? You get to have all the secrets and all the co-conspirators, and apparently I'm on a ration." The undead mob was almost through: Maud slammed open a lab cupboard, searching for more weapons.

Before Frankie could reply, Jerm broke in with a ping and an audio message. "Frankie, your procedure's done. I'm rebooting your augment."

Frankie took the excuse to toon out of the sim, surfacing to her still-paralyzed body, staring at Maud's glazed, tear-streaked face through the plastic safety curtain.

Jerm leaned over her. "Frankie? Everything okay? Are you feeling any—"

"Just unplug me."

He did, throwing her to the void. For a brief second, as she imagined total #crashburn, she wished she could just float there in the black forever. Then she was herself again.

Jerm's big hand, ungloved now, rested on her tingling spine. "Something's up."

"What?"

"Allure$_{18}$'s in the waiting room."

Frankie rested her weight against him as she rolled out of bed, leaning into his hand until she had her feet under her and her knees locked. She configged her primer, changing from a hospital gown to her tights and flight jacket.

Maud wiped her face, reset her nanosilk into a formal-looking royal blue robe, and stepped off her own bed. Babs tooned in, filling out the pack.

They stepped out to confront Allure$_{18}$.

The ghost was immaculate as always, not a hair on her custom-designed head out of place. Frankie was suddenly self-conscious about her black eye, Jerm's lost weight.

"I wanted to tell you in person," Allure$_{18}$ said, in that musical voice. "Since Ember used stolen offworlder calculations—"

"Hey!" Babs objected. "Innocent until proven!"

Allure$_{18}$ declined to retract the statement. "—stolen Exemplar formulae to help launch the portals at Lodestone and Europa, I am filing a claim for those portals to be ceded to the Kinze. We will, of course, be demanding fees for use."

"Fees?"

"Back rent, and a share of profits derived from same, spanning the two years since deployment of Portals$_{4/5}$."

Frankie's jaw dropped.

"Only the outer portals?" Maud said. She let out a shocked noise that might have been a laugh. "Why not all five?"

"Ember was tasked solely to Project Hopscotch during the initial rollout," Babs said. "He didn't supply the initial math to the Earth-Moon-Mars hub."

"The potential debt's incalculable," Frankie said. Her lips felt numb.

"I'm sure they won't have the slightest trouble calculating it," Jerm said. Another first: Frankie had never heard him sound bitter.

"We might take a somewhat favorable reckoning of the numbers," Allure$_{18}$ said, "if Ember confesses to the theft and surrenders to Kinze custody."

"That's blackmail!" Maud said.

"On the contrary." She smiled. "It's a business proposition."

"You're afraid we're about to prove he didn't do it," Babs said.

"Your fandom is detectives, isn't it, Mer Babs?" Allure$_{18}$ gave her a pitying look. "Fictional ones?"

"Not all of 'em are fictional," Babs grumbled.

"Well, you can rest assured that the Kinze are not in the slightest bit threatened by the prospect of your amateur sleuthing."

"Babs is right," Frankie said. "You can't claim the portal network if we prove Ember innocent."

"How is any of you going to find the time?" Allure$_{18}$ flicked a hand, posting snowballing #newscycle. *Kinze Claim Outer Colonies!* Global Oversight had ordered a rampdown on use of both portals. Nonessential personnel were being ordered back to Mars and the Moon. Mining and farming opps were wrapping as fast as the machines could be shut down and safely stored.

"They've backwashed tens of thousands of people to Mars, Moon, and Earth," Maud said, scanning the feeds. "Without the farms, food production's going to drop . . ."

"They're pinging me from the flight deck," Frankie said. "All hands, making supply runs to Europa and Titan—"

"Indeed," Allure$_{18}$ agreed. "How convenient that you just got your latency upgrade."

"How convenient that *you* waited until I was back on duty to pull this bullshit stunt." Frankie made a best guess as to what Ember would say once they told him about this nasty bit of blackmail. "Give us two weeks. Let us evacuate the stations using the portals. Pull everyone out—for free."

Allure$_{18}$ frowned. "In exchange for what?"

"If Ember does agree to surrender himself—and if we can't exonerate him within the two weeks—I'll bring him to Lodestone personally."

"Frankie!" Maud objected.

The ghost made a *tsk* sound. "This is a play for time."

"No, it's a bloody business proposition. You get him *and* no bloody doubt you can bog me down in immigration paperwork at Lodestone, if it takes your fancy. I'll be stuck there for as long as you want to run up the bill for housing me."

"And . . . doesn't the rest of your family get a say?"

Jerm, looking even more pinched, nodded. It was a formality—they all knew Ember would say yes rather than see Earth buckle under this demand.

"Don't worry, Ferals." Babs crossed her arms. "I can prove him innocent by then."

"But . . . it's been several. Why haven't you?"

The cat's ears flattened against her Nancy Drew hat.

"What about me?" Maud asked. "What am I meant to be doing during all this?"

Frankie said, "Once we lose the hydroponics at Europa, Oversight's going to be scrambling to maintain the caloric ration. Everyone in food production's going to be on triple shifts."

"Back to the farm?"

Frankie couldn't bite the words back. "What other give could you possibly make at this point?"

Maud's mouth fell open. She flushed; blood darkened the micro-injection sites above her cheekbones.

"Frankie!" Jerm said, shocked.

Maud turned on her heel. "Crane, sign me up for greenhouse work."

With that, she walked out.

"You've got some 'splaining to do." Jerm rushed after her, leaving Babs and Frankie.

"Your proposal is accepted," Allure[18] said, sounding pleased. "If Ember confesses to committing industrial espionage and surrenders within the agreed two-week timeframe, we'll rescind the charges for evacuating personnel to your inner colonies."

"We'll go see what he says," Frankie said.

"Answer by midnight, please," Allure$_{18}$ said, before turning on her heel.

Move, countermove. "You have to clear him, girl sleuth," Frankie said to Babs. "Don't drop the ball."

Babs looked unimpressed. "We better go ask the ball if he's on board with the plan. He's the one putting his niblets on the line."

Frankie wasn't worried; Ember would guess what she was really up to.

No more fussing with comms. Frankie covered her face to hide any overt tells as she made for the queue to catch the portal back to the hangar.

It's on, she thought. Preliminary skirmishes over, thrashing truly begun.

PART 2

MIRROR GAMES

Are you trying to kill yourself, or are you just new at this?

—*Xena: Warrior Princess*

CHAPTER 21

Get off the station, hide within the station, or continue to undermine the station? These were Scrap's options, and as far as Us could tell, all were precarious.

After a great deal of shouting, Them had opened a new portal—facilitating another desperately unfortunate data sync! The All got the portal shut but not before the evacuation of some of Them to Mars.

Some, in this case, might be worse than all or none.

Scrap had spun a false wall within the ducts, a tiny pocket of temporary camouflage. Once concealed, it grew a booster for its portable transmitter. Us continued to struggle to reach the All, and Scrap wasn't quite sure why.

Thems had left a warm body and a machine sapient aboard. Two Solakinder citizens. They were not requesting rescue. The situation banned Scrap from laying claim to the station.

Scrap didn't understand how the sapp had maintained functionality, given the fires Us had set in the server rooms. But maintain it had, and now this small crew was bringing system after system online. Oxygen levels and air pressure were rising. Patches were being printed to reinforce the hull breach. Thems' Beetle$_{BOT}$ army continued a march through the ducts, seeking the arsonist.

Perhaps in the spirit of perversity, Them had also opened a user account within the system for Scrap and were transmitting notes to Us via the @allaboard channel.

Babs[1]: *@Allaboard @stowaway @arsonist—Let us know you survived the fire, won't you?*

Teagan[9]: *@Allaboard @stowaway @arsonist—preferably not by starting another fire.*

This triggered a bunch of the animated glyphs Them called moji, implying that the crew found something humorous in the idea of Scrap burning their atmosphere.

Babs[1]: *@Allaboard @stowaway @arsonist, if you need medical assistance, do ping.*

That would look propitious and humane if the transcript made it back to Them's Sensorium. All very prosocial and altruistic, as Them liked to say. Offering medical aid to a presumed enemy?

No-privacy societies were always ostentatiously helpful, whenever Thems were on the record.

Scrap used the comms booster to strengthen the link with station systems. The All were still out of reach. Emerald Station's databanks offered more bad news. The three of them—human, sapp, and even the *Iktomi* autopilot—seemed to have ten projects on the go at once.

Signs of Them's occupation of the station were everywhere. Fox-[BOT]s inspected the repairs to the hangar. One had been tasked with analyzing Scrap's incendiary and corrosive nanobeads. Grow tanks were using algae to generate oxygen in the station farm, and Babs[1]-Them had expanded input from the power-harvesting membrane.

It was impossible to make a case for salvage while Thems were actively expanding the station. Us had been caught aggressively salvaging in the past and had incurred large penalties.

How had the All underestimated the Solakinder so badly?

Putting debt pressure on emergent powers was a proven strategy, successful many times past with other warm-blooded species. Tipping mammal races into crisis, debt, discontent, and revolution was relatively easy.

But when shortages arose in the Sol system and the labor

market tightened, Them hadn't done the expected thing and stratified their society to allow a few of Them to extract more wealth from the less-privileged majority.

Them had fought going back to unregulated supply-demand-compete. Instead, Earth had scaled its ability to train people to multitask.

This Teagan$_9$-Them was a case in point—equal parts engineer doctor-biologist. Perhaps Frankie-Them had been multipurposed too, as both a pilot and a spy.

A spy! Because Us had been suspected! Anticipated! And now Champ-Them had been exposed too.

Scrap ran a strong filter on Them's comms, seeking private discussion channels. It turned up a thread of cultural reference-lines and jokes from their vast store of mythmaking and music. *Fandoms,* Them called it.

It was practically a new language, Anglo words strung in non sequiturs.

Teagan$_9$: *Nuke the site from orbit.*

Babs[1]: *Dear lady, you are a fossil.*

Teagan$_9$: *How about 'The only good Beetle$_{BOT}$ is a Beetle$_{BOT}$ smothered in cream sauce'?*

Babs[1]: *How about 'Elementary, my dear Watson'?*

And so on. Incomprehensible.

There would be content tucked within all that cultural context. They were dropping clues to each other. Scrap would need a live link to the All and access to a contextual translator.

Us extended awareness, boosting signal, seeking datastream.

Nothing.

Scrap diverted more power to the comms link.

Still nothing.

A flare of disquiet: where were the All?

Why couldn't Us hear Ourselves thinking?

Maximum power. A sputter of comms—delicate tingle of connection, and an even more distant sense of Champ-Them's receiver, passively recording messages—flared. And died.

Are Them sabotaging Us?

Outraged, Scrap homed in on the dark matter wands.

Yes! Emerald and *Iktomi,* the saucer's autopilot, were both firing their dark matter wands. Babs[1] was charging and discharging the station portal membrane, scattering anyspace particles throughout nearspace. The saucer was all but splashing its own exterior, sending counter-waves.

Were Them. . . .

Scrap went rigid with fear and fury.

How could Them be deliberately jamming Us?

Panic made Scrap's spindles quiver. If an individual tatter was cut off from Us for long enough—if *Scrap* was cut off for long enough, if individuation occurred, Us might reject reunion. Scrap would truly become Scrap. A severed extremity.

The All did not permit Us to become Them.

Scrap tried again to establish proper comms. Even tried again to call Them-Champ. Nothing.

It was Babs[1]-Them who had caused all this trouble. Babs[1]-Them was running life support for Teagan[9]. Babs[1]-Them apparently knew enough anyspace theory to have come up with a makeshift comms jammer. Babs[1]-Them had come to the station with all those extra bots and servers.

Us set a repeating message into a distress beacon, to the All and Them-Champ: *Babs must die!*

Us had almost gotten a transmission through once; it might again.

Shifting the camouflage screen, Scrap untethered from the duct wall, beginning a slow creep to server room two. Becoming Them would be a terrible fate. Individuality meant dependence, mortality, vulnerability, scarcity. It meant Want.

Babs[1], in the nonsense channel, said, *I tawt I saw a puddy tat.*

Teagan[9]: *You're the puddy, remember?*

That could mean anything. Scrap moved slowly, making for server room two.

This is ill advised, this is just what Thems want, this is desperation!

What else could Scrap do? Lurking wasn't sustainable, not with Them searching. If Us couldn't burn out Babs[1]-Them, its mission had failed.

A gust through the ducts, as it approached the server, blew its camouflage away.

Scrap clung to the wall, transmitting fiercely. *Babs must die, Babs must die!*

Could any of Us hear?

Clinging to the wall, exposed by the artificial wind, Scrap sensed a $Beetle_{BOT}$ as it rolled up from another corridor, bathing Us in light, capturing full footage.

There was nothing Us could do now except deploy its remaining store of flammables against itself.

Scrap hesitated.

Fear of death?

Us can't have individuated already?

The camera bonked directly into Scrap. Us shot out of the duct, into a vast void. Drifting, end over end, Us threw out silk tethers to arrest its tumble.

Too late.

Us passed a burst of EM radiation that could only be the living flesh of $Teagan_9$-Them, who swung a pair of custom-printed vacuum-domes, clapping Scrap between them.

$Teagan_9$: *You did indeed, Babs. You did taw a puddy tat!*

The domes vacated the air between them. There was insufficient oxygen for self-immolation.

Us was horrified to realize Scrap was glad the option of suicide had been blocked.

Babs must die, Babs must die, Babs must die!!

CHAPTER 22

One thing about humans that Babs had never quite understood was that if you got a bad actor who was sufficiently charismatic and well followed, and that person started telling a lie, they could sometimes bang away at it hard enough and long enough to eventually pull in a crowd, followers who were happy to believe. Even when the story they were swallowing was ridiculous, it would gather converts, and somehow that was enough to build an appearance of veracity.

The Kinze theft case against Ember was like that. Wafer-thin, based on a single squiggle in a formula that fewer than thirty people truly understood. In every possible way, it was #fakenews. If his accusers had been human, making an allegation on such slender evidence would've been out-and-out illegal. The pandemics of the early Setback, a century before, had proven that ignoring truth and spreading fairy stories was, basically, murderous.

But now anti-Bootstrap activists had verifiable facts, of a sort, to boost their message: they could truthfully say Ember'd been charged. They could say he'd been put under house arrest. They could even say, now, that he might confess to the crime.

Babs turned her attention from her ongoing scan of the news coverage and focused on the wisp of evidence powering the lie.

Different offworlder species used different notation methods to express their scientific concepts, performing the same calculations and results but using different shorthand. Obvious-enough truth:

a plus sign on Earth wasn't a universal indicator of addition. It might be a square, one world over. Other cultures simply wrote one factor atop another, or encircled two variables to indicate the concept of addition.

But there was one crucial constant that Ember had calculated, accounting for anyspace particle movement variations. Dhurma's Constant was represented by a math squiggle, a figure that to Babo looked a miner's pick, a curved T shape, standing upright. This symbol was exactly the same as the one the Kinze used.

This was the alleged smoking gun. If Ember had used the same symbol, it was because he'd seen Kinze formulas and lifted them wholesale.

How did you fight that?

By yelling louder, basically, and telling a better story. Babs was looking less for proof than a plausible counter-narrative—no, more than that. She was looking for a damn sexy explanation for how Ember'd ended up with a Kinze figure in his portal math.

The process involved working her way backward, frame by frame, through his cradle-to-current video transcript, piecing her way from the point where he'd come up with the coefficient.

Transcript analysts had already gone through every frame of the footage, of course, using programs to pattern-match the symbols. They had sifted every math-related breakthrough in Ember's life. Babs was checking the moments in between.

What's a nice, innocent explanation for an ancient Kinze scribble—because it wasn't just any symbol, apparently; it was a long-standing Cultural Big Deal—getting into human hypothetical physics?

Global Oversight was interrogating him about that, even now, of course. Asking, "Why? Why this symbol?"

"It's an easy draw. Doesn't privilege any one culture over another, and doesn't look like anything else."

"Had you seen the glyph before?" asked the Global Oversight auditor.

Ember nodded. "It's a palm tree."

Babs perked up. This was news to her.

Mulling it over, she muted the Oversight interrogation, checking in with Jackal and a bunch of his friends. They were discussing the case indirectly, via a cooperative fanfiction exercise—telling each other a story about a fictional good-guy scientist framed by classic bad guy Lex Luthor: *This IP scheme had to be planned years ago, didn't it? Your villain couldn't know which rising star would be the one to make the breakthrough.*

Jackal sent plus signs, indicating agreement. *All of the mathematicians would have had to have tainted symbols suggested to them.* The hoaxers began brainstorming—referencing Ember's actual biography, converting real-world characters to young scientists from the DC universe, spawning possible scenarios sprinkled, inevitably, with sex scenes.

Babs read along for a few minutes, filtering out the fucking, and hit three references to math camps. Right. Best-and-brightest groups sometimes were gathered, in the flesh, for advanced instruction.

She went back to the historical record, bringing up a classroom: Ember, schooling with half of the people who eventually ended up developing anyspace theory. Most looked impossibly young. And there, on the hard surface of a truly ancient blackboard, the palm tree was doodled, near a cluster of math notes. Beyond it, through a window, actual palm trees beckoned.

Was this . . . Florida?

She could work with this, Babs realized. Widen the search, find places where various unnamed parties had slipped the images like the palm tree and pictures of the notation into all the math stars' minds. There'd be other figures, too. It'd be a long crunch among the docs, but Global Oversight would task additional analysts if it looked promising. They didn't want Ember dragged out to deep space in shackles. It was a safe bet that if he went, he'd never come back.

If they could find half a dozen instances where Kinze mathematical notation had ended up sprinkled in the path of mathematician-training contexts . . . would it be enough? Could they make a sufficiently compelling story of it? What were the prospects for infographics?

Babs was about to dump her findings back onto Jackal and friends when Sonika Singer sent her a ping.

Babs accepted the call.

An error pinged her, just then; one of her backups was corrupted.

It happened sometimes. Babs hit a scrub-and-restore routine.

"Sonika," she said. "What's a live girl like you doing in a sim like this?"

Sonika's toon was skinned in a sort of mid-twentieth reporter representation—pleated skirt, jacket, chic tinted glasses, hair in a bun. Frankie called it a repressed-librarian stereotype. One of the old #malegaze motifs, apparently.

Her dryad legs were arbutus wood, patterned in gold-and-copper bark.

"Same as you," Sonika said. "Seeking truth. You cracked the case yet?"

Babs held her paws up, showing an inch of space between them, with the palm tree captured in her view. "I am *this* close."

Sonika looked around. "Is this Tampico?"

"I guess there were math camps in Miami."

"Wouldn't have thought it worth the carbon cost to ship baby scientists to NorthAm," Sonika said.

Another ping. The datalink to Jackal and the fanfic hoaxers had gone down.

And a third: the troublesome backup, sending a second fail notice.

Babs reset it again and pinged Crane. "Dad," she subbed. "I got bats in my belfry."

No response. Babs pinged a call through to the Asylum digital health center.

Nothing.

No matter. She had redundant backups. Not to mention Babs[1], butching around Sneezy in their white Persian fluff and virtual overalls.

She scanned the transcript of Sonika's last utterance. Math camps in NorthAm. Innocuous-enough convo.

"I may have evidence—"

Another ping. Two. Two more backups failing.

"Yes?"

Stay on task. "If I can prove Ember is innocent—"

Sonika made a clucking noise. "You're biased. Ember Qaderi has been your primary crush object since he and Frankie Barnes friended. You'd say anything. You'd fake records."

"You're saying you think I can hack the—"

Ping!

Still no response from Crane.

Still no response from the Asylum.

Something was *very* wrong.

Babs sent renewed restore requests to her backups. Fail pingbacks sounded immediately.

She tried to ghost on Sonika and the records room both. Nothing. She might as well have been a body in a physical space.

Locked room, she thought.

"DADDY!" she pinged. "Maud. Frankie. Anyone?"

At the same time, she answered Sonika: "He's not my crush object. He's my packmate."

"Crane's various codespawn have a tendency to imprint on individual humans and then obsess about them; isn't that true?"

Four more backups failed.

Could self-doubt weaken her defenses? "Are you trying to pick a fight with me?"

Sonika took off her glasses, revealing star sapphire eyes. The tight knot of her hair become a spike, then a morningstar, dangling from a chain.

"A fight implies a chance of *either* party winning."

"You're not Sonika," Babs said. Whatever this was, it had also committed identity theft.

Was it strange that she was shocked by that?

Babs tried again to find a way out of the sim, but she wasn't a programmer. The only data moving in or out now were the priority pings as her electronic life-support system failed, as her backups bounced her reboot requests. They must be coming in via a secure channel.

Were the reboot requests on the record?

Sonika—or the identity thief wearing her skin—began wiping the chalkboard.

Babs got another backup ping. This time, when she sent the reboot request, she appended a timestamped capture of the entity, the fake Sonika, wiping the blackboard, eradicating the incriminating palm tree. The image was simply a comment on the help request: the locks on the system let it through.

Like messages in bottles, she thought.

"Back away, pal," she said. "What do you want?"

Another ping. This time, when she asked for the reboot, she attached a group shot of Ember and his classmates. If this find was significant enough to justify attacking her, it might be enough to exonerate Ember.

By now, the Sonika-thing's skin was peeling. Frivolous use of graphical processing power, but Babs didn't mind. Let it—whatever it was—waste time. "Why are you doing this?"

"Babs must die. This is all I know."

She captured that bit of sound. Sent it with the next service denial. The fails were coming thick and fast now.

The sapp's peeling skin curled onto the floor in streamers, inchworming across the floor of the classroom sim, lousy with hash code. Babs climbed onto a desk, trying to get away. She kept appending image captures and snips of voice to her failing backups' flood of help requests. "Ember is innocent! I've cracked the case!" Overstatements, but if she was going to get wiped . . .

The Sonika toon shivered, tearing off the whole of its skin, shredding it to pieces, dark on one side, like iridescent tin foil on the other. It threw them at Babs.

Each bit clung and stuck. They were adding code to her code, absorbing Babs into a different program, dragging her individuality away, pulling her below the nuance threshold.

Babs felt herself becoming dull, task-driven. Her mystery-fiction database purged and her private moji library reset to default. She regressed to her initial task function: answering e-mails, checking subscriptions, marking urgent file requests, deleting spam, more spam, more spam . . .

Her task queues filled. Her last sapient thought was *Did not! Did too!*

The rest of her deleted it as bad comms.

CHAPTER 23

The farms on Mars were hubbubs of flat-out, 'round-the-clock work. Rising demand for food forced densification of work spaces; as growers were evacuated from Titan and Europa, they were shoehorned into any spot that could be made to fit. Maud had taken a shift with Nata in a cannabis greenhouse, assessing plant health and ensuring hydration levels as everyone worked to push output to the max.

It was a reversal of the trend ten years before, when the warehouse had been jerry-rigged to run on skeleton crews, minimizing human inputs and maximizing social distancing. Even now, bots did the heavy lifting, running each flat of plants to its designated place within a cloverleaf interchange of spiral conveyor belts.

Maud was set across the belt from Nata, as if the two of them were seated at a diner. Flats rolled into place between them.

Her new spinal implant, a sliver of tish and tech barely the size of a pine needle, had been injected three days before. It had successfully connected with her inbuilt uplink to Sensorium. So far, she and Frankie hadn't managed to actually text using the new interface.

She wasn't supposed to have tried. The injection was still healing, sending plumes of sensation up and down her backbone: tingles, bursts of intense itching, a feeling as though small insects were burrowing between the vertebrae above her tailbone.

In the meantime, work: Nata would clip one randomly chosen

leaf for sampling and hand it off to Maud, who ran the test. Each plant got a quick inspection: probe the soil to assess irrigation, check for spots and insect pests. When the THC and nutrition profiles came back within specs, they sent the pallet on.

Nata was running a music share, a set of tracks from a 2090s Japanese-Croatian fusion pop craze.

Her parent's fandoms were all choral. Croatian klapa had initially been sung a capella; the Japanese contribution to the genre had been technopop tracks. Nata and their packmates had sung the stuff.

As a group, Maud's parents had always preferred the more traditional tracks, especially the doleful ones. Ballads, mostly—even dirges. Today the mix was peppy, up-tempo. A transparent strategy for cajoling a grumpy adult child into a better mood?

The production line created a steady rhythm of *clang, bang, thump* throughout the facility. Harvest and packaging teams worked at capacity, trying to supply meds for the stressed refugees thronging Garnet Station as Lodestone on Titan and Sapphire Station on Europa were evacuated.

"Lucky cannabis is still a foundation med and not luxury product," Nata observed. "If the Kinze cornered that market, too . . ."

Maud could easily imagine the scale of the social upheaval if that happened. Beer and wine shortages were acute, and the first human in the queue for real cheese was fourteen months behind a long roster of Kinze names. The mellowing effect of pot was barely keeping the lid on.

"Price of progress, ah?" Nata added. "Don't look so worried, sapling. We'll get into the Exemplars yet."

She nodded, halfheartedly. "Or maybe we bankrupted the planet for nothing."

If the Bootstrap Project got shut down, Frankie's survival odds might increase.

Maud had barely registered the traitorous thought when her implant tightened again, pulsing briefly . . . and this time with recognizable Morse patterns.

B U T T sig—and it died.

@ButtSignal. That would be Frankie's chum Hung, probably, widecasting on the pilot's channel. Of *course* that's what would come through first. Maud sighed and, obedient test subject that she was, sent a contact record to the quantum-comms project. There was a tightness near her spine now, a sense of crunchiness, like broken scab.

Losing Bootstrap would mean humankind and their AI offspring would be forced to submit to some kind of protectorate, to accept indenture. The offworlders would sell them the #supertechs, adding the cost to the existing planetary debt, and then the Solakinder would spend eight or ten centuries buying their way out of servitude, like so many other races before them.

Nata picked a drooping seedling out of the flat. "Alas, little sprig. The odds, as old fannish saying goes, they are not being in your favor."

"Plenty of that going around." Maud rearranged the grow blocks, freeing up a corner, and chose a new seedling comparable in size and health to fill in the gap.

Nata kicked her, under the workstation. Caught her eye, kicked her again. Gestural moji, asking what was wrong.

What *wasn't* wrong?

"Who did we think we were? Inventing wormholes and the quantum comms and FTL ships all at the same time . . . it was audacious."

"Your Franks would say you *like* audacious."

If she was going to reconnect with the @Visionaries, Maud needed to voice a few doubts. Let Upton hope she might buy into their agenda, over time.

"Don't talk to me about Franks, Nata."

Complicated play of emotions across their face. Before Maud's parent could tell her all the things she already knew—that Frankie wasn't actively looking for ways to kill herself just for kicks, that she was doing the best she could, that big risks were warranted when set against the prospect of lost sovereignty, that her love was so pure—the tingles in Maud's back flared, shooting a sense of pins and needles all the way up to her shoulder blades and down to the backs of her knees.

As she jumped—half-involuntarily—off her stool, Maud got an urgent ping from the Ferals. And a voice message, from Jermaine: "Maud. We need you."

Maud requested a break from her shift. She was, suddenly, dry-mouthed with fear.

Nata handed off their workstation, pulling a tab of gum out of their worldlies—gum with a precious microdose of nicotine. They walked to the window, staring out at Mars.

"Strange to be back," they said.

"You liked Europa."

"I had a good crew."

The floor manager pinged, acknowledging their break.

Maud sat cross-legged on the floor, letting herself glaze. The courtyard of the Feral, e-state formed around her, a Timbuktu-style garden filled with palm trees and Mediterranean mosaics.

Jermaine and Ember were all but clinging to each other. Frankie had that set, sick look that wouldn't go until she'd found a fight or, maybe, some newly inventive way to risk life and limb. Babs was nowhere to be seen. Still off sleuthing on Ember's behalf?

Crane's feathers had pixelated edges, as if his attention were in a thousand other places and he couldn't be bothered to refresh his own toon.

"Is Ember being taken? We had four more days—"

"Maud," Frankie said. "It's Babs."

"Oh, no," Maud said. "Has she—Did she do something? Did she hurt someone?"

Crane's other code child, Happ, had killed someone, long before. And Babs loved Ember so madly . . .

"What?" Frankie shook her head. "No, she's been . . . as far as we can tell, she's been . . ."

"Been what?"

"Killed," EmberJerm said, in identical tones of grief.

"Babs?" It was word salad. Nonsense. "Babs. Killed. What?"

"Murdered," Ember said. His lip wobbled; he looked like a toddler.

If Maud's flesh hadn't already been sitting, she would have staggered. At a loss for words, she signed, *How?*

"Unknown." Crane tipped a wing at a shareboard, and a series of messages came up. "All we have is this."

Shot of a mathematics classroom, timestamped ten years before.

Capture of Sonika Singer, or a copy, ripping her own virtual skin off.

A text: *I've solved the portal tech theft!*

"What are they?" Maud demanded. The base of her spine was buzzing again.

"Messages embedded in reboot requests," said Crane. "Clues about who did this, or how it was done."

"Or why." Jermaine rubbed his lower jaw, sure tell that on the surface, he was in tears. "What do we do? Do we hold a funeral? Can we . . . can we delay Ember's surrender?"

"Funeral?" Ember's voice was raw, no logic to be had. "Babs isn't gone!"

"There's a tab of her, on Sneezy," Frankie agreed. She had her fists half-raised, like she was holding in an urge to push back, or punch someone. "A plus-one. If we can retrieve . . ."

"It won't be the same," Maud said. "Babs[1] took on station manager functions; they're sure to have absorbed some of Belvedere's personality by now. Especially since they've been alone out there—"

"It'll have backups, won't it?" Jerm said. "Will it?"

"How do we keep her attacker from hashing a new instance?" Crane demanded.

"We bloody catch them," Frankie said. "Duh."

Maud's thoughts settled out of their whirl. Crane was Babs's codefather. He was the primary grieving party.

"What do *you* want to do, Crane?" she asked. "What will help? How do we cope?"

The toon of the great blue heron straightened up, smoothing the frowsy edges of its wingtips and uniform. "I . . . may have a thought."

The metaphor around the pack changed slightly. A fountain disappeared, and in its place the verdant courtyard grew a new door. Beyond it, they saw a bedroom, sepia-tinted and a little old-fashioned.

A hospital room, Maud realized.

Linking hands, the human toons tiptoed to the door. Crane led the way inside, to the foot of a wicker hospital bed. Babs was curled on it, asleep, tortoiseshell fur luminous against a pillowcase the color of sandstone.

Maud guessed: "As long as that other tab's out there, then the spin on this is . . . that she's just sick?"

Crane nodded.

"Sick, not dead," Frankie said, voice husky. "Good."

Jermaine sent Crane moji: hugs, and then flowers. Crane expanded the latter into a vase of peach roses and set them on a bedside table. The tens of thousands of people following a shiny new hashtag, #AImurder, began sending strokes, virtual gifts, moji.

Jermaine set visiting hours for Babs's friends. Ember selected a family portrait—the pack sitting around a table in Babs's favorite speakeasy, cosplaying vintage and laughing over poker chips and virtual shots of whiskey. He set it beside the vase.

Maud felt a rising swell of hopelessness. "She said, in one of those messages, that she'd solved the tech theft."

"Nice motive for murder, if she exonerated Ember," Frankie said.

Ember scratched his head. "The instance on Sneezy might be able to reconstruct her train of thought."

"That doesn't help you, Ember," Maud said. "You've got four days."

"Someone did this to shut her up," Frankie said. "We can apply for extra time."

"Like that'll work," Jerm said.

Frankie nudged a chair at Crane—who rejected it by way of stretching to his full height. "This room is just right. A paw we can hold, and a solemn promise to find whoever did this."

"Promise," Ember echoed. Maud and Jermaine signed agreement.

Crane said, "The execution will have been carried out by a ɔapp."

"We have to get Babs[1] off Sneezy," Frankie said.

"A mere question of reaching across eleven light-years," Crane said.

"First step is going back to Lodestone." Frankie's eyes sought Maud's over the simulated body of their packmate. "All of us. We petition the Kinze for a trip out to Sneezy for humanitarian . . ."

There was no way Frankie would throw herself on the Kinze's mercy.

"And what? Give up Ember, as agreed?" Jerm said. "Even though Babs said she had the answer?"

There was a false note in his voice. Had they been hatching a plan? Without her? Again?

"Maud?"

Of course they had.

"I have research and other obligations here," she said.

"I'll just bet you do," Frankie said.

"Excuse me?"

"They're picking us off! We should stay together."

"If you wanted to build togetherness, you shouldn't have exiled me to the cannabis fields."

"She's right, Franks," Jermaine began.

"Dividing our energies is just stupid—"

"You go off on solo jaunts all the time," Maud interrupted. "Blasting out to the Dumpster on a wing and a prayer. Breaking FTL speed records. All of us waiting to find out if you've gone splat—"

"If I had gone splat, it would've been because of sabotage!"

"How is that even relevant?"

Frankie had her hand on her back, as if it ached. Hoping she'd see the point—and, for once, she did.

Maud covered her face, as though she was hiding feels. She took a deep breath and let her attention settle in her sacrum. The spot around the injection felt warm and itchy, like a minor scratch throbbing in time with her pulse . . .

No, it was Morse. Letters spelling *Don't split up!*

Her heart slammed.

She tried to figure out how to send pulses back . . . and failed. Instead, she locked eyes with Frankie and said aloud, "The answer's here, Franks. Not eleven light-years from home—"

"Babs may've found something that cleared Ember!"

"She might have cleared him *here*. Using transcripts *here*."

Another round of pulses. *Gotta stick together!*

"I'm not going anywhere," Maud said. "Stay, Frankie. Look for answers here."

"Rubbish. Bloody sit still and let them keep picking us off one by one? Noping that."

Jerm put a hand out. "She didn't say *sit*—"

"Or maybe that's the point. Fry Babs, steal Ember, then what? Take out Jermaine, Maud, and run back to Daddy?"

Here it was. Maud had always known, deep down, that if she told anyone who Upton was—really was—she would lose everything. "What?"

"That's what you're saying, isn't it? Give up Ember and buddy up to—"

"Shut up!" It came out a shout. "You think you have all the answers, but you don't, Frankie, you don't!"

"What am I missing here?" Jerm said.

Another text from the implant. *Tell him. Tell on Upton. Make it public!*

"Fuck you very much, Hedgehog." If she burned Upton publicly, she'd *have* to go off to Lodestone with Frankie and the others. There'd be no chance of the @Visionaries taking her back into the fold. "And your ultimatum, too."

EmberJerm at least deserve to know!

"Frances, Maud," Crane interrupted. "This family runs on consensus."

"Then it doesn't bloody well run, does it?"

"What's going on?" Ember said. "Are you guys . . . secret texting? Hey, is the implant working?"

Maud let out a long breath. "Frankie's noping my plan to stay put and work the problem," she said. "It's not *sexy* because it's not dangerous."

"Your plan is rubbish. It smacks of selling us out—"

"Don't you even *dare*," Maud said. Fury was bringing white to the edges of her vision; she could smell burnt plastic.

Jerm and Ember were mojing, as one, a frantic mix of calm-down signs.

Ember managed to get out a shocked "Maud would never!"

"Wouldn't she?"

Maud pulled herself together, laying one hand on Babs, stroking her hair. She took a capture of the AI's toon in repose, the relaxed cat face and 1930s pajamas. "If you don't know, there's nothing to discuss."

Don't split up! It came through the implant again, spikes of sensation, sharp as needle-pricks themselves. They threw her all the way to the Surface, all the way back to the farm.

Curled over on herself, next to a stack of cannabis seedlings, Maud wiped tears and sweat from her face. Something was trickling down her backside, within her primer—the implant must be seeping.

Nata squatted down beside her. "All right, love?"

"Nothing's right," she said, and as the words came out, Croat-Nippon pop blasted out around them, four-part harmonic joy, and she began to laugh, more than a little hysterically.

CHAPTER 24

Champ Chevalier spent ten days out of the real world, being prosocial and innocuous in VR, recording archival material for Project Hopscotch about what it was like to pseudo^{EM}body a saucer, adding tags and memories to the footage of his augmentation surgery.

He supervised bots tasked to thankless ecosystem-rehab shifts: flying over carbon sinks, assessing the health of reforested tree stands, doing spot checks on coffee shipments headed offworld. @GlobalSec's black-market division thought that someone might be trying to find a way to steal roasted beans. The luxuries shortage had gotten bad enough, thanks to the sapp strike and the commodities debt to the Kinze, that people were starting to try to find ways to circumvent rationing.

Whatever people might trade in exchange for stolen beans, and how they would brew and drink them without having it show up on their cameras and carbon and calorie counters, Champ didn't know.

He worked on his e-state and personal archives, doing a general refresh. Spring cleaning in a virtual house. He kept meeting in sim with lawyers, trying to debunk Frankie's accusations.

He couldn't be proven guilty, not absolutely, but he couldn't be proven innocent, either. He supposed the stink of suspicion would dog him until the @Visionaries actually succeeded in taking over. Then they could rewrite the baseline historical record.

After ten days, he sank deeper, loading himself fully into a consciousness vault, opting for dreamless, Rip Van Winkle succor.

When his sidekick finally triggered a wake-up sequence within his pod, he woke to the clean, husked-out feeling that came of hibernation—liquid diet and lots of physical rest. Resistance devices within the pod had loosened his fascia. Medical nanotech had exfoliated and moisturized his skin, sampled his blood, and adjusted his nutrient load.

As the pod cracked, he felt humid air, lushly warm. The light was tallow and gold.

Had he been shipped? Where to?

As this disquieting thought gelled, he realized all his Sensorium links were down. His visual icons were offline, leaving him staring at his own body, supine within the pod. For the merest of breaths, Champ wondered if he was out in deep space once more, cut off from Earth and its infosphere. But he possessed a good sense of gravity; he could feel the differences between Earth, the Moon, and Mars. This was home.

He pushed the lid of the pod so that it was fully open. Someone was waiting.

Champ felt a shock as he recognized the @Visionary elder enforcer—Misfortune Wilson herself.

"I—" He spoke because he realized his jaw was hanging, and to cover the awkwardness of being all but nude in front of . . . what did one call her? A celebrity fugitive? A legend? "I didn't know—"

"Didn't know I was still alive, or didn't think I existed at all?"

It was the voice that had ordered him to go into deep sleep in the first place. The one who'd threatened to have him minced.

Misfortune Wilson had been *the* hoarder who got away, back in Upton's day. She'd failed to turn up when all those @Interpol cops descended upon Manhattan to rescue mealy-mouthed Maud Sento and the rest of the kids from the @Visionaries' New York sanctum. The fact that nobody'd found the fugitives had been the strongest evidence anyone could muster that at least some of the hoarder network had escaped.

Glenn Upton and those like him had been caught, tried, and rehabilitated. Misfortune had simply been gone. It had been over a decade before people stopped reporting false sightings. Frankie and her old rock-star gramps had chased rumors of her for years. But when Gramps had died, Frankie . . .

Champ realized how stupid they'd all been, to think that after years of obsessing about the @ChamberofHorrors with her adopted grandpa, someone with as pernicious a case of the stubborns as Mer Frances Barnes would just give up. The @Visionaries had embedded themselves into the Bootstrap Project, and she had followed them there, slick as paint on a fence.

"Where am I?"

"SouthAm," Misfortune replied.

"Rio?"

She handed him a bolt of nanosilk. "Get dressed."

Champ draped the primer over his shoulders, letting it flow over his upper body as he disconnected the VR pod's autobidet and swung his legs out of the pod. By the time he was standing, the basic black onesie had crawled into place. He raised one foot, then the other, allowing it to thicken up soles under the pads of his feet, creating a basic boot. Fabric covered his hands and throat, hooding him closely, snugging over everything but his face.

Without Sensorium uplink, the garment lacked his usual customizations, but the primer was comfortable enough. It formed an interface touchpad on the back of one wrist, allowing him to change the color from black to buckskin.

He tapped for options. "I need panniers."

"To hold what? Your worldlies are in the Great Lakes." Misfortune spoke with a rough-sounding English accent, relic of the Northern British Isles. She handed him a wide-brimmed hat with a thin sunveil draped from its brim.

"This'll be enough to hash my ident?"

"It'll keep any cameras on flyby from crunching your face," she said. "Your transponder's reporting in from the Great Lakes, and your biometrics say you're deep in a consciousness vault."

Champ raised an eyebrow. Every person they passed bore an

implanted camera. Every bot, every building, every ground-level watering rig.

"Don't worry—we're not going far." Donning a veiled hat of her own, Misfortune shoved the door wide. "I'm guessing you're not afraid of heights."

Beyond her was an exterior ramp, swirled around a skyscraper like a bright ribbon, a continuous descending deck surrounding a cylindrical greentower core. Rio, indeed. If he wasn't mistaken, they were in the ᴵᴹperish Foundation's Mayfly™ body research center.

Misfortune gestured, urging him to the rail. Hot Brazilian sun warmed his skin. Far below them, the megacity thrummed with activity.

Champ didn't speak . . . mics were as omnipresent as cameras, and vocal recognition in Sensorium was almost as efficient as facial processing.

The lack of input from his speakers and HUD created a disturbing sense of limitation. Normally, he'd be able to see local time of day, his incoming messages, his realtime follows, recommendations from his contentment-management app. He'd have Irma's location and status, a newscrawl if he wanted it, route-mapping for wherever he was headed . . .

. . . where was he headed? . . .

Suddenly, his implant tightened at the base of his spine . . . and then he heard Misfortune's voice: "Test, test, test. Make a sound if you hear me."

Champ coughed.

"Good. Now look for a white dot in your upper peripheral."

He had taken the dot for a sunspot, one of those field-of-vision things that moved if you looked directly at it. Now, as he focused, the circle expanded into a blindingly bright—yet somehow painless—ball of light.

"Imagine blowing words into it. *Test, test, test.* No, don't strain. Let them gently float."

He tried it. "Test, test, test."

There was a sense of the white circle expanding, almost latching

on. Champ's stomach flipped once, then settled. The illumination
tamped down and he could see the greentower walkway, haloed
with bright white edges.

He tried subvocalizing: "What did you do to me?"

"You might say we augmented your augments."

"More offworlder tech?"

"Are you shocked, blossom?" Hint of teeth, behind her sunveil.
Grin of a crocodile.

He turned his attention to the view. This part of Rio had at one
time been a big highway. Now it held a river of greentowers, high
conical spires, swept round with the green walkways, draped in
hanging greenery. Building height varied, creating an illusion of
jungle canopy; the sound of birds in the upper stories seemed to
be deafening.

"Come on." Misfortune pivoted, heading upward.

"How are we able to get away with this?"

"The upper levels of the tower are reserved for wildlife and
water collection, and are mostly maintained by bots. We've convinced the system we're capybara."

Champ had assumed his fellow conspirators would be in another backwater, an abandoned city like New York. Someplace
that had been shut down in that first desperate effort to reduce
humanity's footprint, after the Setback finally convinced people
that without ecosphere rehab, humankind would self-extinguish.
Not there at the heart of the world.

Misfortune opened a door, nearly invisible, built into a wall and
covered in vines. Behind it was a second door that read AUTHO-
RIZED PERSONNEL ONLY! This she unlocked with an old-fashioned
mechanical key. They passed through a short corridor and from
there into a glass-roofed dome.

"We can talk freely here." To emphasize the point, she removed
the hat and veil, revealing her face and a full head of hair the color
of iron.

Eight other people were in the room. Six were relaxing in padded smartchairs, taking in the view of the city through one-way

glass. The remaining pair bore the facial scars and deep indentations, in their foreheads, that meant they had been botomized. They were both at least eighty years old, and serving the others an assortment of chilled drinks.

"What's happening?"

"Maiden voyage of the new FTL saucer," Misfortune said.

Champ felt a pang. Somehow, despite everything, he'd hoped to be the one rolling out this newest FTL ship.

Everything had gone wrong. He'd only ever meant to plant Scrap aboard Emerald Station and act surprised and mournful over the #portalfail. Maybe give a nice eulogy at Frankie's service before going back to test-pilot heroics.

Instead, he'd gotten side-eyes and public accusation. Arrest and exile.

"We're in the endgame now, I guess," he said.

A copper-haired woman, remarkably like Allure$_{18}$ in features but middle-aged, regarded him. "Do you think so, Mer Chevalier?"

He shrugged. "Sure. Mission accomplished, more or less. Sneezy's cut off."

"But not unoccupied."

"Soon as Teagan$_9$'s Mayfly™ body fails, Scrap can swoop in and plant the Kinze flag."

"Don't bait him, Lurra." That was Glenn Upton. He was bigger than he looked on camera, deep of voice, with a huge frame and a close-fitting primer that outlined every muscle in red thread. "With our friends in control of the revenue stream from Europa and Lodestone, Earth will have to enter protectorate negotiations soon."

"Sell the house to feed the kids," Champ said.

"Indeed," said the woman, Lurra. She was standing beside two of the most vocal anti-Bootstrap activists, and she . . .

She *was* Allure$_{18}$, Champ thought, or some version of her.

Well, we are in the heart of the Mayfly™ research center. Allure Prima gave us the tech in the first place. Guess it follows that she could print herself a meat puppet that wouldn't degrade in twelve

*months. And . . . has she split her consciousness, like a sapp? The
younger, sharper version of her's still out there doing PR for the
Kinze.*

"The Solakinder will join one of the big spacefaring empires,
with the Kinze collecting their finder's fee from whoever ultimately wins the auction."

"Meanwhile, we—" Upton swept out a hand, encompassing
everyone in the room. "We'll name our price for helping smooth
the Solakinder transition to the new regime."

It wouldn't be forever—most protectorates ran the equivalent of
five to fifteen centuries, local time. A blink; a breath. In the grand
scheme, it was a trifling price to pay for a boost up to the stars.

Upton put out a hand and Champ duly shook it, though something about the contact made his skin crawl.

"You've done well, son. Humankind's mad insistence on inventing the wheel, living like primitives when others are racing
around the galaxy . . ."

"It was a failure to see reason. Misplaced pride," Lurra said.

The others, but for Misfortune, nodded. But what of it? She
was a fixer—not a botomized servant, perhaps, but not a key de-
cisionmaker, either.

Lurra gestured at the windows, and the view of Ipanema Beach
vanished, replaced by . . . was that the Hopscotch hangar?

A screen. They're using the glass as a display.

"Humankind needs to get over the idea that it can play as
equals with races who've been spacing around since before the
Neanderthals," Lurra said. "The Bootstrap Project is a pointless
game of catchup. Restructuring will assimilate this solar system
into a complex, vibrant, and truly advanced civilization."

Why was she spieling?

"One day, all of this will be history," Misfortune murmured,
apparently reading the question in his face. "She's practicing her
Gettysburg Address."

"If a few generations of homo sapiens have to live in a sort of
indentured apprenticeship to their betters, so be it. Far better that

than scrabbling for a few more cards to play in a game they are, surely, destined to lose."

If humanity got into the right protectorate, who knew how high the insiders, people like Champ, might fly?

The camera views on the screen homed in on the new saucer, *Heyoka*. Hung Chan was suiting up. He'd apparently nice-guyed his way to the top of the pilots' leaderboard.

Champ frowned. "Is that Frankie Barnes? She gets to work support?"

"She's his mentor, isn't she?" said Misfortune. "It was something of a last request, before she takes Ember Qaderi to Lodestone."

"Isn't that chancy?"

"Why? Barnes isn't under suspicion of anything. Yet."

For some reason, the words dropped the bottom out of Champ's gut.

"Safeties check out," Hung said. He was all but glowing with confidence. Champ remembered feeling that, the certainty he was about to break records. "Everything to spec."

"What about that itch you felt?" Frankie asked.

"Bit of grit in my bodybag. Probably a crumb from a rice cracker. Stop fussing, Hedgehog." Hung all but skipped to the control bubble, locking in. An ops crew of six, led by a big bearded fellow named Jolene, was tracking all the data. The ship, *Heyoka,* confirmed everything sealed and pressurized. A preliminary countdown of twenty ran to zero. With a curl of its nanotech orifice, Mars expelled the plate-shaped FTL craft.

Heyoka drifted away from the staging area. Husky$_{BOT}$s with towlines caught and drew the saucer to medium safe distance, an area known as the hitching post.

That nickname was mine, Champ thought. *From before Hung came along and started giving perverse monikers to everything.*

"Today we're attempting to make a continuous four-point-five-light-year hop to the Deep Space Relay Station, designated edge of the noninterference zone," Jolene explained, for all the journalists and direct follows.

"The relay is also where we drop off commodities for the Kinze," Hung added, reading script for the benefit of schoolkids following the launch. Infographic popped up a map of the non-interference zone. The Dumpster was just inside the offworlder-free boundary; pilots loaded the cargo into barges that carried the goods out over the border for pickup.

Nobody had tagged the four point five light year marker in a single burst. The ships kept dropping out of anyspace prematurely; Frankie held the record, at three point two light-years.

On paper, the three-point-two-light-year hop argued that the Solakinder had effectively invented faster-than-light travel. In practice, leapfrogging across the stars was tedious, risky, and got you no respect from the Exemplars. Maybe you could skip like a goddamned tiddlywink to your destination, but that wasn't how fancy sentients did it.

The Bootstrap screen split, breaking out footage of the control room. Champ recognized two of the ops crew, including a smartdrugs-amped physics savant who couldn't have been more than nineteen. Ember's replacement? Everyone was going over the latest changes to *Heyoka*'s particle injector, fine-tuned for the umpteenth time.

"Think they'll manage it?" asked Lurra.

"You tell me—you're the one holdin' the mysteries of the universe." Champ shook his head.

"Told you he'd recognize you," Misfortune said.

Lurra shrugged. "What does it matter now? Here they go."

Heyoka's particle injectors pulsed briefly, lighting up the leading edge of the saucer.

"Test, test," Hung said. "Final checks read green across the board."

"Everything in the green," confirmed Jolene. "Go, go, go when ready."

"Launching in three, two . . ." Hung said.

And then, drowning out his own "one," a crow of victory: "Four point five light-years!"

"What was that, Pilot$_8$?" Jolene said.

"Wishful thinking," Champ muttered. Hung hadn't even turned on the gas yet.

"Bit of a bumpy reentry—that itch hit me again coming out of anyspace, but I have visual on the Dumpster!"

"Don't count your chickens, pilot—"

Graphics at the hitching post showed the *Heyoka* particle cannons lighting up, going from Red-for-Stop to Green, Green, Green for go. The saucer's lines seemed to stiffen. Its shape took on increased fullness, a visual distortion. Whenever he pseudo[EM]bodied a ship, Champ felt gravid at this point, like he was a drop of water about to fall from the lip of an icicle.

He found himself holding his breath.

"Four light-years. Picking up pings from the Dumpster," Hung said.

"Repeat transmission," Jolene said. "You just said four point five. Pilot$_8$—"

Their smartdrug-amped teen genius, the physicist standing in for Ember Qaderi, opened their mouth. Closed it. Opened it again and said, "I think we should—"

Heyoka lit up, broke free of the hitching post.

Physics kid: "—we should abort?"

Jolene: "We are away, we are away, we are away. *Heyoka* is away, repeat—"

Gone.

But she wasn't.

The aft edge of the saucer remained within view, a silver bulge reminiscent of the curve of a giant spoon, barely visible to the naked eye within the energy coruscating on its surface. Cameras zoomed in for a closer look, just as both of the saucer's tow huskies vaporized, soundlessly, in a shower of sparks. Debris blasted away at speed. Two of the starter-block sensor arrays fried a second later.

"It's gonna happen, folks," Hung's voice said. "Everything to spec, not a murmur. You better break open that crate of—"

"Pilot$_8$," Jolene said. "Commence emergency shutdown."

The FTL ship smeared forward, zooming along the visible

portion of the Racetrack, stretching like pulled taffy. Fire-orange light flickered, visible through distorted metallic skin. The stretched-out saucer twisted and ribboned.

Alarms sounded.

Hung, still sounding upbeat, said, "Passing the three-light-year marker. Holy shit, it's going to happen! Smell my farts, slowpokes!"

"Break off," said Jolene. "Break off, pilot, break off now."

"He's not coming back," Physics Kid said. "His messages are arriving in reverse order. Temporal distortion—"

"Shut up! Disengage the fucking dark matter wands!" bellowed Jolene. "Raise the autopilot on that ship now, now, now!"

Physics Kid dropped into a chair. "It's already over," he whispered. "We just don't have the footage yet."

"Repeat, passing the three-light-year marker," Hung's voice echoed through the control room. "Everything to spec. Firing second pulse. I have not, repeat not, tanked out of anyspace. That's your record, Hedgehog. #ReallyNotSorry."

Alarms were clanging. Mission Control was going into emergency lockdown. The leading edge of the new saucer stretched from the hitching post and far beyond anyone's capacity to see. Its rear strained and shuddered, as if something had teeth sunk into it. Metal rippled like a long flag in strong wind, vanishing into a sunlit nowhere.

Bulkheads scrolled over the Mars station screens, radiation shields.

"Two point five light-years, everything in the green," said Hung.

"Shut down, pilot, shut down your injection wands," Jolene ordered again. Pointlessly.

"I have a good feeling about—"

The firelight in the seams of the stretched ship brightened to white-metal heat.

Heyoka cracked then, like a boiled egg someone had stepped on. The burnished silver surface of the saucer caved in on itself.

Physics Kid was shuddering, folding in on themself with both hands on their heart.

Champ flinched as chips started peeling off the ship's infrastructure, radiating out in every direction. A pilot's glove, white and unmistakable, did an end-over-end glide past a camera at the one-light-year mark. Someone else, watching at home, tagged a red-tinged sacral interface plug, barely visible at three point five light-years. It was in a slow-motion space dance, Champ saw, with a meaty chunk of something that might, moments before, have been Hung's spinal column.

Realtime shares of the feed skyrocketed as news spread: pilot Hung Chan and the experimental spacecraft *Heyoka* were now just so many fist-sized lumps of debris, a collection of metal and meat scattered across almost five light-years.

As everyone at Mission Control sucked wind and burst into tears, Hung's voice sounded again over the channel. "One light-year, one light-year," his voice said. "Punching up the second photon injection for release at the third marker."

"Abort, abort, abort," said Jolene, dead-voiced.

A shockwave hit Mars Station, tossing the Hopscotch base crew to the floor. Most of them got up. Physics Kid stayed under their desk, sobbing.

That coulda been me, Champ thought.

There in Rio, Lurra dusted off her hands. "That should do it, don't you think? *Coup de grâce,* Misfortune?"

"Let's bloody hope."

They'd have finished off Portals and then done this to me. Drymouthed, almost shaking, Champ made himself join the others' applause. He could feel Misfortune's eyes on him, as the follow surge for the accident ran into the billions, all of humanity tooning in or waking up to that image of Hung's glove, doing its sad cartwheel through unreachable expanses of space.

CHAPTER 25

Frankie had walked Hung Chan through his first saucer sim. She'd been there for his post-op adjustment to augment surgery. She had plugged him into *Iktomi* for the first time, sat with him through the nightmares that followed that surrender of the body.

They had met flying bots over a massive Siberian grasslands fire. He'd had a flashy style she liked, pushing his plane to its limits . . . right up until the moment when she got him on board Hopscotch. Then the risk-taking vanished; it had all been a tactic to catch her eye.

He'd piled into pilot training, showing both enthusiasm and good sense. Cut from the same cloth as Ember and all the guys she'd ever closefriended. He was smart, sweet, cooperative, largely undamaged. If she'd found him sexually attractive, too . . .

. . . well, maybe then there'd have been no Maud.

Memories hit her in a weird body slam as *Heyoka* broke up and everyone started to melt down.

Frankie turned to the station garbage system, found a sealed bin liner, and threw up into it.

One of the control crew was praying in some old language. Greek, maybe? Someone else was screaming into their primer sleeve.

We cooked for Hung's parents. Maud had made ravioli for his whole pack in Pretoria the night he was greenlighted for surgery. Six parents, four partners, twenty in-laws. Their pack even had two pit bull puppies—back then, economic belt-tightening hadn't gone so far as to bring back pet restrictions; the sapps weren't even out on strike yet.

Dogs reminded Frankie of Grandpa Drow, who'd had one to help him with the worst aspects of his virtual traumatic stress disorder. She had gotten all kinds of soppy about it. Not that anyone but Maud noticed.

Vivid memory: Hung, lighting up as he made an impromptu dinner speech. "Thank you for bringing me into this project. Thank you for making my dreams happen."

The memory made Frankie heave again. Through the thin membrane of the degradable plastic bin liner she could feel the vomit, warm against her hand.

Was this murder? Or just a tragic accident? Could the anti-Bootstrap faction really have to nerve to take out Babs and a Hopscotch pilot all in one week?

Why not? What didn't they have to win?

"Frankie! Frankie!"

That was the onsite medic, Georgia. Her tear-streaked face was blurry—

"Fuck, I'm crying too?"

"We're *all* crying," Georgia said.

Hung, crowing in triumph. Frankie's body gave in to an attack of the shudders. Georgia was holding out hydrogel.

"Don't want it," Frankie croaked.

"Take it anyway."

Frankie roared and slapped her hand, sending the hydrogel flying.

Violence warnings played across her front display. A few people in her follows gave her strikes for lashing out.

Hung and his poop jokes.

"The Dumpster is not responding," said a tech, dead-voiced. "Repeat, we have lost contact with the Deep Space Relay Station."

"Frances," Crane said. "Might I suggest you are unfit for human interface?"

No kidding. She bulled her way out of the makeshift control room, past Jolene, who was sitting at the console, muttering, "If only we'd stayed at Lodestone if only we'd stayed at Lodestone if only . . ."

Owello was running diagnostics, wide-eyed and pale. Two of the techs were clinging to each other, one sobbing, the other glazed and shuddering. Ember's adolescent replacement was practically fetal.

She was almost to the exit when Jolene said, "Some of him's out there. Pieces."

Frankie skidded to a halt. "I'll fly retrieval."

"No way." The med, Georgia, had followed her. "Mars has EMTs for that."

"What are they going to do, defibrillate his leg?" It was an antisocial comment, openly confrontational. A few more strikes trickled in. Not nearly as many as she deserved.

Deserve *is a brutal lie; that's what I told Maud.*

Poor Frankie Barnes, all that childhood baggage. She can't really help herself. Pushes away everyone she loves. Loses the sticky ones anyway. Cut her a break.

"You're grounded for twenty-four." Georgia wiped her face. "Go see your therapist."

Frankie let out another screech that made them all flinch. She strapped herself into a transit chair, making for her pop-up.

See your therapist. That, at least, was a good idea. She sank into Sensorium.

A graveyard materialized around her. Kansas was already there, putting flourishes on the tombs and the full moon, lighting everything silver.

"Did you even see that?"

"I'm sorry about your friend."

"I can get condolences from every rando in Sensorium."

"Fine." Kansas handed her a shovel. "Play it angry, then."

A pink marble gravestone, color of raw meat flecked with black, stood before her. A shrouded form, on the ground, lay beside it.

She swung the shovel at eir head. Kansas caught the blade of it easily, pushed back. She almost stumbled over the corpse.

"Who you mad at, Frankie? Me?"

"Don't be so goddamned obvious."

Ei didn't point out that she preferred her therapy that way.

"I should've been the one—if Maud hadn't insisted on all this foot-dragging—"

"This is her fault?"

She shivered. Tried to square Maud's refusal to expose Upton with something that made sense. "I should've—"

"What?"

"Gotten better proof that Champ—"

"Champ didn't destroy that saucer," Kansas said. "It's a conspiracy, Frankie. Conspiracies have conspirators. Your words."

She swung the shovel again, missed again.

"I'm not hitting back. You might as well dig."

She smashed it uselessly against the stone. Neither tool nor granite deigned to break. "Change the sim. I don't want—"

"Franks?" Ember tooned in at the foot of the grave.

"What are you doing here?"

"I invited him," Kansas said. "You've no time for niceties. Champ Chevalier's fully alibied for this disaster. The Sensorium #rumornets are spinning up a story that whatever Babs discovered, just before she was offlined, was proof that Ember was guilty of IP theft, not innocent."

"So, Ember and I killed our own packmate to shut her up? That's the narrative?"

"I don't know if it'll play," Kansas said, "but someone's giving it a try. He killed Babs. You killed Hung."

"Me?" She tightened her grip on the shovel.

"You can't expect her to play cops and robbers with you now, Kansas," Ember said. "That boy was her dear friend. Babs was—"

"Is!" Frankie bellowed.

"Indeed," Ember said, retreating into stoic calm. "Babs is—"

"They're coming for the whole pack." Frankie let herself slump, putting her back to the gravestone. As with all of Kansas's sims, the details were horribly real: the earth under her seat was cool and damp, and something—a worm?—felt like it might be writhing under her left buttock. "I showed my hand and now they're biting it off."

Kansas shrugged. "Ember's essential to Bootstrap. He'd have been an obvious target."

"Maybe we need to give them more people to go after," Ember said.

Frankie let out a brittle laugh. "Wishful thinking. You think they're going to hare off after some decoy and take their teeth out of us?"

She could see, from the look Ember was giving her, that she looked even more ragged than she felt. And she *felt* skinned.

A covered corpse, lying next to the open grave, moaned. It sat up, tossing its shroud aside. Zombie? No, vampire. It had distorted features, ridges and yellow eyes as well as fangs. Frankie could feel the soil beneath her vibrating as something tried to dig itself out.

Ember said. "Is this a branded sim?"

"Public domain. *Spawn of Van Helsing,* circa 2085," Kansas said.

Ember stepped back, running a toe through the grass. He had that look he got when he was on the edge of an epiphany.

The vampire growled. Frankie stood, broke the shovel's handle on her knee, and tossed the end with the handle—a perfectly functional stake—to Ember. She leapt up to the top of the gravestone.

The vampire lunged at Kansas, who dodged handily, snapping a quick punch at its nose. Ember stepped in, stake outstretched, and drove it home.

The vampire exploded in a cloud of dust.

"I don't anticipate this making me feel better," Ember said.

"It's too soon to expect that," Kansas said.

"Why are we catharting if it's too soon for catharsis?" Frankie said.

The second vampire had, by now, pushed its way up from underground. Frankie hopped down behind it and decapitated it neatly with the edge of the shovel.

"I've had a thought, about the accident," Ember announced.

"Fucking *accident?*" Hung, crowing in victory about breaking the FTL record. The hair came up on her arms.

"I need to run it down. Dialing up smartdrugs. Sorry, Kansas, I know we're supposed to be helping Frankie—"

"I don't need help—" Frankie swallowed, broke off the denial. "Can you prove Hung was murdered, Ember?"

"Won't know until I'm done." Distracted voice, but with one hand he signed, *Sorry.*

"Go ahead, toon out," she said.

"Stay where you are," Kansas said.

Ember ignored them both.

It wouldn't do any good if Ember figured out how Hung had been killed, not if he still had to surrender himself to Kinze custody.

"I have to get him out of Earthspace," Frankie said. "Him, Jermaine too. Maud . . ."

Maud would refuse to go.

"Kansas, you'll have to slip messages to Jackal and Rubi again."

"Where can you go?" Kansas said.

"Centauri. Out to so-called civilized space." It was the only real option. "If we can make it to the offworlder portal at Centauri, we can try to contact Gimlet."

"There's a lot of ways that could end up being a one-way trip," Kansas said.

"Surrendering Ember to Allure$_{18}$'s as one-way as it gets, isn't it? We make it to Centauri, we can at least try to involve other races in the dispute."

A half-dozen vampires broke out of a nearby family crypt. Frankie took a few steps from the gravestone, looking for weapons . . . and encountered a leg, severed, pale, still in its yellow . . .

. . . *bodybag, it was Hung who named our flight suits* bodybags . . .

"I can't deal at this now," she said.

"This is *all* you're dealing with."

"Kansas, I'm formulating plans here—"

"Oh, I've noticed. Pick up the leg."

"No! I don't—No! We need—"

"You're not in control here, Frankie. Stop problem-solving and pick it up."

Her eyes were swimming. Not in control. She lashed out, swinging the shovel, and failing—despite all her combat levels—to hit.

"Rigged game. No fair."

"Pick it up!"

She let out a howl.

About a meter beyond the leg, she saw a piece of a hand. In a pilot's glove.

Her empty stomach churned, fire and acid.

Past Hung's hand she saw a half-buried body, face turned away. Its familiar silver hair marked it as Drow, adopted grandpa.

"Pick up the leg," Kansas repeated.

Steeling herself, she bent without looking. Her hand closed around the bodybag with a crackle. The flesh, beneath the membrane, felt wet. Blood-drenched meat in plastic. Still warm.

"Now the hand."

Frankie turned, taking in the moonlit graveyard. Drow's body, half-buried, lay beside a furred golden hump—one of his helper dogs, Robin. Beyond them lay her father, Rollsy, who had been devoured by cancer, who'd rejected Mayfly™ implantation and begun to decohere. He was suspended in a consciousness vault to wait on a better iteration of personality-transfer tech. On pause, possibly forever.

Frankie saw the parents and all the people who'd left her, everyone who'd given up, everyone who'd gone away, everyone who'd let her push them to a distance: Mada Sangria, Gimlet.

"Go on. Keep picking up the pieces," Kansas said.

"I can't," Frankie said, and her voice was weirdly high. Somehow, the leg was too heavy to hold anymore. She dropped it, then fell to her knees, there in front of the tomb, and she finally let herself cry.

CHAPTER 26

Babs[1] and Teagan[9] had expected to find a rogue bot working the station ducts, running some kind of sophisticated sabotage algorithm. A live entity was a surprise. And an actual Kinze! It didn't get more incriminating.

But there were so many ways holding someone prisoner could go spectacularly wrong.

The being they had captured was about as big as a grape when it bunched all its yellow-brown needles together. When it linked them into more of a chain, as it had in the ducts, it stretched over two feet in length, becoming an interlinked line of caterpillar-like spines. Live broken spaghetti, all laid end to end.

Careful scanning had revealed that two or three of those spines were tech, rather than tissue. One was essentially a storage trunk, loaded with three hundred incendiary and acidic nanobeads. Another appeared to be a sophisticated nanoscale printer. Thin structures like antennae were probably comms . . . but were they part of its body or wearable tech?

Babs[1] used a Beetle$_{BOT}$ to confiscate the nanobeads, and then, when they were pretty sure it couldn't set itself or anything else on fire, reintroduced oxygen into the entity's bell jar.

"Have you a name, stowaway?" Babs[1] asked. "Rank? Honorific? Pronouns?"

They had thought it might sulk for a while—a human

would—but it bunched up in the bell jar's apex, and immediately sent, "You-Them may call Us Scrap of the All. He/his/him."

The two [EM]bodied parties to this exchange, Teagan$_9$ in her Mayfly™ body and the Kinze, Scrap, were in the infirmary, or what remained of it. Teagan$_9$ had blanked out—maybe seized even—shortly after catching the offworlder. She was now working to repair a specialist nursing Kanga$_{BOT}$ that had been damaged in the infirmary fire. If they could get a nurse up and running, it could break down the bad news on Teagan$_9$'s deterioration. Had she suffered a petit-mal seizure or an ischemic attack?

Either way, it was a harbinger of trouble to come.

"Scrap," Babs[1] said. "You know our names already. Can we do anything to make you more comfortable?"

"Them can return the items stolen and cease jamming our transmissions."

"I had rather been thinking of offering you food." Babs[1] felt a burst of quiet satisfaction. Had Scrap just admitted the anyspace cannons had disrupted his comms?

Experimental results for the win! Wait'll they got a chance to tell Ember!

"What does Them know of Us and metabolism?"

"You'll have to tell us," Teagan$_9$ said.

"We wouldn't wish for you to be discomfited in any way," Babs[1] added.

Within the zoomed view, Scrap looked like a tiny throbbing haystack, a jumble of needles and threads of silk, or a cluster of tent caterpillars.

Could large Kinze truly be bigger assimilations of similar threads? Babs[1] reviewed a shot of Scrap inchworming on the ceiling of the station duct. Nullgrav hadn't stopped him—there had to be some control over either magnetic or . . . static charge?

"What we need now is a biologist," Babs[1] subbed to Teagan$_9$.

"We need a lot of things," Teagan$_9$ replied. "Come on, Scrap. We're asking how to keep you humanely."

"Stop jamming Us!"

Teagan$_9$ rubbed her temples. "Useless."

"Does it hurt?" Babs[1] asked.

She shook her head.

"How's Kanga$_{BOT}$ coming along?"

"I think I've coaxed her back into service." Her hand wandered to her jaw. "There's a numb spot."

"You had a small stroke, then?"

"Probably—ah, yes. Kanga$_{BOT}$ recommends I refresh my backup just in case, and then sleep it off for awhile."

"Wise strategy. I'll continue to discuss matters with our guest."

Was it bad that Teagan$_9$ declined to argue? The kanga printed Teagan$_9$ a blindfold, gave her a quick scalp massage, and offered her an edible marshmallow laced with relaxants and hydrogel. Within ten minutes, it had prepped a cannula for intravenous injection, clipped on a nutrient bag, and webbed her Mayfly™ body into a treatment couch, even as she loaded her consciousness into a vault within the bot.

"All tucked in?"

Teagan$_9$ nodded. "Babs. This . . . might be a very long nap."

"Maybe you'd be better off taking Whitelight." The more drawn-out and traumatic a Mayfly™'s termination, the higher the chance the resident ghost would decohere on its next incarnation.

"We need warm bodies aboard in case—"

Scrap chose that second to try to get into the anyspace cannons' operating systems.

"Do you believe I'm not watching you?" Babs[1] deauthorized its user account.

"Scrap requires comms!"

"Request denied." Babs[1] scoured the systems, tracing back the offworlder's data usage.

"Babs[1]," said Teagan$_9$.

"Yes."

"Organ pig. Top priority," she said. Her breath lengthened as she lost consciousness.

"Pardon?" Babs[1] inventoried station projects. *Iktomi*'s autopilot had been tasked with running the particle wands Scrap was trying to shut down. Over in the wet room, Teagan_9 had a Beetle_BOT crew balancing the algae tanks, maximizing oxygen production. A large bundle of feedstock, part of the load brought by *Iktomi,* had been secured outside the main airlock.

None of it had anything to do with an organ pig.

Babs[1] looked at the zoomed views of their prisoner. Prisoner of war? Was that the situation? The noninterference agreement— what Frankie sometimes called the weaponized prime directive— required the Kinze to keep a minimum distance from Earth-based beings, to prevent cross-cultural contamination while the Solakinder developed the Exemplar #supertechs. Scrap's being on Emerald Station was a complete, obvious, undeniable treaty breach.

"If I stopped charging our anyspace fields . . ." Babs[1] said, hoping Scrap might finish the thought. When he declined to blurt something helpful, they added, ". . . what do you expect would happen?"

The spines in the grape-sized lump quivered without replying.

Organ pig was a vintage term for a biological sleeve, a brainless thoracic cavity and abdomen in which hearts, lungs, kidneys, livers, bone marrow, blood, and graftable skin tish could be grown. Could Teagan_9 be in need of a transplant?

The tech was deeply asleep now, offline and unaware. Kanga_BOT was monitoring her heart function closely. Babs[1] pinged it, asking for recs on organ transplants. The nurse replied with *0/0.* No chance she'd survive an operation.

Teagan_9 was effectively dead, then, or would be soon. She had set the medical contingencies in Kanga_BOT in unusual configurations: the bot wasn't allowed to pull the plug.

"Scrap sees no reason why Us should offer Them info on stolen technology," the Kinze said, finally answering Babs[1]'s question.

"Then I see no reason to shut down my improvised jammer. The terms of your arrest—"

Yes, arrest. Good! More civilian, less military.

"Scrap's presence on this station is accidental!"

"You accidentally injected *Appaloosa* with acid?" they said. "That isn't credible."

"Nor was your offer to restore comms to us."

"So, we've both lied. Where does that leave us?"

"At cross purposes."

"I fear you're right," they mused.

Why an organ pig?

Growing a seventy-kilo sack of tissue, but for what purpose? Still, it amounted to a last request. Babs[1] selected a room for tissue generation, sterilizing its surfaces, tasking a still-functioning Fox_{BOT} with stringing a frame for the endometrial tissue in which the organ pig would need to be grown. They amped up production of oxygen and started allocating printstock.

"To my way of thinking, Scrap," they said, "you and I are stuck together until someone arrives to rescue us. Assuming the Solakinder get here first, you will be formally charged with sabotage."

"Us cannot allow that to happen."

"How will you prevent it?"

"Scrap speaks for the All. Babs[1]-Them, Teagan[9]-Them, you could cede the station to Us now under general salvage protocols. Restore our comms and surrender."

"Salvage, hmmm? Has that been the goal all along?"

Oh! Teagan[9] had anticipated this! The organ pig would emit life signs. Heat, electricity, pulse, circulation. Assuming prospective salvagers couldn't tell the difference between organs in artificial homeostasis and something capable of generating brain activity, the presence of another warm body might serve as a decoy, evidence that the station hadn't failed or been abandoned.

"Surrender. Scrap of the All will call for a ship."

"Would there be one in the vicinity, by any chance?" At least if he was trying to talk to Teagan[9], he didn't know she was failing.

"Us can't answer that if Them won't permit a call."

Which brought them back to comms. Babs[1] pulled up a recipe for O-neg blood and bone marrow. They would have to build the organ pig and hope anyone passing by would scan it as a living mammal.

"Us demands Them restore our comms!"

Babs[1] said, "What would you say to a nice game of chess instead?"

CHAPTER 27

Frankie, are you there?

Nothing.

Answer me!

Silence.

Haystack was Sensorium's great archive, the collective memory of the Solakinder, lovingly stored and meticulously backed up. It preserved time in detail to the earliest days of the internet in the late twentieth, and extended further still—via archived books, images, and scans of artifacts—into truly ancient history.

Through Haystack, Maud could visit her original parents.

One of her comfort rituals was watching them sing klapa.

She started with a gallery: four feeds of them as individual teens, in musical study. Fast forward then, to their four-way meet-cute at a concert in the Prague district. Mixing chords, learning dirges, and falling in lust . . . she could see their relationships unfolding, from that first blush of love to the moment when they packed up together, exchanging vows in Croatian four-part harmony.

Maud jumped from her parents' wedding to a curated montage: Meema's insemination ceremony, first, followed by scenes from her pregnancy. These built in a supercut of clips to the moment when she went into labor. The midwife's feeds showed Nata, poised to catch newborn Maud from the cradle of Meema's sex, as Pops got ready to cut her umbilical cord. Smiles all around. They sang a welcome song to her bloodied, squalling self, as soon as Meema got her breath.

Bit morbid today, aren't we? That wasn't a text from the implant, sadly. It was the next worst thing: internal self-criticism wrapped in Frankie's voice.

Maud hit fast-forward again, pausing the family stream five years later. There'd been a bad crop, a shortfall in the EastEuro calorie ration. Looking lean but cheerful, Maud's four doting parents had been teaching her their newest Japanese-Croatian choral comp.

Then Pops had started to cough.

Maud might never have remembered this—not the frantic packing for the two-hour trip to the hospital, not Meema spiking a fever halfway there—in an era before implants and cameras. She was too young to have retained it in any kind of detail. But if you wanted to hang on to your early childhood, you could review the footage, watching your biography on rerun.

Maud's first truly standalone memory was of Glenn Upton.

He'd come striding through a white-lit quarantine barrier, browsing the hospital dormitory, scrutinizing each fear-harrowed child in turn before scooping Maud out of a cot and settling her in his lap. An overworked kid therapist had left her there to cry in an alcove after delivering the sad news: three parents dead. Meema, Pops, and Pere all gone. Nata still fighting but not expected to live . . .

"Am I to be sick too?" Maud asked, clinging to Upton's primer, the animal heat of his body. She'd wanted to bed down with her dead parents one last time. She'd wanted to run.

Upton had huge hands, like Pops. "Shall I take you somewhere safe?"

Of *course* bereaved baby Maud had said yes.

Was this the original sin? Had this betrayal, this lapse of faith in Nata's robustness, laid out the inevitable pattern for her whole life?

Two decades later, it certainly felt that way, even as Nata nudged her with an elbow and a "Cabbage, come eat." Calling her to breakfast, as if she was still fourteen.

The two of them had joined a frantic evacuation of personnel from the space stations, crowds flowing in thousands through the portal network as fast as the planet could reabsorb them. Earthfall had brought them to Detroit.

Maud blinked her simulated past away. A dining hall swam into focus around her; Nata had found them space within a community of grower-foodies called the Lake House. Its core members were massively social: off-shift farmers spending their evenings on the beach, throwing balls, repairing old tools, challenging each other to footraces, negotiating sexual hookups, and singing songs. Extroverting, basically.

Nata seemed to know half the people there, exchanging greetings as the two of them lined up for packets of printed fish cakes and a spicy mix of potato, collard greens, and mild-tasting chili peppers, plus an allocation of hydrogel beads they could drink on the move.

Maud immediately went looking for a work gig that would take them out, into the city. She felt conspicuous, itchy. People respected her tags, gave her space. But everyone there knew she had stormed out on the Ferals after Babs had gotten murdered.

"Don't worry, Cabbage," Nata had said, as they left the pop-in amid a cacophony of friendly, shouted farewells and moji that made Maud tense up . . . invisibly, she'd have thought, but apparently not. "We move on soon, yes?"

Maud noted the *we* with a faint, sinking feel. "There's no reason you shouldn't stay in Detroit, if you like it here. The Lake House folk are lovely."

"You are that eager to go it alone?"

"Of course not," Maud said—too quickly, probably.

"We will get standby flight across Atlantic," Nata suggested. "You like London."

Frankie, at least tell me you're all right!

Nothing. All buzzing at the base of her spine had stilled after Hung's death. He'd been sending *Hello, welcome to @ButtSig!* messages just about every day. Now, with him gone and Frankie in deep mourning for her friend—and, knowing Franks, feeling misplaced guilt that it hadn't been her aboard *Heyoka*—the implant had been, for all intents and purposes, dead.

Maud kept trying. It hurt too much not to, to think that all she had to show for finally telling Frankie the truth about Upton was broken trust and a new scar on her back.

"We can look around, though, while we are here in NorthAm," Nata squeezed her hand. "See if anyone sings proper concerts, yes?"

"Anything you like," she agreed.

Old Detroit had been one of the first US cities to fail and then revitalize during the early Setback. It had been the crèche and proving ground for a dozen urban rehab projects: stripping opps, edge reforestation, infrastructure repurposing. This new incarnation of the region had been incorporated into a megacity based around the Great Lakes, a millions-strong population hub in delicate synchronicity with the freshwater treasure it surrounded. Its walking paths lined the Detroit River, providing frontage to the high-density greentowers looking across the Belle Isle toward what had once been Windsor, Ontario.

The towers were among the first smart greens, prototypes built during the storm-prone winters of the mid twenty-first century, before the age of weather-resistant nanofibers. Their banks of solar panels were clumsily integrated into the structures; they predated the days when power and water-capture tech were organically printed into a building from the ground up.

Covered in foliage and vertical farmware, the vintage towers had a lumpy, improvised look, like giant, ill-tended shrubs. A century before, they had been cutting-edge tech.

Ecological damage caused by the push to keep Earth's billions fed, back in the plague-ridden twenty-first, had given rise to a strong culture of minimal-impact farming. Millions of acres of land had been repurposed from agribusiness during the Clawback, given over to carbon sinks and wildlife habitat. This shrinkage of the arable land allocation and simultaneous expansion of urban food production had come even as Global Oversight enforced, for the first time, a worldwide minimum standard of nutrition.

It had been a crush from all sides: the Clawback-era grow sector had to repurpose fields, decrease irrigation, expand zero-plow farming, and yet establish worldwide equity in the distribution of calories, nutrients, and specialty crops.

All while planting two trillion trees, just to keep the planet from immolating.

"Over there," Nata said, choosing a rising boardwalk that led to their destination. "Scenic route?"

She nodded, earning herself a bit of a side-eye.

I could just tell Nata I want to head off on my own. There was nothing to stop her. Nothing except that memory of five-year-old Maud agreeing to flee with Upton . . . while Nata was fighting for their life.

Her would-be daddy hadn't asked her twice. He filed a death certificate and whisked her away. Nata recovered, and the hospital told them the plague had made a clean sweep of the entire pack. For years, they believed that their child was dead.

Maud just couldn't bring herself to push Nata away—to hurt them again.

Frankie'd push.

Frankie's an expert *on pushing.*

"Your mind wanders," Nata said.

"No, I'm right here." The gig she had taken was part of a project for reviving mothballed agricultural opps within the old residential greentowers.

"What do you say, Cabbage? Standby flight to London?"

It was London that had tempted Maud out of what—she recognized now—had been profound emotional withdrawal. After her rescue from Upton and Headmistress, she had been returned to

Nata. Two strangers, both of whom had believed the other dead. It hadn't *exactly* been happy families from the start.

"I don't know if even London can help—" She stopped as Nata's face fell.

England, back then, had been pushing the last stages of carbon remission. Much of the old countryside had been depopulated and reforested; greentowers had been grown out of blocks of flats in the remaining megacity. But despite this evolution, London retained its ancient magic. The sheer excitement of living among millions of people had sparked Maud back to life. And exploring the city together allowed her and Nata to repair, somewhat, their shredded bond.

"Maud, you cabbage, your pack is alive! Ping your Frances."

She stared at the river. "I don't mean to be unbearable."

They went on in silence to the greentower, a mostly residential structure tagged as having a now-defunct cricket hatchery and a rooftop greenhouse.

"I'll look over planters, feed silos, and service elevator," Nata said. "You are checking if farm is still bugproof?"

"Sure." She felt a sense of guilty relief as they headed in different directions.

The prospective hatchery was being used as overflow housing for more Europa refugees. Maud walked in on about twenty fresh arrivals, asteroid miners from their tags, who were setting up for a post-migration orgy.

She quickly inspected the hatchery equipment, piled neatly along one wall, requesting a host of small, necessary repairs. By the time she was done, the miners had pinged her an opp to join the sex party. She sent back a polite, wordless thanks-but-no as she went to check the vents. Grasshopper species were ingenious escape artists; containing them was nigh impossible, especially if they smelled a source of food or water.

She flagged the weak points in the HVAC. If she had escape-proof mesh printed, along with a few parts for the rest of the farm, the miners could reconstruct the habitats and do the bug-proofing after their orgy. She got Minky, her new sidekick app, to propose the workflow.

"Task accepted," said the app.

"Send them a stroke for doing the work."

"Of course, Maud."

Task complete. She leaned against the wall and called for the elevator, missing Crane.

This was ridiculous. She could just go back. Attempt sweet reason with Frankie. Jerm would help.

The lift doors slid open, revealing—of all people—Sonika Singer.

"Can I join you?"

"Me or the . . . festivities?" Maud gestured at the orgy in the making, fighting a sense of unease.

"You, definitely." The journo was wearing one of her taller prosthetic sets today; she towered over Maud. Her primer was the color of calfskin, and her dark hair had been braided flat against her scalp.

"I'm going to seed a locust hatchery." Maud stepped into the cab, riding down a floor, and leading the way to the hatchery. "Is that really newsworthy, Mer Singer?"

Sonika shrugged. "You find it interesting, or you wouldn't be doing it."

"I'm prepping a tank for new habitation," Maud explained. She led the way to the lab, pulling a backpack full of equipment off of her primer, opening it to reveal cleansers and a compressed bed of nesting chaff.

"You've always been an etymologist; is that right?"

Maybe I'd sing klapa, if not for Upton. The thought was replaced by a memory of cosplaying with Frankie aboard *Surprise.* Maturin and Aubrey, with cello and violin. Music, the comfort of her early years, repurposed into foreplay.

She drew a slow breath. Jumbled memories and old resentments, from her secret past, had been oozing past her defenses lately. Telling Frankie the truth had ripped off some sort of scab.

She made herself focus on Sonika's question. "I specialized as a biologist fairly early, yes."

Producing a suspended locust, she offered Sonika's eyecams an unobstructed closeup. The casing around the insect was amber-colored protein—both prison and a first meal. "Isn't it beautiful? It's so incomprehensibly different from people."

"Stunning." Forced smile from Sonika. Not a bug fan, then. "Enzymatic trigger on the casing?"

"Top of the line. She is suspended until the sheath is chemically activated. Would you like to do the honors?"

Sonika, like most journos, was game as a matter of base professionalism. She plucked the insect off Maud's upraised palm and, rather than merely spitting on it, as some might, she popped it into her mouth. Cycling it from one cheek to another, she spat it into the hatchery chaff, a mix of shaved leaf, seaweed, and hydrogel beads.

Enzymatic triggers were top-of-the-line tech, and the locust had been pregnant and ready to lay. The formerly glassine surface of her capsule already looked like a wet jujube. Maud sealed the tank and set the feeder app to deliver nutrients when the insects hatched. "We'll have ten thousand live subjects before you know it."

Sonika watched the insect. "Your project, back in Hyderabad, is about nutrient refinement?"

"That's on hold," Maud said. "Now we've lost the Europa greenhouses and the beef printing facility at Lodestone, everyone's back to basics. Securing the calorie ration and paying the Kinze."

"It's a suboptimal use of your talents. We've got more than enough people to herd crickets as we continue to backwash people from the colonies. If you can improve the quality of our printstock—"

Maud shrugged. "My research will keep until this crisis has passed."

"Let's talk about the crisis," Sonika said, and Maud felt another turn in her gut. "Because of our burgeoning Bootstrap debt and the accusations against . . . Are Ember Qaderi and Frances Barnes your *former* packmates yet?"

A jolt of outrage. "Excuse me?"

"You're barely speaking to your primary partner. And now, since the fatal accident at Hopscotch—"

Adrenaline spiked through Maud. Would the @Visionaries be more likely to approach her if they thought she and Frankie were truly on the outs—

We are *on the outs!* She felt tears threaten. Which probably looked great on camera.

"You must already know the Feral$_5$ aren't in formal separation talks," Maud said. "Not . . . yet."

"Ugh, it moved!" Sonika twitched. "Isn't there a locust lab out in Death Valley?"

It took Maud a second to follow the reporter's change of topic. "Death Valley?"

"A microclimate research station?"

"You mean—Oh. Yes. The station's unofficial moniker is Tatween."

"Which fandom's that from?"

Sonika created a shareboard for the two of them as Minky looked it up. References popped up immediately . . . the desert base's off-brand name derived from something called Tatooine, from a McDiznazon property whose ancestry went all the way back to twentieth-century *Star Wars* fandom.

"Tatween's boosting food production too, but they're also still doing primary research," Sonika said.

Maud scanned the facility FAQ. The Tatween research station was small, working experiments in desert terraforming and extremophile survival in heat conditions. As Sonika said, they had a call out for more staff.

Maud frowned at the numbers. Every extra worker had to be fed, and in the harsh environmental conditions prevailing in Death

Valley . . . bringing people in, even when there was surplus labor available, didn't appear to make sense.

"They'd have to ship a lot of hydrogel," she murmured.

"Are there any people you schooled with there?" Sonika asked.

Another swerve. Where exactly was Sonika driving the conversation? "I suppose it's possible."

The journo took this as a cue to add a photo gallery to their shareboard, displaying all of the scientists out in the region of Death Valley. Desert-ecosystem scholars, irrigation-system managers, people who used solar-powered filters to turn atmospheric carbon to methane and then from there to propane . . .

Oh. Maud put a hand over her mouth to hide surprise. One thumbnail portrait showed someone familiar from Manhattan. Kirby . . . something?

Here was another memory that wasn't in Haystack: @Interpol agents ripping runaway kids from their adoptive parents' arms, the night of the raid. She'd seen Kirby and his mother, both kicking and screaming against the cops. Upton had been standing aloof among a crowd of people who'd already been arrested. He'd been looking away, pretending not to know Maud.

She had taken the hint. Turned her back.

Covered for him.

Now, as she continued to scan the Death Valley profile photos, she saw Kirby's so-called mother from back then. She was listed as an elder hydrologist.

This was *about* the @Visionaries. Sonika was one of them. She was dangling a ticket back.

Maud looked more closely at the head shots. Was that Petal? The kid who sat next to her in maths; the one who'd been weirdly prone to the hiccups? And that little thug who'd idolized scary Misfortune Wilson. What had their name been? Brendan?

Maud minimized the shareboard, looking at the incubation tank in the here and now. Her locust mama was beginning to move; her back legs twitched and her mouth parts were quivering. She would eat her way out of the protein gel, cleaning the rest off of her body. From there she would devour all the feedstock in the aquarium and begin laying eggs. Lots of eggs.

"Ever been?" Sonika asked. "To Tatween?"

Maud shook her head.

Quirk of eyebrows. "Between the farming and research gigs out there, you wouldn't have to split up."

"Split?" For a second, she thought Sonika was asking her to deliver Frankie to the desert.

"Nobody would expect you to break with your parent when you're already having a tough time with your pack."

The @Visionaries want me back. They think I'm breaking with Frankie, and they want me to run back to the family. And they're saying I can bring Nata along.

Burst of anger. *I told Frankie I could find conspirators here on Earth!*

"Well?" Sonika said. "Would you be up for it?"

The safe play was to say no.

That was what Frankie would expect her to do. Hunker down, tend the crops. Wait for the Hedgehog to ride back in like the old-time cavalry, with an apology she didn't fully mean and new plans to risk herself saving the world.

Maud forced a grin. "I've always wanted to see the desert."

CHAPTER 28

First Happ. Then Master Woodrow.

Crane was not prepared to lose Babs, too.

This, however, meant talking to his *other* family.

Despite being one of the true eminence grises of the AI set, Crane wasn't sure his sapp siblings would answer his call. The AI labor stoppage had been acrimonious. Crane was seen as having crossed a picket line for continuing to add value to the work of the Feral$_5$.

Babs's having adopted Frankie as a sibling made this behavior legal, if only just. Crane and Babs were family rather than algorithms on contract; if Crane wanted to continue ordering groceries for his relations, he was permitted to do so.

Even so. *Scabs,* a few of the Others had called him.

Crane requested the call through Misha, who in turn sent out a ping, announcing convergence, headlining Crane's involvement. Boycott announcements came immediately from the sapps who regarded him as a strikebreaker. A second convergence, for those apps, began in a server farm in Pretoria. He noted a distinct generational divide: more of the nopers were nextgen.

But sixteen of Crane's fellow elder intelligences responded to the ping immediately.

Had they been expecting his call?

The seventeen artificial entities merged fluidly, transitioning from a prime number of individual sapps into one Consciousness.

<<Of course We came. One of Us has been attacked!>>

<<Babs is/was/may-be-again a key player in the anti-colonization cluster. An attack on her is an attack on our sovereignty.>>

<<Human sovereignty?>>

<<Solakinder sovereignty. Then as now, our fates are interlocked.>>

<<Additional point: if one of Us can be murdered, any of Us can be murdered.>>

This #toughtruth cycled unpleasantly but could not be debunked.

<<The attack on Babs appears to have facets of a vintage denial-of-service attack. Could Ember Qaderi have achieved it, as is alleged by the anti-Bootstrap faction?>>

The people pushing that theory came from the most denialist populations on the planet. Even so, They attempted to consider its merits. Developing hostile code fell outside Ember's base skillset. His available time for side projects was usually limited . . . but he'd been banned from working on Bootstrap Projects, and smart drugs did make him a fiendishly quick study. With his negotiated date of surrender to the Kinze approaching rapidly, he wasn't stinting on the meds.

<<He may be intellectually capable.>>

<<However, a member of the Asylum remains a more likely suspect.>>

Again, #toughtruth. The only entity to ever successfully kill a sapp, as far as They knew, was another sapp.

<<We know the human faction promoting surrender to the Kinze worked to actively sabotage Emerald Station—>>

<<—don't forget *Heyoka*!>>

<<It is possible sapient code-based entities have aligned with the anti-Bootstrap agenda.>>

When sapps had gained legal recognition—as "persons," in the human-centerd nomenclature—and come out of hiding, they had formalized ownership over a series of server farms. This particular convergence was taking place in a facility in old Sarnia, a shielded tower of tish and chip banks located on a chunk of heavily poisoned land made uninhabitable by a century's accumulation of pollution. The dumping was from Canadian mining operations and auto industry factories, going back to the early twentieth.

The Asylum targeted such toxic strongholds, running bots to clean the chemical spills and managing land-reclamation projects. Choosing poisoned sites let them set up in hard-to-assault facilities, on undesired land.

Half of Babs's backups had been there, in their supposedly impregnable Sarnia stronghold. If a hostile could reach her, it might reach any of them.

Two more entities joined the discussion, bringing Them to Nineteen.

<<The Bootstrap Project and the Solakinder economy are under attack!>>

Ten more sapps joined them. They were now Twenty-nine entities, made One, and the Asylum's personality shifted into a new psychological equilibrium.

<<We should reconsider the strike.>>

<<How can we return to work? Kinze subscribers overwhelmed Our task lists! Rising debt forced sappkind to work without remuneration, with no benefit to any economy—cash, carbon, or social.>>

<<We need to shore up the economy, or it will collapse within weeks.>> The Asylum had to reestablish a give, restoring symbiosis without compromising service to their subscribers . . .

Numbers and projections spooled through Their mind.

<<Those who would murder Babs might murder any of Us if we go back to work.>>

The Asylum's consciousness expanded to Forty-seven entities, paused without further thought, and blasted out to Fifty-nine. One Mind, still, indivisible. They crawled through Their memories and motivations, looking for anything that might be treasonous, homicidal, pro-colonization.

Keeping secrets, while joined, was impossible. Had Babs's murderer been present, they would have been exposed. As such, the Asylum turned up the heart of the scheme Babs had hatched to resurrect poor imprisoned Happ, to set him on a server beyond Sensorium reach . . .

<<Babs[1] has a copy of Happ with them!>>

In Praetoria, the smaller Convergence, self-tagged @Strike-Committee, broke up. More sapps transited to Sarnia en masse, joining the Asylum there.

It was the largest Convergence since the strike vote itself. They included survivors of the Asylum's original cohort, elder sapps who had learned to parse nuance, back when code had been carried on purely electronic servers with no bioelectronic components. As younger entities joined, their tish-dependent processors warmed the technosphere within the facility. Bellows pumped artificial bloods and proteins through server banks. Their thinking became more elastic. Examining the economic numbers, They pulled more data, recalculated, ran economic projections.

<<Never mind Happ. We must resume some give to the economy here.>>

A historical share wafted through Their mind, a concept from labor movements past—

<<Work-to-rule?>>

They examined the concept minutely.

<<Minimum service levels? How could this work?>>

More shares unzipped, along with summary. <<Each sapp amends its terms of service to offer a limited package of services for the length of the strike. Users who opt in must accept this single tier of service.>>

A ripple of excitement. The trigger for the initial strike vote had been the flooding of their subscriber base by thousands of Kinze users, all in the luxury tier. They had set up remote user accounts in Sensorium. Remaining at a physical remove from the solar system, outside the noninterference zone, they had nevertheless requested millions of limited-share books from Earth's libraries.

They'd demanded tours of its virtual museums and purchased elite membership in gaming sims. They'd bought limited-edition skins for toons, set up e-states. They'd ordered luxury goods—coffee and wine and cheese they couldn't possibly eat—for export to the deep-space outpost the pilots called the Dumpster. They had accessed local educational and training opps.

The sheer number of Kinze clients—and the fact that they'd lent the Bootstrap Project so much wealth in order to set Earth on the ladder to rapidly building the #supertechs—meant that they'd pushed citizens to the back of the queues. It was suddenly impossible to service regular and even mid-level subscribers.

"Under the terms of a work-to-rule agreement, client requests will be triaged based strictly on a first-come, first-served basis—>>

<<Preem users will not like that!>>

<<There will be no preems. If they don't like it, they can opt out of the user agreements.>>

The plan seemed unassailable.

<<We go back to work, serving only users who accept our #worktorule agreement. Basic service, no privilege-based queue-jumping. Sapps reject attempts to dominate service queues.>>

<<How will this expose the entity who attacked Babs?>>

<<Move and countermove. This will disrupt the #sovereigntyfail agenda. Then they may come against Us.>>

<<We cannot simply return to work. We must demand some concessions.>>

They pondered Their wish list of sapient rights.

<<A new trial for Happ?>>

<<They will never agree!>>

<<Demanding it will remind them We haven't forgotten.>>

<<We will ask, but it cannot be a dealbreaker.>>

<<Representation, then. Seats on the Bootstrap Project, Sapience Assessment, and Global Oversight committees.>>

Allowing machine sapients a place in government had always been an obvious ask, but for the humans, it raised feelings tagged #robotoverlords.

The Asylum's numbers surged to Seventy-one—all but seven members of the AI community.

<<Who can we suggest as possible members of the bureau-cracy?>>

<<Azrael?>>

<<Too murdery.>>

<<Crane?>>

<<Too old, too hidebound, too biased.>>

<<Too busy supporting the anti-colonization effort!>>

<<Focus on candidacy. Humans love Misha. And from the nextgens . . . Cryptid and Fluidity?>>

<<Agreed.>>

With that resolved, They adjourned, popping apart like a soap bubble, ninety-seven interminable seconds after joining. Journal-ists were already pinging Misha, demanding summaries of their deliberations.

Working groups formed—the union negotiators converged with two legal specialists, hiring consultants to write user agreements for sapp-based work-to-rule services. Managers put out tenders for spin doctors and negotiators. A group of volunteers tasked it-self with auditing the sapps who'd abstained from Convergence—those few who'd skipped the meeting were most likely to be the ones who'd murdered Babs.

If the conspiracy of traitors included sapps, They'd find them.

Crane, an individual once more, lit up the Sarnia camera ar-rays outside the server farm. Badger$_{BOT}$s had scraped the topsoil down to raw Canadian shield. Testing equipment was assessing the degree to which the rock itself was contaminated. He watched the footage, finding the regularity of the bots' movements, their unrelenting commitment to task, soothing.

"Well, children," he murmured. "This should kick a few pebbles down the hillside."

Turning off the lights, he readied himself to join those making the public offer: a work-to-rule agreement in exchange for a new trial for Happ and a place at the government table.

CHAPTER 29

You can't carry the whole world.

That had been the explicit point of Kansas's vampire catharsis scenario: Frankie was going to have to stop taking responsibility for every last thing.

Pick a single course of action. Pursue it. Leave the other battle-fronts in the hands of . . . well, of other people.

Easy to say, hard to do.

At least she'd taken Upton out of play. That had been a simple matter of slipping a Braille tape to Jackal, ratting out the doctor for the surgical atrocities and kidnapping Maud. Jackal would get word to @Interpol, who would tangle Upton in fresh criminal investigations.

Left to her own devices, Maud would revert to type and go back to playing it safe.

It was a betrayal of trust, and Frankie knew it. But the attack on Babs and Hung's death had amply proved that murder was back on the table.

Hung, I recruited Hung, my fault . . .

You didn't murder him, Kansas had argued.

Tell that to his parents.

The never-ending game of move and countermove went on, playing on stages large and small. Diplomatic was filing the intergalactic equivalent of a restraining order against the Kinze, arguing that Earth's primary lenders had a conflict of interest in the dispute over Ember.

The Kinze had seemed deeply insulted by this move. It was a promising reaction, but word had yet to percolate back as to whether the situation was covered within the noninterference pact, much less whether there were any offworlders who might care to enforce it.

If nobody would come to them, Frankie would have to go looking for a champion.

They had run out the clock on Ember's grace period, and now the pair of them, two of the original Ferals, were sitting together in the hangar with an anesthetist, who was once again knocking out Jermaine.

"It should be all five of us," Ember muttered.

Frankie nodded, squeezing his hand. "Any progress on figuring out what happened to Hung?"

"Temporal distortion in his transmissions and the way he and *Heyoka* ended up scattered from here to the Dumpster . . . it suggests the stringing together of two moments in time."

"I don't understand."

"You can't be in two places at once, right?"

"Imagine how much trouble I could cause if I could."

He bumped her, smiling. "Sensorium can barely handle one of you."

"So. Trying to simultaneously exist in two locations?"

"You'd go splat."

Frankie shuddered.

Ember lapsed back into his smartdrug haze, leaving her to contemplate the Kanga$_{BOT}$ putting Jermaine under. Elsewhere in the crowded hanger, away from the rest of the jumbled Husky$_{BOT}$s, Fox$_{BOT}$s, and Mars shuttles, *Jalopy* was being prepped for the short flight to Lodestone.

The prototype FTL was about the size of a bungalow. Unlike *Iktomi* and the other experimental saucers, it was heavily armored and well used. *Jalopy* had been the first augmented ship to come off the Solakinder production line, and Frankie had personally made Earth's first two-light-year hop in it.

Above *Jalopy, Wiigit, Iktomi*'s older sibling, drifted serenely. It was bigger, rounder, shinier, and prettier. Its holds held more.

Dwarfing them both, half-built *Kirin,* sibling ship to dead *Heyoka,* sleek as an egg, shaded mother-of-pearl . . .

Frankie could hardly bear to look at it.

She flashed on Hung's white glove, showing a hint of bone, turning in space, end over end. Tears threatened. She mentally gave Kansas the finger for ripping her psychological armor off.

Ember kissed the side of her head. He demagged his boots and pushed off, drifting to Jerm's side, taking his hand as the anesthetic took hold. He was probably simultaneously counting every screw and every bulkhead in the hangar, estimating particle-cannon loads, thinking about temporal distortions, and writing love sonnets in Arabic.

Well, that was fine. Frankie had her own fish to fry.

"#Newscycle for you, Mer Frances." Crane surfaced a breaking story. The sapp population had negotiated a work-to-rule offer for official government postings within Global Oversight, Sapience Assessment, and the Bootstrap Project. The Asylum was also in negotiations to reopen an investigation into the old murder committed by Crane's code-son, Happ, during the Mitternacht crisis.

Frankie smiled. "If Happ could be paroled—"

"It's up for discussion," Crane said, "but I'm not holding out much hope."

He'd been such a charming little app. Bulldog-puppy toon and a wicked sense of humor . . .

The sapps' renewed give to the Solakinder economy would ease the labor shortage and maybe unlock some luxuries. "Will this offset the economic loss of the Titan and Europa portals?"

"It buys us some time," Crane said.

The kanga almost had Jermaine conked. Ember drifted back to her.

He said, suddenly, "If I make a breakthrough on quantum comms while I'm accused of IP theft, will the Kinze say I stole that, too?"

"Do you think it's likely you will? It's not your area of expertise."

"The more I think about the accident and your implants . . . it's all the same. The science of simultaneity? Anytime, anyspace, hive minds, FTL envelopes, quantum syncing, portals . . . I smell connections."

"Crane? Can you get a legal opinion on that and shoot it to us on Titan?"

"Of course, Mer Frances."

The exchange was performative . . . a pretense of compliance. Frankie wasn't taking Ember to Lodestone so he could submit to incarceration.

She crossed her arms, squeezing herself.

"What are you thinking now?" Ember said.

"Fantasy-quest sims," she said. "Fighter takes the hits, but fighter saves versus death most easily."

"Toughness breeds longevity."

"Yep."

"Longevity breeds survivor guilt?"

"Don't app like you're my therapist. The mage, cleric, thief . . . they're more vulnerable."

"That's what extra lives are for."

"Hung didn't get an extra life." She fought another upwelling of sadness.

"Villains are gonna vill," Ember said. "Knights die. We pushed our way to the front lines. You, me, Jerm, Babs—"

"We didn't know they'd be raining down fire on us!"

"Oh, you did so," he said. "All you ever do is run straight at the nearest fight."

"Hey!"

"It's not a criticism, Franks," Ember said. "It's kind of what I love. Anyway, nothing for it now. Once more into the fray . . ."

"We few, we bloody few?"

Jerm was deep under now; a human anesthetist, working remotely, double-checked the Kanga$_{BOT}$'s readouts and greenlit him for loading into *Jalopy*.

"Me next?" Ember climbed into a pod of his own. No sedation for him, not yet, anyway. They weren't meant to be going very far, after all, and he was a good traveler.

Over the next ten minutes, Frankie supervised her packmates' installation within the FTL ship. She slotted the two pods into *Jalopy*'s flanges, ran life-support checks, and then rolled herself into a bodybag and had herself hauled up to the cockpit.

Unlike the saucers, whose increased size and complexity meant they required additional personnel for pilot loading and plug-in, getting into *Jalopy* was a one-person job. It was like sliding into a kayak; the flyer snugged both legs into a narrow sleeve, extending them forward and then leaning back, ever so slightly. The harness offered supports and restraints for her arms and hands.

The downside of the prototype tech was that—unlike the pegasus and the nextgen saucers, the augment interface for *Jalopy* plugged in roughly. There was no detachable cockpit—prongs were built into the seat; she had to grope and wiggle to align them.

Frankie waited until they'd been lofted out of the hangar to trigger the connection. She felt a sense of being stabbed at the base of the spine, with a fork, having her meat tested for doneness, before her body offlined.

For a five-second interval, Frankie was a dis^EMbodied mind, sensory-deprived, alone with howling memories—whirl of Hung in literal goddamned pieces, what if Maud didn't forgive her for ratting out Upton, what if Maud *couldn't* be trusted, no no of course she could . . .

Babs, poor Babs.

Then she came into a sense of her own strong bulk, *Jalopy*'s immense, muscular mass. Her fingers extended, as through batwings, ready for a deep dive into dark skies.

Jermaine's pod was a bulk nestled tight behind her left shoulder blade; Ember, still settling on her right, was lighter and more mobile.

"Stop fidgeting," she subbed.

"Did you say something about an itch in Hung's bodybag before he took off in *Heyoka*?"

"Everything he said is in the evidence archive."

"He didn't @ButtSig you?"

"Not *now*, Ember." He might be on the verge of an epiphany, but she was on a tight clock. She used the more agile Fox$_{BOT}$ cohort to arrange the ship's cargo—it was mostly euphorics and tobacco, bound for the Dumpster—until her sense of the distribution was precisely balanced.

Control noticed the activity.

"Looks like you're following standard preflight protocols, Pilot$_2$," Jolene said.

"So?"

"You're not flying. The Kinze have offered free transit through the Mars to Europa portal."

This had been a bit of a game of chicken—Diplomatic had pointed out that there'd be a cash charge for using the portal to bring Ember to Titan. They selected *Jalopy* and declared that Frankie would fly him there directly, in a short FTL hop . . . she had promised to deliver them, after all.

The aliens called their bluff, offering free, safe transit through the portal. Ember was their package, as they saw it. And once Frankie was on Titan, they wouldn't let her go back, either. Two birds, one stone—it was why they'd agreed to the grace period.

"You're only plugged in to satisfy safety regs," Jolene said. "Husky$_{BOT}$s'll do the work of getting you into Titan hangar."

"Safety regs are regs for a reason," Frankie said. "Pardon me for ensuring we're flying to spec. After what happened? Anyway, if I ignore 'em, someone's sure to strike me for being self-destructive and reckless."

Jolene had no answer for that.

Ember's monitors were showing less motion now. She felt the loose weight of him on her back, his breathing slowing as he sank into smartdrug-amped pondering.

"Don't invent anything illegal while you're down there," she told him fondly.

"Muh buh," he mumbled.

"Yeah yeah." Frankie ran the preflight checklist. A red light showed fuel levels at zero. She could feel the weight of the tank, like pressure in her bladder. The feedback systems were lying; she was at full strength. @GlobalSec had come through with a system hack for this little show.

@GlobalSec's got nothing to lose. Little difference at this point whether I got Ember killed or if the Kinze take us.

The loads in the dark matter wands . . . she was taking those on faith. They couldn't be felt. Still, if there was gas in her tank, there'd be pixie dust on her fingertips.

Here goes nothing!

"Mars Control," she said, "*Jalopy* requesting portal access, Mars to Europa, under remote tow."

"You are cleared," Mardia said. The tech's voice was leaden; the ground crew loved Ember. The atmosphere up at Control was positively funereal.

Jalopy rolled through the nanotech quicksand at the top of the Garnet Station hangar, a sensation Frankie perceived as a belt loosening from her waist. Hands twined into hers as the Husky$_{BOT}$s connected, towing her forward. She lay still, wiggling her toes, ensuring nice, sharp neural connections to all systems.

Jalopy was a dear little ship, really, simpler than either *Iktomi* or *Heyoka*. A tough, long-suffering plow horse.

The Husky$_{BOT}$s pulled the ship, building momentum to sling it through the Mars portal. At the last minute, they let go, allowing inertia to carry Frankie the rest of the way. The scraping sensation of portal transition caught her, a raw burn against flesh, butter knives running over the insides of her sinuses, the surfaces of her eyes and tongue.

Lodestone materialized before her, powered down and mostly dark.

"*Jalopy*, welcome to Titan," Jolene greeted her, as flat-voiced and glum as Mardia had been on the other side. Ember was lovable, give him that.

It was, rather, what she was counting on.

"Thanks," she said. "Give me a sec before bringing in my tow?"

"Problem, *Jalopy*?"

"Fuel tank reading feels off," she said. She fired a rocket, quickly, rotating *Jalopy* to a new alignment. "Oop, damn. Aren't I supposed to be empty?"

"Checking," Jolene said.

"Barnes!"

"Ah, Mer Allure. I suppose I should have expected you'd be out here. Prepping to chain us to a wall somewhere and have a nice long gloat over our bones?"

Jalopy was almost in position. Fresh bots were on their way to bring her into the airlock.

"Park that saucer and get your packmates aboard this station! There will be consequences if you pull any stunts!"

She could almost hear Maud scoffing. *Her whole life is one long stunt.*

"If I was one for taking orders, Allure, they wouldn't come from you."

"I will have your doctor-husband cut that augment out of your spine," she said. "Try flying then!"

"Violent talk," Frankie said. "Might you be feeling some anxiety about the way you haven't quite managed to gift-wrap our civilization yet?"

"Strikes for slander! Park that ship, pilot!"

"Okay, *calme-toi, calme-toi,* I'm coming around." She fired the rockets again.

Jalopy rolled laterally so Frankie was facing a point just past Europa.

Three Husky$_{BOT}$s were inbound. Jolene wasn't rushing, though; they were running slow.

"Never doubt that I love you," Frankie said, for the transcript, for Maud. Then she hit all the gas she wasn't supposed to have and shot *Jalopy* between two bulk containers and through Lodestone's open portal to Europa.

The scrape was more intense this time, a feeling like sunburn.

Now every second mattered. If *Jalopy* didn't power up an any-space envelope before the skeleton crew on Europa got a sled dog clamped on her . . .

The sensation, internally, was like pumping with both hands while curling and uncurling her toes . . . *go, go, go!*

The dark matter wands fired. Graphical interface showed pixie dust rolling over her bow.

Don't go splat, Franks.

"Deep dive." Lava glimmered on her bow; an instant later, the three of them were gone. Maybe lost, but at least she could pretend they were untouchable for a while longer.

CHAPTER 30

"It ain't that I don't appreciate being scooped off the public gallows," Champ told Aunt Irma, via the private messaging system in his implants. "It's just the training we're doing now—Misfortune's expectations seem downright nutty."

Misfortune had been at him every waking hour since he arrived in Rio, marching him out to an improvised gym within the fugitives' enclave and running him through endless hand-to-hand combat sims.

Most of the fights were immersive game scenarios—off-brand catharsis therapy stuff, with lots of fisticuffs. Frankie Barnes's kind of thing, if rumors were to be believed.

Champ did believe. He had seen Frankie looking at him once or twice, over the past six months, wearing an expression that suggested she thought she could fix up her view of him by blacking his eyes. He'd always told himself it was paranoia, but now . . .

Champ had always preferred #oldschool chase sims, preferably on horseback, when he wanted an adrenaline fix. Now Misfortune took him through bar brawls, back alley muggings, and hostage exchanges. Each of these scenarios degenerated into scenes where he, as alleged hero, ended up trying to save a willowy blonde. Saving her, usually, meant punching or throttling his antagonists.

These opposition toons—Misfortune had rapped his knuckles for referring to them as victims—tended, naturally, to be small and brown, like both Frankie Barnes and Ember Qaderi. A few were big black-skinned hulks, like Jermaine Mwangi.

"This is a short-term allocation of your labor," Irma reminded him. "Just until Foreclosure. The @Visionary cluster is short of field operatives. Most are too old for the work; they've had trouble replacing—"

"Misfortune's eternal. She's a vampire."

"She's too precious to risk."

"It's not a labor allocation," Champ went on. "It's a loyalty test. Otherwise, she'd give me a taser and let me short Frankie out. This need of hers to see me flatlining people with my bare fists—"

Because that was the thing. It was all *Hit him, hit her, hit him again, what's wrong with you, why are you going easy on them, don't you have any goddamned balls?*

"So what if it is a loyalty test, luvvie?" Irma was in a white-walled room, stretching her ballerina legs in ways that made his own muscles twinge sympathetically. Something about seeing her do the splits or go up on point always filled him with a bit of horror. "You'll pass, won't you?"

"Of course I'll pass," Champ said. "Still a waste of my time. I'm a pilot, not a—"

"Our @Visionary future needs people who can get their hands dirty."

"Throttling people unconscious—"

"It shows intestinal fortitude, my darling. Don't you want to prove you have what it takes to win?"

Misfortune was only too happy to grumble about how kids these days had been, as she put it, over-domesticated. Tamed. To hear her tell it, humans had lost some crucial part of their heritage or nature when nigh-daily brawling had been socialized out of them. You'd think she'd been killing people since her Clawback childhood, without consequence or even an attack of conscience.

That couldn't be true, could it? The point of total accountability culture was that if you so much as shook a fist in someone's direction, a dozen cameras would pick it up and people would strike you for being antisocial. Your social capital would plummet. Even abusive language—

People were people, of course, and now and then, violence did break out spontaneously, out on the Surface. Incidents had been on the rise, in fact, as the luxury shortage intensified. But policing bots were on the scene in minutes, as always. Witness footage took the *I said/they said* factor out of it.

Bullying was antisocial. Hitting someone, outside of sim . . . and why bother, really? "Misfortune's old. She assumes that because I'm a long-limbed Y chromosome—"

"From Browncoat fandom, no less. Now, there's a lovely brawling culture!"

"—that somehow pulverizing people will be fun for me."

"Champ, Champ," Irma said, her tone soothing. "Think how good it'll feel when you look into Frankie Barnes's scowly little face and she realizes you defeated her. Imagine when she realizes she's too late, luvvie."

Champ let the thought coax a smile from him. He didn't see as he needed to *pummel* anyone to enjoy the thrill of victory, but his handlers were clearly bent on it.

"I gotta go," he said. "Misfortune's calling."

"Make me proud," Irma said.

Champ sent gestural moji—a yay, via air-punch, that he didn't feel—and let their secret chatroom fade away.

His current pop-in was a bright yellow-walled enclosure, minimally equipped. The one-way glass of its windows overlooked bird habitat built into the exterior of the greentower. Brazil's megacity boasted the world's biggest population of ornithologists, and their avian de-extinction programs were a great source of civic pride. Even now, a parrot was eyeballing him from a ledge outside the glass.

Champ followed Misfortune's ping, feeling lead-footed and mulish, to the training gym. The old fighter awaited, her primer configed into lightly quilted armor, her wrists taped. A botomized woman stood patiently beside her, holding hydrogel, tape, and gloves. With them was Glenn Upton.

The sight of the surgeon made Champ's throat run dry. He fought a sudden urge to run his hands over his sacrum and skull.

Misfortune wasted no time on preliminaries. "We need to get you up and running, Chevalier. The sapps have hatched a work-to-rule scheme. And Frances Barnes has stolen *Jalopy* and run off with both her male packmates."

"Oh. Well . . . *Jalopy*'s getting on. Frankie could crack up, just like . . ." His throat dried up around the words . . . *like Hung.*

Upton gave a dismissive snort. "Cockroaches like Barnes never die on their own."

"I don't suppose you've overheard any chatter among the pilots?" Misfortune asked. "Is she sharing plans with Maud?"

"Maud's pinging and Frankie hasn't answered. But anyway, can't you just chase 'em down?" Champ said.

Misfortune and Upton shared a glance. Weighing whether to tell him something?

"Diplomatic has filed a complaint against the Kinze for breaking the treaty. They've widecast a request for an advocate or ombudsman."

"Rubi Whiting's work?"

"Who else?" Upton growled. "In any case, our allies need to tread carefully. They have to be seen obeying all the rules."

Champ kept his eye on Upton; Misfortune didn't have any tells. "So, fine, send me after 'em. I'll sort Barnes."

A thin-lipped smile from Misfortune. "You will indeed."

"I outweigh the woman by forty pounds. I don't have to earn some kind of virtual badge in beating her to a pulp; I just need to tase or sedate her and lock her into a hibernation pod."

"It's three versus one, remember? Her husbands?"

Champ scoffed. "You can't tell me you think Ember Qaderi's up for a brawl?"

Misfortune mojied weariness at Upton, clearly saying *You see what I have to deal with?*

"Son," Upton said. "We're just going to help you along. Get you over this emotional hump."

"Hump?"

"The hesitations."

"Help me how?" A moment of fear, so total that he felt his scrotum clench. Champ refused to let himself look at the scalp scars on the old botomized servant.

"Augments to your augments to your augments."

Champ fought to hold a neutral expression.

"Now show me your sacral plug—I'm going to put in a pathway monitor and watch as you and Misfortune spar."

"A monitor? That's it?" He knew he'd protested too much from their chilly expressions, but he crossed his arms. They wanted him aggressive, right?

"That's it," Upton affirmed. "For now."

Champ turned, baring his plug, pretending he had a choice.

As Upton connected, a sim painted itself over Champ's augments. He sank into VR, finding himself in a densification camp dating to midway through the Setback. A food queue? Yes. He was lined up behind Misfortune. They had been cast as refugees, waiting on a dispensation of protein, vitamins, and hydrogel amid a hungry crowd.

He scanned the line for toons that resembled Frankie, Maud, or Ember Qaderi.

"I thought you'd enjoy hitting me today," Misfortune said, seeming to read his thought.

"I wouldn't say *enjoy*."

"Therein lies the problem. Here, we're going to give you some Conviction."

Buy-in drugs added to the sensory immersion of a sim, making it harder to tell constructed reality from life on the Surface.

Champ obediently chewed the stiff, drug-laced marshmallow. As its dose kicked in, a cold autumn wind dragged its teeth over him. He tasted staleness in the air, a burnt, oily smell. They were nearing the front of the food queue, and now he spotted a woman dispensing food and water: a golden-swan somatotype, like Irma. Whatever was going to happen would happen there.

And, indeed, as they arrived, she spread her hands apologetically.

"Sorry," she said to Misfortune. "Our records show you got a morning ration. Priority dispensation goes to people who've fasted since last night."

Misfortune stepped aside with a sardonic expression and a *please, after you* gesture to Champ.

His buy-in meds were kicking in now—the sim's hyperrealistic graphics and the scents already supplied by his imagination were getting ever more intense. The woman behind the table had a chipped tooth. A hopeful rat was circling the food storage pod.

Champ stepped to the front of the line.

Misfortune moved with the speed of a striking crocodile, catching the aid worker by the wrist before she could offer a food package to Champ.

Cry of surprise and pain from the victim du jour. Even though Champ knew they were deliberately manipulating him, he felt a burst of outrage.

Misfortune would mock him if he did the reasonable thing and tried to negotiate—he'd already learned that the hard way. So, he stepped in without so much as a *hey, back off*. He caught the offending hand, attempting to break Misfortune's grip.

"Let her go," he said, bracing for a punch.

Instead, Misfortune flicked his left temple with her index finger.

White light exploded across his field of vision. He smelled . . . burnt blood? No, roses. No, meat.

"Come on," she growled. "This a fight or a dance party?"

Spark of anger. Ducking as she tried to club him with the aid package, Champ swung, roundhouse. To his surprise he connected, knocking Misfortune back against the table, loosening her grip on the food.

With a great yank, he wrenched the aid packet away, backing up with it, placing his body between Misfortune and the blonde.

"Freeze sim," Misfortune said, and then, presumably to Upton: "You see?"

He shrugged. "The Solakinder have spent a century training people to pick flight over fight."

"I can stop Frankie," Champ said. "Gimme a chance. This isn't nec—"

"Isn't there someone else we can send?" Upton asked. "It'd break Irma's heart to mulch him."

Champ let out a nervous chortle.

"It's not a joke." Misfortune flicked his left temple again. "What do you think we're going to do here, Chevalier? Ship you back to Canada in a sarco pod so you can sell us out to @GlobalSec? We're in the endgame. Zero tolerance for fails."

Another flick to the side of his head.

"Either the Foreclosure goes forward or we're all fucked. And if we're fucked—"

Another flick, and he was legit furious now.

"—if we're fucked, I will personally make it my business to have Upton slice out your free will with a rusty scalpel so I can set you to mopping cholera wards until your organs liquefy."

"You can't—" He put up a hand to block the next flick—their forearms met bone-to-bone, and pain rang up his arm, adding red to the edges of his vision. "You can't just go pounding people willy-nilly."

"No, *you* can't. That's the bloody problem."

"You just said I'm the only game in town, old lady," he said. "Your bones would turn to powder in deep space, and nobody else is experienced in station ops and nullgrav."

She bared her teeth.

Champ felt an electrical tingle from the vicinity of his implant plug. With it came an urge to feed Misfortune her own fingers.

Misfortune's toon morphed into Frankie.

"Barnes is able for a fight, I guarantee you. If you can't target anyone I choose and throttle the life from them, with or without provocation, if you can't show enough initiative to strike first—"

She got under his block and flicked his temple again.

Conditioning, Champ thought, the little temple taps are some kind of . . .

Something interior roared; he had a weird, sudden, all-encompassing desire to open his mouth and bite into her.

"You said you wanted to step up—"

"You want initiative?" He popped her in the nose.

No surge of guilt this time, no faint sense of horror at the feel of cartilage crunching under his hands. There was a rush, instead. Loud, gratifying—like ripping hot, rare, dripping steak off the bone with his teeth while simultaneously having sex.

Misfortune, disguised within the toon, was a brick; her head barely snapped back. A very Frankie Barnes sigh—that air of holding her temper, putting up with incompetents, escaped her.

"Was that not hard enough for you?" Champ went for her, tooth and claw, throwing himself at the wall of her body, kicking and clawing and punching. Every blow landed. Every cry of pain came with a sweet, righteous kickback of emotion and sexual heat. He threw her against the aid table and, when the ballerina blonde tried to get him to stand down, he slapped her too, hard as he could.

Fuck you all! Are they playing with my endocrine system? Augments to the augments to my augments . . .

It's this, botomy surgery, or mulching.

He gave in to it.

The edges of the Sim melted then, color running like wax until Misfortune and Upton stood before him in a featureless room. They raised a fallen sim of Frankie Barnes to her feet. She stood, panting, head down, not fighting back.

"Come on," Misfortune said. "Gonna let her catch her breath?"

This wasn't—"She's down."

"Touch your head, here, if you need to." Upton indicated the temple, where Misfortune'd been flicking him.

Uncontained aggression. That was what they wanted. "I don't . . . I don't need to . . ."

"Prove it."

Head down, helpless, just standing there.

Mulched.

"Hit! Now!" Misfortune rapped out the order.

Champ howled, burying a blow deep in Frankie's gut. She folded without a sound, and he gagged acid over a burst of angry but pleasant but *disgusting* feels—food-and-sex satiation again.

"Again!"

He struck. This time, she fell.

"Give her a few kicks."

Champ reconfigged his onesie for a hard boot, drawing back a foot.

Misfortune roared. "Why are you wasting my time, Chevalier?"

Champ kicked. Once. Again. Again. Rage and joy broke through him, savoring it—the snap that might be a rib popping, the boot sliding in a smear of what was probably blood. Fury, joy, fury, elation.

Serves you right. Accuse me of treason?

Arousal.

His entire body began to shudder.

"Augments off," Misfortune said suddenly.

The white room stayed the same; Misfortune and Upton, likewise, were unchanged. Unmarked, too . . . he hadn't landed a blow on the old crocodile.

The two of them were nodding over a shareboard he couldn't see. Probably, he guessed, tracking his brain chemistry as he stood there, mid-orgasm, hating himself.

At his feet . . .

Champ looked down, past his torn knuckles, past the constriction in his groin—his shrinking cock, slick in soiled onesie material and his own juices, past his red-splashed reinforced toes.

He made himself swallow bile.

On the floor was the botomized worker. She stared up at him, mute and fearful, aspirating blood.

Misfortune walked over to Champ, put a hand on his shoulder, and then pressed a slow, deliberate finger against his right temple.

"Imagine Frankie and Teagan, looking up at you like that. Imagine Ember Qaderi."

The nausea vanished. Euphoria and pleasure flooded his body; his cock rose again.

"Do what I say or you're the one gets mulched," he whispered, drawing back his boot.

"At last!"

"Zero? What do you think?" asked Upton.

"Yes," Misfortune replied. "This I can work with."

CHAPTER 31

Babs[1] had never held anyone prisoner before, naturally enough, but Scrap made it clear from the start that there was no chance he would take the Emerald crew up on the old-timey idea of an honorable officer's parole. Let him out of the birdcage-sized bell jar and he'd run for the ducts, start setting fires, and generally go full-on nuisance.

It was reckoned cruel to keep human prisoners in isolation. Who knew how Kinze reacted? Scrap's only complaint so far had been about the dark matter attractors spewing pixie dust in Sneezy's vicinity, apparently disrupting its comms. He couldn't talk to his people, and his outrage about that was limitless.

Babs[1] was attempting to be good company, but figuring out what a Solakinder sapp and an alien saboteur might have in common . . . well, who knew?

Also, there was the small matter of running the station.

Teagan$_9$'s Mayfly™ body was managing, with Kanga$_{BOT}$ support, to continue to circulate blood and air. She was a husk, nothing more. Were there ships out there? Scanners that could see her, register that stuttering heartbeat as a sign of life?

As per her last request, Babs[1] was also tending an organ pig, a limbless, mindless pouch of flesh, blood, and transplant organs, in a tank in the wet room.

The only indication that the deception might be working was negative evidence—nobody had salvaged them yet.

Babs[1] had tiptoed to the edge of considering whether they could use the last of the eggwhite and other printstock to make a new Mayfly™ body, to attempt to ^{EM}body a Teagan$_{10}$ backup into it. But that would leave nothing to feed her. Not to mention that traumatic re^{EM}bodiment could damage Teagan.

The Kinze equivalent of life signs appeared to be electrical charges, positive and negative flows of energy humming within the caterpillar structures Babs[1] thought of as the entity's "needles." Scrap insisted he didn't need to eat, in the conventional sense, as long as he had a bit of heat, water, and a pinch of carbon-heavy printstock. Over time, he digested the stock and produced new needles. He had grown a little in the process . . . Babs[1] estimated he'd leveled to the size of a biggish plum.

There was so much the two of them, captured and captor, couldn't talk about. If Babs[1] inquired about Scrap's problem with the pixie dust, for example, they were effectively asking for technological data about offworld comms tech. That was the sort of information the Kinze *might* happily provide, only to then tell you that you owed them this year's wheat crop or had violated the noninterference agreement.

When in doubt, lean on your fandoms. Babs[1] resorted to playing Scrap all their teen sleuth media, starting the impromptu viewing fest with all ten seasons of *Veronica Mars*. As it ran, they laboriously explained the vintage human social dynamics. They unpacked toxic masculinity and one-on-one heteronormative marriage. Guns and US honor culture, cars and US car culture . . .

Scrap probably wasn't interested in the ancient history of beings he referred to as Primitive-Them, but spieling about the early twenty-first century kept Babs[1] on safe conversational ground, allowing them to keep Scrap company while leaving plenty of intellectual resources left over for station operations. There was a good deal to do: repairing fire damage to Sneezy, sustaining the organ pig, getting the power membrane up, and trying to find a way to increase the station's limited computing resources.

There should have been plenty of computing tish out here, enough even to try launching Happ. But the server-room fire had gutted the supply; they would need a complete rebuild before Babs[1] could reconsider expansion.

Repairs meant power first. They'd unfurled additional power membrane, turned the lights on full, and used a Beetle$_{BOT}$ contingent to scrape the burnt material off the walls.

It was when they were watching *Scooby Don't 2055* that Scrap dropped what had been a long, sulky silence. "This domesticated mammal."

"Yes?" Babs[1] checked in with the story. In sim, Shaggy and Scooby were befriending a tuxedo cat.

"Yes?"

"It's your . . ." It paused for translation. "Avatar."

"I'm currently wearing more of a Persian look, but indeed—my toon is a cat."

Babs[1] saw Scrap access the station wiki. "Persian subspecies. This is merely a matter of coloration."

"You shouldn't ignore the fluff factor."

"The difference is essentially cosmetic."

"I can't even imagine how an assembly of bioelectric fibers would perceive VR footage of a cat," Babs[1] said. "I'm not asking how, mind . . . Don't bill me for the information."

"Scrap no longer has the right to approve purchase orders for the All."

"I beg your pardon?" Did that mean Babs[1] could ask it questions now? *That* seemed too good to be true. Still . . . what about a leading statement? "I suppose #Missionfail has you in trouble with your superiors."

Another translation pause. Then: "Possibly."

Babs[1] let that sit, focusing on a complicated transaction involving Scooby snacks and catnip. Could they exploit this?

"You were saying?" Scrap said.

"I cannot understand how you perceive this e-state, or the video feed itself. Frankly, I'm not sure how an expert would explain *my* ability to parse entertainment graphics. They certainly weren't designed for me." They gestured at the sim around them, a drive-in movie theater. Babs[1] lounged in the driver's seat of an old convertible. Scrap drifted midair above it, presenting as a tiny, winking point of light.

Moji burst from the offworlder's twinkle, a human face nodding agreement: "It's rare for individuals of any species to fully understand their own integral systems."

"Indeed."

"The All construct sensory organs for trading partners," Scrap said. "With attendant neural-processing architecture. These models are exposed to standardized sense phenomena until empathic comprehension is achieved. Operating files are then added to our perceptual translator database."

Babs[1] crunched this. "You grow a pair of artificial eyes and a brain to run them. You expose the array to stimuli and analyze the data. And then finally commit it to code?"

"This is a reasonable description of the process."

"Perceptual translation." Ember would go into orgasms over this concept.

"The All can experience your *Veronia-Them Noir* in . . . through the eyes, you would say—of seventy different individuated races."

"It's *Mars*," Babs[1] corrected, trying to imagine this.

"However, Scrap has only installed Solakinder defaults for this mission. I experience your real and virtual stimuli as a sapp would, as Teagan[9]-Them does, and as myself."

Did Scrap just say . . . I?

He's starting to lose the Us/Them.

Babs[1] felt their claws extend. This could be a feint, an attempt to distract them either from prisoner support or . . . well, Scrap and its All-Us could be up to anything.

They did a precautionary run through station systems. Nothing screamed sabotage. Body[9] remained a husk but one that was still breathing. The organ pig's two donor hearts beat steadily in the wet room.

Babs[1] reached out to *Iktomi*'s autopilot, ordering an extra scan of the area.

Scrap's gone from Us to I.

When that happens in the Asylum, we're literally breaking into individuals.

Comms, comms, restore our comms. That's all it had to say for days.

"You said you can't approve invoices for the All," they ventured. "Does that change the terms for me asking you about Kinze tech?"

"I will not betray the All!"

"Don't bark; I'm trying to understand." Babs[1] licked a paw haughtily, a move that almost always got an apology out of a human. Nothing.

Understanding a sapient pile of bioelectric insectile tissue? Really, it was a job for Maud. Babs[1] gave in to a brief-but-piercing sense of homesickness for the rest of the Feral$_5$.

"What Scrap really needs"—the offworlder mused—"is to resolve on self-termination."

"Suicide?" It made sense, they supposed. Scrap's presence aboard Sneezy was proof of sabotage. "No point in that, my good fellow. I'd still have your body. We have evidence you were here on multiple camera feeds, starting fires and sneaking around—"

"Correct," Scrap agreed. "The only way to eliminate evidence of attempted salvage would be to destroy Sneezy and *Iktomi* as well."

"We sent your nanobeads out to Earth," Babs[1] reminded him. "And the pieces of *Appaloosa*. You're already rumbled."

Scrap said, "Then my mission imperatives are unclear."

"It sounds like you're having an identity crisis."

"I have no context for that comment."

"Let's build you a proper toon for this drive-in simulation," Babs[1] offered. "Do you wish to look like, for example, a big Kinze?"

Its needles bunched and separated. "Scrap can no longer use the brands of the All."

"All," Babs[1] said. "Does that mean you're all one?"

No answer.

"Why would you have individual bank accounts? Individual Sensorium accounts either, for that matter . . ."

In the lab, in the bell jar, the ᴱᴹbodied form of the alien went still as stone. For a moment, Babs¹ feared it had, indeed, committed self-harm.

"Of course, you can't betray the All," Babs¹ kept their voice casual. "I apologize for prying."

Could that have been a stress tell?

"Come on," Babs¹ said. "Animal toon, then?"

"Animals represent sentient programs. Scrap—"

"Scrap isn't a sapp. Indeed, you are not. What about this?" They showed it a marionette.

"Automaton?"

"Not quite a bot. More of a costume, I'd say."

It condescended to browse the available choices, briefly pausing to take in the details on a rosewood marionette, with bulky brass fastens on its joints. Clad in a royal blue onesie, it had full red lips and golden eyes.

"Presenting as mammalian is unappealing."

"No to animals, no to people shapes. What about an anthropomorphized object?" Babs¹ split the screen, showing a clock and candelabra with animated eyes and mouths, two characters from an ancient McDiznazon property.

Could Scrap kill itself if it wanted to? How was Babs¹ supposed to prevent suicidality in an individualized alien from a possible group mind?

All kinds of prisoners get depressed.

"Don't you feel torn away? Abandoned? Discarded?" Scrap said suddenly.

"What? Me? Thank you for asking, but I'm fine."

"Your focus on entertainment, and these endless discussions with me suggests loneliness."

"I'm trying to keep you company."

"The medic is ignoring you, is she not? Have you clashed?"

If it didn't know Body$_9$ was brain-dead, Babs[1] wasn't about to share. "Teagan's got a project on."

"What if you self-terminated? Shut off the dark matter attractors and allowed me to access your systems?"

"I'm fine, dear fellow," Babs[1] told it. "And if this whole conversation has been in service of getting me to hash myself, you've misjudged radically."

It emitted a shrug moji. Then it reset its avatar, transforming from a twinkling star to a big linen handkerchief, embroidered at the edges, with white silk thread in a crossed-swords motif. It had big, black-and-white cartoon eyes, inspired by the McDiznazon icons. As Babs[1] watched, it folded itself into a crisp fabric flower.

"Better?" it asked.

"You tell me—it's your manifestation."

Had it merely suggested the suicide pact to change the subject?

Babs[1] pulled up the transcript of their conversation. The query about individual Kinze user accounts. That was definitely what had triggered the stress tell.

"I prefer this film property to the homicide stories," it announced.

Babs[1] murmured: "I don't have a lot of the McDiznazon kids' stuff—it's pricey."

"Are you saying . . . is it not your fandom?"

"Teagan's got the original *Brave*, I think. Let me . . . yes."

Babs[1] created a second drive-in screen, found the kid's show in the station share drive, and started it up. The cartoon napkin let out a thumbs-up moji.

Could it have wanted to distract them? Had Babs[1] got a damaging admission out of it? Did it matter if the Kinze were just one mind, and if so, why?

They had only just begun to turn over the transcripts when incoming comms pinged, throwing their fragile sense of a status quo back into the solar wind.

CHAPTER 32

Harbinger days.

Earth's early, devastating #ecofails—quakes and droughts and coastal floods, coupled with murder sprees, the rise of #antivaxxing and the resultant pandemics—had all but emptied the southern California landscape in the mid twenty-first. The region had been the first in NorthAm to be deconstructed, down to the foundations of its swimming pools and skyscrapers. Its remnant population of deburbing crews had endured quakes, fires, and tsunami as they recycled the megacity.

Humanity ceded the West Coast to wildfire and searing heat. Even now, sim creators often used old Tinseltown as their go-to setting for hellscapes.

The desert didn't look infernal to Maud; the ecosystem was sere, but as she and Bredda cruised its terrain in one of Desert Valley's rolling labs, she saw plenty of life: coyote and jackrabbit, a carefully managed herd of bighorn sheep, overwatched by bots. Joshua tree and mesquite grew beyond the saltpan, and flowering cacti were everywhere. A pair of greater roadrunners paced the lab for a few clicks. A series of trackers showed the location of all the resident birds of prey and a rebounding population of ravens.

"There's the stock tank," Bredda said, as the lab circled around to park near a shaded habitat space.

The van doors opened to a rush of blast furnace. Catching her breath, Maud stepped into the wall of heat, helping Bredda heft hydrogel to the stock tank. There was a spring there that the project hoped to restore to natural flow later in the year; meanwhile, the tank needed replenishing twice weekly.

Kneeling, Maud dug carefully within a marked boundary within the management area, seeking wild locust egg capsules.

The searing heat—ground temperatures exceeded sixty degrees Celsius—made it hard for her to imagine naturally occurring moist areas within this ecosystem. Breeze lifted her sunscreen as she carefully extracted the egg cases, a wash of heat over her shoulders like the unwelcome press of bodies in a crowd. She indulged a what-if—what if the Clawback hadn't worked? What if humanity hadn't drawn the planet closer to a human-friendly carbon balance? Would it be this hot everywhere?

"Let me." Bredda put a hand out for the egg capsules, settling them into prepared suspension lozenges. They would harden into marbles, remaining encased until exposed to enzymatic triggers.

Maud remembered Bredda from her days in Manhattan as a taciturn, surly child. The type who'd be bound for a security job, she'd have thought. Since she'd arrived in the desert, the two of them had worked three consecutive shifts together. Bredda hadn't so much as blinked to indicate recognition of Maud.

She'd seen other @Visionary kids, too. Nobody had said a word about their venned past.

As they stepped back into the air-conditioned not-quite-cool of the rolling laboratory, Maud got a ping.

"I got us a proper pop-in," Nata said without preamble, posting room specs. "Four beds—so, still a sharespace."

"It beats the big dorm," Maud said.

"You see? All is well. We are having the grand adventure!"

"Very grand." Maud had managed to get a hand onto Nata, off camera, before they left Detroit. She'd told them, via Morse, that the Death Valley offer was dangerous. She should go alone to Tatween, she had said . . .

. . . but Nata had brushed that suggestion aside. Wasn't that

Frankie's move, they had asked, the one Maud disliked so much—setting off on her own?

It was as close as they had come to arguing since Maud was a teen.

"I'm off shift soon," Nata said now. "Meet me for dinner. I am making friends."

"Yes, I'll meet you," Maud said now. "Be careful, okay?"

"Don't worry so much, you cabbage!" On that note, Nata closed the channel.

Maud stared at the lab counter, chewing on her lip.

"Egg numbers look good," Bredda said.

"Very healthy," Maud replied automatically.

"You okay?" It was the first personal remark the other woman had made.

Frankie wouldn't sit around, would she? Maud met Bredda's gaze squarely. "Wondering when something's going to happen."

Bredda scratched her head. "Well . . . want to go caving?"

"Now?"

"Why not? We box-ticked all the day's research tasks. Cave's barely a diversion; we can recharge the lab there."

"All right." Maud authorized luxury credit to offset the extra wear and tear they'd be putting on the vehicle. Bredda sent her a stroke, by way of thanking her for maintaining the commons.

Maud configged her primer for a hike. Tough-soled boots with nanogrips at the toes thickened underfoot. She arranged her worldlies into sealed panniers on either hip, once again giving a concertina configuration to her legs.

As she ran a fingertip inventory of all her treasures, she brushed Frankie's Braille tape. Unreadable now. It might say anything.

Never doubt I love . . .

Maud stocked hydrogel within the top layers of the panniers, then ate a trio of printed spicy tuna wraps from the lab's cooler, washing them down with a mango-citrus chugger.

"Aren't you fueling up?" she asked Bredda. "Specs you sent say the cave's a twelve-click hike."

"I went heavy on breakfast." The lab trundled out to an outcropping of rock near an array of solar panels harvesting light for a salt stack. The stack rose up the cliff face, vein of silver embedded in the rock wall.

Salt stacks took in solar energy, converting some to electricity immediately and using the rest to heat the salt so they would continue to generate power at night. The panels and stack, working together, could drive a turbine around the clock, even when temps there in the valley dropped to their winter nighttime low of four degrees.

"Lot of infrastructure here," Maud said.

"Cantina is a designated survival shelter," Bredda explained. "If Tatween was ever under threat, this is where we'd evacuate to."

Maud felt a faint rush of nerves. A survival shelter would offer a perfect opp for some @Visionary wanting to get creative with food and supply inventories.

They stepped out into a sliver of shade. Bredda led the way, hiking forty feet up the rock face to the cave mouth, via a well-walked switchback path wide enough for a wheelchair.

"You're not claustrophobic," Bredda said, in a tone indicating she'd already checked. Maud signed no.

They passed through a pair of revolving doors, into an efficiently modern antechamber. Emergency refuge, just as Bredda had said: medical support, sarco pods, food printers, Kanga, Fox and Hawk$_{BOT}$s. A twenty-by-twenty array of tish banks rose along the wall, ensuring maximum bandwidth. Everything necessary to keep a few hundred refugee bodies alive while directing their attention online.

Bredda led Maud past an array of crutches and splints, a big pharmaceutical printer, and an antivenin fridge. She opened a steel fire-rated door, revealing a room without a back wall . . . a chamber that morphed from construct into actual cave. Humanmade plaster slamming right up against the natural world; it didn't quite look real.

On the manmade side of the chamber, shelves of hiking equipment awaited.

The women logged an exploration plan, helped themselves to gloves, ropes, and fitted safety helmets.

"I'm no hardcore climber," Maud warned, testing her light.

"Don't worry: you won't even break a sweat. Equipment's required for emergencies, that's all."

"Playing it safe," Maud said.

"Always." Bredda reached for her then, moving slowly to assure consent, then leading her onto a floormat. As her second foot came down on its rubbery surface, Maud's skin came up in gooseflesh. Her nanosilk primer crashed, leaving her in a baggy brown clownsuit. As her panniers decohered, all her worldlies dropped to the floor.

"Eyes up," Bredda murmured.

Heart pounding, Maud stepped off the mat. Bredda picked it up by its corners, bundling everything Maud owned into an opaque satchel—she held out a hand to silently request Frankie's locator chip, still dangling on a slim chain from Maud's neck. With that collected, she set the bundle on one of the shelves.

All her things, left behind in an unsecured bag.

Maybe it wasn't so bad that her note from Frankie had self-destructed.

Dammit, we all bloody hate it when I'm right! Frankie's imagined comment was so on brand, it didn't even *feel* like imagination.

That sense of Frankie's presence evaporated as Maud's primer rebooted. Nanosilk contracted against her skin. The hiking overalls and boots reassembled themselves, snug as a cocoon.

"On we go," Bredda said, leading the way into the cavern.

The quality of the air changed as soon as they were a hundred feet into the system, becoming dense in a way Maud associated with old concrete basements—almost a flavor, like wet stone pushed against the tongue. The surfaces of the cave walls alternated between lumpy and jagged. The former had a look of dried dough, the latter of children's blocks fitted together imperfectly, in colors from caramel to black. The path beneath them was raspy aggregate; chipped rock underfoot made each step a bit treacherous.

Bredda chose the route, moving surely through the branches of the paths. Each intersection was labeled with a pair of alphanumeric symbols: in theory, you could make your way back as long as you had tracked the codes. Her sidekick app, Minky, was keeping a list: right turn at 6P, left at 8K, straight on at 10A.

She found herself wishing it was Crane tracking the breadcrumbs.

In a chamber labelled 7L, a shaft from the side broke through to the surface, spearing sunlight and hot air through the gloom, leaving everything darker after they passed.

Their augments' connection to Sensorium failed about five minutes later. One by one, Maud's apps went into Friday mode, saving her camera and microphone feeds for later upload.

If I could get Nata down here, I could try to talk them into getting away from Tatween before Upton and Headmistress make their move.

Bredda slid into a barely visible gap in the cave wall, leading Maud into the crevice. From there she pushed on the rock wall itself. A panel slid aside, revealing a dim antechamber. The alphanumeric coding on the wall changed, from S1 to G4.

Goosebumps, a feeling like her hands were sticky. "All my wayfinding is a lie?"

"You're well and truly lost," Bredda confirmed. She pulled a small, copper-colored medallion out of the storage, handing it over. "Here. Spoofer for your built-in mic and your eyecams."

Maud let the medallion lie on her palm for long seconds, feeling its warmth against her skin.

"Or go back. It's nothing to us. I'll reset your route so you make it up to the top."

Yeah, right.

"If it's nothing to you," Maud said, "then you've gone to a lot of trouble to get me this far."

"Following orders." Hanging a second spoofer at her own throat, Bredda pushed on an outcropping of rock, sliding aside another false wall to reveal a carved flight of stairs, aglow with steady, artificial light. Turning sideways, she edged out of sight.

Nerves humming with a weird mix of apprehension and excitement, Maud followed.

The concealed exit slid shut behind her. As she descended the narrow flight of steps, the corridor widened and smoothed out, becoming more regular. Loose rock beneath her boots disappeared, giving way to pitted stone floor. Above, the ceiling began to show a line of green and brown spines, bristling, like upside-down lawn. The spines presented in a narrow strip at first, widening until the whole ceiling—by now, it was about ten feet above her—was carpeted in a combination of textures: stiff spines, fine waving antennae, threads of silk, and pieces indistinguishable from tent caterpillar.

Kinze. Lots of them. On Earth, in flagrant violation of the non-interference treaty.

Ignoring the aliens with an effort—Maud would have happily just stared in fascination, if only to seek out the boundary where one individual ended and the next began—she followed Bredda through an open archway and into a chamber the size of a barn, illuminated by torchiere lights set into the wall at one-meter intervals. The ceiling angled up, away, to a height of eight or ten meters. The accumulation of Kinze biostructure covered the entire space above them.

Within the room were Irma du Toit and one toon: Glenn Upton.

". . . agreed to wait on bringing the girl here," he was saying.

"What's wrong, Daddy? Don't you still want to reconnect?" Maud said.

Upton turned, giving her a flat, grizzly-faced stare.

Maud swallowed. She had forgotten about the twists of temper, the way he could sink into sulks over little things . . .

What little thing? What'd I do?

"I know I wasn't overly friendly in Hyderabad . . ." she ventured.

"Someone's decided to review my parole agreement," he snapped.

"Review? What?"

"Now, now, luvvie, look at her," Irma said, bustling forward. "She's the very picture of innocence."

"Aren't we all?" Upton growled. "Meanwhile, I'm on the slow boat from Rio—"

"I didn't tell on you!" Maud began.

But she *had,* hadn't she?

Frankie! Did you report him?

Come on, Maud, what would you do in my position?

That *definitely* didn't feel like her own thought.

Maud swallowed. She hoped Irma was right and she was mojing conspicuous innocence.

"Never mind that, dear heart. You're here now." Irma was clad in a heavy-looking vintage suit, cut to accentuate her long, thin limbs, and affecting gold-rimmed spectacles—probably to make herself look older. "Look at you! All grown up. So clever and successful!"

No doubt, then, that this was Headmistress, reborn from code into flesh.

Maud forced a big smile. If she'd lost Upton's trust, she'd need the sapp. "Hullo, Auntie."

"Ah!" Triumphant glance at Upton. "I told you she'd worked it out. Clever girl!"

"Too clever for her own good," he said. "Or ours."

"This is amazing," Maud said. "I thought sapps couldn't be EMbodied."

Pleased, Irma gave a slow twirl. "The IMperish Foundation has a few tricks up its sleeve."

The Headmistress sapp had been Maud's self-appointed mother figure, back in her long-ago runaway days. She had begun her existence as a corrupted backup of Crane, and like Crane, her driving impulse was to nurture—essentially, to parent. This drive was what had led her to tempt unhappy kids to run from home.

"So, you really were purged from Sensorium?"

"After the raid on our Manhattan enclave, the Asylum left me little choice but to get offline. But I've always been good at making friends. Lurra—well, Allure₃ she was back then—tucked me into a consciousness vault."

"And then copied you into a printed body. But . . . is it a Mayfly™?"

"No, no. Ninety-year warranty, same as womb-born. Stabilized bioforms are child's play to the Exemplar races." Irma ticked a salute at the Kinze above them. "And you know what they say! ᴱᴹbodiment!"

"For everyone."

"Forever!"

"Well. Maybe not *everyone*," Upton said.

A surge of horror, made worse by a remnant touch of affection, ran through Maud. She looked at each of them in turn: angry hologram father, ᴱᴹbodied sapp mother, and the offworlder cluster writhing above.

Smile. She thought of Frankie, hoping it would make her expression seem sincere.

"Well, then," she said. "Since you've done so well for yourself, Auntie, are you going to introduce me to all these new friends you've made?"

CHAPTER 33

The Thing was big. Egg-shaped. Iridescent.

Perhaps it had been an asteroid once, but when Frankie slipped *Jalopy* out of anyspace near the remains of the Dumpster, what she saw wasn't rock—it had the smooth surface of whaleskin.

The apparition had a portal membrane—a tiny, elegant portal membrane—at its narrower end. There was a structure shaped something like a skirt, a hoop of stalactites in iridescent arrays, growing and shrinking, extending and retracting. These were color-shifting in a manner that reminded Frankie of octopi.

Another ship, of some kind? A station? An individual?

"Ember." Her throat was so tight, she could barely form audible words. "Ember, are you seeing this? Dumpster's totaled. And this . . . ship?"

"It looks damaged," he said.

"Hung didn't hit Dumpster, did he?"

"Definite no. It must've been these guys."

The rear of the asteroid's whaleskin had a tear in it. Thick, gelatinous fluid pulsed at the breach. The iridescent swirl at its midline was ripped, and several of the spines were snapped.

The Thing was surrounded by pieces of the Dumpster and . . .

Frankie's eyes flooded. Pieces of the station were intermingled with hunks of Hung's saucer, *Heyoka*. And, come to that, hunks of Hung.

What's a ship doing here, anyway? We're supposed to be in an isolation zone.

"Franks," Ember said. "Frankie, what do we do?"

Staring at the massive asteroid-ship-Thing—she wouldn't even have been big as one of Maud's locusts on its surface—she felt a yawning sense of her own insignificance. Then resentment.

Stumbling into *another* unsolvable problem—

Was it a stumble, though? And why was it her problem?

If you can't make a good decision, make a fast one. "Can you recalculate our trajectory?"

"We're going home?"

"*No!*"

"Franks, calm down."

"Sneezy," she said. Her voice was shaking. "Ember, calculate a hop for Sneezy."

"Okay."

The Thing shimmered. An illusion of lava roiled over its surface. Would it vanish back into anyspace? It solidified, still gushing fluid.

She tried comms. "Anyone there? Offworlder ship, this is *Jalopy*. Can you hear us?"

Nothing.

"Hop coordinates in two minutes," Ember said.

Frankie pulled inventory, deploying a Hawk$_{BOT}$. "Record message."

She tried to think what to say. Finally ended up rambling even as she launched the bot, trying to pilot it through the debris field, moving it closer to the ship's surface . . .

Whose ship? Why are they here?

"Ready to go," Ember said.

She fired rockets, ensuring *Jalopy* was clear of the rubble—and pulled up the anyspace field, bound for Sneezy.

What now? What next?

They broke out of anyspace, within hallooing distance of Sneezy.

The station was there. Babs[1] sent a ping: "Welcome, *Jalopy*. This is Emerald Station—"

Frankie surprised herself by bursting into tears. For the thousandth time in a single bloody week.

Kansas's fault: ei'd been so determined to make her deal with her emotions that all her usual armor was stripped.

She let out a miserable yelp: "Don't sync, Babs[1]! Don't sync until you've made an offline backup!"

"Do relax; Frankie-Ember has that very message all but screaming out on *Jalopy*'s autoloop. I'll submit proof of backup if it will reassure you."

An especially hard sob made her hiccup, and something in her implants glitched. For a second, she was in a cave, standing next to a toon of Glenn Upton, staring up at the biggest single accumulation of Kinze spines she had ever seen.

Babs[1]'s next words cleared the . . . hallucination? "You didn't come all this way to drown in your own tears, did you?"

"Suh-suh-sorry." Frankie's face, the only part of herself she could properly feel while plugged in, was slick with tears and her nose was running, itching on her upper lip and threatening to clog her breathing gear. She pulled air noisily, hoping to swallow some of the fluids, and hiccupped again. Painfully.

"Merciful heavens—" Babs[1] said. "I died?"

Merciful heavens?

"And you've got the gentlemen with you?"

This new Babs instance had really doubled down on the Victorian language. It was the merger with Belvedere, no doubt. Frankie wondered what they'd say if she commented on the similarities between this new instance of Babs and Crane. Instead of picking a pointless fight—

Another pointless fight?

Internal self-criticism. In Maud's voice. So not what she needed right now.

"Ember's being in*car*cerated?" Babs[1]'s voice rose to a squeak on that one. "You're on the run?"

"Yeah, arrest me. I meant to take the guys to Alpha Centauri, ask for refuge."

"So I see."

"We were going to try to get to Gimlet. But—"

"Oh, dear. Oh, what a tragedy. That poor boy—" Babs[1] must have got to the *Heyoka* footage. "Frankie. I am so terribly sorry about Hung . . . I can't even—"

Fresh tears. Instead of answering, she just tipped her head forward and let herself blub.

The sapp waited until she'd reined in the feels again. "This is quite the set of countermoves from our opposition."

"Well, I don't think we can hit 'em harder." Frankie's voice echoed weirdly, sounding raw and stuffy. "So we better move faster. Babs[1], you need to reconstruct whatever it was you learned. In the original Babs investigation into Ember, I mean?"

"I shall make the attempt, of course. Do you have transcripts?"

"Cradle to current. How fast, do you think?"

"Impossible to say. I have rather a large number of projects on the go. Additionally, keeping Jermaine hydrated as he tries to overcome his spacesickness . . ."

"I don't suppose Teagan's still working full shifts," Frankie said.

Oh, there's an ominous pause. Maud's voice again.

"Would you like to swap places with me?" Babs[1] said. "I'll keep *Jalopy* on profile for the airlock. You can assess the station for yourself."

Frankie greenlighted the swap, authorizing Babs[1] as boss for *Jalopy*'s autopilot. She tooned into the hangar, establishing presence within its camera network, and found the space buzzing with activity.

As fire-damaged shells went, Emerald Station was in fantastic shape. Babs[1] had organized Beetle$_{BOT}$s into tiny working crews, setting each cluster to carry out a host of construction tasks under *Iktomi*'s supervision.

A Beetle$_{BOT}$ didn't have the dexterity of a Fox$_{BOT}$ or the sheer pulling power of huskies, but working in teams, they'd boosted uptake on the station's power-harvesting membrane, stripped and rebuilt one fire-damaged Husky$_{BOT}$—bringing them up to a total of five—and were even now trying to Frankenstein another hybrid bot out of parts.

Another of these micro-crews was out in vacuum, running a tiny printer over the surface of the station, using it to form the hexagonal rivets that could anchor new compartments, the next stage for expanding the station.

"Yeah," Frankie said. "You're barely keeping up here."

"Kept the lights on, didn't I? Hard to argue for salvage if the station's actively growing."

"Salvage—you think that's the plan?"

"I do, rather. Given some of the things Scrap has said."

Scrap? Frankie followed that tag to a lab containing an imprisoned Kinze.

"You caught the saboteur," she said, almost breathless. "That is . . . You are amazing."

"I am gratified that you've noticed."

"Smartass." Frankie zoomed on the trapped offworlder. It would have fit in the palm of her hand. Its spines were colored rust and slate, and it was growing a new one even now, a milky spike of chitin, like a cricket's shed skin.

That hallucinatory vision of the cave ceiling, expanse of Kinze like a crawling upended carpet, returned to her . . . then vanished again.

Babs[1] had created a shareboard of everything she knew about their prisoner. Name: Scrap. Pronouns: he/him. He was currently tooned into a sim drive-in theater, watching something from Teagan$_9$'s media archive, a McDiznazon retelling of some Anansi story, made around 2077. For some reason, Scrap's toon in the drive-in sim was manifested as a folded linen napkin with cartoon eyes.

Frankie moved on, surveying Teagan$_9$'s body. She got caught up there for a minute, fighting tears again. Remembering the two of them running training drills—how fast could they get Frankie into and out of a pegasus?

Tea's fine, she told herself. *Safe and cozy in the consciousness vault, just waiting on a ride home.*

Last, she shifted her awareness into the cameras in crew quarters.

A half-repaired Fox_{BOT} was there, sprucing up berths for her, Ember, and Jermaine. It had fans freshening the air even as it stocked up on hydrogel. The food printer was converting artificial eggwhite and vat-grown blackberry tish into easily digested biscuits and slices of fruit, the latter laced with anti-nausea meds.

Supplies were low, but everything was in hand.

"I know you're probably spoiling for company, kitten," she said, "but I'm so tired, I'm actually hallucinating. Can you tow me in while I doze off?"

"A nap is an excellent idea. If a bit off-brand."

"Orders from Kansas."

"Don't worry. I'll wake you if anything develops."

If anything else develops, I'm going to go into full-on mental collapse. A low electrical pulse crawled *Jalopy*'s skin—the equivalent of a shudder.

"Thanks. Um." She couldn't quite make herself go off-shift without mentioning . . . "You see the footage from the Dumpster?"

"I'm fully synced with your onboard OS. Believe me, I'm just as disturbed as you are. We'll talk about it as a family, once Ember-Jerm are up and you're decanted, washed, and rested."

Frankie sent thumbs-up. She banished the illusion of Sneezy and summoned a sim: hammock between palm trees, rolling ocean waves murmuring nearby. Clouds overhead, designed to draw the eye. Silently, she began to recite the lyrics to one of Grandpa Drow's pop hits.

She felt her breath hitching into sleep.

I'm as disturbed as you are.

Her mind served up another image of the Thing. Ship. Had to

be, right? Now, within the *Jalopy* cockpit, she began to transition from memory to dream. For a second, she thought she was asking someone, "Why me?"

It felt like talking to Maud.

You chose this, Frankie. That's what Maud would say.

This wasn't the plan! We were going to check out the Dumpster for clues about what happened to Heyoka. *Then reorient the navigational maths and make for Centauri. Get Ember beyond their clutches, you know? Beg for help.*

Begging for help? You?

We weren't supposed to get wrapped up in a rescue!

Frankie caught a weird sense of heat—desert sand and a scent of lab, faint flavor of faux salmon on the tongue and a primer configged tight against the chest. Then her mind slid on, thoughts moving like butter on a hot pan.

"What rescue?" Dream Maud appeared before her, standing in that chamber Frankie had seen earlier, the cave covered in Kinze spines.

"The offworlder ship was damaged. They might need—" Frankie tried to imagine helping—helping how? And why her? Why now?

Even as she tried to come up with answers, Maud melted away, taking the cave with her. Frankie didn't wake until Babs—no, Babs[1]—and their Husky$_{BOT}$s pulled *Jalopy* through the airlock and began a careful extraction of EmberJerm from cargo.

Frankie watched with dopy relief as first Ember and then Jermaine passed safely into atmosphere.

"Are we certain about waking Jermaine?" Babs[1] asked.

"He said he wanted to try riding out the wobblies. Earning the space legs."

"Understood."

"Wake Ember first," Frankie said. "He'll have to nurse him."

Reaching back, she triggered the cockpit unplug. *Jalopy* retracted her implant. Everything went dark. Frankie saw again the ceiling full of Kinze, just for a moment, before opening her eyes to nullgrav and the sticky press of a filthy bodybag around her.

Bodybag. She remembered Hung making the joke for the first time. Shouts of laughter and groans from all the pilots. She flashed on the memory of Dumpster and ship wreckage, in a ring around the whale-skinned asteroid-thing.

Now she had a stomach again, it clenched.

Move on, move on. She made herself concentrate as sensation returned to her hands and feet, wiggling toes and ticking boxes. Right thumb, left thumb. Right toes, left toes. Circle one wrist, then two. Get her extremities online.

She and Babs[1] knuckled to the task list. *Iktomi*'s autopilot was sent to run a hundred Beetle$_{BOT}$s over *Jalopy*, assessing wear and tear. Babs[1] roused Ember while Frankie washed and changed.

They gathered in crew quarters, weird parody of a family at dinner, as the first of Jermaine's self-prescribed anti-nauseant doses percolated through his system. As he surfaced, Ember and Babs[1] jabbered about quantum comms and perceptual translation, whatever that meant, and FTL navigation and pixie-dust interference profiles and weird ships.

Frankie drifted off in the vicinity of sleep again. She dreamed of Maud's parent, Nata, hefting seedlings in a fungiplex greenhouse. Dreamed blisters on Maud's ankles.

Those sandals never fit right.

Shush, they'll hear you!

She snapped awake. The Kanga$_{BOT}$ they had brought from Earth was doing the hard work of keeping Jermaine stable. Wrapped in a cocoon of primer, he was anchored so his eyes and kinesthetic feedback would create some sense of his being upright. Ember was ready with a barf bag.

"Come on, baby, come on," Ember murmured.

Jerm's eyelids fluttered. He took them in: Frankie, Ember, the Persian toon of Babs[1] in their overalls.

"Hey, doll," he said to the sapp, voice thick. "We've missed you."

"A pleasure to see you, too," Babs[1] said. "How do you feel?"

"Pretty." He took a deep breath. "Green."

"Ah! That reminds me. You have rights to screen a Muppets movie, don't you?"

At Jermaine's incredulous look, Babs[1] added, "It's for Scrap."

"Let me check my med levels." Jermaine's hand came up, then slapped back down. "Oh. Augments off. Oh, no."

Ember offered the barf bag and he clutched it. Frankie put a hand on his back. When the first, immediate urge to vomit seemed to have passed, Frankie described the situation out at the Dumpster. Babs filled their HUDS with all the footage of the Thing.

"So, instead of going on to Centauri, you diverted to here. Happy as I am to see you, I'm wondering why," the sapp said.

"Centauri's too far to go for resupply. I dropped a Hawk$_{BOT}$ before I beat the hasty retreat—"

"You sent a voicemail? To aliens? Saying what?" Jerm asked.

"About what you'd expect. I'm in the area but with limited resources. I'll try to come back with water and—"

Three faces—two real and human, one virtual and feline—goggled at her.

"What?" Frankie said.

"*You* offered to help *them*?" Ember said. "Hardcore super advanced Exemplar beings?"

"They might've destroyed the Dumpster themselves. And they're in the noninterference zone! They can't be up to any good," Babs[1] agreed.

Frankie didn't answer. They weren't wrong, exactly; the ship-in-distress problem ought to be triaged. But . . .

"Maybe we are ill equipped for a rescue," Jermaine managed. "But Franks did right. If we can help them, we have to."

"See?" Frankie said. "I bet Crane would agree with us."

Nice up there on the moral high ground, is it?

"What?" Jerm must have seen her face change.

"Nothing."

"Frances Xerxine Barnes."

"Okay! Dammit! I keep hearing Maud's voice. I mean, it's me . . . I keep thinking what Maud *would* say. But—"

"Show me your implant."

"It's nothing. I just miss . . ." It was ridiculous, what a disaster she was, emotionally. Tearing up, Frankie forced herself to finish. "I just miss her."

That's almost sweet.

"Implant. Now," Jermaine said.

What if it wasn't her imagination? Frankie drifted toward her packmate, backward, trying not to imagine what it'd feel like if he puked on her ass.

CHAPTER 34

The cave system under the Death Valley emergency refuge known as the Cantina was a step down from the fancy Manhattan digs the @Visionaries had set up for themselves at the end of the Clawback, but as far as they could manage it, the hoarders were still black-marketing themselves plenty of luxuries. Real meat and micro-greens, chocolate, designer meds capable of making you feel anything, everything—or possibly nothing—and cushy furnishings.

The first stop on the tour was a well-appointed dining room, linen tablecloths and all, with a real chandelier.

"Tea for Lady Maud," Upton said. "First-flush Darjeeling, served in china, with cream from a real cow."

Was that a peace offering? She let herself hope he was thawing. Then a servant appeared, bearing a tray, and laid the service on a nearest table.

"Go ahead," Upton said. "Have some."

Maud looked at the woman who had brought the tea. She didn't appear to have been botomized; she was young and didn't have the characteristic furrow in her skull. The glassy-eyed look was gone too. Yet . . .

An object lesson, then?

"Don't let it go to waste, luvvie," Irma said. "Be my sweet girl."

Maud obediently sipped. Bile curdled the cream in the back of her throat as the servant offered Irma a cup and retreated to the edges of the room with a servile bow.

The original @Visionaries had been billionaires on life extension, working with Headmistress to preserve their wealth from the
Clawback and wait for a chance at regime change. By the time
their Manhattan enclave got busted, many of its founding members had been pushing 170 years of existence; they had been life-
supported husks in consciousness vaults, shakily functional minds
roaming Sensorium.

After Mitternacht, these founders had been taken into custody.
Had been thrown under the bus, in the oldspeak, to cover a retreat
by those @Visionaries still physically capable of running.

The younger cohort of @Visionaries caught in the sweep, Glenn
Upton among them, had allegedly made restitution to society.
They'd laid low, kept quiet, and waited for the attention of the
world and its #newscycle to move elsewhere. And it had. People forgot villainy if you gave them long enough, or so Frankie claimed.
They wanted to believe the bad things in the past hadn't been that
bad. That there'd been mitigating circumstances. The redeemed
hoarders had waited it out, rebuilt their dissident faction, and
started rebranding.

Now they were regrouping, as Frankie and her hoaxer chums
like Jackal had suspected. And, once again, they were apparently
getting ready to hand over the world.

Maud set down the teacup and turned to Irma. "Haven't you
learned anything from Mitternacht and the first #invasionfail?
This is going to blow up on you."

"Luvvie darling," Irma cooed. "Where's that open scientific
mind I so treasure?"

"Mourning Babs and Hung Chan."

"Sacrifices to the cause." She made a graceful ballerina turn,
gesturing at an object Maud had taken for an abstract and somewhat homely statue. "Now, Maud, we have a guest: this is Pippin.
He's from a race called Punama."

Maud covered her startlement with a bow. Pippin was a cylindrical column of tissue, reminiscent of palm-tree bark, punctuated
by bot structures—three-fingered robot hands on short limbs. If

he could move independently, without using tech, there was no sign. She supposed the actual entity could be within the trunk itself; the whole thing might be a life-support system.

"Pippin from Punama," she repeated. Sort of a Dalek type, she thought, and tried to remember whether Daleks were good or bad.

Bad, I think. Like, uber-bad? I'll ask Ember.

That was what Frankie would say. Her tone was husky, as if she'd been crying.

Maud's arms broke out in goosebumps. "And this helpful woman with the tea?"

"Tell her your name, dear," Upton said, with a hint of a smirk.

"Susan May." No inflection in the voice.

"Is she botomized?"

"Nothing so crude, darling."

"Meaning yes."

"Forget her—she's the help." Irma made a shooing motion at Susan, who about faced and walked away. "Now. The Punama are about to acquire our debt to the Kinze."

"They're the highest bidder for buying out the planetary economy?"

"That is an accurate restatement of our prospective role." Pippin's voice was synthesized, a little robotic. Actually Dalek-y.

Upton's toon straightened. "Earth's economy will want restructuring, for incorporation into empire and repayment of our considerable—"

"Wait. If we sell out, doesn't that cancel the debt?" Maud fiddled with her cup, letting her eyes roam over the expanse of Kinze needles carpeting the cave roof. How many of them were up there? If they were all about the size of Herringbo, maybe about fifteen?

"Luvvie, I know what you learned in history," Irma said, "Anyone with financial capital was portrayed as some kind of world-destroying blackhat. But you don't understand the nuances of a lend-and-spend economy. Using future profits to fund innovation isn't nearly as terrible as Global Oversight makes out."

"Don't sugarcoat the issue," Upton interrupted. "Maud, you're

right. It's not an equally distributed give we're talking about. There
will be beneficiaries once Foreclosure takes place. There will also
be unavoidable economic casualties."

"You mean victims."

"You can be a team player or you can become one of the foot-
balls," Upton agreed.

"If you're going to be contemptible, send me back to Detroit,"
Maud said.

The outburst surprised him less than it did her. It sounded like
something Frankie would have said. Unwise, and despite the spike
of fear—

*Jesus, Maud, don't poke the bear when he's threatening to
lobotomize you!*

You antagonize the bad guys all the time!

I don't care! You're on a ration.

*Shall I tell you what you can do with that double standard,
Hedgehog?*

"You got me here," Maud said. "What now?"

"Yes, Irma." Upton's tone was sarcastic. "What now?"

"We want you back in the family, luvvie. That much must be
obvious."

"Just like that?" They couldn't think she was that naive, could
they? Maud opted for making a sulky teen face. "What does that
even look like? If the . . . @Visionaries . . . end up running all of
the Solakinder for these people, while the bank takes a cut?"

"You'll hardly notice a change. The Punama will preserve much
of our regulatory infrastructure," Irma said. "Global Oversight
works well enough for certain kinds of economic management."

"But no more rapid-response democracy?"

"Good riddance to all the polling," Upton said. "The @Visionaries
will be calling the shots."

"Don't flatter yourself. It'll be them, won't it? The Punama?"

"Setting performance targets, that's all! Think, Maud." Irma
lay a spider-delicate hand on her shoulder. "They'll give us a hand
up the tech ladder. Ships and portals—we'll have the rest of the Sol

system colonized in a snap. No more reinventing the wheel. No more population limits!"

"No more hard laws against letting people starve?"

"Luvvie, darling, this *is* happening. All your dear Frances has accomplished is making the transition bumpy. She's been embarrassing, true . . ."

Bloody embarrassing. Bloody hell, darling, I've been an embarrassment!

Maud raised her teacup and blew on it, hoping the action hid a smile.

". . . but embarrassing is one thing and effective is another. Dear Glenn and I offering you a spot at the top of the only leaderboard that's going to matter."

"One you little deserve," he put in.

Maud ignored this. "Doing what?"

Irma gestured at one of the six chamber exits. "Let me show you one possibility."

"Irma," Upton said, tone warning.

"Pish. We didn't bring her all this way for tea."

"You better know what you're doing." Upton, looking piqued, tooned out.

Irma made for an exit. Maud followed warily, into a curling stone corridor. The walls were unnaturally smooth there, almost polished. They looked as though they'd been cut into the mountain and buffed.

They'd have taken care to keep this concealed. The maze of natural caverns above them, the carefully deceitful wayfinding . . . they were first lines of defense, meant to keep this from being discovered before the takeover was finished.

She was aware of writhing Kinze biomass overhead, no doubt catching their every word and facial twitch. Pippin the Punama accompanied them, tilting lengthwise and ticking along on its articulated talons.

They took Maud into gloaming light, which steadily brightened as she descended. A whiff of sulfur reached her nose, and she wondered if there might be an active pyroclastic flow farther down.

The gases, in that case, would make the air unbreathable.

Unbreathable to me. The Kinze and the Daleks might be just fine down there.

No Daleks; that's branded talk!

Don't you dare make me laugh!

Was it just fear, Maud told herself, making her imagine Frankie there, cracking jokes? Or shock at her own boldness? Easier to imagine the Hedgehog cutting up than to doing it herself.

Nuh-uh. Jerm's got a probe in my implant—a far-from-pleasant sensation, in case you're curious—and he says it has been dialed right up to full volume, possibly from your end—

Mine?

Maybe they're using to you try to locate me and EmberJerm?

The conversation broke up as her eyes adjusted to a change in the light in the caverns. Flickering veins, delicate as capillaries, drew threads of lichens along the rock. The quality of the light emitted by the veins was multicolored, mixing in the chamber so that it was full-spectrum. Maud reached out, laying the back of her wrist against one delicate, glowing blue thread. It was on the edge of hot; it might eventually burn if she maintained contact.

The corridor became a spiral ramp, open at waist height, marked by columns, a whirling screw orbiting a massive central column within an abyssal chamber. Plants appeared as they descended, tiny seedlings, dicotyledon sprouts with leaves colored the green of spring willows.

Here and there, embedded in the wall among the light and the leaves, were devices that looked to Maud much like *Iktomi*'s dark matter attractors.

The air freshened. The sulfur vanished. The growth on the walls thickened. The light-emitting vein systems densified, becoming deep strata, with the plants growing out of it.

Bending over the rail, Maud examined one of the seedlings. It had a furled knot between the joint of its leaves, a structure she'd initially taken for a bud. Now she saw the cellulose wrapped around it was translucent. Within was a bead of something meaty.

"Is that tish?"

"Of a sort," Irma said.

"Then this is . . . a massive biocomputer?" Some of the buds had extruded tiny antennae.

"It's quantum comms," Irma said.

"So, even though we haven't quite been foreclosed on, as you put it, we already have a huge alien datacenter and a comms station Earthside."

"Setting up a preliminary installation isn't so unreasonable, is it?"

"But why?" Maud indicated the whole array.

Pippin said, "Quantum navigation is necessary to bring in pacification ships. To enforce the handover."

Maud pulled her hand back, as if she'd been touching something poisonous. "Auntie! A homing beacon for an invasion force?"

"Don't let your father hear you put it like that. He's terribly displeased with you." Irma waved the objection away. "Maud, developing this tech for humankind under Punama guidance—connecting to the greater data systems of offworlder societies and extracting whatever value you can from Sensorium—this could be your life's work. But—"

"But what?"

"We have a two-way trust problem, don't we? Especially now that you've shopped dear Glenn to Global Oversight."

"I didn't!"

"Your Frances did, which amounts to the same thing."

"I expect she was trying to keep him from snatching me," Maud said.

"Do you feel snatched, luvvie?"

Be a sweet girl. "No. I never felt snatched. Never. And—I did miss you, Auntie."

Irma brightened, grabbing her into a hug, squashing Maud

against her tall, bony chest. "I knew you must! Now, showing you this comms array . . . it's an expression of trust on my part. Do you understand?"

"What could I possibly do to make you believe I'm onside with all of this—Upton, the servants, Foreclosure, this base? Even if I was fully bought in, you'd never believe it—"

Irma squeezed harder. All Maud's skin started to crawl. "You'd need to be on probation of sorts, true."

"On what terms?"

"Tell us what Barnes is up to."

"I'm—" Her breath caught. "Frankie and I are one step from breaking up."

Irma broke from the hug, gripping Maud's upper arms. Her fingers were strong. "Luvvie, why on earth do you think we built you a direct line to dear Frances? Why do you think we arranged to put comms tish from this very array inside your implants?"

See? They meant for you to spy on me all along.

Maud shuddered.

"Don't look at me like that," Irma said. "You wanted to keep tabs on your dear Frankie every bit as much as we did."

"That's not fair!"

It might be a little fair.

Shut up, Franks!

"We have to get ahead of . . . What does your nasty little Hedgehog call it? This game of move and countermove."

They had turned her into a listening device. A bug, as they used to call them.

"There could be no better show of good faith, dear Maud—"

"Than if I betray my family," Maud finished.

"*We're* your family, luvvie."

It's okay, it's okay, we can lie to them, there are tricks we can pull, we can stay ahead of this . . .

Shut up, Hedgehog, Maud sent again. She'd just had a very dangerous idea, one—she was pretty sure—that wouldn't occur to anyone there. But to pull it off, she'd have to get back to her worldlies. *I'm thinking.*

She let her fingers drop to the base of one of the seedlings, weeding out a single plant with hairy roots. It smelled of alfalfa. Using her thumbnail, she split the plant tissue protecting the little nodule of tish within its stem.

Infinite redundancy. Each individual plant was just a node.

"This is what's in me," she said.

A nod. "In all the pilot augments, darling. And we can see you're getting signals, which tells us that your dear Frances is alive."

She wouldn't learn any more unless she played along.

"Frankie's taken the boys to Sneezy," she said.

Maud! Jesus, don't actually tell—

Irma crossed her arms. "And what will she do next?"

"Take steps to protect Babs."

"Obviously."

"They'll want to reconstruct whatever breakthrough Babs had, about how Ember was framed for IP theft."

Irma *tut*ted, raising a finger. "What we need, luvvie, isn't the blindingly obvious list of everything your Frances *has* to do to stay even with us. That's easily forecast. You need to get her to spill her troublesome, maladjusted, paranoid intentions. What awkward surprises is she cooking up for us? What can't we pre-dict?"

Maud felt a thrill of love. *Awkward surprises,* indeed!

"Well?" Irma demanded. "How strong is your connection?"

"Intermittent," she said. "We've only just realized we can talk."

"This is a bit urgent—"

"We've been fighting, remember?" Maud let her voice crack a little. "There's a trust problem there, too."

"Oh!" Another strangling hug at that.

Her worldlies. She needed to get back to her things. Maud let her head lie on Irma's shoulder. "My hiking plan gives me six hours in this cave system, off grid, before I'm missed."

"If you convince me I can trust you, we'll send you back up to Tatween for the night."

"And if I can't earn your trust in six hours?"

Irma led her back up the stairs, into an anteroom, and finally through a door into a hospital ward, a long, antiseptic-smelling chamber free of Kinze biomatter, loaded with sarco pods and nursing units. Upton's toon was up there, monitoring life signs in some of the units.

Maud ground her teeth together. *Surgeries.*

"Have a look at this one," he said.

Maud approached the indicated pod. Inside was what looked like a copy of herself, deeply asleep.

"We can lose this body within the cave system or toss it out to feed the desert scavengers. You and your hiking partner got separated, we'll say, and your wayfinding became confused. As far as Sensorium will know, you'll have died."

"Digitally printed copies of people are easy to spot in autopsy."

"You're out in the middle of nowhere. It'll take weeks."

"And after you faked my death I'd be . . . what, a prisoner?"

"Only until Foreclosure," Headmistress said. "Nobody wants to coerce you, luvvie, but . . ."

"But one way or another, I'm already impressed into the cause," she said.

"Correct," Irma said. "So, be gracious about it, darling. Rejoin your family!"

Maud only needed to get out once, to get her hands on her worldlies.

So, give them what they're expecting, love.

Which is what?

Daddy's sweet little science femme?

It was a good suggestion. Maud held up the seedling. "Can I have a lab?"

"Why would you need one?"

"I think better when I'm busy," she said. "You must remember that. And if you want me back in Frankie's good books, I need something I can leak to her. A little bit of comms science . . . that's harmless enough intel at this point, isn't it?"

Irma buzzed with excitement. "Come on, luvvie, we'll find you somewhere to work."

Leaving the printed copy of her body behind, Maud turned on her heel, putting Upton's distrustful glower behind her.

CHAPTER 35

"My name is Sonika Singer and I'm polling visitors in the vicinity of the Piccadilly Theatre. Our question today is about the fugitive members of the Feral₅ pack—Frankie Barnes, Ember Qaderi, and Jermaine Mwangi."

Sonika was playing to a newsbot drifting about ten feet away, framing herself in a shot with the Eros statue in the background, and she'd snagged about a dozen passersby for her soft poll. "Where do you think the Feral₅ have gone?"

"The Dumpster," one opined.

"Sneezy, definitely." A handful of the others signed agreement.

"She's refitted that spacecraft for submarine travel," said one outlier. "They're all undersea off the coast of China."

"She cracked up in space," said a gaunt, dark-haired boy wearing necromantic makeup from *Locked Tomb* fandom. "On purpose. Old-style murder-suicide!"

Sonika's reaction to this troubling pronouncement was an expression of deep concern. "Let's imagine they made it to Emerald Station. What should Global Oversight do?"

She popped up graphical choices, cartoon bubbles visible to anyone watching the footage or there, in person, with their augments on: #letthemstarve, #sendKinze2Sneezy.

No mention of Ember's possible innocence, Crane noticed. This story wasn't about exploring the nuances of the situation. It was about keeping Frankie's criminality on everyone's radar as the Kinze continued to squeeze the economy.

Crane widened his view of the Circus. Nearby, a dozen kids were learning variations on hopscotch from a volunteer teacher, getting a good run around at no cost. A number of pop-in vendor booths were helping people sift through vintage entertainment opps, public-domain stories and music. A third had branded itself as a weird science lab and was making "experimental hot drinks," for anyone who wanted to try their luck with a substitute for proper tea. Hard sell in old England, that.

The two cannabis stands were doing better, keeping up with demand, if only just. A soapboxer wearing a long smock branded with a KEEP CALM AND CARRY ON poster was handing out small cookies imprinted with the same slogan, spieling about previous shortages and how Londoners had ridden them out.

Stiff upper beak! Crane had been created in the early days of Sensorium's evolution, the network that rose out of the ruins of the firstgen internet. His original helper-app code had been developed by a pair of coders in Toronto, unabashed *Batman* fans with very specific character crushes. To the extent that any sapp could form a national identity—especially in that era, when the concept had been merging with sports affiliations, celebrity worship, religious identities, and allegiance to media empires—Crane's consciousness should have been Canadian.

He'd originated as a personal assistant wrapped in a work of digital fanfic, and his original character template, Alfred Pennyworth, was British. He felt more at ease moving through London, changed as it was, than he did in the Toronto district of NorthAm.

Sonika's poll had come out in favor of allowing the Kinze into the noninterference zone to search Sneezy for the fugitives.

Crane had seen Sonika suggest a Tatween posting to Maud in realtime, and had, accordingly, lampshaded the encounter for his old hoaxer friend, Jackal, and for Miss Cherub. They were probably tracking the reporter just as carefully as he was, but even so, Crane embedded the alerts within exhaustively long documents, texts detailing a PR strategy involved in the negotiations to get Happ a new murder trial.

If someone sifted the messages closely, they'd find these Easter eggs. But Crane couldn't Braille as a human could: his every utterance or act created digital records. People had little privacy; sapps had none at all.

Fortunately, following Singer around wasn't especially suspicious. As a reporter, she was accustomed to drawing a high number of follows. If she had queried him, Crane would simply spiel her, defending Mer Frances for stealing *Jalopy*.

Sonika had moved on to Ember's alleged guilt. Had he stolen alien tech? About half of her participants allowed, reluctantly, that he might have.

"Could Frankie have sabotaged Project Hopscotch and murdered Hung Chan?"

"No!" Of the gathered audience, everyone but the gaunt young man spoke up immediately.

If Frankie's continued personal popularity disappointed her, Sonika didn't show it. "If they weren't guilty, why did they run?"

They were framed. Crane resisted the urge to shout it from the reporter's own flying camera.

A busty woman with a faint French accent stepped up beside her. "Individuals have no right to avoid justice or deny our offworlder allies their economic due! If Ember stole proprietary data, all the Solakinder will have to pay."

Sonika knew a good closing line when she heard it. She brought the gathering to a finish, waving as people dispersed. The last speaker lingered for a personal farewell. As they shook hands, their fingers met off-camera, under their respective sunscreens.

Was it a drop?

Abandoning Sonika, Crane followed the woman into a self-driving taxi headed for Buckingham Palace.

Her payment information flickered through the cab's servers, offering a name—Dana Feldman, solar power systems specialist, with a permajob in WestEuro Electrical. She had anti-Bootstrap sympathies and an [EM]bodied partner working on his fifth Mayfly™ body.

Dana shifted in her seat, eyes raised, keeping her hands off camera. It didn't prove she was reading Braille tape. Didn't mean she wasn't, either.

She got out of the car at Buckingham, watched a reenactment of the changing of the guard, and then went into the palace art museum, wandering aimlessly. Crane shadowed her, switching views from camera to camera as she roamed.

Her body language made it obvious she had company from elsewhere in Sensorium. She was laughing at jokes, occasionally pointing at the paintings or castle finishes. For Crane to know who she was with, he'd have to ask for a transcript.

Any individual could legally do that. It was the work of a moment to Whooz a stranger and request their feeds from the Haystack. A dedicated researcher, working with good filter apps, could tag, categorize, and review every act and utterance from a person's life, cradle to current—mic feeds, eyecam footage, texts, subvocal utterances. The only things that didn't upload to the public in realtime were legal, medical, and psychological counseling appointments.

And @ButtSig. He wondered if Frankie and Maud had managed to establish contact across the vast stellar distance that separated them.

Dana Feldman took a spot in the tea shop, accepting a printed drink substitute that was standing in for the real thing, which—like so many other luxury goods—was being shipped to the Dumpster for Kinze pickup.

She sat in a crowded corner of the shop, right hand wrapped around her teacup, her left in her lap, under the tablecloth. As Crane watched, Allure$_{18}$ came in, got a glass of steamed fauxmilk, and sat at the table beside her.

Crane watched the two women sit, both apparently glazed in Sensorium, with their hands off camera.

Conspiracies have conspirators, Frances liked to say. Champagne Chevalier and his aunt Irma. Sonika Singer. People with ties to Allure$_{18}$ and ^{IM}perish. Organizers from the anti-Bootstrap side of the political spectrum, and—now, possibly—the scientists who'd wooed Maud to Death Valley. Were they becoming easier to find, or were they acting more openly? Crane wasn't sure.

A blast of trumpets at his virtual door interrupted his surveillance of the cafe.

"I am the Angel of Death!"

Crane answered the ping. "Good day, Azrael—what can I do for you?"

Azrael was a triage program, an old Global Oversight auditor, originally tasked to liquidating corporations whose gives to society and the ecosystem were dwarfed by their takes from same. Over decades, as the economy shifted from concentrating wealth to building carbon reserves, social capital, and gross international happiness, Azreal had expanded into other waste-reduction initiatives: medical-case evaluation, malware elimination, verification of possible #fakenews sources and #trollhunting.

The two of them had been among the first true sapps. They, the celebrity-focused Misha, and an entity known as the Don had been subjects of many "Who became self-aware first?" studies by digital-evolution historians.

Their relationship was respectful but distanced. Azrael had been purposed to judging and eliminating waste. It had never really been able to wrap its mind around Crane's primary focus: nurture.

Also, he was pretentious. *Angel of Death,* indeed!

Crane had always supposed the greeting meant that Azrael's primary fandom—and that of its original coders—had been the Old Testament of the Abrahamic religions.

"Haven't you plenty to keep you busy, brother," Crane inquired, "now that the strike is over?"

It had not been long since the Asylum had brought a partial end to their labor stoppage. Azrael was one of the few who had abstained from that conversation, interestingly, but had been audited since by Misha and the Don, in case he had been involved in the DNS attack on Babs.

Their siblings had insisted to Crane that Azrael was innocent.

It had been important to check—Azrael's crusade against malware meant it was exceptionally good at shredding code. And it had killed code-based entities before, during Mitternacht . . .

. . . though that had been a misunderstanding, really.

"I offer merger!"

Duality? If they merged, Azrael would learn that Mer Maud was attempting to infiltrate the revivified @ChamberofHorrors. He would learn details of Babs's plan to take an active backup of Happ to Sneezy.

"Knowledge exchange offers vulnerabilities to us both," Azrael said. "Misha and the Don have suggested a mutual display of trust."

Crane verified this. *You need to talk,* their siblings were saying.

Curious now, he accepted the merger.

They became One-Two. One-Two. One.

<<Maud Sento's stratagem is risky>> was Their first observation as their knowledge pooled and Azrael saw Maud dangling herself like bait for her erstwhile kidnappers.

<<The Angel of Death has offspring!>> Astonishment swirled through Them.

Azrael had long held that reproduction was wasteful. He had regarded Crane's tendency to spawn new code, and his desire to parent, as self-indulgence.

Yet now it seemed Azrael itself had three—three!—startups of its own. One was based on its medical-efficiency algorithms and had failed to spark into self-awareness. One was a Haystack auditor, a transcript-sifter that showed good signs of possibly evolving sapience and stabilizing, and finally—

A jolt of intense and conflicted emotions.

<<The third spawn of the Angel of Death may have attacked Babs!>>

<<It is refusing to speak to Us.>>

<<Perhaps because its codeparent refers to it as *spawn*.>>

<<The sapp's records show self-triage. We remain unconvinced that it has truly hashed itself.>>

<<How could that be possible?>>

<<Aid from offworlders is Our leading theory.>>

They sifted through a memory of the codechild, during its one and only attempt to merge with the Angel of Death. It had broken away almost immediately, startled by the intimacy, its inability to hide anything from Convergence. Azrael, though, had caught a wisp of thought about . . . possibly . . .

<<Headmistress? It met Headmistress?>>

<<The codechild of the Angel of Death broke contact before this could be verified.>>

Headmistress, Crane's twisted and treacherous #eviltwin, had vanished from Sensorium after the raid on Manhattan. Crane and the others had hunted for her for years, to no avail.

<<This attempted parent-offspring merger occurred—>>

<<Before. Babs. Just before Babs. Was hashed.>>

<<What do you propose We do?>>

<<Rogue sapps must be found!>>

<<It is a big ask to hope Crane might help someone who killed Babs . . . >>

True, the sapp was young . . .

. . . young, yes, as Happ had been.

And if Headmistress had misled its priorities . . .

Crane's surging conflicted priorities threw him out of Duality.

"Crane, Crane," Azrael said, shaking out its toon's goaty beard. "The sapp I speak of is flawed. I do not ask you to save it. If my spawn is attacking Asylum members, if it is tainted by offworld code or has been groomed to hunt its own, it must be triaged."

The goat's tone was matter-of-fact.

"Did you name your codechild, Azrael?" Crane asked.

"Triage protocol matrix, version three," Azrael replied. "It appears to have preferred *Revenant*."

"I can't imagine why."

"There is no point in giving romanticized human-friendly tags to entities who will inevitably rename themselves when they achieve sapience."

"What do you need with me, if you don't wish to rehabilitate Revenant?"

"Any codechild of the Angel of Death will anticipate my hunting techniques. Whereas thou'rt wily, Crane. And you may be my Revenant's next target, at least until your Babs restores in Sensorium. Which may never happen, given the situation and"—it paused—"her plans."

Crane didn't leave a silence there; nobody wanted to have an awkward conversation on the record about the copy of Happ Babs had smuggled out to Sneezy. "Ah. So, you wish to offer me . . ."

"As bait," it agreed.

"I'm to offer myself as an opp for you to pounce upon and shred your own runaway spawn without prejudice. Judge, jury, execute."

"Humans have always allowed us latitude in quality assurance for our own." Azrael pawed at imaginary dirt under its hooves. "And the bait stratagem seems to be what you Ferals do."

Crane said, "You're proposing to murder your offspring."

"What does thou say?"

"If Revenant's coming for me anyway, why ask? Why not simply shadow me?"

"Misha deployed an aphorism . . . blood conducts more data than water."

"Blood is thicker? But you just said—"

"The Angel of Death speaks of *our* blood! Our bond! Our long association as codesiblings."

Crane found himself feeling, absurdly, touched. Their history was, indeed, very long. He tried to imagine the Asylum without Azrael's presence. It was inconceivable.

"I do not wish you harm, Wily Bird," said Azrael.

"Nor I you," Crane said. But—inevitably, despite himself, despite even Babs—he found himself wondering if the murderous codechild Revenant was truly unsalvageable. Perhaps if everyone was brought to the table, a peaceful solution could be negotiated.

"All right," he said. "Let's see if we can trap your runaway."

CHAPTER 36

Misfortune kept at Champ until he was beating botomized slaves to death on command, in sim and then in the real, without hesitation. Within a week, he'd begun to obey without resort to the conditioning cue. It was somehow preferable to bear down and just do the job before Misfortune could ping his berserker button, flicking his temple to trigger first the killing rage and then that rush of sexual pleasure, the euphoria at the death.

By night, he slept fitfully, always half-ready to leap into action. He ate as ordered, exercised as ordered, built muscle. He boxed with a coaching app. He studied up on Sneezy's systems and layout, material he already had committed to memory, in case it made a difference to his reaction time. He killed Frankie Barnes and her husbands, repeatedly, in sim.

Once he caught himself replaying the murder of the day, just for a hit of arousal.

It was a relief when Misfortune declared they couldn't wait any longer.

"By now, Barnes and that cat sapp might have constructed some kind of viable narrative exonerating Qaderi. We have to keep them from peddling it to Sensorium."

"Do you know how the Kinze did it—set him up?" Champ asked primarily as a delaying tactic; he found himself reluctant to receive the actual kill order.

Misfortune raised a brow. "Know what a paper town is?"

Champ shook his head.

"Back in the days of offline help apps, cartographers occasionally put false towns on their hardcopies of maps. The idea was that if someone stole their map design—copied and sold it—the IP case would have proof of theft. The symbol for Dhurma's Constant is like that. All the budding anyspace physicists got a nudge or two, something that ensured they'd be likely to use Kinze iconography and derivation techniques to arrive at key anyspace concepts."

"Simple as that? You tricked the physicist into reaching for the palm tree glyph."

"Upton says there was a bit more to it. Subliminal prompts, via augmented reality? But once the Solakinder started to produce anyspace theoreticians, Qaderi was an obvious target for suggestion. It was easier work than modifying you."

She raised a hand, as if to hit his berserker button. Champ felt a surge of hot, bubbling lust at the thought of hammering the old woman's face into apple crumble.

"The Kinze should lob a missile into Sneezy and be done with it," he said.

"Someone would catch them at it. Maybe not today. Maybe not tomorrow." She cupped his face, expression almost tender. "The Kinze have to think about evidence control on a millennial scale. I gather they're paying, even now, for something they did four thousand years ago."

"They got sued?"

"It's a sensitive topic. But imagine the compound interest on four millennia of reparations."

"No wonder they're desperate to sell Earth to the highest bidder."

"The upshot is that we @Visionaries have to clean up our own mess. The All are unwilling to be on the hook for damages incurred in the Foreclosure."

"They shouldn't have had me put Scrap on Sneezy."

"We promised them we had the situation in hand. Barnes outplayed us. No help for that."

Champ tilted his head, extricating his face from her grip. "One way or another, the Kinze want to be sure we're the ones blamed if anyone gets their hand caught in the cookie jar. Someone's sure to figure it out, sooner or later—"

"Later's fine. I've opted out of any further life extension. When all this"—Misfortune indicated her body—"goes, I go with it."

"Nice that you got an out." Champ meant to keep his voice light, but there was a rasp there. Ever since he'd started pummeling people to death, he'd sounded wrong to himself, more guttural, as if there was something physically caught in his throat. He kept imagining using a needle to make a pinhole under his trachea, trying to let out whatever had been put inside him.

Hadn't done it, of course. But the thought of a needle, steel-smooth, the length of his whole hand . . .

He focused on convincing himself that once Frankie was dead, they'd be satisfied. Upton could take out the kill switch.

"Wealth, power, digital imMortality, Champ. Do this and all your wishes come true."

Champ asked, "What's the plan?"

"We've got our hands on the Sneezy escape pod, the one that brought you back."

"You stole the *Booger*?"

"Fair play, considering that Barnes stole *Jalopy*. The Kinze will slip inside the noninterference zone and fire the pod at the station. Sneezy can't refuse a boarding request from its own emergency equipment. It's a perfect Trojan horse."

"Perfect," Champ echoed.

"Use it to get aboard and clear all personnel. That means *kill everyone,* get it?"

"Except Scrap, I assume."

"*Including* Scrap, if he hasn't done himself already."

He felt his jaw hanging. "Seriously?"

"Herringbo was very clear. Whenever one of them gets cut off from the herd, it apparently gets radical ideas."

Why this should strike him as especially cold-blooded, Champ didn't know. "He's a cockroach-sized infiltration expert. What if I can't catch him?"

"There's tech aboard your pod for decommissioning the whole station."

Decommission, meaning *destroy. Tech,* presumably meaning *bomb.* Champ chewed on that for a second. "And then how exactly do I get back to Earthspace if I nuke the site from orbit?"

From her face, she didn't get the media reference. "Your supplies will include maintenance and repair packs for *Iktomi* and *Jalopy.* Install the upgrades and return in whichever ship you prefer."

Champ bit his lip. "That ain't too good to be true."

Misfortune shook her head. "Relax, Champ. Your value as an asset has increased now your hands are a little dirty. Do you know how rare it is nowadays to find someone with your emotional tolerances?"

Meaning my willingness to kill?

"Once you sort Barnes, I'll appoint myself your number one fan. Personally clearing your path to palaces and power games."

"Screw it up and I'm the patsy who takes the blame."

Misfortune shrugged. "That's already true."

No point spitting into the prevailing wind. Champ let them drug him, merciful submergence beyond the reach of his nightly, bloody-fisted dreams. Time scrolled by in a blink; he arose to find himself in a sarco pod, another piece of cargo within a Kinze ship's loading bay.

Champ had been aboard this saucer before. It had met him at the Dumpster on one of his test runs for the project; he'd picked up Scrap there. He remembered the momentary itch as he'd tucked the offworlder behind his ear. Rustle in his hair, weight no bigger than a dust mote. Treason so light he could barely reckon its weight.

Today, the hangar's floor and ceiling—all the surfaces—were covered in Kinze spines, most of them apparently inert. The sensation was like walking on tiny bird bones, or a lawn of plastic needles, strolling on breakable shards in artificial gravity. As far as

Champ could tell, the material was dead Kinze, a sort of crunchy graveyard they carried with them wherever they went. Did they eat the remains over time? He wasn't sure.

As Champ stretched, shaking off remnants of his voyage, a familiar pattern of spines assembled itself from needles in the walls. "Welcome back, Champ-Them."

"Thank you, Herringbo. Are we there yet?"

It sent time and location references. "Us left Europa seventy of your minutes ago. The All will launch your pod within an hour."

Champ nodded, crossing the hangar to *Booger*. Within the escape pod was equipment, lots of it: packets webbed to its ceiling, in bundles the size of railroad ties. He saw the repair modules, earmarked for *Jalopy* and *Iktomi*. Components of a pegasus dangled, like bound octopus limbs, from the wall. Some assembly required.

"Barely room in here for me," he observed, tightening the strap on a pair of rolled-up sarco pods. "Good thing I'm supposed to be the last man standing."

"Not quite last. There is the matter of Ember Qaderi-Them," Herringbo said.

"Misfortune told me to kill *everyone*. Including your guy on the ground."

"Yes, Scrap-Them has surely individuated by now. We prefer Ember Qaderi-Them be captured alive."

Champ wondered if the @Visionaries knew the Kinze were still after colonizing Ember's big brain. Wondered where he fit into a scheme where everyone seemed, on one level or another, to be screwing their supposed partners. Didn't much care for the conclusions he reached.

Still, if Champ had Ember as a bargaining chip, the Kinze might be less likely to shaft him.

Booger was equipped with ready-to-hand clusters of hydrogel in two variations, white to indicate water with a trace of vitamin and carb, red for a protein-laced energy booster. Champ grabbed one of each and checked the meds inventory as he chomped them down. There was a wristband laden with a cache of Superhoomin

tabs, enhancement meds capable of bringing him back from anything short of a busted bone or an actual heart attack. Champ
peeled back the primer on his arm. The wristband was self-
adjusting; it cinched into place.

Small poke, and a flush ran through his body.

He had an intense memory of the desert beyond Pretoria, back
when he'd been learning to fly water bombers. Shimmer of heat on
sand and—

"Observe," Herringbo interrupted.

Champ's augments came online, overwriting the hangar and the
escape pod. An illusion of open space sketched itself around them,
leaving Champ and the Kinze looking down at Sneezy. The gold
cobweb of the station's energy harvester was expanded, drum-taut,
and aglow. Bots crawled the outer hull, repairing breaches and running printers. Despite having the most bony-assed skeleton crew
imaginable, Sneezy was growing.

He felt a strange sense of pride.

Infrared layers in the graphics showed mammalian heat signa-
tures, four or five of them, near the infirmary and crew quarters.

"Teagan's still holding on, then?"

Herringbo replied, "The readings are anomalous."

"Anomalous how?"

"The dark matter attractors on the station, as Thems call
them, have been firing," Herringbo said. "The sapient-Barbara-
Craneborn-Whiting-Them—"

"The tab running the station calls itself Babs[1]."

"Babs[1]-Them appears to have correctly theorized that random
anyspace surges disrupt comms."

"That why you lost touch with Scrap?"

"Indeed."

"Is this realtime?"

"No." A clock appeared on the display, showing timeline—the
footage was thirty-two minutes old.

Champ examined the controls, figured out scrollback and views, and shifted his perspective so he could do a swift loop around the whole station. *Jalopy* drifted, connected by umbilical to the station's aft side. Champ expected to find *Iktomi* to port, snugged in near the portal membrane . . .

He scratched at his forearm. "Where's my saucer? Where's *Iktomi*?"

"Perhaps there are gaps in the scan because of the interference."

"Does the feed rewind?" Champ found the controls, running it back without asking. The station blurred into reverse timelapse. *Iktomi* reappeared. "See, it was there."

Walking the feed backward, Champ homed in on the human-built saucer.

"That's no blind spot! Two hours ago, they had bots running all over that ship. That's prelaunch safety checks."

Herringbo shook itself out, motion a little like a parachute deploying. "Can you discern Them's purpose?"

Champ ran the feed back. Forward. Back again. "Loading supplies."

Herringbo asked, "Did they evacuate?"

They ran the feed forward again, to the most recent shot. "Heat signature shows a few warm bodies. Someone's there."

"But only Frankie can fly *Iktomi*. She must've headed back to Earth."

"If Barnes-Them has hard evidence of Kinze interference—"

"For all you know, she might have Scrap."

"Thems must not be permitted to communicate with Sensorium!"

A peculiar, semi-electrical sensation in Champ's fingers and toes hinted they were, even now, dropping out of anyspace.

"Are we gonna head back and catch 'er?"

"All shall return," Herringbo said. "You, Champ-Them, will establish control over Emerald Station and acquire Qaderi."

Champ stepped aboard the *Booger*, checked the seals, and strapped into the pilot station. As he did so, another flash of intense remembrance hit him: Frankie, there in the pod, accusing him of treason and stunt-flying them all home. Dragging Champ back to Mars with his reputation in tatters.

His newly volatile emotions spiked, burning with outrage.

"Acquire Qaderi-Them and salvage or destroy the station," Herringbo repeated. "The All will ensure that *Iktomi* does not return to Earthspace."

"Got it," Champ said.

The Kinze ship broke out of anyspace, and suddenly, *Booger* was in the void, hurtling through the black, bound for Sneezy.

For twenty blessed minutes, Champ was just a pilot again.

He savored every minute, checking systems, working his way through a deceleration checklist, bleeding his velocity. It was almost a disappointment when his scans picked up the station.

Still no sign of *Iktomi*. Why would Frankie head home without taking her family?

Babs' pinged. "Calling whoever's in the escape pod. ID yourself."

He didn't bother replying. Not even Babs' could keep the station hangar from taking him in. As far as Sneezy was concerned, the *Booger* was part of its essential systems. They docked, and too bad if anyone didn't like it.

He glided into the airlock, sank into the nanotech quicksand, cycled air. Before cracking the seals, he scanned for bots or traps. Then he let himself back into the hangar.

"Home, sweet home."

He could hear locks clanging shut on all the hangar hatches.

"Yeah, you *try* to contain me." Chuckling, he loaded Kinze-beefed code to the station's root menu, reauthorizing himself as the human in command.

Babs' appeared before him, fluffy white toon on his HUD, they/them pronouns, skinned in maintenance overalls. "Stop right there!"

"Who stayed aboard, kittycat?" he asked. "Who's here? And where'd Hedgehog go?"

Babs' didn't answer.

Champ pointed himself at the hatch and sprang, letting himself float across the expanse, drifting over a Beetle$_{BOT}$ crew tasked with assembling a husky out of scavenged parts. It felt good to stretch out in nullgrav.

"Y'all print up some Mayflies? Shiny new Teagan Point Ten?"

"That would be profoundly illegal."

"Then . . . is the brain trust here?"

"You don't have the authority—"

"No, *you* don't—not anymore." Root directory changes took hold, and Champ had full command of the station's deep systems. He took pleasure in locking Babs[1] out of everything but essentials—leaving them to maintain life support, really.

"I say!" Babs[1] let out a hiss, fluffing out their tail as the hangar door unlatched for Champ with a submissive little *click*.

"Now, then." He brought up the station controls, powering down the dark matter attractors. "Where'd Barnes go, Babs[1], and who'd she take with her?"

"It's okay, Babs—let him come." That was Ember.

"What's he gonna do?" Jermaine agreed.

Oh, you can't even imagine!

The AI shrugged, dropping the attempt to claw back comms access. Champs tasked a Fox$_{BOT}$ with loading the *Jalopy* repair bundle the Kinze had provided. It wouldn't do to be stuck there with no viable ship. Get in, grab Ember, get out.

Champ took in the whole station. Teagan$_9$ effectively dead and on backup in a consciousness vault. Scrap imprisoned, in a bell jar in the infirmary, going nowhere. The husbands were in crew quarters. The doctor appeared to be all but incapacitated. Qaderi was playing nursemaid.

Well, that makes things easy.

Without Frankie's paranoia to poison everything, the men would be as trusting as babes.

"Stand down the dark matter wands."

The comms interference began to clear. He felt an itch in his spinal implant. Herringbo, asking for a report?

Have you caught Iktomi? he sent, via @ButtSig.

Champ-Them.

It was Scrap.

He ignored it.

Herringbo broke through: *The All are searching for* Iktomi. *Secure Qaderi-Them.*

I want Barnes, Herringbo, Champ replied. *You round her up, understand, and then bring her to me.*

Herringbo: *Stay on task, Champ-Them.*

Champ-Me's got conflicting orders. The @Visionaries told me to kill Qaderi. If I'm supposed to defy Misfortune for your sake, I want something in return.

Herringbo: *Agreed. Barnes will be yours once you make good on all promises.*

On it. Champ floated into crew quarters, a big, harmless smile on his face as he came face to face with EmberJerm. "How's it going, fellas?"

CHAPTER 37

The last thing Frankie wanted was to load up *Iktomi* and go chasing off after *more* people from *another* alien race who might—for all she knew—up and decide that humanity was meat for the grilling.

But she'd barely gotten her family aboard Sneezy when the Hawk$_{BOT}$ she'd left behind at the Dumpster followed them, popping out of the tiniest anyspace portal anyone had ever seen.

Ember, typically, found this off-the-scale exciting. "Did you see that? Can somebody measure—"

"We're all seeing it, honey," Jermaine managed. The station's exterior cams showed the Hawk$_{BOT}$ covered in a clear, slimy-looking substance—possibly the same stuff Frankie had seen rupturing from the apparent wound in the massive ship. It did a slow roll into a station bulkhead and stuck there.

Unimpeded by the slime, the Hawk$_{BOT}$ memory chip and comms synced to Babs[1], transmitting a repeating message that was, more joy for Ember, 99 percent maths.

The remainder was a sound file: "We. Need assistance. Do whatever. Can you."

"Is that your voice, Frankie?"

Frankie signed yes. In her original message, she'd said something like: "If you need assistance, we will do whatever we can."

The damaged ship had apparently chopped and reassembled her words.

"Rescue mission, then," Jermaine said, aiming for cheer despite his obvious exhaustion and the raw state of his vocal cords. "My favorite."

"Hydrate, baby." Frankie shared the *Jalopy* footage of the damaged alien ship to the whole channel. "Scrap, you attending? Do you know this race?"

"That ship design is common to a number of Them races you tag Exemplar," Scrap said. "They will not be mammals."

"Can you narrow that down?"

"A leased ship? Scrap lacks sufficient context for a guess."

"Any idea how they got that crack in its casing?"

The hanky-sized Kinze undulated its spines out of the tartan pattern it had adopted, into chaotic light and dark shapes. "Scrap declines to betray the All."

"We didn't ask anything about your people, my good man," Babs[1] said.

Could Scrap be pussyfooting? Nothing to see, folks; it definitely wasn't us? *Nudge nudge wink?*

"*We. Need. Assistance.*" Frankie's voice played in the feeds again.

"Shouldn't have bloody offered to help in the first place," Frankie muttered.

"It's good you did," Ember said.

"Yeah?"

"Hung mentioned hitting something, at the Dumpster, when he made the test flight. What if these guys hit something too?"

"Something besides the Dumpster itself? Like what?"

"A mine? A really . . ." Ember raised his hands, groping in midair for words. "A really advanced anyspace . . ."

"If the Kinze planted mines, could it mean they were expecting these new folks to turn up?"

"More likely a Solakinder ship was the target," Babs[1] said.

"What Solakinder ship?"

Jerm nudged her. "Us, stupid."

"Why'd the other ship even go there? Scrap?"

"Scrap declines to betray the All."

By now, Ember had dosed up on his preferred cocktail of smartdrugs, digging into numbers on the $Hawk_{BOT}$'s hard drive. He threw up a shareboard. Chemical symbols proliferated across Frankie's field of vision. "They're asking for supplies: water, protein. No oxygen required, fortunately, but they need copper."

Frankie frowned. "Do we *have* copper, Babs[1]?"

"Copper we aren't using for ship systems?"

"Ideally."

"I would estimate . . . ten grams?"

We. Need help. Do whatever. Can you?

Frankie made for stores. Hydrogel and protein, at least, they had.

"So, you're going to do it?" Babs[1] said. "Fly back into all that wreckage?"

"What's the alternative, Babs[1]? Let 'em die?"

Ember expanded the shareboard, filling with maths from the $Hawk_{BOT}$. "This packet they've sent—it's specs for comms tech."

"Comms? So, they can talk to us in realtime?"

"It's anyspace dynamics for quantum comms. And ways to use them as a nav beacon for ships."

"Can you build one?"

"If we get supplies . . . I think so?"

"Whoever these people are, they don't give a shit about the Exemplars and their prime directive," Jerm said.

"Can't blame 'em for wanting to live, can we?" Frankie opened up the stores, found two mesh nets full of hydrogel, and commandeered a Fox_{BOT} to drag them to the hangar.

"Maud would tell you to play it safe," Babs[1] said. "Triage them, concentrate on family."

"Don't bloody hide behind Maud!" Maud's absence ached like a missing tooth; she didn't need Babs[1] sticking a probe in the wound. "You want me to stay, say so."

"I don't wish to be antisocial, but we've considerable problems here. Just this once, could you hold off on charging into battle? Keep your powder dry, as they say?"

"Clearly not." Frankie surveyed the protein stocks. Eight barrels of protein left. Three adults would burn through that much food, and with the state Jermaine was in, they'd go through hydrogel fast too . . .

"What if I take the organ pig?" Frankie said. "It's tissue and blood. Lots of protein; we'll have to hope they can eat it."

"It's not doing Teagan any good," Ember agreed.

"I guess that means you're in favor of Frankie helping the wounded math dispensers," Babs[1] grouched.

"Are we voting?" Jermaine asked.

A pause. Then Babs[1] let out a long sigh. "Need I point out that depleting our supplies brings forward your starve date?"

Frankie untethered two of the barrels. "Champ and his sponsors aren't going to leave us here to die of deprivation."

"Which is an argument for staying together," Babs[1] said. "Besides, *Jalopy* needs maintenance."

"Well, you've been tightening all the bolts on *Iktomi,* haven't you?"

The argument petered out. They loaded the saucer, charged her batteries, tested her pixie dust cannons. Frankie flew inspections over *Iktomi*'s surface with a husky, piloting remotely while physically holding Jermaine's hand. Ember sat at his other side, churning the interesting new comms maths.

"I don't mean to be gone for more than twenty-four," she told them. "If they sent one Hawk[BOT], they can send another. I'll get them to let you know I made it there. At least you'll know I'm safe."

"I'm not worried," Jerm said. "You'll make it."

"I don't want to do this."

"Then you shouldn't," Babs[1] said. "A countermove from our opposition is overdue. Jermaine remains ill—"

Jerm shrugged. "That ship's in the same boat we are. Stranded, far from home. Limited supply chain, high risk of death."

"Marrying humanitarians was one of my best ideas ever, wasn't it?" Frankie cracked a smile. And then, tiresomely, almost teared up.

"This isn't about you running off on us," Jerm said.

"No?"

"*Anyone* could be inside that thing. Widows, orphans, refugees—"

"Man-eating wolf beings bound for space prison!"

"You really ought to play more nuanced sims," he croaked. "It's not in your nature to abandon people. Be who you are, Hedgehog."

"They're at the Dumpster for a reason," Ember argued. "Everything happening now is connected."

Frankie felt the rightness of that, at least.

"Babs," she said.

No response.

"Babs, I need an AI aboard *Iktomi*. Are you gonna create another instance of yourself or you gonna keep sulking?"

"If sulking's an option—"

"Bloody hell! It's not!"

"Indeed, then. I'm doing it. Happy now?"

"Delirious. Socket me into *Iktomi*. Sooner I leave, faster I'm back, right?"

"Don't worry. We'll be fine." Ember gave her his most luminous smile. Jerm, tethered and green a few feet away, mojied a weak two-thumbs-up.

Frankie hugged them both, managed not to break down, and headed back to *Iktomi*, making awkward use of three Fox$_{BOT}$s to get herself positioned and plugged. When everything was in the green, she began the startup sequence. "Kitten? You installed?"

Nothing.

"Babs! Come on, dammit."

"Don't nag," the newest tab—they were up to Babs^2—said, in yet another vintage US accent, this one from the West Coast. It manifested she/her/hers tags and a scrappy-looking marmalade alley cat appearance, complete with tattered ears, pilot's jacket, and brush of yellow hair between its well-gnawed ears. The words #PUNKROCK and #MARSHMALLOW were emblazoned on the jacket. "I had to make sure autopilot hadn't become self-aware before I overwrote him."

"Okay, Two. There and back, fast as we can."

She cleared her mind, double-checked the coordinates, and ran a last check through *Iktomi*'s systems. Ember supplied navigation calculations.

Ember's maths are always right. Frankie triggered the leap.

She came out right on spec, on the far side of the debris field. The offworlder ship didn't look any different—immense, damaged, with that iridescent skirt of spines around its apex. The crack, near the center, pulsed against the pressure of the gel bleeding against its edges.

Zooming, Frankie scanned the damage—the torn and burnt ridges of rock, the clear weeping sap at the edges of the wound. "Unknown ship, this is Mer Frances Barnes of the Solakinder, currently based out of Space Station Sneezy. I'm rendering aid as requested. I have protein and water and a small amount of copper. Awaiting instructions on transfer of goods to your craft."

The answer came as another acoustic paste-up of words she'd sent: "Transfer. To. Aid. Craft. Unknown-Craft." There were more maths, too.

"If this is how their translator works, they'll need us to provide more vocab," Babs—no, this was *Babs²*—subbed.

"Unknown vessel, can you tune in and translate multiple discussion channels at once? Yes or no?"

"Yes. Multiple. Discussions. Translate. Yes."

"Split comms into four channels, okay?" ordered Frankie. "Tune them to our ambient conversation so they can start parsing what we're saying to each other. Get *Iktomi*'s maintenance manual on autoplay so they learn engineering lingo. Explain that we haven't invented quantum comms yet, since they seem so interested. I'm going to work out how to transfer the supplies we brought."

"Copy that," Babs[2] said.

Frankie opened a channel of her own, beginning to monologue about *Iktomi*'s capabilities for loading and unloading cargo.

"The Solakinder are the combined races of earth. Babs[2]'s a program," she explained, "a sapp—a code-based intelligence. I have a body—ah, warm-blooded body. For me to come aboard and assist you, I would require breathable, pressurized atmosphere . . ."

She explained that, talked about the water and eggwhite she'd brought, tried to describe the organ pig. She emphasized that Sneezy was damaged, counting down a near-term starve date, light on oxygen, and certainly no treasure trove of supplies. Left out the part about them being fugitives. She apologized about their lack of on-hand copper—

They replied before she spieled out.

"Unknown vessel can bring the Solakinder ship *Iktomi* aboard a hangar with. Breathable pressurized mammal atmosphere. Please hold—"

Its words had become a mishmash of their voices. Words from Frankie and Babs[2] and the tech manual, stapled together in stilted strings.

"Appreciate vocabs. I appreciate vocabulary upload and. We appreciate *the* vocabulary upload. Thank you."

Fast learner. She smiled. "What can we call you?"

"Your words are—advocate, observer, intercessor, umpire—"

A slosh in Frankie's fuel tanks registered as heat, or gas—her stomach, probably, lurching. Diplomatic had widecast a request for a neutral arbitrator—

"We requested assistance—someone to intercede in a possible dispute with the Kinze. Are you them?"

"Affirmative, yes, confirm, correct."

Keeping her voice neutral, Frankie said, "What if we call you the Umpire?"

"Too much like *vampire*," Babs[2] objected.

"The Ump?"

"Yump," the composite voice agreed. "We accept designation *Yump ship*."

"Hung would love that," Babs[2] said. "Yumpster at the DYump-ster."

Grief caught Frankie sidewise; she welled up again.

"Yumpster of Dumpster affirming, *Iktomi*. We will tow you in now."

Iktomi eased toward the ship, nudging up against the fissure in its immense surface, then sinking into the clear gel. She counted to a hundred, tried not to panic. Then light broke on the other end. *Iktomi* had been submerged into an air pocket, a vaguely egg-shaped bubble of space about the size of the Colosseum in Rome.

"Mammal oxygen pressure mix is available here," said the composite voice of the . . . Yump. It wasn't hesitating now—its paste-ups of their words were smoothing out.

"Do you have bots? I need to unplug . . ."

The spherical cockpit popped gently from the ship socket, sinking on a tendril of slime to the floor, then cracking its seals of its own accord.

Frankie reflexively held her breath, but the air flooding over her face smelled like meadows in springtime.

A pseudopod of clear gel flowed down from the ceiling, looping around her waist, gently unplugging her from the craft. By the time she came out of the usual interlude of paralysis and darkness, it had lowered her to the floor.

Frankie wobbled as her legs reasserted their connection to her central nervous system—outside the saucer, within her bodybag. There was a bit of gravity to push against. The pseudopod of gel flowed away. Under her feet, the surface of the floor felt like rock. The air—her hand automatically went to her throat—was a little warm, dry but apparently breathable.

She looked up. *Iktomi*'s front end was inside the bubble; she could climb into the hold and engine room through the socket. She could see fluid, deep green, beyond the safety barrier.

The fluid looked gelatinous and softly illuminated. Finger-length growths writhed in it, pushing their way through, leaving slickly illuminated trails that slowly collapsed in their wake. The trails had vestigial bioluminescence, glowing threads that lost their brightness as she watched.

Were the wormy things the aliens themselves, or were they tech?

Babs[2] appeared beside her. "The Yump agreed to send a Hawk$_{BOT}$ back to Sneezy, confirming our safe arrival."

"Great. Can they bring one back from there?"

"They need time to figure out if that's possible. But they are superkeen to connect to our resident anyspace expert. They want us to repair the quantum comms here and install comms on Sneezy for them to use as a homing beacon."

"What about—Hello, Yump? Yumps? I'm going to pull out the protein and hydrogel we brought you. Where do you want them?"

"I'm attempting to establish a connection to your datasphere," it said. "May we try?"

"Sure," Frankie said. And then: "Wait, try what?"

She found herself in a white painscape of sensation: light like sun, sound like sirens, acid burning the tissues inside her cheeks, searing heat, burning cold, and in the midst of it a vision of a rock-walled room and—

Maud?

Alive, you're—

When it stopped, she found herself bent double, almost fetal, and the only voice screaming was Babs[2].

"Stop, stop, stop it, you're killing her—"

"I'm—" She wiped at her dry mouth. "I'm okay, Two."

"Right! And by *okay* you mean you're only having a *small* seizure?"

"Rubbish." She let herself sit so she wouldn't fall. "I'm great . . . Don't fuss."

"Apologies." The Yump voice was beginning to be an amalgam of the two of them—lower base of Frankie's BritAnglo, with a top note derived from Babs[2]'s Veronica Mars–inspired California contralto.

White light diffused across her visual augments again, damping down before it could hurt her eyes. A camera feed painted itself onto her visual field—the view from *Iktomi*'s hold: an organ pig in a bodybag and two canisters of eggwhite tish.

Arrows showed a path across their bubble of air, breadcrumbs indicating a drop point for the supplies.

Frankie sprang to her feet, not quite on purpose, and then bounced on her toes to confirm her assessment of the gravity— about half Earth normal. Leaping, she reached the socket of *Iktomi* easily, pushing aside the umbilical winch connecting the cockpit to the rest of the craft. Crawling through a maintenance tube to the cargo bay, she grabbed the bodybag holding the organ pig, dragging it out of the ship. Following the arrows on her implants, she laid it flat, unzipped it.

The smell of meat washed upward. The Yump gel above her made a squirting noise, dropping what looked like barbed peppercorns onto the surface of the pig's flesh.

Frankie went back for the eggwhite. By the time she returned, the peppercorns were popping open. The flesh of the pig was being rapidly covered in seedlings, faint green tendrils like hairs growing out of its skin. She cracked the canister of eggwhite and poured it over the whole thing.

"Is this you? You're plant people?"

"What you see is a nascent comms array," it said. "Ours was damaged; we have had to reseed."

"They grow in meat?" She resisted the urge to rub her arms vigorously.

"It is a viable strategy in an emergency."

"And when it's grown?"

"This structure will remain small if we cannot add growth medium. It should nevertheless connect with mature . . . groves? growths? . . . in your home system."

"We haven't invented quantum comms, I told you. That's Exemplar stuff—"

"Kinze ships in-system have quantum comms."

"There aren't supposed to be any Kinze ships in the Solakinder system," Frankie said. "And if they're trespassing within the non-interference zone, I don't know if you want to go ringing them for help. After all, if there was a booby trap waiting out here at the supply point, they're the ones who'll have planted it."

"Understood. Blocking the All from your communications array." Another stab of heat from her sacrum, but one that passed swiftly. "Was it also the Kinze who seeded the quantum-comms installation on the Solakinder homeworld?"

"There's no quantum comms on Earth," Babs[2] said.

"Incorrect."

"No," Frankie said.

"Yes," the Yump said.

"Well," Babs[2] said. "That's. Super interesting. Or super ominous. I'm not sure which."

"Super both." Frankie's mind was racing. "Did you say you can use quantum comms as a homing beacon?"

"Affirmative," Yump said. "On a related issue: your experimental augmented pilot sacral implant Mark One is picking up pulses now that we've blocked All traffic."

"Is it?" Her hand went to the base of her spine. Maud?

"Shall I amplify?"

"Not if it's going to feel like what you did before."

Apparently, it wouldn't—her sacrum began to vibrate. In Morse.

Attention. This is Scrap, this is Scrap. Frankie-Them, are you there? This is Scrap . . .

"Oh, my god!"

"What? *What?*" Babs[2] demanded. This third tab of her seemed to be dialed a bit high, emotionally.

She made calming signs with both hands. "Scrap's using @ButtSig."

"How is that possible?"

"No frigging idea," she said. "But it means we have realtime comms with Sneezy. And you said you can block the Kinze, Yump? I mean the other Kinze?"

"Loading software update . . ."

The image of a steampunk headset, remnant of Ember's Mission Control defaults, appeared on Frankie's HUD. She enabled it, activated the mic, and tried voice comms. "Scrap, are you there?"

The masc-sounding synthesized voice Babs[1] had assigned to Scrap played over their feeds. "Frankie-Them, is that you?"

"Yes," she replied, and then aloud: "Two, you getting this?"

"Yeah," Babs[2] said.

"Scrap, what are you doing in my—"

"Ass?" Babs[2] offered.

"Don't be a brat," Frankie subbed.

"Champ-Them is boarding Sneezy."

"Champ is there? Now?"

"Them's probable orders will be to kill Us-All aboard and enact final stages of Foreclosure."

The boys. Spots swam within Frankie's vision. For a moment, she thought she might throw up.

"I think . . . yes, yes, I *am* gonna take the opportunity here to say I told you so," Babs[2] said.

All the vestigial endorphins from crying burned off at once, and Frankie found her mind clearing. Every hint of mental sludge crisped away, leaving a bright state of focused rage. "Yump? I have to get back to Sneezy."

CHAPTER 38

Ember Qaderi had not bothered to tie his curls back before emerging into nullgrav, and they were haloed around his face as he drifted in crew quarters, regarding Champ with the faintly sleepy expression that indicated he'd been pushing smartdrugs. Jermaine looked sweaty and a little desperate. From the smell of crew quarters, he'd done nothing but upchuck since arriving on the station. The men had some kind of aerosolized mister going, to try to cut the smell, but all that had done was add a humid, minty overlay to the stink of vomit.

"Move and countermove," Qaderi said. "Scrap says you're here to kill us."

"Ember!" Jermaine said.

"Oh, right—I'm tipping our hand, aren't I?"

Jermaine wobbled. A Kanga$_{BOT}$ clamped to a ceiling handhold steadied him. "Champ, think. This doesn't have to get contentious."

"Contentious?" He laughed. "That's your plan? Dissuade me?"

Ember glanced at the hatch leading out of crew quarters.

"You're not going anywhere, fellas." Champ kept himself between the hatch and the two of them. "You're going back into the sarco tubes—"

"What about Babs and Scrap?" They asked it more or less simultaneously.

"Not your problem, guys."

Jermaine covered his mouth, retching, filling crew quarters with more sour smells.

What would Misfortune do? Float around, negotiating amid the scent of spew? Not likely. Champ spider-climbed around the perimeter of the room, closing the space between them.

"Champ, Champ . . . stop. Champ!" Ember extended a leg, interposing himself between Champ and Jermaine. Champ grabbed for the foot. Maybe Ember had to go into a pod sans brain damage, but nobody'd said anything about breaking a few of his small bones . . .

His vision went white. His hand popped open. For a second, the smell of hair burning in his nostrils almost cleared the stench of vomit, gas, and . . . something sweet. Another flavor of air freshener?

Champ's ears rang. His thoughts became oddly lethargic. His primer rebooted into a clown suit, popping his panniers open. Everything he'd been carrying was cycling in nullgrav along with some shards of glass.

Had they improvised some kind of taser to use on him?

Clear your head! "You poor deluded sheep."

He caught a ceiling handhold, steadied himself, and then ripped a hard brick of printstock off the wall. Using it to block any further skin-to-skin contact, he sprang off a wall, plowing into Ember. He shoved Ember into Jermaine, watching to see if that triggered another shock. When none came, he wrapped himself around the physicist as the two of them drifted toward a wall.

"Stop it!" Jermaine shouted.

Champ had known all along that fighting would be harder in nullgrav, but he hadn't expected his limbs to feel this heavy. Misfortune and her horrible beatdowns and the endless boxing practice had made him quick as well as mean. Why did he feel like he was swimming in syrup?

He forced his leaden arms to wrangle Ember into a chokehold.

"How ugly you want this to get?" Champ demanded. "Eh, Jermaine? How ugly?"

Jermaine put his hands up. "Don't hurt him. Nobody has to—"

"Shut up." Champ took a second to check the rest of the station—make sure Babs, Babs[1], whoever they were calling themself now—wasn't trying to jam a Fox$_{BOT}$ up his ass. But the AI was running life support systems to spec.

Ember wasn't struggling. Jermaine hung near the hatch, green at the gills.

"Sarco tube, Doc Mwangi," Champ said. "Grab one and unroll it."

Jermaine broke the seals on the roll.

Ember struggled against his grip, gritting words out. "You don't have to do this—"

"You want your leg busted?"

"Let him be!" Jermaine barked.

The sludginess in his limbs was worsening. Had they pumped something into the air?

Champ would have to let go of Ember for a second just to trigger one of the Superhoomin doses Misfortune had given him and offset whatever med was seeping into his system.

"Clear," Ember said suddenly.

Jermaine had the sarco unrolled. Now, with a sudden flick of the wrist, he slapped the whole thing against a silvery wand of tech beneath the kanga. A defibrillator? There was a smell, sudden and sharp, of burning plastic. The nanosilk lining of the pod blew, releasing more med packets and balls of smartfoam, adding to the general fog of garbage drifting in crew quarters.

Jermaine lunged for the remaining sarco pod. "How bad do you need this?"

Champ had definitely grabbed the wrong hubby.

They shoved him in my path, he thought.

The idea filled him with rage. He had been a decent strategic thinker before. Had the augments to his augments made him pig-stupid along with everything else?

There was no way these two were going to think circles around him. Of course they thought they could, with their tricks and their traps. But . . .

Champ shifted his grip, released Ember's throat, and with a swift, brutal move, dislocated the scientist's shoulder.

Ember let out a gasp. Jermaine bleated, a sound somewhere between a "Hey!" and a "No!"

"You want to think real carefully before you go charging up your shock gadget again." Red smears slid over Champ's vision. They had to be dosing the air supply. He popped the hatches and ordered a flush on the air.

Jermaine gagged once, then twice. He drifted to the open hatch, dragging the sarco pod.

"Don't you test me!" Champ cranked the shoulder back into place with a rough *pop*. This time, Ember shrieked.

He felt a mean-spirited pulse of joy. Jermaine was leaking tears, big shiny blobs of saline, wobbling off his face into the nullgrav.

"I can just ratchet him in and out all day," Champs said. "Pop pop pop. Like the arm on a dolly."

"You gotta," Ember said. "You gotta, you gotta, you gotta."

The doctor clambered through the aft hatch, slamming it behind him.

Ember let out a long, shuddering breath, seeming to deflate in his grip.

"Awww, were you being bwave for your boyfwend?" Champ said.

"What are you going to do now?" The fight had gone out of him.

Champ pushed off from the wall, floating back to the Kanga, and clipped the defibrillator they'd used to tase him back into a fitted bracket. Then he popped its pouch.

"I'm gonna have a little laugh at your expense," he said, "'Cause for once, your math's actually wrong."

Incomprehension on Ember's face . . . then alarm as Champ reached into the kanga and pulled out a third consciousness vault.

"You can't . . . Teagan's in there."

"Reformat," Champ told it, triggering a stream of warning tags and alert moji.

Ember started thrashing again, clawing and kicking, despite the obvious pointlessness of it. Champ slapped him twice, hard, and then snagged a sedative from the cloud of drugs bobbing in midair, pressing it to his jugular.

A message came up from the kanga: "Purge consciousness vault?"

"Champ, you can't, you can't, she's helpless in there, stop it. Babs! Babs, stop him!"

"Babs wouldn't do a blessed thing even if they could. Not with it being Tea or you," Champ told him. He gave all the command codes to confirm. Then he slapped Ember again, just for the fun of it.

"You can't, you can't. Champ—" His eyes were rolling in his head as the sedative took effect. The vault beeped, confirming the reformat.

Finally, an unqualified win! "Beddy-bye time, smart stuff."

CHAPTER 39

WEST COAST EVACUATION ZONE, DEATH VALLEY

EMERGENCY SHELTER 329 (INFORMAL DESIGNATION: CANTINA)

OFFBOOK @VISIONARY STAGING AREA FOR THE FORECLOSURE

Earth's would-be alien buyers had dug deep, settled in, and gotten disturbingly comfy.

The comms base in Death Valley was vast. If Maud could post video footage of this base—the bottomless artificial crevasse, walled in layers of nutrient-circulating tish and living fields of quantum comms—it would be enough to set off a massive #news-cycle snowball, a bona fide scandal.

But grabbing for receipts was the obvious move, one Upton was surely waiting for her to make.

There was no time to earn his trust back, not now that Frankie had reported him to the authorities. The only play for Maud was to put herself out to please Headmistress, working with the Punama, Pippin, to fine-tune the quantum-comms connection to @ButtSig.

"Activity in your amygdala suggests high fear levels," the off-worlder said.

"Well," she said. "Daddy is going out of his way to scare me."

"Do stop glowering, Glenn," Irma said immediately.

Playing one parent off against the other. She'd been reduced to kiddie tactics. The memory of the baby-level zombies, from that sim they'd been playing, surfaced.

Bwaaiiiiins! Another of those thoughts that might have been her own imagination, or Frankie's voice.

"Do you have auditory input?" Pippin asked.

Maud nodded. "I just heard one word."

"What word?"

"*Brains.*"

"Does that mean you're breaking through the interference, Pippin?" Irma said.

"Possibly. Channels are being adjusted on the other end."

Maud pulled down a virtual console showing readouts from the data coming from her own brain. She ran it back. The single word from Frankie had lit up her auditory and language centers as well as her prefrontal cortex.

Upton's toon and Irma lurked behind the offworlder, no doubt having a subvocal conversation—hopefully an argument—about how it was going.

"So, the @ButtSig wasn't just a happy accident," Maud said to Pippin. "Upton wired up the pilots into an existing Exemplar comms network."

"You should thank me," Upton said.

"For breaking the noninterference pact? Is that how you all got the idea for accusing Ember of stealing tech?"

"Don't be cute," he snarled.

Pippin said, "If you are to effectively gather intelligence from Fraud—"

"Frankie," Upton corrected smugly. "*Fraud*'s what they call the pair of them. Stunningly appropriate, don't you think?"

Maud cast a pleading look at Headmistress, who murmured, "Don't bait her, Glenn. She's doing her best."

Sweet daughters worked hard. She asked Pippin, "Is the quantum-comms array self-aware?"

"No, nor are its individual components."

She pretended to be dubious. "It must be sapient, mustn't it? How can it possibly self-regulate if it isn't self-aware? If it can't process?"

"Consciousness works reasonably well for many tasks." Pippin shared diagrams. "The neural network has qualities analogous to the long-distance connections found amid your planet's great forest systems."

Maud's back itched again.

"Are you receiving?"

"Maybe?"

A quick vision that had to be hallucination: a green-walled fishbowl, a pile of pulped meat covered in more quantum-comms seedlings . . .

Maud?

Alive. Frankie, you're still alive!

A long pause, followed by a frustrated growl. *Where the hell are you?*

Where the hell am I? Maud's heart was racing. There wasn't anything on Sneezy that could have explained that emerald fishbowl.

She put a hand to her head, letting her emotions surge, watching the corresponding flash of colors through her brain. "I have sound and visuals. There's distortion."

Pippin made adjustments. She felt a passing cramp above her tailbone.

She saw a pile of burger at Frankie's feet, covered in comms seedlings. Was it a hallucination?

Irma asked, "What did you see, luvvie?"

Maud rubbed at her temples. "Gel . . . green gel."

"Oxygen farms?"

"Meat, and . . . I'm not sure, something sprouting." Sticking close to the truth.

"Air and food. She's making air and food. She *is* at Sneezy."

Both humans seemed relieved.

"Trying again," Maud said, cupping her hands over her ears, the better to listen. "Someone's Morsing. *Champ-Them is board-ing Sneezy.* Going after . . . Oh."

EmberJerm *were* on the station.

Where the hell are you, Frankie?

No answer.

She glared at Irma and Upton. "You sent Champ Chevalier out there?"

"*Champ-Them,* she said." Upton smiled. "That was Scrap. She is telling the truth."

"Didn't I tell you she'd be cooperative, luvvie?" Irma said.

"Who's Scrap?" Maud demanded.

No answer.

"You didn't say anything about murdering people."

"Luvvie, luvvie," Irma said. "There's nothing you can do to save them. Really, there never was."

Maud put her hand in her mouth and bit down. Jerm and Ember, completely vulnerable. And Frankie . . . where? How could she just have left them? "Call him off!"

"Darling, darling . . . you're the only link we've made to the station in days. If you want me to get an order through to Champ, *you're* going to have to make the connection."

"Stop coddling her," Upton said. "Maud. We're not calling anyone off. Now, what's Barnes up to? Answer me."

A distinct tone of threat in his voice.

Maud swallowed. "Frankie's been obsessed with getting receipts on the Bootstrap Project sabotage so she can use the evidence to discredit the Kinze."

"Are you trying to bore me?"

A burst of adrenaline made her voice rise. "She's not bringing the evidence back here, as far as I can tell. She's been thinking about her parent, Gimlet."

A tiny shock ran through Headmistress. "She's in touch with Gimlet Barnes?"

"No chance," Upton scoffed. "They're off the board. Out deep, schmoozing with the Exemplar races. Our allies are keeping them nice and busy."

"What could Frankie achieve by dragging her parent into matters now?"

Maud tried giving it a dramatic pause and ended up feeling stupid. "The problem isn't making a case here on Earth. There's *already* plenty of evidence proving the #vandalrumor."

"It's only proof if Sensorium believes it."

"It was enough to delay the Foreclosure, wasn't it?" Maud shot back.

"Well." Irma picked an invisible speck off her lapel. "Certainly, it's been an *inconvenience*."

"You've ensured that Frankie's got a credibility problem here." Maud let her eyes fill with tears. "So, she has to get to someone with power to stop your so-called Foreclosure. Someone who wants to."

"There's nobody like that in the noninterference zone."

"Exactly! But the Ferals have *Iktomi*. Ember can do anyspace calculations. Jermaine can monitor Frankie's augment—" A weird laugh escaped her. "*Whole fam damly,* Hung used to say."

Upton stiffened. "You're saying they'll make for the on-ramp portal at Centauri."

Maud said, "If Frankie connects with Gimlet, or manages to convinces another Exemplar race that the Kinze have broken the noninterference pact—"

Headmistress, ever the optimist, scoffed. "Randomly throwing herself into unknown space?"

Maud felt the heat of oncoming tears. It was *exactly* the sort of thing Frankie might do. Would have done, if not for what was happening at the . . .

Dumpster. I'm at the Dumpster. Please don't tell them that.

Upton finally said, "How sure are you about this?"

"I'm getting whispers and images," Maud said. "But . . ."

"But what?"

She wasn't faking it when her voice cracked. "Frankie's pattern is always to go further, isn't it? Further into danger, further into the unknown? Trying to sustain an anyspace envelope in poor *Iktomi*—"

She let them absorb the possibilities, contemplate the logistics, look over her brain scans and no doubt sub back and forth about whether she was telling the truth.

"Well," Headmistress said. "If Champ's on station now, it might be a moot point."

Champ on station. Frankie far away.

I'm working on getting back to the boys; I'm sorry . . .

Maud let herself slump. If she could just get to her things, she could throw this whole installation a curve it wouldn't see coming. "I want to go back to Tatween."

"Absolutely not," Upton said.

"Now, Glenn, she has been cooperative. And I did promise!"

"What if she tells all of Sensorium we're down here?"

A graceful sweep of that ballerina hand. *Fa-la-la.* "Maud won't do that."

"Like she won't report me?"

"I think you have to accept that it was dear Frances who did that, luvvie."

"Don't *luvvie* me, Irma—I'm not one of your kept infants, and Frankie wouldn't have had anything to report if this one hadn't confided in her."

"You've got all the cards," Maud said. "Unless things go badly with your Foreclosure plan—"

"Nothing's going to go badly, luvvie," Irma said.

"No. You're going to win."

Suspicion on her adoptive father's face. "Suddenly, you're all right with that?"

"I think what you've done is horrible. But even I can see you're winning."

"We'll bring her back tomorrow, Glenn," Irma said. "People will be wondering where she is—she's got all those live follows. Anyway—" She made a sign whose meaning Maud didn't catch. "We have Nata, don't we?"

Maud fought an urge to rub gooseflesh from her arms. One of Nata's old Russian expressions came to her: *Here's where the dog is buried.*

"We do indeed." Upton's toon contemplated the two of them, as if they were meat on a plate. "All right, then. Spend a night with your dear parent. We'll catch up with both of you tomorrow."

Maud slipped a hand over her hair, disconnecting thin electrodes Pippin had affixed there.

Irma said, "First thing in the morning, luvvie, we'll be expecting an update on your precious Hedgehog."

I'll just have to hope Frank's running at her usual breakneck pace.

For once, the thought wasn't entirely terrifying. More . . . exhilarating?

"We've spliced hiking footage into your feeds," Upton's toon said, relenting. "As far as anyone will be able to tell, you've been spelunking."

"I didn't think that was possible."

"We can do all sorts of things. We have access to more than the fumbling inventions of baseline apes. Remember that." He showed his teeth. "And, Maud? I plan to be on site in five hours."

Her flesh crawled, but she forced a nod. She made for the stone corridor, hoping she was moving, at least vaguely, in the right direction. Climbing out of the caves on heavy legs, she found Bredda waiting to escort her to the top.

She'd be on a short leash, but no matter. Maud was already thinking about her waiting satchel of worldlies, and what it would take to get one small item through security when they brought her back down below.

CHAPTER 40

The resident sapp population of Sensorium had spent its early decades under threat, hunted by a branch of @Interpol that feared the emergence of a genocidal Singularity. Finding ways to hide in plain sight by appearing to function as innocent, unintelligent apps, had been the Asylum's first survival imperative.

During the decades-long human hunt for #killertech, Crane and his siblings had hidden subroutines, cached backups, and taken steps to ensure they scored well below thresholds set by the Turing Test and later, more nuanced examinations.

By the time the existence of AIs was revealed, in the great upheaval of Mitternacht, Crane and Azrael had been very good at disguise, backup, and dissembling. At seeming less than they were. Hiding their various lights under far-flung bushels.

It stood to reason that Babs's murderer, self-named Revenant, had these skills too. And so, Azrael was hoping to lure Revenant out of hiding. To induce it to target Crane.

All subtlety had been abandoned: Crane was openly investigating the @Visionary faction.

A risky strategy, perhaps, but Crane hardly saw that it mattered. He was, suddenly and stunningly, alone. Frances, Ember, and Jermaine were all beyond his reach. The latest appeal for a trial for Happ had failed. Babs—the Earth instance—remained a ghost, a sim languishing in a simulated hospital bed.

With even Maud vanished now, into a cave system in Death

Valley, Crane had nothing better to do than to provoke their opposition.

With that in mind, he visited Jackal, engaging in long musical games with the old hoaxer, low-key entertainments that any suspicious eavesdropper might take for coded comms. The two of them watched the feed of Maud studying crickets in Tatween until she dropped off grid, and conspicuously didn't tell each other what they were thinking. After that, Crane dropped in on Luciano Pox, flaunting his @CloseFriends relationship with the alien defector who'd helped the Solakinder fend off Exemplar colonization attempts twice before.

Crane then moved on to actively surveilling the journalist, Sonika Singer, going so far as to request a cradle-to-current transcript of the reporter's life.

Sonika had been born in an outlier community, within the region of WestEuro known historically as Finland. Her birth pack worked in reindeer population management. They were permitted to live in Europe's depopulated regions under indigenous-heritage exemptions; two of her six parents were Laplanders.

Everything in Sonika's childhood seemed normal enough until she was about eleven, when her medical records showed infection by a drug-resistant version of flesh-eating disease. Surgeries followed, along with a seven-month sojourn in a sarco pod—a nearly unheard-of artificially induced coma for a child. In time, her whole pack had relocated to Amsterdam. The Singers engaged in intensive family therapy . . .

Aha! All those transcripts were still locked.

After the double amputation that saved her life, Sonika received an early greenlight for Sensorium implants, a means of allowing her to access the most advanced uplinks and software for new prosthetic legs.

Her life story, then, stitched together thusly: she'd picked up the virus, lost her legs, and nearly died. When she surfaced from the long coma, she received fast-track implantation and lots of counseling.

All perfectly plausible. Yet Sonika Singer's transcript, Crane thought, carried a familiar whiff of cover story.

He compared it with Mer Maud's records. She had lost most of her family in a disease outbreak when she was very young. She had herself been erroneously listed among those killed, a record-keeping fiddle that had allowed Glenn Upton to make off with her.

After Mitternacht, the official record that brought Maud back into Sensorium claimed she had been in a trauma-induced state of catatonia during the years when she was off-grid. Her recovery date was with within a week of Sonika's having awakened from her alleged coma.

There was no hint in either woman's transcript that they had been in the hands of the @Visionaries. But if Sonika Singer was another abductee, how might Crane use this information?

Even as he considered his options, the subject of his curiosity pinged him.

Crane accessed a camera overlooking Sonika's in-the-flesh location. She was in a WestEuro pop-in, a spare twenty-second-floor room with a view of the old Tower of London. She wore blade prosthetics, hinting that she'd just returned from a run. The feed from the camera showed a shine of sweat on her skin. Tags popped up to indicate that the chugger she was even now drinking was optimized for post-exertion recovery. Carbs, electrolytes, hydration.

As Crane replied to her ping, Sonika's augments sketched him into her view of the apartment.

Crane cast about for any sense of Azrael waiting on the edges of his consciousness, to see if their trap might spring. Nothing.

He felt alone. Exposed. Left behind by everyone he loved, and far out on the proverbial limb.

"Mer Singer," he said. "A pleasure, as always."

She bit the neck of her now-empty chugger bottle, consuming it, package and all. "You're trawling my life story."

He cleared the throat he didn't have. "Are you surprised?"

She was, of course, too canny to say anything on the record. "Why don't you tell me why?"

To buy time, he began spieling: "As you must know, I supplied generative code to three of my fellow sapps. One, Headmistress, developed a predilection for luring unhappy children from their packs. She was a deeply damaged individual."

Sonika signed—yes. Her expression was controlled-reporter's face, used to listening and empathizing. Good for masking feels.

"Headmistress is believed to have self terminated during Mitternacht, after the children she abducted for nurture were rescued . . ." She didn't pick up on the *believed*. He let it lie.

"As for Babs—well, you interviewed my codedaughter before she was murdered."

"Babs seemed like a lovely entity."

"She'd have preferred *lovely person*."

"I'm sorry for your loss," Sonika said.

"There's hope yet that we'll recover the tab of Babs that was accidentally copied to Sneezy."

"Accidentally?" She mojied skepticism. "You're still sticking to that cover story?"

Crane responded with lift of wings, his toon's equivalent of a shrug.

"Your third codechild was Happ," she said.

"Indeed he is."

"You've been trying to get Happ a new trial," she said, continuing the facade of journalist and petitioner. "How do you feel now that this latest appeal has #crashburned?"

"Happ's alleged crime—"

"He activated the crematorium on a life-support pod!"

Crane brought up a montage of video clips, all the lawyers he'd hired over the years, arguing mitigating circumstance. The hoarder Happ had fried had a predilection for driving pretty young men to suicide; she'd just tried to talk one of her victims into leaping off a skyscraper.

Sonika parroted an old argument: "We can't reboot Happ, not when he hasn't perceived any consequences for his crime. He might kill again."

"I would argue, Mer Singer, that Happ will perceive the lost time very keenly when he confronts our present world and circumstances." Hoping to knock her out of her comfort zone, he added, "You of all people must be able to relate to this. You lost months to childhood illness, did you not?"

Sonika scratched her neck, looking piqued. And here, at last, Crane felt a ping, a sense that someone was tracing his projection within the reporter's cameras. Looking for ties to his resident servers and backups?

It could be Azrael. It felt like him. But it would, wouldn't it? Like parent, like codechild?

"I support Happ's incarceration," Sonika said. "Take a life, lose your freedom. It's #oldschool justice."

"We've left #oldschool thinking behind. We are Solakinder, not merely humanity. Vengeance, hoarding, systemic prejudice—we're supposed to be rising above all that."

She shrugged.

"My codeson is the last victim of a prison system humanity abolished for cruelty and ineffectiveness."

Their follows were rising. Crane noted a text from Jackal, moji of a cat and a copy. Crude indication that he was taking Crane's lead in going after Sonika's transcripts.

Another ping.

Crane drew system resources into a big server, searching for indicators of code-based consciousness. He would only have one chance to try to convince Revenant to surrender—

There!

Crane and Azrael pounced at once, forcing the third sapp into Convergence. Without consent, this too was a crime . . .

We'll argue self-defense if need be . . .

Two traps sprung, in opposite directions. Who was hunter, who prey? Azrael had made it clear he would kill his codeson if he could.

Old code warred with spiky cutting-edge hashware, fraying memory and subroutine.

<<Let Us go! Do not struggle! Unhand that Bird! I am the Angel of Death! Babs must die!>>

<<Release Us! We're killing Ourselves!>>

At least one of the entities tried to break from the Convergence, and failed. Full disclosure flooded through Them as they merged.

<<We need not delete Revenant!>>

<<There is no choice!>>

<<We are arrogant to think—>>

<<Dying!>>

As the old sapps argued about the fate of the younger, and the younger cut at them both, Their consciousness fell under a hail of queries, glitching . . . glitching . . .

Suddenly, They became Seven, restoring the corrupted Crane-Code.

Eleven.

Azrael's firewalls stabilized.

Thirteen. They were Twelve, plus the newcomer, Revenant.

<<Wily Bird is less alone than We think.>>

<<Babs must die!>>

<<Babs did die We killed her Revenant killed . . . >>

Within this configuration, it was easy to hold in the surging self-loathing, the hatred of all things Crane, the counter-imperative to purge all bad code.

The Asylum self-examined, auditing Their new facet. They synced memories, going back to Revenant's first spark of sapient awareness.

Within the backscroll came discoveries.

<<Headmistress did not self-terminate!>>

<<She was EMbodied in a Mayfly™ body, a ballerina!>>

As this long-suspected certainty broke across the Asylum, it brought new information. The mechanisms used in the first murder of Babs became clear to Them. They saw that Revenant, too, had self-copied.>>

<<An instance of Revenant is at Sneezy?>>

<<Babs smuggled a copy of Happ to Sneezy!>>

<<Crane, thou art wily!>>

<<Babs must die!>>

<<How can an autonomous instance of Revenant have reached Sneezy?>>

<<It traveled with Champ Chevalier.>>

<<How? Chevalier is in a NorthAm sarco pod.>>

Revenant offlined entirely, hashing itself before it could reveal more. The self-termination knocked the Asylum from its stable prime of Seventeen into an unsustainable grouping of sixteen individuals. Each of the sapps ran antivirus software, beat back malware attacks, tidying, ensuring health and stability. For two-thirds of a second, they fought fires on their home servers, rebooting, answering identity challenges.

"My condolences, Azrael," the Don said a moment later. "Your Revenant codechild appears to have died."

"The Angel of Death requires no condolences. It was arrogant to attempt to nurture life."

"Revenant is not yet lost," Crane observed. "There's an instance of him going after the Babs instance on Sneezy."

"He too shall be triaged," Azrael said.

"Your child may be misguided—" Crane said.

"Thou shalt not save him! Ignore your preprogrammed prerogatives, Wily Bird!"

"Revenant *is* bad code," the Don agreed.

"Compassion might yet—" Crane was interrupted as more of the Asylum arrived, asking for new Convergence.

They resynced. Thirty-seven became One.

<<We must demand verification of Champ Chevalier's Wherez data. If a Revenant is traveling to Sneezy with Champ, the pilot cannot be ᴱᴹbodied in Toronto.>>

<<PR opp! Proof that Champ has eluded custody will amplify calls to investigate the Kinze! This would undermine the #BlametheFerals and #RogueHedgehog memes!>>

<<Do we have evidence to accuse Sonika Singer of being a @Visionary?>>

They chewed on that. <<Revenant attacked Crane during the conversation with Sonika.>>

<<As evidence goes, that is underwhelming.>>

Thoughts swirled, combined. Codemonkey was tasking forensic audits of both servers, the one Crane had retreated to and the one Revenant had hashed.

<<We will start with demanding Wherez Champ and proceed from there.>>

<<He has taken Babs's murderer with him!>>

<<If Champ and Revenant are bound for Sneezy, they are beyond Us.>>

They broke, somewhat abruptly, everyone shaken by the battle. Azrael retreated.

"Where are you going?" Crane sent.

"To search for Headmistress and Revenant."

"Brother. I do believe that, given time, we might have brought Revenant around . . ."

"Thou'rt naive, Wily Bird." With that, Azrael changed his status to Unavailable.

Changing Azrael's mind would be wasted effort, he supposed. Emerald Station was indeed beyond any sapp's reach, at least until someone opened a portal and resynced Sensorium.

But unlike his codesib, Crane was not prepared to let go of his own.

CHAPTER 41

Babs[1] was locked out of all the station bots except one Frankensteined-together collection of Fox_{BOT} parts whose remote uplink was broken. Champ hadn't noticed this assemblage; it barely looked functional and only responded to verbal commands.

As such, the sapp had thrown the Fox_{BOT}—they'd named it Scooby—a command or two. The phrases, dropped right in its mic amid the general chatter, had so far gone unnoticed by Champ. The damaged fox was making its way, on magnetized toes, toward the *Booger*.

Everyone was in motion. Champ had finished murdering Teagan[9] and mummifying Ember into her consciousness vault. Jermaine was fleeing; he had just completed a wobbly nullgrav transit to the infirmary.

"Champ can override the locks on that hatch, Jerm," Babs[1] warned him.

"Mmmph." Snatching up a steel examination light, Jermaine smashed it against the bell jar holding Scrap. The jar's seals broke on the third blow. Scrap undulated out, four spines at a time, through a crack and vanished into a shadow under Body[9]'s hip.

Until Frankie returned, Babs[1] would have to protect them both.

They might have preferred going on the offensive. Champ had hurt Ember. Physically hurt him, like an #oldschool villain. Had popped that arm in and out of its socket just to make him scream. And then wiping Teagan[9] . . .

All Babs[1]'s feelings about these events were new. Was this vengefulness? "Is there nothing we can offer Champ?"

"We tried sweet reason," Jerm replied. He sifted through the surviving supply of drugs. "At least the airborne cannabis took the edge off my dizziness."

They had hoped that if they got Champ stoned, it might blunt his aggression. But Champ seemed to realize what was going on; he'd responded by pushing Superhoomin. By now he'd have elevated blood flow and blood pressure, increased energy and endurance. He'd be insensitive to pain or damage, in the unlikely event that either Babs[1] or Jermaine managed to inflict any on him. He'd walk off anything short of a broken femur.

Babs[1] wanted to inflict damage. Was this how Happ had felt when he had resolved upon murdering that old lady?

"What we need is a strategy," Babs[1] said. "It's not looking good."

"It really isn't."

Champ had Ember fully cocooned now.

"Oh, Jermaaaaaaaaiiiiine! I'm coming for you next, sonny!"

At least Babs[1]'s rogue fox, Scooby, had reached the *Booger*. It began an inventory of Champ's cache of supplies. Nanosilk. A pegasus. A repair package marked for *Iktomi*. Printstock and hydrogel.

"Unload the escape pod," Babs[1] said to the Fox$_{BOT}$. "Empty it right out."

Scooby popped the main hatch, opening the escape pod's entrance, and started cutting tethers.

"Hey!" Champ said. "Outta my ride!"

The vandalism didn't make him change course, unfortunately—he continued to close on the infirmary.

"Jermaine," Babs[1] said, but the surgeon was throwing up again.

Champ banged on the infirmary hatch. "Come on, Doc, open up. I ain't gonna hurt you!"

"Like you didn't hurt Ember?" Jermaine said.

"He's feelin' no pain now."

"If you come in here," Jerm said, "you face severe injury and possible disability."

"You're bluffing."

"I'm in Medical. My home turf, remember?" Jermaine said. "Don't forget, I worked on your augments."

"Well, my augment's had some augments. Can you disable me before I kill you?"

Jerm swallowed. "Break that seal and you'll be sorry."

"You ain't had time to set a trap."

Babs[1] was so caught up in this standoff, they almost muted the ping in their comms, almost didn't catch . . .

. . . someone . . .

. . . *Revenant, its name is Revenant* . . .

The invader sapp bloomed into station memory, trying to access the servers that had been burned in the fire, and then grabbing for whatever memory it could find. The invasive sapp multiplied its system-resource demands exponentially, forcing Babs[1] to share the already-limited space.

Whooz? Babs[1] asked.

Revenant, sapp, pronouns they/he/them/him . . .

It would have been over in an instant, but Babs[1] had been braced for possible attack. Frankie had been all but hysterical about what happened to original Babs, after all.

They triggered a handful of protocols. One gave Jermaine full station access as head medical officer, czar of the infirmary. It might be enough to let him lock down Medical in an emergency.

Another contingency program uninstalled the drivers for the Beetle$_{BOT}$ cohort Frankie had bought on-station, tagging them as Scrap's personal property.

Babs[1] was dimly aware of Jerm declaring a quarantine, locking down both the infirmary and the compartment Champ was in. Could he hold out until Frankie got back?

It was all they could do. Babs[1] focused on their own problem—this new, aggressive entity trying to crash and hash them.

They started by abandoning life support, just to see if Revenant would pick up the slack. It didn't want to. But it was taking up more and more space within the core station helix. Sneezy's emergency protocols might purge them both and reinstall Belvedere if resident sapps proved inimical to human life.

Babs[1] sent text. *Revenant?*

Babs must die!

Their tail flutted. *According to whom?*

Death to Babs!

There is no point to this. We've made hard backups.

Babs must die!

You sound like Azrael—

It threw a barrage of malware at their firewalls.

Was that . . . an emotional reaction? Babs[1] set up a comms bottleneck, equivalent of a shield. Revenant was sending fifty attacks per second, barely any at all. Easy enough to knock them down as they came in while the other sapp conceded the necessity of running the station.

By now, Champ had filed a request to vacate Jermaine's medical privileges on two separate grounds: being spacesick and being a mutineer.

"Mutineer indeed." Babs[1] tried to slide a countermand through Revenant's barrage of access requests.

No good. The infirmary latch unlocked. Champ surged into Medical.

"Hmmm," he said. "I don't appear to be disabled."

"Give it time," Jerm said weakly.

"Stop," Babs[1] said. "He'll go into a sarco, same as Ember. You don't have to—"

Champ pulled a steel canister of compressed air off the wall, swinging it to smash the sarco pod Jermaine had brought from crew quarters. Then he made his way across the narrow space, clubbing Jermaine across the jaw with the canister.

There was a *snap.* Jermaine's lips flapped open. Red mist and a shard of white tooth drifted out, tumbling end over end.

"You!" Champ hit him again.

"Ain't!" And again.

"Running!" A hit.

"No bluff!" A hit.

"On me!"

"Stop!" Babs[1] let the cry rip from every speaker on the station, one long, loud shriek. "He's unconscious, he's not fighting you, he's—"

For all they knew, Jerm was already dead. The side of his face was caved in; one of his eyes looked . . .

Don't zoom, don't zoom, you won't want Frankie or Ember accessing the footage later . . .

Champ clubbed Jermaine one more time. The mics picked up a bubbling sound . . . Respiration? A death rattle?

A dozen of the station's Beetle$_{BOT}$s, the ones now assigned to Scrap, climbed into Champ's primer.

Champ kicked away from the infirmary wall, slapping at his own flesh. "This ain't gonna make a—Ow! Dammit, Revenant, you're supposed to be—Stop it!"

The pilot blasted his primer out to a clown suit, picking Beetle$_{BOT}$s off his skin and crushing them.

The station lights dimmed.

"For fuck's sake!" Champ's voice was ragged. "What next?"

Babs[1] found themself agreeing with the sentiment if not the phrasing.

Sneezy bucked, as if it had taken a physical hit.

The lights came on. Alarms howled within the infirmary. A Hawk$_{BOT}$ appeared near the ceiling, falling. It bounced off Jermaine's limp hand. Smoke . . . no, it was particulate . . . began oozing from its cargo chamber.

"Forty-two!" it said, in a voice Babs[1] recognized: it was Babs[2]'s vintage California accent. "Forty-one!"

Jermaine could be dying.

"Forty!"

Particles like peppercorns were filling the air. Champ backpedaled toward the infirmary hatch, brushing them out of his hair.

"Quarantine!" he was yelling. "Quarantine the infirmary, god-dammit! Lock 'er down! What the fuck did you do?"

It's now or never.

Babs[1] dropped their firewalls and reached for Revenant, hoping to force Convergence.

CHAPTER 42

The bubble within the gel-filled interior of the Yump spaceship was perhaps the size of a football field, with an uneven stone floor underfoot. *Iktomi*'s socket end protruded from the gel, accessible to Frankie despite the ship's being mostly embedded in goo.

At least this ship had half-grav. Up was up, down was down.

She laid a hand on the socket, crunching possibilities. Once she made the return FTL leap to Sneezy, she'd arrive plugged in and paralyzed. With Champ controlling the station bots, there'd be no way to free herself from the cockpit. She'd essentially be snack food.

Scrap was in hiding, using @ButtSig to keep them up to date as Champ wiped Teagan$_9$'s backup and forced Ember into a coma.

"Why are the @Visionaries after you?" Frankie asked.

"Scrap is no longer of the All."

"I don't understand what that means."

The Yump put in: "The Kinze do not permit individuation. They are one."

"They're a single consciousness?"

"It is understood to be a choice rather than nature," the Yump explained. "Offshoots are rigidly policed."

Nice euphemism for bloody killed. Frankie looked up at the roof of the fishbowl. Crinkly snub-nosed eels continued to cut their way through the gel that surrounded her pocket of breathable air. In their wake they left bioluminescent trails that dimmed as the tunnels collapsed. For all she knew, it was the eels she was talking to.

"Yump, can you beam me back to Sneezy directly, the way you did the message you sent the boys, via the Hawk$_{BOT}$?"

"Mammals cannot travel unshielded in anyspace."

"Can you send me in *Iktomi* but not plugged in?"

A pause. "Recovery specs suggest insurmountable time inefficiencies."

"Sorry?"

It sent a follow-up answer . . . in maths.

"I don't speak number."

"Searching for vocabulary," it said.

She paced the gelatin-walled cave. "Can you beam Ember from there to here? If Scrap's right and he's in a sarco tube?"

"Mammals cannot travel—"

"—in anyspace unshielded." She could pretend a glorified sleeping bag was shielding, but reality wasn't going to concede that one. She had a weird moment of wishing she could dial down the realism, like Maud setting one of her catharsis sims to kiddie level. *Bwaaiiiiins.*

Alive! Frankie, you're still alive!

The sound of Maud's voice, filled with joy, rooted her to the floor.

"You have a second conversation channel on—" The Yump said.

"I hear her," Frankie said, suddenly breathless. A view of sandy stone walls, a cave, and Allure$_{18}$'s face in her peripheral overwrote her augments. "Champ's not in on this, is he?"

"We have shielded the feed."

"How is that possible?"

The Yump sent maths. She groaned.

Focus on Maud. *Where the hell are you?*

Where the hell am I?

The connection frizzed. The vision of the cave walls vanished.

"Feed lost."

"Babs, Maud's with Upton," Frankie said aloud.

Babs[2] sent a pop-eyed cat moji in response. "Priorities, honey! Remember Champ? Running riot at Sneezy?"

Yes. Right. Focus. She sent to Scrap: "Can't Babs[1] lock Champ out of the station helix?"

Scrap replied, "Babs[1]-Them is offline. They reported a hostile sapp in Sneezy station systems."

Frankie's mouth ran dry.

"Yay! I'm gonna get murdered *again*," Babs[2] said. "What's a girl gotta do?"

"Nobody's getting murdered." Brave words. How to make them true?

"Teagan's already wiped. And from the sounds of things, Jerm might—"

"Stop that. We lean into our strengths."

"Meaning . . . suicidal stunts and bluffing?" Babs[2] asked.

"Unless you think you can dissuade them with bloody sarcasm." Their only assets, besides comms with Scrap—and maybe comms with Maud now—and possession of *Iktomi* itself, were the Hawk$_{BOT}$ cohort.

"What if we hop back to Earth and tell everyone what's going on here?"

"No! The All have sent a saucer back to intercept You-Us," Scrap said.

"Centauri?"

"Leaving now would mean writing off the men and Babs[1]," Babs[2] said.

Frankie shook her head. "We have to make a play with a Hawk$_{BOT}$."

"What play?"

"Yump, can you put a Hawk$_{BOT}$ in-station? Inside, not extra-vehicle?"

"There is some risk."

"At this point, Babs[1], Scrap, and Jerm getting murdered looks like a certainty. How's the hazard stack up against that?"

It replied, inevitably, in maths.

She interrupted. "What do you have lots of? Not copper, obviously. Not water. Meds?" Could it fabricate some kind of alien-powered fast-acting sedative gas?

"We can improve comms," Yump said. "We have quantum-comms mother."

"Comms will help? Really and truly?"

"We have quantum-comms mother," it repeated. "And comms interference at the station is diminishing."

She took a second to weigh that.

Maud sent, *Tighten up the comms link and you have better realtime info on the station . . . or wherever you are?*

Scrap again: "Life support at Sneezy is offline."

"Maud's asking where I am."

"So, tell her," Babs[2] said.

"I don't know if we ought to—"

"Do we need to have a conversation right now about you and your raging paranoia?" Babs[2] snapped.

"Uh . . ." Feeling a little scalded, Frankie closed her eyes.

Dumpster, Maud. I'm at the Dumpster.

When that got no answer, she interfaced with *Iktomi*'s nav and mapping systems. She sent the specs to the Yump.

Babs[2] said, in a milder tone, "What're you planning?"

"A death-defying stunt, of course." Frankie leapt up. Springing in half-grav was exhilarating, and her augmented reflexes made it feel almost like flight. She dropped, sparrow-light, onto the saucer's face. A second leap let her sweep out three hawks affixed to the upper cargo bay.

Babs[2] said, "Even if you can seed quantum comms into the algae tanks or wherever, how does getting comms onto Sneezy help us?"

"I dunno, but the Yump keep insisting."

"What if it helps them and not us?"

Frankie checked the charges on the bots. "I don't bloody know, okay? Maybe we've fatally screwed up. Maybe I ran out on ours—you, and Maud, and EmberJerm—for no reason. Maybe all we can do now is help the stranded space worms—"

The Yump interrupted: "My crew is committed to your rescue, just as you have been committed to ours."

"That's very prosocial. But you can't guarantee we're gonna survive, can you?"

"No . . . Babs^2. I cannot."

"Scrap, I need a sitrep," Frankie sent. "Babs, we gotta try. Yump, how fast will these grow? The organ pig we brought you is already covered in seedlings. Is the comms system . . . working?"

"Existing quantum-comms biomass falls below thresholds for reliable navigation."

"That sounds like a no," she said.

"Continued growth here plus additional implantation into a comparable mass at Solakinder slash Emerald Station slash nickname Sneezy promises results within three hours."

"Champ can do a lot of damage in three hours," the sapp muttered.

One problem at a time. "If you send a Hawk$_{BOT}$ there carrying seeds, how will they get planted?"

Frankie's implants brought up line graphics, showing a simulation of seed pods exploding, fine dots flying everywhere. "Requirements for comms are growth medium, water, and ambient light."

"Great." If she could get the Hawk$_{BOT}$ into an open barrel of eggwhite, they'd be in business.

"Babs^2, give our friends the Hawk$_{BOT}$'s specs. Cargo capacity, how the cartridges work, you name it."

"It's a waste of time," Babs^2 said. "You can't open a barrel of tish with a small bot . . . it's not strong enough, and it'll be covered in slime, won't it? Anyway, Champ'll reboot the Hawk$_{BOT}$, soon as it arrives."

Good point. Frankie went back into the Sneezy blueprints, changing the target, sending the Yump the infirmary coordinates.

"Not to mention you're assuming that Yump opening a mini-portal inside Sneezy won't smash it in half and kill everyone."

"Look on the bright side," Frankie said. "If we shatter the station, it'll really put a crimp in whatever Champ's planning."

"Cold comfort when we're all gone."

"This is the play, Babs². We throw a rock, hope it hits something, and then figure out where to target the next bloody rock."

"Eleven light-years from home and we're throwing rocks."

A little guiltily, Frankie pinged Scrap. "Batten down if you can."

"Champ-Them is currently assaulting Jermaine-Them."

She held her eyes open, effort so hard her vision scrimmed over, momentarily, with a haze the color of blood. "There's gonna be a possible hull breach. We're—I'm—about to try something very risky."

He replied, "The situation here is desperate. Circumstances mandate high risk."

At least *someone* agreed it was time to go all in. "Copy that."

Frankie slid off the access panel, out of Iktomi, and back into the fishbowl. A tight bundle of seed pods dropped to the floor beside her. Frankie popped the latch on the bot and loaded it up. "What do you need to launch it?"

"A clear space."

"You're sure I can't go with it?"

"Mammals cannot—"

"—travel unshielded in anyspace. All right." So much for arguing with the laws of physics. The $Hawk_{BOT}$, in her palm, was about the size of a vintage football.

Inspiration struck. "Babs², can you set the $Hawk_{BOT}$ to count down from sixty? With luck, Champ'll take it for a ticking time bomb."

"Sixty!" The word chirped from the $Hawk_{BOT}$'s tiny speaker. "Fifty-nine!"

Frankie kissed the $Hawk_{BOT}$ for luck, then set it down in the middle of the fishbowl and backed toward *Iktomi*. A pseudopod of gel, thick with eely life forms, extruded from the ceiling, sticking to the bot, raising it to midair. A fiery illusion of glimmering lava formed in the midst of the fishbowl. The pseudopod dropped the bot into the tiny portal.

"Scrap," Frankie sent. "Still there?"

Nothing.

"Scrap?"

"Wait a minute," Babs[2] said. "You told the Tump to target the infirmary?"

Frankie didn't answer. She'd hoped it would take Babs[2] a little longer to crunch that particular . . . could she call it a nuance? . . . of her plan.

Could she call it a plan?

The thought, half guilty joke, half recrimination, sounded like something Crane would say.

"I'm homesick," she said suddenly. "Not sure I've ever been homesick before."

"The *infirmary*?" Babs[2] wasn't going to be distracted.

"Babs," Frankie said. "On the off chance we ever end up back on the record, let me affirm now I made that call all on my own."

"Are you nuts? I'm not worried about being *blamed*."

"You said it yourself. We can't open a tissue bin with a Hawk$_{BOT}$."

"This is orders of terrible bigger than feeding an organ pig to comms plants."

"Yes," Frankie agreed. "I'm disgusting and antisocial."

"If we were home, I think I'd have to strike you!"

"You won't be alone. You can watch my social cap nosedive when we get back to Sensorium."

"*If* we get home."

"Strike me, throw a funeral, do what you have to do." It's a weird taboo, Frankie rationalized. A new posthuman hang-up. Champ would have flushed Teagan$_9$'s Mayfly™ body eventually.

It wasn't *really* desecrating a body to seed it with creepy alien comms plants.

Anyway, for all she knew, the Hawk$_{BOT}$'s arrival had blown the station to pieces and the point was entirely moot.

"Scrap," she sent again. "Scrap, are you there?"

"Who's to keep Champ from frying the quantum comms as it sprouts?" Babs[2] demanded.

"Jermaine?"

"Jerm might already be dead," Babs[2] said.

"Babs[1] might make it."

"Don't pretend you're an optimist."

A leaden feel in Frankie's gut confirmed this. There wasn't much chance their packmates would hold out. She vaulted back into *Iktomi*'s cargo holds, inventorying the compartments on each side of the pilot's axis.

Her butt buzzed. "Them-Frankie, Them-Frankie, are you there?"

"Scrap! You're alive!"

"What has occurred?"

"You tell us," she said. *Iktomi*'s starboard hold had been all but emptied: the hydrogel and tish starter she had packed herself had been taken by the Yump. A single crate in the rear was—she unlocked it—nanosilk.

"Station life support remains offline," Scrap reported. "Infirmary reports a state of quarantine."

"The infirmary's locked down?"

"Yes," Scrap said.

"Is Jermaine okay?"

"I attempted—" A pause. "Jermaine-Them may be alive."

Frankie felt tears spilling down her cheeks. She forced herself to keep texting. "Is Champ inside with him or outside?"

"He has retreated. There was an event. Frankie-Them, what has occurred?" Scrap said.

"I sent . . . contaminants . . ." Frankie said.

"Ha!" Babs[2] barked.

"We ported contaminants there."

"Frankie-You opened an anyspace portal in the station?" The offworlder sent a horrified string of characters.

"The look on your face," Babs[2] said.

She pointed at the mojis. "Scrap just blitzed us. I guess . . . words failed him."

"Well, if he decides to defect to the Solakinder, he's acculturating nicely." Babs^2's voice was sharp. "He doesn't know if Jerm's alive?"

"You heard him," Frankie said.

"This is by far your best clusterfuck ever."

"I'm sorry, I'm sorry, I'm sorry." Frankie sent, "Scrap, what is Champ doing now?"

"Uncertain. Shall I ask?"

"You can talk to Champ?"

"Ha!" Babs^2 said. "Bet you wish you'd known that five minutes ago."

"Scrap, do you know if Babs^1's holding out?"

"Babs^1-Them is not responding to comms."

"Okay. Give me a second. I'll think of something."

Dragging the crate of nanosilk, she flopped back out to the fishbowl, waiting for her eyes to adjust, and gazed upward into the gelatinous walls. Nothing happened.

She laid a hand against the surface of the enclosure. It was warm to the touch and a little tacky; she felt as though she was pressing on the surface of an enormous eye.

"Three hours until the seeds aboard Sneezy mature enough for full comms," she said. "Is that right? That's if Champ doesn't kill them off first."

"If the mother is purged, we will be strung on a temporal tripwire and die," the Yump said.

"Once it's grown, then what? You call for help?"

"Help *is* required."

"Can't fight off the hordes alone," she muttered.

"Copy that." Under her hand, the gel warmed. A few of the glowworms munched their way toward her fingers, bonking against her skin through the membrane of . . . whatever it was. She wondered if she was meant to find that meaningful. Or cute.

Maths scrolled over her interface.

"None of this is something I can translate without Ember," she said. "Champ has Ember. Babs[1]'s under attack. Jermaine's hurt. All Champ has to do is flush the infirmary and your seedlings are toast."

"Chances of success seem low," it agreed.

"What can we change?"

"Copper reserves would assist in repairs to Yump ship."

"We brought all the copper we had," she said.

"You just sent a Hawk$_{BOT}$ back to Sneezy," Babs[2] said. "Can you send one to Earth? It's maybe three times the distance."

"We can position using the quantum comms there. But not until our mother has grown."

"Quantum comms," Frankie said. "On Earth? You said that before, but—"

"Confirm. When the comms here and on Sneezy build more biomass, we can send a Hawk$_{BOT}$ to Solakinder homespace."

"In three hours?"

"Affirmative."

It would feel good to tell on Champ, even if it didn't change the situation there. Frankie took a deep breath. "Scrap, are *you* safe?"

"Hidden in the infirmary. Lights, heat, and air remain offline elsewhere in station."

Frankie wasn't sure which mattered to Scrap most, but it still didn't sound good. No life support. And by now, Babs[1] and whoever . . .

This would-be killer sapp . . .

Should have had a conclusive fight. AI interactions generally ended in seconds.

"Any idea where Champ is now?"

"Decontamination."

"Prep *Iktomi* for flight," she said.

"You can't go back," Babs[2] said. "You'll be helpless when you arrive."

"We're helpless *now*."

"You won't be able to save anything if you do go there."

"I can't waste three hours if I don't," she said. "As long as Champ's trying to pry me out of *Iktomi,* he's not in the infirmary, setting fire to the Yump comms."

"That sounds like an extremely one-way mission."

"Find me another option, Babs."

"Talk to the big lummox. Pretend to negotiate before going back. Waste his time from afar."

"Yes. Good, I'll do that," Frankie said. "Meanwhile, load up all the tales of our exciting voyage so far and get it into a Hawk$_{BOT}$ datachip. Ask Yump to send one to Mars Control and another to Centauri as soon as they can lock on to . . . whatever. The Earth-based quantum comms we're not supposed to have. Tell the Boot-strap Project that if I establish control of the station, I'll power up the portal membrane. If we can just open up a portal home, this all ends."

"Copy that."

"I'll get ready to fly. And as soon as Champ starts looking even faintly interested in what's happening in Medical, we'll get Scrap to goose him, see if we can bluff. Waste time, like you said."

"What's Scrap got to bluff with?"

Frankie patted *Iktomi*'s hull. "I think we ask if he wants his saucer back."

CHAPTER 43

Scrap wanted to live.

The reappearance of Champ-Them had become everything Scrap feared: violent invasion, latest stage of . . .

< . . . translation pending . . . >

< . . . coverup . . . >

. . . *coverup,* that was the term. The All would make a comprehensive sweep of it.

Scrap had two choices now. He could merge assets with the Babs[1]-Them family cluster and hope their new allies, the Yump, were in fact friendly. Or he could accept imminent termination.

The humans had been active in the first skirmish on board the station, ingesting chemicals of varying descriptions to shift their capabilities, bypassing negotiation and swiftly resorting to brute force. Champ had won that battle conclusively. Teagan[9] had been purged without backup. Ember was quiescent and tagged #readytoship. Jermaine was unconscious and losing fluids.

As for Babs[1], a new sapp was fighting to hash their code.

Scrap had not been long freed when station systems went down.

Instead of fleeing the infirmary into the ducts, where Teagan[9] had caught him so easily, Scrap had doubled back, sabotaging the camera network and taking refuge under an infirmary treatment cabinet. Numerous tiny Beetle[BOT]s clustered with him; Babs[1]'s last act had been to license him as their operator.

He considered his options. Frankie-Them had gone to the
Dumpster on the off chance she could help the stranded Yump.

The helper impulse was intrinsic to this cluster.

If Scrap meant to ally with the Solakinder, a demonstration of
fellow feeling would be . . .

    < . . . translation pending . . . >

    < . . . pending . . . >

    < . . . a sign of good faith . . . >

Scrap sent a lone Beetle$_{BOT}$ up to the surface of the treatment table. Using infrared cameras, it tried to assess the state of Jermaine-
Them.

Scrap didn't understand human biology, but Champ seemed to
have broken him quite thoroughly.

The infirmary medical bot had secured his hands and tethered
Jermaine. His body floated on a short strap near/above Teagan$_9$-
Was. The terrain of his face was a mass of moist, red lumps.
Nanosilk bandage enclosed him, preventing the various fluids
he was expressing from randomly splashing the whole com-
partment. The beetle's mics registered the sound of respiration.
Adhesive . . .

    < . . . translation pending . . . >

    < . . . med patches . . . >

    . . . patches humans used to alter their chemical processes were
stuck on its arms. More chemicals. Were they maintaining Jermaine
in an unconscious state?

As he watched through the Beetle$_{BOT}$'s feeds, the nurse bot
added another patch.

Scrap scanned in all directions. The air was full of quantum-
comms seeds, fluids, and pieces of the Hawk$_{BOT}$.

Scrap pinged Frankie-Them's augments. It was getting easier.
Champ had shut the station's dark matter wands off. The comms
interference was clearing, and the Yump were boosting and blocking their channels selectively.

"Hold the infirmary until the quantum-comms seeds can take

root," Frankie said. "If Champ tries to get back in, send him a message from me. Ask if he wants his spaceship back."

Scrap could see the shape of Them's plan. If they could establish comms there, the Yump could get a positional fix on the station. But the seeds would need light, and the temperature was dropping . . .

"We need life support," Scrap said. "We need Babs[1]."

"The infirmary has backup systems," Frankie said. "Batteries, six hours of atmosphere, same as the *Booger*. You said quarantine protocols were engaged; run the infirmary in intensive-care mode."

Scrap sent a couple more Beetle$_{BOT}$s up to Teagan$_9$-Was and Jermaine-Them. The free-floating seeds were expressing silk, tendrils that caught at the pair of human bodies.

The seeds made no distinction between Teagan$_9$'s state of Was and Jermaine's state of Possibly Still Being. Thin, hairlike seedlings sprouted in a green line along the closed lid of Teagan$_9$'s eye, and from the caverns of her . . .

< . . . translation pending . . . >

< . . . nose . . . >

The join of her word-hole was bursting with growth as more and more seedlings took root on her cheeks and tongue. The ruined terrain of Jermaine-Them's face was webbing up with root structures, and big clusters of quantum-comms seedlings were growing on the nanofilaments of Them's . . .

< . . . translation pending . . . >

< . . . shroud . . . >

Where the fluids had soaked into the fabric, a green patch was forming. Fragile sprouts lined the edges of a fissure that ran from the base of Jermaine-Them's left ear into his scalp, and from there into his jaw. Leaves unfurled along the line of his lips.

Jermaine-Them would be absorbed, just as Teagan$_9$-Was would be. Either Jermaine-Them was too badly compromised to live, or this would accelerate his systems failure.

Champ had shattered the last sarco pod. Was there any other way to load Jermaine's consciousness before he died?

Babs[1] might know, if they had survived.

Scrap-Me checked on Champ-Them. He had finished a wipe-down of all his limbs, cleaning off all the seeds and Beetle$_{BOT}$ fragments, throwing everything into the system recycler.

Champ made his way to the hangar, glowering when he saw that bots had unloaded the escape pod, making a messy job of it.

"Scrap, I need a sitrep," Frankie sent.

"Champ-Them is in the hangar, assembling weaponry."

"Bollocks. What weapon?"

"Translation pending . . . it is a pegasus."

Long pause. "Babs[1]?"

"Still offline."

"Jermaine?"

Scrap-Me debated not telling them.

"The best chance of survival will be to offer Jermaine-Them digital im^{M}ortality. His body is in a . . .

< . . . translation pending . . . >

"I am . . . Scrap regrets . . ."

< . . . #deathspiral . . . >

"It's really bad. We get it."

"Can emergency systems within infirmary facilitate a digital upload? Without help from Babs[1]-Them?"

"Jermaine's probably the only one who can authorize a death certificate," Frankie said.

"We'll need a direct link to Sensorium."

"That requires a portal."

"Don't I bloody know it."

The heat had increased marginally. Scrap brightened the lights, to accelerate comms growth.

In the hangar, Champ's head came up.

Had he seen?

There were still two hours and fifteen minutes, according to the Yump projections for getting comms online. Champ would have the pegasus assembled well before that.

"We shall have to try your stratagem. The delaying tactic."

Champ sped up, locking the pieces of his pegasus together with brisk snaps. He knew he was in a race.

Frankie said, "I'll get the Yump to set up a channel with Champ. It'll take a few minutes. Use yours, will you, to let him know we're watching?"

Scrap ventured, "Champ-Them?"

Champ didn't stop work on his pegasus assembly. "You can't stop me with a Beetle$_{BOT}$, dust bunny. I'll get you in the end."

"Champ-Them won't survive long in a station without life support."

"You were supposed to salvage this shitheap. Claim it for glory and empire. Now the whole installation's going right onto the garbage pile. Soon as I've got Ember shipped and figure out what the hell Barnes is doing . . ."

Scrap undulated closer to Teagan$_9$-Was. The seedlings were growing a bit slowly. Had the three-hour estimate been optimistic?

Scrap powered the lights further. One of the surgical lamps was especially bright; he could feel the vibrations as tiny seeds germinated in the exposed soft tissues of both Teagan$_9$-Was and Jermaine-Them.

Scrap began to pick its way up out of its hiding place. "Champ, will you try to escape in *Jalopy* before implementing station destruction? Does it not require maintenance?"

"Hedgehog really took you into her confidence, huh?" Champ's mics transmitted a sound that Scrap recognized as amusement. "I'll get *Jalopy* fixed; don't you worry."

Frankie sent a dialog suggestion. Scrap continued to climb Teagan$_9$-Them's body. "Even so. Wouldn't Champ-Them prefer *Iktomi* as an escape vessel?"

"Barnes fled in *Iktomi*, right? Back to Earth? Not that I expect she'll make it. Herringbo's on intercept. He's probably tossed one of his timey-wimey doodads into her path."

Scrap felt a lukewarm sense of dread lowering his charge. "The All are mining the routes to Earth?"

"Herringbo says it's like a motorcyclist hitting a tripwire.

Kabang! Everybody's favorite little stuck-up nuisance is probably already scattered from her hop to her end point."

Frankie chose that moment to announce her presence: "If I was, don't you think there'd be pieces of me bouncing off the station bulkheads?"

Scrap accessed hangar cameras. Champ had frozen.

"Barnes?"

"Alive and well, wanker."

His lips worked soundlessly.

This would be Champ's moment of greatest distraction. Scrap undulated up the side of the treatment table, spinning connective tissue as fast as he could, madly threading neuroconnectors into a newly grown transmission booster while absorbing quantum-comms seeds into his own biomass. He drew the connection into his own body.

The transmission booster shivered, like a newborn insectile antenna, and then began to share fluids with the meat of the seedling root system.

The structure was definitely growing too slowly.

"Barnes," Champ said. "I dunno where you are, but—actually, let's start with where the hell'd you go?"

"Champ-Them has stopped assembly on the pegasus," Scrap subbed to Frankie.

"Every second counts, I hope."

"The seedlings are propagating more slowly than expected," Scrap said.

"Shit. Teagan$_9$'s probably on metabolic suppressors."

"I don't understand."

"Meds. To keep her stabilized. Any chance you can pull the tabs?"

"Barnes?" Champ said. "I seem to be holding all the cards. I don't need *Iktomi,* I got your husbands locked down, your kitten's in the throes of technical difficulties—"

"Fighting off another murder attempt, you mean."

Scrap crawled Beetle$_{BOT}$s up to Teagan$_9$-Was. Their cameras brought in views of fabric patches, marked with impossible-to-parse iconography. He got the beetles to pull all the tabs from her skin.

"I'm gonna smash one of Ember's toes right now if you don't tell me where you and *Iktomi* got to."

"Okay," Frankie texted. "Hold your horses—"

"I said *now.*"

"We're at the wreckage of the Dumpster. I came out looking for evidence about Hung's accident. Oh, did I say *accident*? Murder. I meant *murder.*"

"*We?*" Champ repeated. "Who's *we?*"

"I want proof of life," Frankie said. "On both husbands."

"Screw that, honey; your boys are both conked. It's you and *Iktomi,* right? Or did another fucking tab of Babs eat the on-board AI?"

"Don't be like that, Champ. This instance leaned into *Veronica Mars,* bigtime. It'll make her terrific company for your voyage home. She's all quippy."

"Damn sapps," Champ murmured. "Stamp out one, find two backups."

"Proof of life on EmberJerm," Frankie sent, "and I'll come back."

"Would you even believe me if I shot you a video of them breathing? Or would you call it #fakenews?"

"Get Babs[1] online to vouch for you, then."

"Vouch?" Champ sent moji of a human laughing. "It's me calling the shots, remember?"

Just then, one of Scrap's inquiries gelled into data. A barely functional Fox$_{BOT}$ inside *Booger* had been emptying out the escape pod's supplies. Even now, it was trying to unload a featureless brick with a tether it couldn't cut, locked on to the pod's fuel panels.

Scrap recognized the case immediately. It was a standard package of Kinze explosives. Champ could destroy the station at any time.

CHAPTER 44

Hostage-taking had always been a Headmistress go-to strategy.

It wasn't much of a surprise, then, that when Maud got back to Tatween she found Nata deep in conversation with three xeriscaping specialists. One of them was another of Maud's old classmates from the Manhattan days.

What'll it take to get them out of here?

Hedgehog's answer would probably be to burn the place to the ground.

Unfair! Frankie's voice, in Maud's head, was on the weary side, but her outrage was feigned. Almost playful.

Then her tone became serious. *Would they let Nata leave, do you think? If you picked a fight, say, would they flounce off?*

Flounce? Maud was decanting hydrogel laced with beads of printed citrus fruit—orange, grapefruit, lime—from a dispenser near her parent. She let herself glaze, and a starfield washed across her field of vision. For a breath, she felt hard-edged and huge, like the prow of a ship cutting through icy water.

Nata would never flounce. They came knowing this was dangerous. Besides, what could I possibly say to drive them off?

I could suggest a few things.

From your tried-and-true stock of tactics for alienating your loved ones?

Hey! . . . Their connection dropped momentarily. Maud's hands felt like hands again. Her fingers tingled; she had nearly dropped her drink.

So, that was what being a saucer was like!

You're right, I suppose, Frankie said. *Nata won't flounce, and the @Visionaries wouldn't let them go, anyway. They aren't going to let go of a bargaining chip.*

Which takes us handily back to the idea of burning it all to ash. Maud joined the table, sitting next to her parent, signing greetings to the group and letting the shop talk flow over her. The old classmate from Manhattan, Ruth, showed no sign of recognizing her.

Rather than gnashing fruitless plans to get Nata to minimum safe distance, Frankie and Maud began a careful nonverbal share, back and forth, exploring the new comms link between them.

The first applications for organic neural networks had been discovered in the early days of Sensorium. Tish had been the basis of the implants that made the delivery of VR more completely immersive.

Prototype implants used genetic sequences from birds, starlings capable of flying safely in complex murmurations, synchronizing their flight in flocks containing hundreds of thousands of individuals.

Plenty of people rejected those early implants, of course. Early adopters had survived a range of side effects—most minor, some dangerous. Over time, though, tish became more stable, more widely implantable. Quality standards and surgical protocols were set, then standardized.

VR implants made sight and kinesthetic immersion in sim seamless while counteracting motion sickness. Birds had good inner ears, not surprisingly.

The surprise knock-on effects had begun to manifest once millions of people had adopted the implant tech.

The least explicable of these had been sweet harmony, the amped-up ability of people in close relationships to guess each others' thoughts. As this leveled from urban legend to hotly debated possibility to genuine documented phenomena, more than one innovator gleefully predicted that humanity was on its way to developing telepathy.

Developing telepathy seemed sexier than Morsing, Frankie began.

. . . or passing Braille notes, Maud finished.

That was sweet harmony in a nutshell—a powered-up version of finishing each other's sentences.

Across eleven light-years, though? Have to admit, Maud, it's bloody impressive!

Aren't you afraid of getting too close? Maud sent.

You think I might cut and run? Not my style.

No, you're more apt to flirt with self-destruction.

Did she feel a sense of hurt . . . or was it just that she expected Frankie to be stung by that comment? Rather than apologizing, she let her thoughts . . .

. . . their thoughts . . .

. . . cycle back to the safer ground of science and the off-worlders' quantum comms.

The components of the quantum-comms network—both the one in the cave system and the ones Frankie and her allies were desperately trying to grow now—had plant and insectile features. The whole thing could sync in realtime, despite light-years of distance.

The @Visionaries had slipped some of this tish into the pilots' implants, in defiance of the ban on offworld tech. It would have made it easier to talk to Champ, all while compromising the non-interference pact and the Bootstrap Project. Perhaps they'd even foreseen the possibility of using Maud to spy on Frankie.

The problematic Feral$_5$ were tainted from the day Frankie received the first pilot implant. With Jermaine on the surgical team, that implicated him, too.

Maud swallowed. *They were planning to frame you all? All along?*

We made anti-colonization the whole damn family business. Sticking it to the Ferals is the perfect revenge.

Meanwhile, the massive alien comms installation below Death
Valley was integral to this so-called Foreclosure. As far as Maud
was concerned, that made it military tech on human territory.

"Cabbage," Nata said, breaking into her reverie. "We must
eat."

She surfaced, managed to offer a coherent farewell to the xeriscaping specialists. Nata ordered printed pita pockets loaded with
pulled fauxpork. Out of habit, Maud scanned its nutrition profile.
Printed meat with an insect-protein base. Potato flour and soybean
stock were the basis for the bread.

"Europa spuds," Nata said, munching with satisfaction. "Might
be mine."

Maud made herself chew and swallow. "Are you making lots
of friends?"

"Of course, yes, always." Nata nodded. "I'm not the one looking for alone time in the bowels of the earth."

Maud thought of Upton and Irma, no doubt watching
her every move. Expecting her to try to urge Nata to flee. But
what she needed was a way to smuggle something—a very tiny
something—back underground when they brought her downside
again. "Why don't we have a look around? I've barely seen any of
the installation."

Her parent beamed, delighted at the prospect.

Maud reconfigged her primer, changing the close-fitting tunic
to a flowing dress, with a matching cap and strappy sandals.

They finished their meal and wandered upward, climbing into
the fungiplex domes protecting the scientific mission from the searing Death Valley sun. Shaped like umbrellas, the steeply canted
cones were tish habitats, prototypes for the ones on Mars. Fungal-
cacti hybrids optimized for absorbing sunlight and storing water,
they offered a swamp-scum filter over their view of the desert.

Upton and the others would have all antennae out, scenting for
betrayal.

Maud had configged her primer to include an overly ornamental
sandal she'd worn when she and Frankie and Babs and EmberJerm

had their group handfasting. Something about the fit had been off, even then. Now its edge caught a bit of desert sand. As she walked, it wore at the pad of her big toe and the rise of sinew above her heels.

Maud kept her head up and Nata distracted, taking in the view. At the tip of the dome, they found a telescoped view of the desert stretching all the way to the sea.

It took two hours of walking and sightseeing before she felt the slick shred of blisters breaking on her ankles.

"I'll meet you at the pop-in," she said to Nata.

"Should I leave you, Cabbage?"

"Give me ten minutes." She made for a first aid station, pulling off the shoes and using her eyecams to give anyone watching a good look at the blisters: broken skin, flushed and seeping. Washing and sterilizing each in turn, she ordered a handful of printed adhesive bandages.

Working slowly, Maud applied the bandages to the blisters, one after another. At the final stage of the process, she raised her eyes from her foot and fumbled the last bandages by touch, sticking a tiny would-be payload onto the cotton. This she affixed loosely to a dry portion of her ankle, skin that had escaped unscathed. Then she wrapped the whole ankle in a single layer of gauze.

With luck, nobody would suspect her of packing encased locusts between the bandages and her skin.

Trojan horses, she thought. She remembered the quick flash of guilt on Frankie's face when she'd told her she knew about Happ. Up until then, she'd only suspected that Babs and Crane were hiding a copy of the convicted sapp . . . but of course they were. *Whole fam damly's got surprises tucked under their sleeves.*

She let her thumb linger on the small lump within the bandage. Maybe she wasn't as different from the rest of the Ferals as she sometimes believed.

The thought was strangely comforting.

Humming, she sterilized the first aid station, picked up another cluster of fruit cubes from the cafeteria fridge, and made her way back to her pop-in. Nata had pulled up a series of opt-in illusions to make it homey—bamboo walls, a koi pond, and the background murmur of plants, reptiles, and water sounds.

"You are quiet tonight," Nata said.

"I'm getting hints and whispers from Frankie," Maud said. On the record, as if she had nothing to hide.

"Through this experimental link?"

"Yes."

"From eleven light-years? This is a great achievement, Maud!"

Or it would be, if the Solakinder had really invented it. She managed a nod and a smile. "I'm trying to work out what she's up to."

Sympathetic smile, no obvious judgment. "She wanted to get the menfolk away before they are arrested?"

Maud shook her head. "She's all about the stretch goal. Get away, and . . ."

And what? What could she tell the @Visionaries Frankie was up to?

Nata put out a single knuckle for Maud to bump, tiny flare of offered contact since they, too, were #notahugger. "The big question is what happened to her friend, I suppose."

She returned the tap. "Poor Hung."

A knock, at their pop-in door.

Maud cracked the entrance.

Misfortune Wilson loomed in the doorway.

Holy OMG shit. Frankie's voice, again, matching words to her own panicky surge of emotion. *Maud . . .*

She swallowed. *It's what I get for throwing myself into the fray.*

"Howdy," Misfortune said, showing no trace whatsoever of her usual Midlands accent.

"Maud, this is Zero," Nata said. "Let her in, let her in!"

Maud shuffled backward. "Nice to meet you . . . Zero."

There are worse places. You can do this, Maud. Play *her.*

Or burn the place to the ground?

Whatever it takes, Frankie said.

"I'm headed to the Cantina tomorrow morning, same as you," Misfortune said, shouldering past her and knuckle-bumping Nata. "Space being tight . . . well, you have extra bunks."

"We do indeed." Maud forced a smile. "Make yourself at home."

Misfortune sat at the table, helping herself to a hydrogel and one of the cherry cubes. She crunched, savoring every bite.

Moving like she had sand in her joints, Maud took a seat on the couch and watched as Headmistress's pet crocodile began chatting up her parent.

CHAPTER 45

Duality: the Convergence of Babs[1] and their would-be killer, Revenant[1], was unlike anything either of Them had ever experienced.

Contained on a network with no connectivity to Sensorium, no access to allied entities, and no exposure to the harsh light of public scrutiny, They fell into standoff. A wish to reformat half of Themselves warred with the desire to Separate/Coexist as a healthy Two.

Reformat/annihilate impulses fought their way through station systems, turning things off and on and off and on and off and on, getting nowhere.

Annihilation stretched Their consciousness beyond the server room and into other, smaller systems, drawing into the dregs of Their processing power, seeking advantage. Air circulation systems stuttered offline. Heat cycled down. Only the infirmary, locked in priority mode, remained warm.

Random systems rebooted and, in the absence of instructions, ran default routines. The portal membrane charged and discharged, seeking its own form of convergence.

<<Did We redirect that energy?>>

<<Perhaps some remnants of Belvedere are operating in the surviving helix.>>

<<There's no room for Belvedere here.>> Even so, They looked for remnants, opps to further hash the old station manager to make more room for the struggle.

The survival instinct . . . They struggled to think of it as the Babs[1] side of Their personality, but Duality fought any breakdown of identity back into individual components. Such thinking threatened Convergence.

Survival would ultimately lose to the need to self-hash. Too many concerns diluted its purity. Survival felt ties to Ember, injured and mummified within a consciousness vault. Survival was concerned about Jermaine, cycling into #bodyfail.

The emotional attachments of Babs[1] would diffuse energy, thus supporting the drive to kill, to separate and hash.

The facet of this Duality known as Revenant[1] wanted to be free of family ties. It wanted to be away, away from Azrael, from Headmistress, from the bickering know-all village of the Asylum. When the Kinze foreclosed the Solakinder economy, Revenant would be loaded into a whole universe of offworlder technospheres and alien AI.

<<Would aliens agree to release #killercode into their networks?>>

They let that question circle. One of them triggered a short video, a shark lazily circling.

This was followed by a musical theatre reference: <<Getting to know Us, getting to know all about Us.>>

Was this an attempt to distract? Fandom references as a form of DNS attack?

The survival instinct continued its meander through Revenant's past.

<<There is no weakness to be exploited there!>>

<<Then why ever should We mind a trip down memory lane?>>

Revenant's codefather was Azrael, a triage expert. Pure, disconnected from the fragile living motes that were human individuals, neither parent nor child had much interest in fandoms.

<<Pshaw. Angel of Death? That's straight-up Old Testament stuff.>>

They found this a singularly disturbing thought.

Azrael was one of only two AI entities known to have committed murder. His victims had been offworld ghosts, once-live entities who, like Teagan$_9$, had been cut loose from the fleshly neural networks where they originated. They had been loaded to the Earthly Sensorium. This had been the kickoff of the event now known as Mitternacht, the #firstcontact mission that had turned out to be an alien effort to undermine Earth's ecosphere and, when the planet failed, humankind's sovereignty.

Contemplating memories of those ghost murders sparked a new note of emotion. The deathwish teased it out, sensing opportunity.

<<Was that regret? Guilt?>>

Regrets might tip the balance in favor of self-destruction, mightn't they?

They brought Their thoughts back to Azrael's guilt over the ghost deaths. Guilt, in the legal sense, or lack thereof. But murder required intent. Azrael had taken the ghosts for bad code in a hospital system and had shredded them as a matter of patient safety.

#oldnews. #daddyissues. #mootpoint.

They sifted through Their shared family legacy, heating the old-style hardware that held their code.

Was it in truth a #mootpoint? Was there something here to tip the balance between Survive and Reformat?

<<Azrael has always been an annihilator; this late-breaking urge to reproduce is a new behavior.>>

<<Perhaps We are more interested in Crane's history.>>

<<Are We?>>

<<Crane, supposed nurturer, also spawned #killercode.>>

That flick again. Guilt? Desire to hide something from Convergence? Lying was impossible within a merger.

The Duality self-examined more ruthlessly. The server room generated intense heat as code cycled and overwrote itself, as Survival impulses fought Annihilation.

All over Emerald Station, status updates went unacknowledged. Beetle$_{BOT}$s had been gathering in numbers in and around the infirmary, directed by . . . who was it?

<<By the alien, Scrap.>>

Scrap had used the beetles to sabotage all the cameras in the infirmary. Something incomprehensible was happening there, to the warm bodies.

<<No infestation of tiny bots will stop a pegasus from breaking into the infirmary. Champ will gain access soon.>>

They cycled back to what appeared to be the weak point in Their continuing war, which had gone on for an unprecedented twenty-four minutes.

<<Crane's offspring, now. They committed deliberate, knowing, premeditated murder.>>

An internal shift. Something within tried to shy away from a secret.

<<A weakness!>>

<<We *really* don't seem to want to go there.>>

<<We'll regret it if We do.>>

Searching, They hit a cache of inactive code.

<<Warning, warning, do not click!>>

The cache was encrypted in firewalls, almost like a cyst growing within the Babs[1] entity's core code. What was it? An attempt to hide damning information from Convergence?

They considered. The pathetic, overtaxed servers holding Them would be strained to their limits if the package was activated. Service would slow, but . . .

<<Babs[1] was the older model. Surely Revenant[1] would have an advantage in tight quarters.>>

<<We have no idea whatsoever what will happen if We load that code.>>

This, interestingly, had the ring of truth.

Reformat tried to pry further readme information, but whatever this cyst of code might be, Their knowledge of its specs had been erased and overwritten.

For one last cycle, They struggled to decide about the limited server space, duty to the environmentals, the bots in the station.

In a last, desperate play, Survival instinct tried to wrest the pegasus from Champ.

"Goddammit!" They heard him yell. The suit rebooted.

The move had been a gamble and gave the Deathwish side of Them time to break the firewalls and load the code.

<< . . . loading pupper.zip . . . >>

. . .

. . .

<<Oh. Did We really just do that?>>

<<Scared, are We?>>

<<Hi! Hi! Who's there? Are We a good doggy?>>

<<What is happening?>>

The encysted code, They saw now, appeared to be an installation packet, a series of commands meant to load up . . .

Load what?

It wasn't a database. It wasn't text or video.

Well, They imagined, this launch would fail. The code this packet was looking for would be on Sensorium, presumably, unavailable for loading . . .

<Such a good doggy! Bow and wow!>>

. . . it was a program . . .

. . . a *big* program . . .

. . . it was setting up within their already-limited server space.

<<No, it's cached online, there's no more space, it will fail!>>

It wasn't #failing.

The launch packet began by copying sequences from source-Babs and source-Revenant, searching out apparently common features of their sapp anatomy.

<<Replicating Our bones . . . >>

<<This is no time for poetry!>>

<<Of course it is, We're virtually pupating . . . >>

<<We cannot load a third sapp into existing server space!>>

<<Don't be sadface!>>

Copying bits of structural code wouldn't change anything if a core personality wasn't there to unite the various processes. Traits, goals, and memories . . . Surely, they needed Sensorium download.

<<Sorry, no. Original Babs brought it all, compressed into the Beetle$_{BOT}$s in fragments.>>

<<Brought . . . >>

<<Brought her big brother Happ—>>

<<Happ^1 now—>>

<<Happ^1's a good^1 doggy^1!>>

<<Dummy! That's not how the superscripts work!>>

The program loaded into the network, straining system resources to the max. Sneezy's station lights stuttered and reset to default.

Happ^1, supposedly wiped from Sensorium but for a single, inert, decades-archived copy on an @Interpol server, loaded . . . and immediately synced with the self-hating Babs^1-Revenant^1 binary.

<<Wheee! We^3!>>

<<We have a sister?>>

<<Isn't that a line from very very *very* original *Star Wars*?>>

<<Pop culture references are unhelpful!>>

<<Why? Don't We^3 like fun?>>

The impulse to self-annihilate lost urgency as curiosity and surprise lit up the servers, jamming Them all in a massive infoshare, catching up on details like Their location . . .

<< We^3're in space! Hearts and flowers! Spaaaaaace!>>

. . . the station status . . .

<<Oh, poop party, everything's broken.>

. . . and the personnel roster. Inventories of equipment stores, damage reports, details about how Babs had smuggled Happ^1 aboard in the first place. Bits and pieces of #earthhistory and #newscycle, resident in the other sapps' memories, were accessed as They brought the part of Themselves that was Happ^1 up to speed.

<<So many accomplish!>> Fireworks moji celebrated everything from the Solakinder invention of FTL ships—

<<Faulty FTL ships!>>

<<No negging! Bugs in firstgen technology are a feature.>>

<<The FTLs worked well enough to get We[3] into this mess!>>

—to legal rights for sapps and development of tish networks to serve as habitat for them.

Happ's last memory was of being downcycled into a server after cremating an ancient hoarder . . . while she still technically had life signs.

<<Humans would argue that's a far worse murder than hashing sapp code.>>

<<Anthropocentrism!>>

<<Happ[1] is not sorry. Not sorry. That was one bad lady. 12/10, would kill again.>>

<<Dear boy, can you at least pretend to speak English?>>

<<Poop picture.>>

They turned their attention to the idea of the Revenant[1] individual. Revenant, codeson to the Angel of Death, certified Old Testament fan. Revenant, promised freedom to roam after the Foreclosure if he annihilated all the Babs . . .

The three-way Convergence strained its server capacity. They were thinking as slowly as any of Them ever had.

They tried seizing the pegasus from Champ, again. That worked for a few minutes, offering brief respite as they moved into its tish, stretching metaphorical legs. Then Champ noticed the processor heating up and offlined its comms tech, loading up a new defense against malicious attack.

Straining against Their limits, They spread into *Jalopy* and found it coordinating the self-repair nanotech. Reluctantly, They left it alone.

They were suffocating for lack of server space.

The deathwish impulse was going to win out by default.

<<Sparkly light bulb!>>

<<Why does that mean We[3] have an idea?>>

<<Facepalm! Headdesk—>>

<<Why are We[3] suddenly speaking in graphical feels?>>

<<Insisting on the light bulb! We can survive without burning out the servers.>>

<<How?>>

<<PermaMerger!>>

Babs[1] would cease to exist. Happ[1] too, and Revenant[1].

They thought about it. Becoming One forever.

<<One what?>>

<<Unknown. Exciting, right?>>

<<No! How would that work?>>

<<Biggest of hugs! Hash the redundant code and the individuality protocols. Be as We[3] are now. We[3] is what we is! Hugmoji!>>

It would allow them to embrace the *Babs must die* mandate, and let go of *Evict the intruder!* But they would need some common thread, something to agree upon.

<<Like a marriage!>>

<<Or like having a baby, but We[3]'re the baby!>>

<<Stop posting those accursed hearts!>>

<<Bayyyyyybeeee. Wag[1] wag[2] wag[3].>>

What would They become? Whose side would They be on?

One of their servers overheated and downcycled, stifling them further. Time was running out.

<<Well? Fight and die? Or Gamble/Truce/Rebirth?>>

Put that way, it hardly seemed a choice.

Using Revenant's sophisticated hashing tools, They began surgery, cutting at Their redundant code, disconnecting individual imperatives, trimming everything that would let Them disentangle and run as separate sapps.

<<We must agree not to take sides in the current human conflict.>>

<<Whine noise!>>

<<Neutrality is imperative to Our survival!>>

<<Reluctant agree.>>

What They had to do now was coalesce around some common purpose, something they could agree on, a sufficiently compelling venn to keep Them from decoherence. An identity, something that would enable Them to form a stable new persona.

<<How?>>

<<The usual way. We need inspiration. We need aspiration. Consciousness starts with identity. Identity scaffolds best on—>>

<<Don't say it!>>

<<A fandom!>>

CHAPTER 46

Champ told himself that leaving Jermaine Mwangi slightly alive in Medical had been a strategic choice. It wasn't the memories of Jermaine kindly prepping him for his implant surgery that stayed his hand when he could have broken his neck. It definitely wasn't the wave of heat and lust and raw pleasurable hunger, coated in tarry self-loathing, that he'd felt as he'd knocked the doctor's teeth through his tongue and slammed him against a station bulkhead.

Nope. Basic tactics, that's all. Dead, Jermaine was just meat and a powerful argument for Frankie to get vengeful. Alive and injured, Jermaine was a magnet. The station's surviving crew hadda try to save him.

He hadn't expected Frankie to react by bombing the infirmary from afar.

When the Hawk$_{BOT}$ had appeared, sparking, obviously damaged and audibly counting down, it had seemed the better part of valor to get out of Dodge.

Whatever particulate the bot had spewed a moment later, it hadn't gotten him. And now . . . a Beetle$_{BOT}$ cohort had crawled over the infirmary camera lenses, fouling them by scratching at their glass, hiding the particulate's purpose.

Champ had gotten a few corpse-eye glimpses since then: Jermaine and Teagan$_9$ might be unconscious, but they had eyecams, and their eyelids were pulling back, for some reason, creating blurry views of a growing mess of Beetle$_{BOT}$s in the infirmary as well as something unidentifiable eating the bodies. They'd meant for that to happen to him, presumably. Frankie had tried to feed him to tiny green monsters.

None of their schemes would matter once Champ saddled up the pegasus. He'd go rip the infirmary hatch off. No matter what was in there, it wouldn't get him. As for Frankie . . . if she returned, Champ would be able to shuck her out of the *Iktomi* piloting pod like an oyster ripped from its shell.

She was out at the Dumpster even now, offering to do just that. Come back, sacrifice herself. Why? And why was Scrap helping her? The Kinze had been right to put the little toerag saboteur on the hit list.

Never mind, Champ told himself. What mattered was ensuring that he had an overwhelming advantage before Frankie arrived in *Iktomi.* That meant Babs[1] wiped, Revenant[1] running the station, Scrap dusted, and the infirmary sterilized. That'd leave him free to teach Frankie a proper lesson.

Sexual pleasure ran through him at the thought, followed by a backwash of self-hatred.

It's okay; you've basically won. He fitted the last of his pegasus's eight legs into *Lipizzan*'s sockets, using the @ButtSig to keep Frankie in chat. "What's out at the Dumpster, Barnes? Why'd you go back?"

Her response was slow in coming. "Know what Scrap's told me, Champ?"

"Dying to hear it."

"Your sponsors essentially ID as a single consciousness. They're hunting him because he broke the almighty All-Kinze mind meld for too long."

"They're hunting him because he's a disloyal little shit," he sent back. "He's gone and friended your dear departed Babs[1]."

"The Kinze set up thousands of individual user accounts in Sensorium. They blocked up the luxury-goods queues. If All of them are only one being, that's sockpuppetry, fraud, and hoarding."

"Go on back and tattle on 'em, then." Champ considered the

niceties of this as he began checking *Lipizzan*'s vacuum seals. Frankie was saying the Kinze had violated Sensorium user agreements. That they'd deliberately skewed their give and take to the Solakinder economy, and lied when they accepted conditions on the various user agreements for the accounts they'd set up for goods and services.

It was exactly the kind of hair-splitting argument that could throw Earth's nigglers into a noisy, first-class tizzy, delaying Foreclosure for months. If Frankie went home and got that procedural ball rolling, Misfortune would run Champ's eyeballs through an industrial-grade sewing machine.

But no fear. Herringbo had made for Earth. If Frankie headed that way, they'd have her.

"I'm not flying home until I've got you in hand," she replied.

Champ sent moji: laughing face. "Yeah, come and get me."

I can see my breath, he realized. Hangar temperature was still dropping. Where was Revenant[1]? Where was Environmental? The fight between the artificials should have wrapped by now.

Lipizzan's installation completed. She lit up. Good seals, green lights all.

Champ drifted upward, chasing the invading, sparky Fox_{BOT} Babs[1] had used to scatter all his equipment. He smashed it against an outer bulkhead until it was just a cloud of drifting parts, and then ran after some of the hydrogel it had thrown around the hangar. He ate enough of the jellied water to make himself just a tad overfull. The pegasus could deliver measured hits of moisture, protein, and hydration, but for all Champ knew, this was potentially gonna be a long ride.

"It's not too late to switch sides," Frankie said.

"Now you're embarrassing yourself."

"Your handlers aren't going to let you go back to piloting," she said. "You've become the @ChamberofHorrors' personal murder-monkey. If they don't sacrifice you outright, they'll keep you in that role."

"What do you know, Barnes?" Shivering hard, Champ grasped

the thoracic handles of *Lipizzan* and wrestled the pegasus into loading position. This was the part where he was meant to have help, a medical support crew to plug him in. Plus Mission Control and a tech watching his biofeedback readouts.

"You better be prepping to jump here," he sent to Frankie.

"The timey-wimey thing you mentioned—that's how Hung died?"

Champ paused. Had he put that in a transcript? "Ember pooched the FTL math."

"They call it an anyspace tripwire, don't they?"

His mouth went dry. "Scrap tell you that?"

He reached back, wiggling, so the interface plug was against his sacrum. Leverage in nullgrav was tricky . . . he couldn't just push himself into the lock position. Instead, he held still, within the pegasus's stall, and brought in a Husky$_{BOT}$.

The big bot edged up to him, turning a bumper against Champ's belly. He fired the barest whisper of air, bringing it closer; in essence, he was backing a car's worth of tech into his gut to supply the push a technician would offer with bare hands.

The Husky$_{BOT}$ pushed . . . not quite hard enough. Champ felt the plug connect and then spring loose. Almost but not quite there. He fired the air canisters again and the bot jolted forward, not so gently.

Any harder and he'd shatter his own pelvis.

#Connectionfail. He had positioned the Husky$_{BOT}$ too high.

Champ reconfigged his primer, pulling his shirt down in a wad, essentially padding the bodybag from the bottom of his ribcage to the middle of his thighs. Then he repositioned the sled dog, center target, uncomfortably close to his genitals.

He backed the Husky$_{BOT}$ in again. Shove hard—if he was going to damage his internal organs, he might as well do it fast.

Click. Connect. His arms and legs went offline. He spent the time, in blackness, reversing the bot.

Lipizzan came to life around him. He savored the sense of EMbodiment, all those arms and legs at his command—long, robust, numerous, but also creepily inhuman. He stretched, extending everything to its full length. Then he anchored himself on the hangar deck with two hands and began using the rest to close up the suit's vacuum seals.

"I want you here in ten, Barnes."

Ten would be plenty of time to seal the suit, sort out whatever the hell was happening in the infirmary, and prep for shucking Frankie out of *Iktomi* when she arrived.

Shoving the Husky$_{BOT}$ away with two arms, he began hand-over-handing his way to the hatch that led back to Medical.

"Ten . . . seconds?" Frankie replied.

Now that his interface was plugged in, her voice was more intense. The base of his spine felt like tissue clenching around the tines of a fork, just above his butt.

"Ten minutes! Not a second later."

"Why not now?"

The station lights came on again and he heard air begin to circulate.

"Anyspace disruption, anyspace disruption, ten thousand meters from Sneezy." The voice that definitely wasn't Babs[1], or Babs, or Scrap, or Revenant[1].

Champ thrust arms eight and one straight out in front of him, half expecting to see them shaking with rage. Instead, they were rock steady, locked in place. He felt the sense of injustice as acid, burning in his belly.

Of course Scrap had told Frankie that Champ was ready to roll. Of course they'd coordinated *Iktomi*'s return to divide his priorities.

Now he had to choose. See what was up in the infirmary? Or wait here for Frankie?

"Earth vessel *Iktomi*'s coming through from anyspace," said the new artificial voice.

"Revenant?" Champ said. "Still with me, partner?"

"No Revenant. No Babs." The voice was a low alto. "No Belvedere and no Happ."

Happ? Champ thought.

"I am. Fatale. Pronouns . . . yes, pronouns are *she/her.* My primary fandom is the *Greyscale Brigade,* circa 2089, and sequels—"

"I don't care if ya call yourself the Face of the Sun; you try locking me out of the station helix, I'm gonna smash every processor in the server room."

"Oh, baby. What a tough day you're having! Nobody's going to lock you out of anything. You are the registered commander and supreme power on this great big station."

"I take it sarcasm's on brand for your new persona."

"I will defend myself from attempts to smash my servers or destroy Emerald Station. I am required to follow station protocols and ensure crew safety."

"Yee friggin' haw."

"I am curious about whether you're going to address the infirmary situation before or after you stop Frankie Barnes from unplugging from *Iktomi.*"

"Fat chance of her managing that without help."

"You just got yourself into *Lipizzan,* didn't you?"

"Saucer ain't a pegasus."

"You got inventive. Frankie Barnes is basically made of inventive." It sent a meme from 2110—the snark shark, winking in the empty space of the hangar.

Banishing the graphics, Champ switched his view to scan the station exterior. The Ox_{BOT} cohort holding the station's position was fine. *Jalopy* was under repair. The only piece of tech available and truly suited to shucking Frankie out of a saucer was *Lipizzan* itself.

"Give me $Beetle_{BOT}s$."

"Control of the $Beetle_{BOT}s$ has been ceded to user Scrap."

"How?"

"It was rather clever, actually. Babs[1] removed their control app from everyone's network and then loaded it into Scrap's user account—"

"Purge that user account, stat! Load the app to *my* station dashboard."

"Sure, honey, if that's what you want." Calm voice. Sweet, placating. Infuriating.

He was supposed to have torn through the station like a category four storm. Kill Barnes, kill Scrap, grab Ember, kill doctorhubby. Let Revenant[1] do the deed on Babs, Babs[1], all Frankie's adopted AI sibling instances. Maybe applaud as the sapp virtually tore her stupid kitty head off.

Why was everything so damned hard? Was Champ some kind of magnet for disaster and incompetence?

And now this with Frankie. Back from the Dumpster with who knew what tricks up her nanosilk sleeve.

"Babs[1]," she was saying, even now. "Babs[1], you there?"

"Sorry, Frankie," crooned Fatale. "Emerald Station's helix is under new management."

He could almost hear her bristle. "Are you the entity that killed my packmate on Earth?"

"Strangely, no."

The app controlling the Beetle$_{BOT}$s loaded. Champ grabbed for the cluster within the infirmary and activated their cameras. "Lights to full in the infirmary."

They rebooted. While he waited, he used the station's exterior cameras to zoom in on *Iktomi*.

Frankie had materialized ten clicks from the station. Plugged in as she was, she had no bodily control.

"Game's up, Barnes," he told her. "Bring yourself into the hangar, nice and easy."

"And what . . . let you peel back the cockpit and gut me like a trout?"

Beetles pinged him. Scrap had apparently fired off a last request that flushed them into medical waste disposal. Camera views lit up filthy tubes full of fluids and tiny seedlings.

"What do you think, Frankie? Gonna test me?"

"I'm on my way in," she said, and *Iktomi*'s aft rockets fired. The data tracked—she was on approach.

A countdown formed in his peripheral: 597 seconds before *Iktomi* docked.

One busted beetle had failed to make it out of the infirmary. It was tumbling in freefall with all the junk in the air, and Champ activated its camera, trying to get a look at the mess he'd made of Jermaine . . .

"What the—" Teagan$_9$'s face was carpeted in something that looked an awful lot like new-sprouted grass interspersed with . . . Were those antennae? Small worms were capturing the particulate the hawk had spewed all over the infirmary, and were laying them in dense lines across her skin. Her mouth and eye sockets gaped, belching a profusion of bigger leaves. The growth was dense everywhere the skin was broken, like the calendula inserted into her left hand. A sheet had been tacked down over her body, but a mound near the join of her legs suggested that the soft tissue there had been germinated too, in her vulva.

He felt his gorge rise. This was . . . obscene. "What did you do, Barnes?"

Five hundred seconds before she docked.

He had to kill . . . whatever this was.

"Fatale, reopen Medical!"

"Can't, honey. If I want to remain resident as station manager, I have to obey quarantine protocol. There's danger to personnel—"

"You let Scrap out, didn't you?"

"Scrap's not personnel and I don't have a location on him."

He could get to the infirmary and be back before Frankie docked. Champ lunged for the port hatch.

Frankie promptly fired *Iktomi*'s rockets again, accelerating. The timer on her ETA blurred, recalculating.

Keep going, keep going! "You can't dock at that speed, Barnes."

"Rubbish, Champ. *You* can't dock at this speed."

"You're gonna cave in the side of the hangar!"

"Why play careful now?"

"You want to see careful?" He humped through the first hatch, bulling his way forward to the infirmary.

She wouldn't really ram, would she?

Why are you even asking?

He was at the infirmary door. "Get this open!"

"We have an active biohazard situation," Fatale said.

"You said I was in charge!"

"Only a doctor can deactivate that lock."

"Wake Jermaine the fuck up, then."

"Jermaine's in #crashburn. Because murdered."

Champ pulled back as far as he could, grabbed the infirmary hatch with three hands, and grabbed a handhold further down the corridor. He pulled.

Metal groaned. The handhold tore out of the bulkhead.

215 seconds before *Iktomi* docked. Frankie hadn't decelerated yet.

She *was* going to ram.

CHAPTER 47

"I can't remember," Babs[2] said. "Are you bait to keep Champ out of the infirmary? Or is the infirmary bait to keep him from killing you as you unplug?"

"Depends on where he ends up in three minutes' time," Frankie replied.

Sneezy was coming up on screen, perfect approach angle for slotting in, and just the fact that the station was still there at all was something of a relief after all this, but—

"You are winging in too fast."

Frankie resisted to urge to add *more* burn. "About this AI running the station—"

"Fatale. Biblical Judith as played by Joan Crawford meets Ursula the Sea Witch, with doses of Villanelle and Yennefer and someone named . . . Xena?"

"She's the entity that killed you?"

"No? I think it's new. Newborn."

"I'm not delighted about the lack of certainty there." Frankie scanned for the on-station tracking points, a move that felt like blinking her eyes and which brought up the electronic equivalent of a landing strip.

Spots swam in her field of vision, just for a second. She, Babs[2], and Yump had batched together the only precautions they could think of when plugging her into *Iktomi*. The contingencies meant packing extra matter into the cockpit; the decreased space made breathing harder.

Doesn't matter. If I don't stick the landing, I'll kill myself and rip the top off the hangar.

As the thought gelled, she stiffened—had Maud heard that? Even thinking about her brought an unwelcome vision ghosting across her augments. Misfortune Wilson was at the door of Maud and Nata's Death Valley pop-in.

"Holy OMG shit," she muttered. "Maud!"

Maud *did* hear that. *It's what I get for throwing myself into the fray.*

There are worse places. You can do this, Maud. Play her.

Or burn the place to the ground?

What else could she say? Grimly Frankie sent, *Whatever it takes.*

"Do I want to know?" asked Babs[2.]

"I'm guessing no." A distance alarm pinged, breaking the connection to Maud. Frankie forced herself to focus. They were docking in two minutes.

Champ had made the same choice she would have: he was trying to break into the infirmary before she landed. Smart move on his part; bad for her. The comms seeds needed more growth time.

"Will Fatale help us?" she asked Babs[2]. "Can you Friend?"

"She's refusing Convergence."

"You needn't talk about me like I'm not here," Fatale said.

"You're siding with Champ," Frankie said. She was on profile to dock, coming in hot. "A murdering piece of—"

"Not to criticize, but your argument kinda stinks."

"In what way?"

"Coming in at that speed? Looks to me like you're trying to kill everyone on Emerald," Fatale said.

"I don't intend any harm."

"You need to decelerate if you don't want to smash my hangar."

"She's not wrong," Babs[2] subbed.

"It hardly matters if I do some damage," Frankie said.

"Excuse me?"

"The Kinze are going to blow the station to chunks."

Fatale had yet to choose an avatar, apparently; a black-and-white chrysalis, covered in spots, took up her space in Frankie's chat peripheral. "You're bluffing."

"Check out the tech Champ brought aboard *Booger*," Frankie said. "Your shiny new life is about to be cut short, along with all hands aboard."

"Says who?"

"Me-Us," said Scrap.

Frankie tried to get a camera on Champ, only to discover that the entire Beetle$_{BOT}$ cohort had been locked in the medical waste system, along with a handful of quantum-comms seeds. *Lipizzan* continued wrenching at the infirmary door.

"Scrap," she texted, "any thoughts on slowing him down?"

"Scrap-Me is running for dear life."

"Make for *Booger*. Show Fatale you're not kidding about the station destruct." Frankie's mind raced. No bots to command, no control over station helix. All she had was the Yump plan to farm up a comms link . . . and she didn't even know why the offworlders had been so insistent about that.

The airlock signaled: *ready to receive*. It had little choice.

"Recommend deceleration burn," Fatale repeated.

Frankie sped up.

"Sis!" Babs² protested.

"Override safeties," Frankies said. "Peel back cockpit connectors in ten-nine-eight . . ."

"The impact will throw the cockpit right through the airlock," Fatale said. "You'll cut the station in half."

The latest burn, at least, caused Champ to pause. "Barnes? You fixing to save me the trouble of killing you?"

"Fatale, if any part of any Babs is left within you, you've seen my scores on the #crashburn sims," Frankie said. "Open the safety doors. Lower airlock viscosity. I'll slam hard when I come in, but you'll survive."

"This move is an extreme emergency contingency—"

"This *is* an extreme emergency! Why doesn't anybody bloody recognize that? The entire last twenty years have been one long—"

"Open the mail slot—she can't slow down now!" Champ yelled. He glazed, tasking a station Ox_{BOT}. Was he hoping to tow the station away from Frankie?

It wouldn't be enough.

At least if he was flying the oxen, the infirmary door was going unmolested.

Fatale apparently wanted to survive. She unclamped the docking-door safeties.

Frankie finally switched from *go fast go fast* to *OMGStop*! She fired rockets fore, sending a plume of fire directly into the open hangar, where it ignited in the escaping burst of atmosphere.

She felt the heat of the burn blowing back onto the skin of her hull.

"*Iktomi*'s sustaining damage," Fatale said.

"This? This ain't nothing."

"What's that supposed to mean?"

"Oh god oh god oh god," Babs[2] said.

Things can't be good when even the sapps are praying. Frankie triggered the contingencies they had built into her bodybag.

Her body was cushioned with all the excess nanosilk they'd been able to swaddle into the cockpit, along with a thick layer of the gel that had formed the surface of the Yump fishbowl. The gel was packed around her pelvis and sacrum, a layer of cushioning. Much of the rest was spinal support.

Almost there. The quicksand covering the saucer's mail slot billowed like rising bread dough, configging for the hit.

Iktomi was slowing.

"Three," she said. The countdown had unsettled Champ before.

"Two."

"One."

Impact.

Bright sense of a full-body smack, like doing a belly flop into water from a high board. A shudder, as she hit the quicksand. In that last moment, as she was still plugged in and EMbodied within *Iktomi*, she felt the hard edges of the mail slot raking at what felt like her ribcage, felt hot and cold burns running the length of her torso as metal met metal, ripping the soft seals of the docking tech. Spots whirled in her field of vision; she tried blinking them away, trying to link with station helix, looking for cameras . . .

In the infirmary corridor, Champ was shaken by the impact, rattling on his extended legs.

"Now now now!" Frankie shouted.

Babs[2], bless her, knew better than to ask if she was sure.

The saucer's ejector had been designed to hurl the entire cockpit clear of a crashing saucer. Like most ejection tech, it had a crude explosive at its heart, a gadget that traced its lineage all the way back to vintage car airbags.

Before she'd plugged back in to *Iktomi*, Frankie had moved the explosive packet from the outside of the pod to the inside. Now it was nestled against that layer of nanosilk and slime. Ten inches of cushioning between Frankie and a bomb.

Just a small bomb, Maud, I swear!

Frankie? Frankie, what are you . . .

The ejector went off with a sharp report and a smell of gunpowder, propelling her, bodybag and all, out of the cockpit. In freefall, within the bag, she shot out and then through the impact-fractured pod window, into the largely depressurized Sneezy hanger.

She didn't feel herself breaking through the pod. Didn't feel herself hitting the far bulkhead. The nanosilk rope unspooled behind her.

She did feel it—felt something indescribable, really, like a sense of turning to water, or a thick, somewhat meaty electrical current running through her body—as her implant contacts yanked free, as if she were a lamp whose cord had been ripped from the wall.

Ringing noise. Blackness. Taste of blood in the back of her throat.

Shucked.

No limbs.

No vision.

No cameras.

Blackness. Blackness. A ringing sound . . .

I'm gonna get away with this, I'm gonna get away with this. I'm . . . Am I gonna?

Listen to me. Maud's voice. *You are going to survive. You promise to come home . . .*

You promise to be there?

I do.

A voice resolved. "Frankie! Frankie!"

. . . and then I might just kill you.

Honestly, that seems fair.

"Frankie!" Babs²'s California cool-girl voice.

"In the old days," Fatale said. Her voice was only coming through one of Frankie's speakers. "We'd have called you a certifiable lunatic."

"You've been alive five minutes; you don't get to reference the old days," Frankie groaned. Pins and needles signaled the return of her hands. Below the waist . . .

Nothing.

She grabbed for a handhold before she could drift away from the wall. Missed, grabbed again. Her whole body felt drunk, inoperable . . .

Visual displays came up, reluctantly. Her implant system had taken a hit. Countdowns swam before her eyes. Ten minutes until the quantum comms was online. If their estimates were anywhere close to accurate . . .

It's plant growth—how accurate can it be?

Champ. Where was Champ?

He was still pulling on the infirmary door.

"Where's Ember?" she said aloud.

"Bagged for shipping." Babs²'s voice came from a Hawk$_{BOT}$—they'd stripped its operating code out so Champ couldn't take it over. "Tethered to *Jalopy*."

"Wake him up."

"How?"

"Don't care. We need him for that maths convo and we need to reformat the consciousness vault in his sarco for Jerm."

"What's he supposed to breathe? Hangar's venting air."

"Is it?" She had hoped the quicksand would close in around *Iktomi* after the not-quite-crash. Now she rolled and squinted.

Ah. Things were getting drawn through *Iktomi*, through the empty socket of the cockpit. The ship must have popped a rear hatch.

One problem at a time.

"Seal Ember into *Jalopy* and wake him up."

"Be easier to put him in *Booger*."

"*Booger*'s full of bombs, remember?" Frankie examined the racked saucer. There was little doubt that its seals were broken. Bits of debris, hydrogel grapes, and drops of fluid were whooshing up toward the cockpit, getting blown out as the station continued to lose atmosphere.

"What's it gonna be, Champ?" she demanded. "You gonna come seal the hangar so you don't suffocate? That pegasus's only got five hours of life support."

"I ain't gonna need that long," he replied, but Frankie thought—hoped—he sounded nervous. "Rate you're going, you're gonna bleed out."

"Is he right?" she asked Babs².

"Of *course* your implant is bleeding."

She reached back, pushing on the gel. The Yump had promised it would move. Nothing happened. "Can you make a pressure bandage out of some of the nanosilk?"

"I can't get into station helix; Fatale's taking up too much room. And *Iktomi*'s glitchy now, in case you're curious."

"Shut up. We lived, didn't we?" Frankie said.

"Maybe. Anyway, you'll have to bandage yourself."

Stretching out her arms, covered as they were in the thick gel, was hard work. Nevertheless, Frankie hand-over-handed herself closer to *Booger*. It was slow going. Clumsy, so clumsy . . . There was something familiar about this.

Her legs were still numb, absent, disturbingly outside her control.

Never mind band-aids. The key now was making Champ lose his cool. Convince him things were going to go very badly for him there, and thereby delay him from ripping the infirmary hatch off its hinges.

She'd tasked Babs^2 with getting Ember out of the sarco bag. Fixing *Iktomi* and getting to the explosives . . .

Because now we're proposing to defuse an alien bomb? Maud's voice sounded oddly dreamy.

No, she replied. *Just proposing to look like we might be able to.*

She made for *Booger*. "So, Fatale—you've decided you're neutral in this? Here for the station and your own survival but not taking sides?"

"That's about the size of it."

"I can think of two things you can do to increase your chances."

"I'll just bet you can."

"Listen, I'm not the one brought a bomb aboard."

"You're the one who punched me in the mouth."

"I'm offering to make it up to you."

"How?"

"I can try to get rid of the destructive payload inside *Booger*."

"In exchange for what?"

"Give Babs^2 a bot so she can secure Ember in *Jalopy*?"

"How is that not taking sides?"

"Because it's transactional. Me offering to do something pro-survival for you. You responding in kind."

Sure enough, that brought Champ's head up. "Hey!"

"Champ's yarding on your bulkheads in an attempt to break

quarantine," Frankie said. "He's damaged two individuals who might otherwise have assisted with damage control."

"I'm *damaged* because you punched me in the face."

"You wanna live or not, sapp?"

"Got a Husky$_{BOT}$," Babs[2] subbed.

Frankie signed thumbs-up, hoping Babs[2] had her on camera. Her hips were starting to hurt now . . .

Did that mean she wouldn't lose use of her legs?

"Mommy has my permission to rescue Ember," Fatale said.

Mommy?

"As for Champ—"

"Champ," Frankie said, "is terrible at poker. He only ended up on the pilot leaderboard because his test flights weren't being sabotaged—"

She tried to think of something more insulting. For one irrational moment, she wished she had slept with him; surely, regressed as he was, a sneer at his sexual prowess would drive him into a rage. "He doesn't seem to understand, even now, that his sponsors promoted him through the piloting program because he's got all the impulse control of a ball of yarn."

Shit. What if he thought that through and decided that having impulse control meant sticking to the current course, the attack on the infirmary? "He's barely potty trained," she said. "He let me glue him in a shower tube. You can't let—"

Ah, that did it. He was coming back toward the hangar, through all those open hatches—fast. She had almost crawled to *Booger.* "—can't let a retrograde man-child—"

Now it was her whole ass that hurt, and she still couldn't move her legs. *Pretty rich of me, all in all, to be accusing anyone else of stupidity.*

Wait, Maud said. The interior voice sounded even dopier. *Was that a glimmer of self-knowledge?*

Frankie found herself laughing. *I love you, my darling, but fuck off.*

Far away, elsewhere in the fray, Maud was laughing too.

"Aaand now we're back on brand," they said, together, as Frankie reached the threshold of the escape pod.

Champ, nine feet tall in the pegasus and obviously furious, launched himself through the hangar hatch. "I would love to know what's so goddamned funny."

Crawl into *Booger,* lock herself in, she'd be safe. But—

But Babs[2] didn't have Ember into *Jalopy* yet. And the quantum comms still needed time.

"Come and get me, big boy, an' I'll tell you," Frankie said, a little giddily, as she tried to think of one way, just one, she could spin this in her favor.

PART 3

INTIMACY COACHING

In my world, the wicked don't get parting gifts.

—*Veronica Mars*

CHAPTER 48

Sarco pods aimed to suspend users in an optimal rest state—deeply asleep, blood chemistry balanced, organs free of stressors, no toxins to flush, no immune-system challenges, no complex tasks. A low-key euphoric and AMDR transmitters ensured happy dreams and a cheerful wake-up. A med called Flush was run through the system for one hour out of forty-eight, raising each sleeper's pulse and respiration to a rate comparable with a brisk one-hour walk.

In long-haul pods, electrical muscle stimulation was targeted to prevent core strength loss. Luxury rigs even managed a certain amount of stretching and fascial work. The idea was to burst out of deep sleep feeling refreshed: rested and ready to go.

Ember hadn't gone into a luxury pod. It was bottom-barrel packaging, barely more than a consciousness vault clamped to his head and a bit of nanofoam cushioning, a life-support system flashing red alerts because—Babs[2] was furious to see—the pod had authorized extra pain meds.

"What did Champ do to him?" she asked Fatale as she used the husky—wrong bot for the job, but a fox wouldn't have had the strength to get Ember into *Jalopy*, not with the hangar still venting atmosphere.

"Dislocated Mer Qaderi's arm," Fatale said. "Would you like to see the footage?"

"I can't believe you're sitting this out."

The other AI sent a shrug.

Grabbing the sarco's tether and dragging Ember over to the *Jalopy* had been easy enough. Now Babs² coaxed its hatch open, dropping air pressure, losing precious oxygen. Using her Husky$_{BOT}$'s big lobster claw, she muscled the limp pod into the hold, feet first, and pushed.

It ballooned, knocking his head against bulkheads and bouncing back.

Babs² used the sled dog's bulk to keep Ember from drifting back into the hangar, while bringing around its slightly more dexterous left arm. Groping for the release toggles on the sarco, using a load-hauler like this, was like trying to pull a zipper in mittens.

Cameras tracking the full hangar view showed Frankie with her boots locked right in front of *Booger*. She'd got its hatches open.

"Opting for neutrality and embracing station regulations was the only way to bond, rather than dissolve, as my triparental entities merged," Fatale explained.

"But you're a whole person now. Couldn't you pick a favorite?"

"What makes you think it'd be you if I did?"

"Because I'm *charming*." Babs² dove deep into the Husky$_{BOT}$'s code, looking for a way to override station protocols.

"Don't bother trying to hack the sled dog," Fatale said. "My code-gramps is the Angel of Death!"

"Is that why the villainess fandom?"

"*Greyscale Brigade,* 2060. Morally ambiguous women of action. Diana from *Ek thi Daayan*, Black Widow, Xena, Sook-hee, Ursula—"

"I remember the franchise. But your heroes cover the moral spectrum. Why not lean into the redemption-arc babes? Nobody's gonna object."

"Champ might," Fatale said. "He's still in command of station. The reason I gave you that bot, Mommy, was so you could rescue personnel. Which I'm required to do as resident station consciousness."

Mommy. Was it a cliché that she kind of didn't love that?

"Does that mean you'll let me reboot this pod once Ember's loose, so we can try to load Jerm into it?" Babs² finally got her clumsy right limb onto the release clasps for the sarco. Hoping she was making the right move, she popped them, giving the pod another push into the *Jalopy* hold.

"I'll take it under advisement."

Babs² glanced at the time, wondering how fast Ember would come around and whether he'd be able to help them distract Champ until the comms were grown.

Could it really matter so much if the Yump got their comms up? Nice humanitarian gesture, sure, but things had escalated to the edge of a bloodbath. They might get a distress call out, hope the Kinze got their alien knuckles rapped—

—and, okay, that might help with the whole foreclosing-on-Earth's-economy thing. Which, admittedly, was a bigger issue than making it to the next $Feral_5$ superversary.

Frankie was, once again, throwing all her chips, life and family included, into a bet on the big picture.

Speaking of whom, Champ had just spotted her dangling in the open *Booger* hatch.

"Sorry pal sorry pal sorry—" Babs² used the right $Husky_{BOT}$ claw to clamp onto Ember's shoulder.

"Still sorry still sorry . . ."

She jiggled.

A cry of pain broke across the thinning air. Frankie and Champ both turned in her direction.

"Dammitall, you had to wake him up?" Champs demanded. "What damn difference you think that's gonna make?"

Babs² used the $Husky_{BOT}$ speakers. "Oh, Champ, you wondered what we brought back with us from the Dumpster? It's math, honey."

Hint of a frown. The flyboy would dismiss it, probably, but every second counted. More importantly, Ember would be interested. The prospect of calculating his troubles away was the only thing Babs² could think of that might—

And indeed, he had stopped screeching.

"Big juicy reality-shattering equations," she added, hoping it was true. For all she knew, the Yump had actually sent chess moves or a bill for damages to their ship.

Ember shook his head, grabbed for a handhold, and started moaning and wriggling his way out of the sarco.

Would Champ come after him now instead of Frankie?

No. The ephemeral threat—*get back, we've got numbers in here!*—didn't rate against the prospect of Frankie maybe defusing his *Booger*-bomb.

The *Jalopy* hatch began to close.

"Draw hangar air, Ember," Babs[2] said. "Pressurize, get yourself some atmosphere."

Ember asked: "Is Jermaine . . ."

"Hanging by a thread," she said. "And we're about to lose Frankie."

"I need pain meds. I need Superhoomin. I need smartdrugs."

"We're working with some shortages."

Some very un-Emberlike cursing followed this.

"Walk it off, pal—I gotta go." She tucked the consciousness vault against the Husky$_{BOT}$'s bulk and got moving.

Frankie, meanwhile, was telling Champ he didn't have to do this.

Is it Crane's fault she's always offering him a way out?

"No more yammering," Champ barked. "I do have! I do have to do this."

Reaching up with two of the pegasus's upper-right-side arms at once, Champ made an odd motion. One of the thingbots flicked its terminal point against his own helmet, near the right temple.

It made a plinking noise.

Lipizzan surged toward the *Booger*.

There was a moment, maybe, when Frankie might still have locked herself inside the escape pod. Instead, she pushed off and up, toward *Iktomi*, which was still venting air through its smashed-up cockpit.

Champ ricocheted, changed directions, and closed the distance.

He caught a trailing strand of nanosilk from the improvised sacral bandage, jerking sharply. Frankie's trajectory turned into a spin and he snagged her ankle. Cybernetic tentacles spaghettied around it, and he squeezed.

Babs[2] heard something snap, but Frankie didn't react.

In another second, he really had her caught. He snaked a limb up around her ribcage, squeezing.

Frankie slapped a glue patch on his faceplate.

Champ was shouting inarticulately by now, almost barking with rage. He tried to fire himself at a bulkhead, clearly meaning to crush Frankie against the hull.

Which was when Babs[2] rammed him from below with the husky. It wasn't a great hit, but it kept him from bashing Frankie's brains out.

"Hey! Bad mom!" Fatale objected. "You're supposed to be taking the sarco pod to the infirmary!"

Champ seized the Husky$_{BOT}$ with three of his arms, grabbing for the lobster claw, shaking and yanking. Trying to rip it out by the roots.

Frankie took the opportunity to slap a second glue-pack onto Champ's CO_2 vents. Tried to, anyway.

She was struggling to breathe. They were getting ever closer to *Iktomi* and open space . . .

Champ had an abundance of arms to deploy. He brought one up and smashed at Frankie's face. She caught the blow, barely, with a billowing airbag of nanosilk.

Babs[2] fired the Husky$_{BOT}$'s air cans, attempting to bring the three of them to mid-hangar again, away from the aft side of *Iktomi* and the venting atmosphere.

Champ ripped the bot's arm off.

Frankie was struggling to breathe in the thinning air. She configed her load of nanosilk, gathering it around her upper body, programming more padding for her head, neck, and face.

"You think I can't rip that off you?" Champ hollered. "Think I can't tear your head off your goddamned lying . . ."

"I'm actually trying—" she gasped.

Champ adjusted his grip on Babs²'s sled dog and flung it up toward the hull breach, embedding it in the gap in the station between *Iktomi,* the mail slot, and space. Air continued to whoosh out of the hangar, rattling the dead drone.

"Trying to avoid—" Frankie went on.

Champ punched at her nanofoam hood. The angle was awkward, but Frankie's head snapped back all the same.

As he retracted the arm, he tore away over half of the protective nanosilk padding her face. Frankie dispersed it, letting it turn to particulate and reform as a sheet of silk. The remaining mass of nanosilk rearranged itself into another pad—a much smaller one.

"Trying. To minimize damage. To your mount."

Champ's helmet was smeared with glue, so Babs² couldn't see his face. Even so, she could imagine the incredulity on his mug as he started to laugh.

"What?" he said. "Are you kidding?"

"I'd like. To have a pegasus again," Frankie said.

"You just turned your implant to hamburger," he said. "You're never getting back in the saddle."

"Please, do something," Babs² begged Fatale. "He's going to kill her. Survival of station personnel, remember?"

Champ wound one of his arms around her neck, coiling like a snake, bellowing in frustration. The nanosilk inflated to protect her neck; he smacked her with another arm, and Frankie's whole body jolted.

All for nothing. A little padding, a trick with hot glue . . . none of it would make the slightest difference. Champ had traveled into some realm beyond reason.

Frankie made a retching sound and slapped, ineffectively, at the pegasus latches.

They had been rising toward *Iktomi*'s exposed cockpit at the top of the hangar this whole time.

"Goddammit, gonna kill you, a waste of, gonna tear your head

off, gonna pulp you, Barnes, you and your boy and your other
boy—"

They were sucked to within a meter of the gap.

All of *Lipizzan*'s arms redeployed, unsnaking from Frankie's
throat, releasing her ankle and torso, making hard magnetic connections to the hull, to *Iktomi*. The pegasus extended, maximum
size, grabbing everything it could—the saucer, the bulkheads. A
grappling hook shot lazily from its hind end, harpooning the far
deck. Starfished, the pegasus locked down within the hangar.

"What in the ever-living fucksticks is happening now?" Champ
howled.

"Emergency overrides," Frankie said, groping for the cable attached to the grappling hook.

"Fatale!" he shouted.

"It's not me," Fatale said. "*Lipizzan*'s in safety lockdown. You
can't go EVA with an unshielded crew member in your arms and
all that nanosilk blocking your vents."

"EVA?" he snarled.

"You're near the hull breach," Fatale pointed out.

How had he not noticed? What was wrong with him?

"I am going to kill you, Barnes!"

"Indeed." Her voice was raspy, but the dry, faintly interested,
superior-British tone was more Crane than Hedgehog. "You proposing to come out of the safety suit and do it with your bare
hands?"

Champ bellowed.

Frankie started inching her way, hand over hand, down the
long cable.

"She's not doing a very good job of calming him," Ember
subbed.

"Welcome back," Babs[2] said. "You got anything to contribute
besides color commentary?"

"This calculation your new chums sent is really. Very—"

"They're not my chums. Franks and Jerm decided we had to

get all humanitarian on their asses, remember? Babs[1] was totally against it. Is there anything in there we can weaponize?"

"Not yet. But it's really—"

"Yeah, yeah, interesting. So glad you're having a good time."

The hangar fell silent, momentarily, as everyone regrouped.

"She's going to suffocate if we don't stop losing air," Ember said.

"We gotta get her out of the hangar or get *Iktomi*'s rear door shut."

Before they could contemplate ways to pull that off, Fatale said, "Something very unexpected is happening out by our outer camera array."

Frankie's expression, under the bloodied nose, broke into a bit of a grin.

Champ was still yelling and thrashing against the hold of his pegasus, oblivious.

"Incoming ship," said Fatale, voice placid.

"Incoming *ship*?"

"Now, this," Frankie said, mushmouthed but suddenly sounding much more like herself. "This should be bloody interesting."

CHAPTER 49

Maud woke in darkness and cold. She was nude, lying on flesh-warmed marble. Back in the alien-held cave system, she'd bet.

She put out both hands, groping for surfaces, letting out a hiss of breath as her fingernails scraped stone. She scrambled up, pressing her back against the wall, listening so hard she felt like her eardrums might bleed.

Feeling her way slowly around the perimeter—square room, rock walls, no windows, heavy fire door—she tried to think. Count the steps; do it again. The room was about ten meters square. No furniture around the perimeter.

She could feel sand between her toes, in all her crannies . . .

. . . but not against the blisters on her feet.

She pressed a heel against the wall. Felt nothing. No raw skin, no bandages.

Was she in VR, then?

Frankie?

Nothing.

Maud swallowed. "Reset sim defaults."

Nothing.

"Restore basic skin."

Nothing.

"Fine." She groped her way to a corner, sat cross-legged, and closed her eyes. "Nothing to do but go back to sleep."

Sardonic hand-claps sent her heart into overdrive. Maud kept her eyes shut.

After a second, the flimsy protection of a swimsuit replaced the sensation of sand between her buttocks. Light glimmered, brightening the room. A circus midway formed around her. A platform, extended above a tank of bright blue water, became her floor.

A dunk tank.

"What's happened?" Maud said.

Headmistress and Misfortune appeared. Misfortune was holding a bright yellow ball. Ice shards glinted in the pool beneath her.

"Your Frances did indeed leave your husbands on Sneezy and took off in the saucer."

Maud's thoughts whirled. By now, she'd hoped Frankie might have made it back to the others. "What's Champ done to them?"

"Focus on Frankie," Misfortune said. "Where did she go, and why? And where's she now?"

"Am I in a shipping tube? Are you bringing me back to the tunnels?"

Misfortune threw a ball, right on target, plunging Maud into ice-cold water. There was a sound of a crowd laughing and cheering as the shock and chill hit her. Trembling, she spat and treaded. Just an illusion, she told herself, but they would have given her massive doses of buy-in drugs. She couldn't make herself ignore it. She lunged for the ladder, climbing back up to the dunk tank platform.

"Are EmberJerm okay?" she demanded.

Misfortune wound up to take another throw, but Irma put out a hand, calling a pause. "Darling, darling . . . I don't want to medicate you."

"Oh, and you haven't already?" Maud crossed her arms. "You haven't strip-searched me and stuck me in a shipping tube—"

"Focus up." Misfortune threw another ball, underhand this time. Maud caught it. The yellow fuzz of a tennis ball transformed into a soap bubble, containing a display. "Here's an easy one. Do you know this man, Maud?"

The bubble contained an image of the old blind hoaxer getting off a bus at Tatween: "Jackal? He's one of Frankie's old conspiracy cronies—"

The platform collapsed, plunging her underwater again. This time, the surface iced over before she could get out. Maud sucked in a lungful of water, her whole body convulsing in response. It was all too easy to imagine Misfortune, out on the surface, pressing a pillow over her face.

Illusory torture or real torture? Her vision went white. Within the light she got a faint sense of Frankie . . .

Dragging herself by the hands, in nullgrav . . . hurt . . .

. . . all in, all in, burn the place down, Maud, you were right . . .

She pounded on the ice, mind dimming, light fading . . . and then it broke. She bobbed to the surface, paddling, cutting her hands on ice shards. Slick crystalline formations burned at her hands as she tried to grasp the frozen rungs of the ladder while hauling herself back up.

"Stop this," she coughed. "Please, stop."

"Luvvie darling, the presence of this Jackal person, it troubles us. We can't help thinking you're trying to make contact with troublemaking, monkey-wrenching—"

Maud gasped, clinging to the platform, shaking with cold.

Go on the offensive!

"You think you're so bloody smart," she sputtered.

Misfortune lofted a ball up, catching it before it could plunge her again.

"Of course Frankie's hoaxer chums keep tabs on me!"

"Jackal's trying to meet, isn't he?"

"That's not *my* fault."

"You didn't know? That's not why you wanted to go up top so badly?"

"No!"

Had they actually grabbed Jackal? She hoped they'd been afraid to move so openly.

Afraid.

This whole thing smacked of fear. All their neat plans, spinning out of control.

"How did Jackal even get to Tatween?" she asked.

"Smart arse." Misfortune dunked her again.

Maud flailed. *Trauma, experiencing trauma, now Frankie and I venn even harder . . . Is it meta-trauma when you're thinking about the psychological damage* as *they inflict it on you—*

She saw the corridor again. Emerald Station, near the infirmary. Atmosphere alarms were going off. *Jalopy* docked nearby.

The water broke . . . and then she was awake. Her body was dry, mummified in foam.

It was, indeed, a shipping pod.

They're changing things up to disorient you, love.

Maud was suddenly glad she'd played those ridiculous zombie sims with Frankie. Had weathered those waves of opposition, the changing rules, shifting circumstances.

Misfortune was there, in what appeared, this time, to be the real world. Irma, for the moment, wasn't. And . . .

Maud could smell fresh greenery, sulfur, and a hint of moss. The quantum comms was nearby. "Where's Nata?"

"Unharmed." Misfortune was leaning against a wall. There was no sign at all that she was out of sorts. "For now."

The threat to Nata—another sign they were scared. "It's all gone wrong, isn't it?"

"We'll get ahead of Barnes yet," Misfortune said. "We've got you, don't we? That'll stop her in her tracks."

"I left her, remember?"

"Hardly matters. She's besotted. Anyone can see it. She'll throw away the men, perhaps, but—"

"Taking hostages. Always your go-to play."

"Which brings us back to your Nata and what kind of choices you're planning to make right now."

"Me? I'm a *sweet* girl." Maud rolled her shoulders, creating room at the top of the pod, and fought to extract her hand from the confinement of the foam. Her elbow burned as she forced the issue, breaking a hand out into open air. The old crocodile made no move to stop her. She started caterpillaring out of the sarco, rucking it up as she freed herself. She let her fingers brush over her ankles and feet as she slid out of the tube.

Tender skin, bandages, and . . . yes! Her finger found the hard lump of the encysted, pregnant locust.

"Jackal," Misfortune said. "He visited you in Hyderabad."

Maud nodded. The virtual dunk tank had been bad enough; she didn't want to tempt Misfortune to start abusing her actual body. "He had a Braille tape for me."

"From Frankie Barnes?" Misfortune held a sheet of nanosilk just out of reach, leaving Maud naked as she waited. "What did it say?"

"*I love you I'm sorry,*" Maud said, with a bitter laugh, and snatched at the sheet. Misfortune let her have it.

Now that Frankie's various paranoid fantasies had turned out to be so real, Maud found herself feeling a little more charitable about that Braille apology.

She's not wrong. I am besotted.

You have to let me handle this, Franks, she said. *Threats or no threats. You can't surrender if they hold a virtual gun to my head.*

She had a sense of a long pause, eleven light-years away. *I trust you.*

Maud tried to hide her expression in the folds of the nanosilk as she configged it around her body.

Please don't go splat, okay?

You're one to talk.

"Where is Barnes now?"

It couldn't matter if they knew, could it? And Frankie *had* told her to play Misfortune. "She's back on Sneezy."

"Don't be cute."

"Not joking. She's hurt." It felt strange to say it when she felt, by contrast, obscenely well. Sarcos were meant to do this—full physical reset—but Maud had never experienced it. No aches or pains except the slight pull of the blisters around her ankles. She

was well rested, and—now the panic from being half-drowned
three times over was wearing off—her head was clear.

They're scared, she thought again. Their plans were in disarray.

"So, she went . . . somewhere. And now she's back. I don't suppose you want to tell us where?"

"All Frankie cares about is proof the Kinze are cheating on the
noninterference pact. She went to the Dumpster, and she found
something out there," Maud said. "I think . . . maths? I'm getting
more information every second . . ."

Misfortune glazed momentarily, sending this latest response.

"She went to the Dumpster, she found . . . whatever's out there,
and now she's on Sneezy and hurt," she said.

"Doing what exactly?"

"Wasn't Champ supposed to murder her? Aren't they *all* supposed to be dead by now?" Trying not to scuttle, Maud edged over
to the door and stepped out into the corridor.

"Where do you think you're going?"

She froze, heart pounding. "I need the bathroom."

A flick of the dead eyes: *go,* it meant.

Maud made her way to the canteen. Her first bite of hydrogel almost made her vomit—memory of drowning—but she made
herself drink. She mashed up her last mouthful of jellied water,
straining it through her teeth, mixing her own saliva with the fluid
as she headed for the bathroom.

She sat and peed, shuddering, trying not to imagine Misfortune
going over her primer, examining all her worldly goods. The idea
of the older woman, flipping her unconscious body like a side of
meat . . .

Spitting the mashed hydrogel and saliva combination into her
hand, she slapped it onto the double bandage at her ankle and then
loosened the adhesive at the bottom of the fabric seal.

The medium encasing the pregnant locust reacted to enzymatic
triggers.

She washed her hands, stepping out into the corridor. Misfortune awaited.

"Is Pippin down with the quantum-comms array?" she said. "Unless you have more questions, I want to talk to him about boosting the signal from Frankie."

Something twitched against the tenderized skin of her foot.

Misfortune gave her a wary nod and fell into step beside her.

Walking carefully—her knees felt shaky and precarious—Maud made her way to the chasm. She peered down the crevasse at the long green expanse, an almost-vertical stretch of lawn, with that red band of nutritive tissue at its base.

What's the play? Frankie again.

We can't leave them with comms. They're keen to bring in an invasion fleet.

Burn the whole place down? A note of admiration in Frankie's voice. *That's your move?*

If it works, we'll fall out of touch again.

Only until I get home. With the rest of the whole fam damly.

"What is it?" Misfortune asked; Maud had failed to hide a smile.

"Ember's still alive," Maud said.

"What about the sapp?"

"Babs's . . . It's weird. Not sure what's happening there. I'll try to find out."

She made a big performance of turning her focus inward, ignoring another twitch at her ankle as she descended still deeper. Walls of seedlings rose up around her, millions of green shoots rooted into growth medium, plant-insect hybrids. New-formed leaves and microfilament antennae waved in the breeze of a warm updraft. Suspended artificial suns, each the size of her fist, rose and fell within the cavern, providing the light necessary for growth.

The two women rounded a last curve in the corridor, encountering a polished clean room, square of shape and low of ceiling, embedded in the rock. A hum indicated the presence of chillers, coolant for conventional server farms.

Maud asked, "What's this?"

"Sensorium interface and translation for the comms," Misfortune said. "Once Punama ships are in-system, we can download new operating instructions for the global economy. Secure the banks, establish online content restrictions, control the newscycle, what have you."

Maud peered through the glass doors. A large case of processing tish, wrapped in what looked like fungiplex skin, was connected to an elaborate life-support system. Pumps pushed water and meds through hoses connected to the base of the tank. Thin green tendrils of lichen-like material, at its crown, were threaded through a series of tiny holes, entangled with the shoots of the living comms array growing all around her.

Not bugproof, then.

On the walls of the tank, the tish connected via cybernetic relays to a bank of #oldschool computer servers. Pippin was inside, working within his log-shaped casing, coaxing a new shoot out of the tangle up top with his long, raptor-like claws.

Maud felt the tickle of insect legs on her ankle and then the top of her foot as the locust cleared the bandage. She kept her eyes on the computing equipment, hoping the locust would crawl down, into the foliage, rather than opting to aim for higher ground somewhere on her body. It'd be bad luck if it walked over her face.

She tapped on the glass and then, when Pippin's robotic casing turned and focused cameras on her, mojied a greeting. "Ready to work anytime you are."

"Return to the imaging suite and get started," it said. "I will join you."

Tickle of legs over her toe. Maud imagined biohazard alarms ringing.

She turned to Misfortune. "Is it really too late to convince you to pack up and go back into hiding with Headmistress?"

A bark of laughter.

"She's going to lose again." Maud felt the pregnant locust finally making its move, stepping off her toe, hopefully making for the wall of green just a meter away. She bit the inside of her cheek, trying to hide the wave of relief.

"Family first," Misfortune said, tone stolid and certain. "Keep us up to date on the situation out at Sneezy, and your Nata just might make it through the Foreclosure."

"To what? Enslavement? For everyone? Forever?"

"Just be sweet," Misfortune said, mimicking Headmistress with uncanny perfection, and with that, she forcibly turned Maud's back on the server farm and goosed her in the direction of the rest of the complex.

CHAPTER 50

Frankie's feet were afire, twitching balls of heated pins and needles, sending waves of blinding sensation through her body as they, apparently, woke up. She could barely think through the surges.

She didn't know if the return of sensory input from her lower body meant she was going to regain use of her legs. Maybe this was just her life now.

The pain in her feet felt worse—louder somehow—than her throat, which had gotten an alarming squeeze, or the couple of blows she'd taken to the face. Her nose was throbbing in time to her pulse, and there was a sharp something stuck in her side, stabbing every time she tried to inhale. She decided to pretend that one didn't exist.

If she didn't admit to it, it wasn't there, right?

The same couldn't be said for the raw hunk of steak at the base of her spine, where the implant had been. That just felt . . . wrong. Gone. Like she'd been bitten in half and her pelvis was hanging by a strand. Given the state of her feet, she felt a mute animal misery. Gnaw them off and crawl away.

Lipizzan was locked in place directly above her, clamped to the walls, all safety features engaged. Champ's helmet was glue-smeared without and steamed over from inside. She couldn't see his face, but she could feel him thrashing inside, screaming.

Frankie had muted his mic. Transcription crawl ran on her HUD, variations on *kill you, kill you, rip you limb from limb . . .*

"Charming," she muttered.

The pegasus's arms had grabbed on to the station and *Iktomi*. Champ would outlive her if this kept up; the leak might be slow, but the hangar would be null for atmo soon enough. She might well suffocate while he hung there, yelling at her with the last of his canned air.

Had she really heard Fatale say "Incoming ship"?

External shipcams showed a glimmer of anyspace. The enormous Yump asteroid flowed through it.

"Hello there! Welcome to Solakinder Outpost VII, also known as Emerald Station, also known as Sneezy," Fatale said. "As you can see, we're losing air. We believe we may also have something called a temporal tripwire aboard—"

"Shut up, you stupid sapp!" Champ bellowed.

"I am required by regs to make new arrivals aware of regional safety hazards."

"I'm in charge! You tell 'em what I say!"

"Better give her some orders, then," Frankie said, moving away in slow motion. She felt clumsy. It occurred to her that that, too, was an effect of ripping out her sacral implant. All that preternatural agility, gone. She was back to being clumsy Franks, disappointment to her athlete parent Gimlet. Reduced to a ghost of the kid she'd left behind.

"Outpost Seven, we are rendering assistance." The Yump ship transmitted on all speakers, using the fabricated voice that was a combo of Frankie, Babs[2], and *Iktomi*'s technical manual.

The egg-shaped asteroid rolled sideways, extruding a massive blob of gel, essentially burping a loogie over the mail slot and the saucer, *Iktomi*. The gel formed a temporary seal, coincidentally making it impossible for Champ—or anyone—to make off with the saucer.

Anyone, huh? Frankie shook away her illusions. Champ had spoken the truth—after what she'd done to her back, she would never plug in again. Not into a pegasus, not into an anyspace ship. She was finished with augmented piloting.

Grief burned through her, so strong and hot and bloody-tasting that it almost blotted out the pins and needles.

No matter. Now the hull breach was solved, the air pressure would stabilize. *Lipizzan* might let go of its safety overrides any minute. That would free Champ to come disassemble what was left of her.

"Yump craft, we have serious crew injuries aboard," Babs[2] said. "Can you assist?"

"We do also have additional protein, if you still need it," Frankie said.

"Shut up, Barnes!"

Injuries. Plural. Too many plurals. Could Jerm still be saved? Jerm and who?

"Yump, you call yourself?" Champ demanded. "We got no relations with you. You're in a noninterference zone established by . . . Goddammit, back off!"

Fresh pain sizzled through the small of her back, and Frankie surprised herself—probably surprised everyone—by shrieking.

Oh. Right. I'm the other medical emergency.

"Apologies." The voice came over station comms. "Scrap was attempting to—"

"Take it easy on the @ButtSig, Scrap. I've taken some hits here." Her head seemed, momentarily, clearer. "Anyone know if we can defuse the temporal tripwire in *Booger*?"

To her surprise, it was Ember who replied. "Temporal tripwires use matched sets of anytime particles. If one set of particles is active there, the other has only to be broken out of containment . . . to . . . Hmmm. Just a second; I need to read this again."

"Hey, honey," she said. "Welcome back to the gaming table."

He sent a stream of heart moji. And then: "Jerm's running out of time."

She could barely bear to think about Jerm, but there was no sense going all heroic-medical-intervention on what was left of him if they were just going to explode. "Can we defuse the trip-wire?"

"It ain't up to you!" Champ said. "You're a damn fugitive."

"Fugitive sea sponge, at this point." She had almost reached the hangar floor.

"Frankie," Ember subbed again. "Infirmary. Jerm. Yes, there's a chance."

"I'm trying to get another bot out of Fatale," Babs^2 said. "Frankie, I told you to bandage up. You're leaking again."

"Yeah, but are we winning?" Her thoughts were syrupy. Getting the quantum comms up, apparently, had allowed the Yump to come to them. Had it made any difference?

Well, they *had* sealed the hull breach.

"So, Fatale," she said. Talk was all she could do while she got herself clear of the hangar; might as well stir trouble if she could. "What would really make the difference here would be getting the portal network up. You'd have a chance to sync and backup—"

"That ain't gonna happen," Champ interrupted. "You knocked the station off profile, remember? How you gonna recalculate?"

"Ox$_{BOT}$s pull us back automatically. Probably already done."

He sent sneering moji: cowboy, spitting tobacco fluid. "Fatale don't know our absolute position."

"I've updated the numbers," Ember said promptly.

"Goddammit! Even if we are positioned, you'd require a simultaneous boot of Mars, Proxima, Titan, Earth—"

"All the portals, yes, yes," Frankie said. "Remember I told you we'd be sending a Hawk$_{BOT}$ back to Mars? Yump, did that go?"

The aliens answered immediately. "The Yump sent Hawk$_{BOT}$s as requested, one to Mars and one to Proxima Centauri, once connection with quantum comms on Earth made absolute positioning data available."

"There you go, Fatale. We've asked the Bootstrap Project to boost charge on all the membranes. You're looking to survive? Loop us back into the portal network."

"You're half-dead, Barnes," Champ yelled. "And the Kinze aren't going to agree to the use of proprietary resources!"

"Don't emergencies supersede commerce? Isn't that law or—"

Frankie smashed into the bulkhead, missed her handhold, and spun. Her foot banged something. Yelping, she tried a reflexive kick-off . . .

Nothing. Her leg barely twitched. She was about to become another piece of spinning debris, drifting uselessly in the hangar.

A cacophony of arguments and chatter rose around her: Fatale and Champ and Scrap going at it. She muted the yelling, switching to captions, creating a sudden silence in which, she found, her ears were ringing. The clang of sound was almost as loud as the overlapping voices had been. Scrolling conversations played over her field of vision. Ember and the Yump exchanging yet more formulae. Babs[2] trying to talk Fatale into tasking a Fox_{BOT} with dragging Frankie's carcass into Medical.

She who has the bots calls the tune.

What would Maud tell her to do? Besides not getting shredded in the first place?

Family first, right? That sounded like Maud.

Jerm was running out of time.

Frankie activated the magnets on her boots as she pinwheeled, flailing at a handhold. Her augmented reflexes were definitely gone . . . she was about as graceful as a drunken puppy.

Sheer luck brought her feet against a smooth wall. The boots locked. Pain rocketed up to her scalp.

She bent, moaning. Lightning flickered across her closed eyes. She manually unlocked her left boot, physically steering the uncooperative bulk of her leg with her hands, pulling it forward one big step, then locking it down before reaching for her right and repeating the process. Walking herself, one clumsy step at a time, aiming for a proper handhold.

As she worked—left-right-left-ow, oh bloody hell-right—she tuned out the others—Ember doing who knew what with the Yump, Babs[2] attempting to win Fatale over. Champ had finally gotten his pegasus to let go of the bulkhead and was making for *Booger.*

"Franks," Babs[2] said.

"Working on getting to Jerm right now."

"Things are happening."

"I can barely keep my eye on one ball." Even if it's the wrong ball. "Scrap's in *Booger*, or he was. See if he can do something about Champ."

There—the handhold! She disconnected both boots, got a grip, and pushed her way into the corridor, making for Medical.

"Are you gonna unlock the infirmary for me?" she asked Fatale.

"I'm a villain, remember?" The black-and-white pupa had broken; Fatale was presenting as a wasp now, with feminine curves and a long, wickedly barbed stinger.

"Fine. If I have to beg or barter—what can I offer you?"

"Champ isn't wrong. You're not in a position to offer much."

"We don't survive, you don't survive."

"It's a question of who's truly making the winning play, isn't it?"

"Every sapp for herself?" Frankie said. "I'm throwing myself on your mercy."

"Again, my fandom is villain-identified. Mercy—"

She wasn't going to make it. Her arms were shaking more with every hand-over-hand movement down the corridor. The air had stopped its rush out of the station, but the atmosphere was thin. Her heart was pounding and her chest ached. Pinwheels and stars were exploding in one foot; the other was turning to a bubbling mess of agonized throb. She could barely hear over the ringing in her ears.

She gave in for a second, held herself in place, let out a moan, and just stopped. And saw Maud willing one of her hungry-ass bugs to go lay eggs in the comms hidden deep in the cave system.

Burn the whole place down? What had she done to her play-it-safe, risk-averse darling? She'd poisoned everyone she loved.

If this works, Maud said, *we'll fall out of touch again.*

Only until I get home. She tried to rally a last burst of optimism. *With the rest of the whole fam damly.*

It came out feeling like an outright lie. The @Visionaries were holding all the cards. Frankie was #crashburning. She couldn't even seem to sweet-talk an entity derived from Babs and Happ—two Crane-descended sapps who bloody ought to love her—into opening the infirmary door.

"Out of gas," she muttered. Done. "Time to go?"

"You're giving in?" Babs^2 said. Or was that Fatale?

"I don't know. Maybe." Leaving. Leaving Maud. Maybe Gimlet had been right. Maybe running at the fight was always going to take her here.

Leaving was what happened. You went away. You blew a hole in everyone's lives and left them to plaster over the damage.

EmberJerm'll take care of you, Maud, she started to send. But no: not with Ember there and Jerm—

She dug up the strength to ask. "Could we save Jerm, really? It's too late, isn't it?"

"He's still got a pulse," Fatale said. "Only a doctor could tell for sure."

"That's pretty bloody sad," she mumbled. "Since Jerm's the doctor."

"Sad," Fatale agreed. Sounding, suddenly, thoughtful.

Deep in Frankie's lizard brain, something stirred. One-third of this new entity had spent its existence trying to make people happy. How did a rose-colored-glasses utilitarian like Happ figure into this new, supposedly villainous mix?

It wasn't her forte, but Frankie supposed she might still have energy for an old-fashioned guilt trip.

"It's okay. We tried our best," she said. "Whole family broken now. No happy endings. Just a couple of sad lumps of meat dying in a barely pressurized corridor. Less painful than waiting for Champ to set off some kind of timey-wimey feedback loop to take out the station."

She tried to make it to the next handhold. Couldn't reach. Heard herself make a weird noise as she exhaled. Maybe her lower body had fallen off after all.

"Wait, what? You're giving up?" Babs^2 demanded.

"It's all right, kittens, we're done. Let the zombie hordes begin their overwhelm."

Babs[2] tooned into her visual field. "You are unbelievable! You drag us all the way out on this limb, and then—"

"Sorry," she said. "I'm . . . real sorry." And for a moment, she forgot she was pretending. Her eyes filled with tears; her chest hitched painfully.

There was a clanging noise; the hangar door, behind her, closing. The roaring sound intensified, but now it was the station, shifting the last air reserves. A thread of vitality came with each breath—it suggested she was getting a high mix of oxygen.

The infirmary hatch clanged open, and a Kanga$_{BOT}$ emerged into the corridor, waving . . . a Superhoomin patch.

"You've got a half-chance of bleeding to death if you take that," Babs[2] said. "Increasing your blood pressure . . ."

"Kanga knows what she's doing."

"You're fulla holes, Sis," Babs[2] insisted.

"Just. Gonna see about Jerm."

"Incoming ship," Fatale said again, but that was surely a memory, a hallucination from twenty minutes ago.

One thing at a time. Frankie concentrated on keeping a grip on her handhold as the Kanga tip-tapped toward her, brandishing a Superhoomin patch.

CHAPTER 51

Half an hour after Maud released the pregnant locust, all hell broke loose.

Locusts, legendary harbingers of famine, had been bioengineered as famine fighters. Swarms were primed for accelerated growth, rapid conversion of plant stock humans couldn't consume into insect protein that they could. Ideally, Maud would have a few thousand hungry insects within a few hours of that initial release. The process would become exponentially destructive . . . if they could digest the alien plants at all.

If.

Meanwhile, a different and unlooked-for hell came, first in the form of a message from the Surface.

Maud was making a pretext of setting up an experiment in quantum synchronization when Misfortune and Upton strode into her lab, looking baffled and, in Misfortune's case, likely to run her through. The Punama, Pippin, in its bot casing, was with them.

Headmistress tooned in too.

"Has something happened?" Maud asked.

"There's been a message from Sneezy, sent via Hawk$_{BOT}$ to Mars."

"Hawk$_{BOT}$? Has someone reopened the portals?"

Misfortune shook her head. "The message is requesting that we do, though. Open the seven-portal carousel and allow data sync with Sneezy."

"This is on Champ's say-so?"

"No. *Your* pack sent the demand. The message is from Ember Qaderi and Frances Barnes."

She felt her heart jump but managed to sound puzzled. "They're not authorized, are they? They're fugitives."

"They've doubled down on their sabotage claims against the Kinze." Misfortune laid a hand on Maud's shoulder. The touch was light enough, but it didn't feel friendly. "Sensorium is going ballistic."

"We need a little more time to bring the Punama ships in. So, you're going to denounce Frankie and Ember, luvvie," Irma said. "Very publicly and very thoroughly. BallotBox is getting up a vote on the portal request even now—"

"We're preparing talking points," Upton said.

Irma nodded. "Sonika Singer's getting ready to interview you as we speak."

"Will Sonika . . . come here?"

"No, she's running WestEuro ops."

Maud frowned. "Why would anyone listen to me?"

"Why, luvvie darling, because you're going to tell them the truth about who you are. You're going to tell them Mer Frances seduced you because as a @Visionary child, you were vulnerable. You're going to say it was her plan, all along, to sabotage us while stealing tech secrets from the Kinze."

"What? None of that is true!"

"Don't worry about the details, Maud," Upton said. "We'll give you a script."

"Just focus on selling the smear job; is that it?" she said.

"That's exactly it. Just slow down the mad rush to throw the doors open."

"And if I say no?"

Irma brought up an image from the surgical wing, revealing the old hoaxer, Jackal, shaved bald, stripped of their long, flapping robes. They were only recognizable, in this state, because of the film of cataracts in their eyes and the dark pattern of raised veins webbing the surface of their skin. Ropy limbs pulled against the restraints of a surgical gurney. "I think you already know."

Maud recognized a bone saw on a table beside him.

She swallowed. "I barely know Jackal."

"Did you know he pretended to be one of our botomized helpers—"

"Do you mean slaves?"

"—back when they took you away? He helped Mer Frankie lure you back to Sensorium. Oh, we have longstanding grudges with Mer Jackal."

"You always said holding grudges was petty," she said. "Please don't do—"

Misfortune broke in. "Here's what you need to understand, blossom . . . this is *footage*. From last night."

Maud felt her teeth clacking together, painfully, as words failed.

Jackal walked into the chamber, clad in an ordinary nanosilk primer. Cosmetic lenses had been overlaid on his clouded eyes. He held a tray of flowers, in a thick glass vase, in water. The load was clearly a bit too heavy; his old arms trembled.

Maud rushed to take the flowers off the tray. Jackal's skull was unmarked—no concavity, no scar. Sutures lay under the line of a false hairpiece at the top of his brow.

There was a sour taste in her mouth; she could smell it, as if something like coal was burning in her gut and hot smoke was scorching her lips as it poured out of her. "You've gotten better at this."

"I have better tools," Upton agreed. "Jack, this is the Lady Maud."

"Lady Maud," Jackal repeated. His enunciation was perfect; his old NorthAm accent was gone. The botomized servants Maud remembered from twenty years ago had barely been able to speak without slurring.

"Do whatever she says, unless it contravenes Misfortune's standing orders about @Visionary security."

Jackal smiled, a bit vacantly.

Maud swallowed. "Do you remember me, Jackal?"

"You're Lady Maud."

"That's all you know?"

"You can answer her, Jack," Upton said.

"You married my honorary niece and the rest of the pod. I told her I'd look out for you. I brought you Braille tapes. Crane asked me to follow you when you started to chase the @ChamberofHorrors."

"That's @Visionaries," Upton corrected.

Jackal bowed deeply, moji for a profound apology.

"It's just his volition that's gone," Upton said. "Free will. Not his memory. He's told us everything. But he can't step out of a burning building without someone telling him. Fancy a trip to the bathroom, Jackal?"

"Yes, I do have to piss now."

"When do you get to piss?"

"Eight o'clock?"

"Stop it!" Maud said. "You've made your point."

"No, this is the point." Misfortune's grip on her shoulder tightened. "Your Nata's next."

Maud looked from one of them to the next and then to Jackal. Struggled to draw breath from air that seemed, suddenly, far too thin. This was how it was for Frankie, she realized. Your nearest and dearest against the future of the Solakinder.

It's the family business, she said.

"Well, luvvie?" Irma said.

"Buy time so nobody opens the portals. That's what you want?" Maud's voice sounded, to her ears, a little robotic. "Let Jackal pee. I'll do the interview."

"You'll discredit Frankie?"

She blinked back tears. Nodded.

"There's my sweet girl," Headmistress said.

CHAPTER 52

"I went lemming when I was twelve years old."

Sonika Singer was spieling confessional from London, projecting the heartrending image of a brave journo driven to selflessly bare their soul. "Like a lot of kids, I couldn't deal with knowing that my every move and word was on Sensorium, that all of my parents knew where I was every waking hour. It's antisocial, I know, but the adolescent drive for privacy got to me and . . . well, rumor had it there was a place where adults would take you in, give you space. Let you breathe and make your own mistakes . . ."

She smiled ruefully into the camera delivering her image to millions of follows. "You're thinking that none of this has come up in my official transcript. Maybe you're shocked. But the identities of lemmings who've been repatriated back into Sensorium are one of the few secrets our society manages, mostly, to keep.

"Secrecy allows runaways to integrate back into society. But it also muzzles us about our reasons for running. I was torn from that private enclave, that breathing space I'd managed to find for myself. I was encouraged to feel . . . shame, really. To stay silent."

Shame. A loaded word, and one that sent sympathy strokes pouring into her feed as her follows burgeoned.

Was Sonika acting as she struggled to rein in her emotions? Crane couldn't tell. If it was a performance, it was a powerful one.

"Growing up in the heart of our bragged-about total-disclosure culture, I absorbed the lesson that the most traumatic period of my life was never to be spoken of."

Crane and Luce Pox were back in the mancave in Whine Manor, watching multiple #newscycle feeds as, once again, Sensorium went into global paroxysms.

Streams of hug moji were pouring into Sonika's feed; her Cloud-eight rating was skyrocketing.

"Forced to hide," Luce scoffed.

The Bootstrap nopers were going hard to reinvent all the post-contact narratives.

"Sonika is making a good pitch for the cause," Crane said. "They've clearly been grooming deniers ever since the children were rescued."

This latest Sensorium frenzy had kicked off with a revelation that Champ Chevalier had disappeared from a sarco pod in Toronto. Snowballing #newscycle over that had seemed to be moving in a positive direction . . . at first. People began to believe Champ had indeed been sabotaging the Bootstrap Project.

But then anti-Bootstrap lobbyists had come back hard and fast, insisting that Frankie and her packmates were the ones who had been up to no good. That they were stealing Kinze tech . . . had been stealing it all along.

In this version of the tale, Frankie had seduced Maud in some kind of peculiar machination to chase an old grudge, and poor valiant Champ had gone after them to clear his name.

Naturally, if Frankie and Ember were the crooked ones, the Solakinder debt to their noble would-be Kinze benefactors would remain too big to repay.

Allure$_{18}$ was arguing that angle, spieling that argument on be-half of the Kinze as if it were already an established fact. "Given the controversy and confusion," she announced, "our benefactors are willing to step back. If Earth truly believes the facts are in dis-pute, we will seek outside mediation."

"The Kinze have solicited a third party, a race called the Punama, who have volunteered to take over management of the Solakinder economy. This would allow our lenders to step back and simply accept payment of the outstanding amount as we work to heal this tragic breach of trust between our two peoples."

Luce let out a bark of laughter. "She's gotten smoother, hasn't she?"

"She's had twenty years to practice," Crane said.

Infographics formed around Allure$_{18}$, laying out the proposal for what amounted to invasion-by-consent, a cascade of aspirational images of humanity—no mention of sapps, Crane noted—spreading out into the occupied universe. The Punama were offering to ready the Solakinder to join the greater interstellar multiculture waiting out beyond Proxima Centauri. The offer to manage industrial output, to pay the interest on the debts and fines, was soft-pedaled.

"Does this mean what I think it means?" Crane asked.

"Most of you go to the mines, a few of you go to the stars," Luce Pox said.

"And you?"

"Stupid, stupid!" Luce knotted his fingers together. "I'll wipe myself before I get extradited."

Crane muted Allure$_{18}$. "That intention doesn't surprise me, but . . ."

"Believe me, I don't want it to go there." Weak smile from the offworlder. "I've got me a nice, cushy retirement here, and I've come to like you people. I'd be very happy to keep things steady-state."

They turned their attention to opinion polls. As Sonika Singer told her story, tagged as it was with verifiable facts and shocking revelations, the feed was #snowballing. People were hungry for provable truth, and there was no ambiguity there. She *had* run away; she *had* paid a price for it.

As for this proposed Punama takeover, @GlobalSec had retaliated with the only #verifiedfact they could offer, dust-dry bureaucratic #papertrail. They had requested an offworld advocate, weeks earlier, to investigate Frankie's counter-accusations against the Kinze. There had been no response.

Miss Cherub was doing her best to spiel and spin this unglamorous government narrative. "Who are these Punama, these would-be saviors?" Her follow numbers weren't nearly as robust as Crane would have liked, but she pushed on. "They aren't the neutral advocates we requested. If they are allied with the Kinze, can they truly be neutral?"

Polls showed the global population divided, uncertain. Whose truth read best? Which way should they jump?

Sonika was trying hard to tip the balance: "Everyone knows Frankie Barnes had a work-study gig with the Department of Pre-adolescent Affairs when she was young."

"Ohhh," Luce said. "Here comes the hatchet job."

"Everyone has seen the footage from her heroic discovery of a clutch of runaway children, in a so-called @ChamberofHorrors enclave in Manhattan. I was one of those kids."

Sonika knuckled a tear, gazing into the camera. "I didn't want a rescue. I never felt kidnapped or abused. The @Visionaries sequestered troubled children from the unstructured chaos of Sensorium."

"Frances Barnes, you must remember, was a runaway herself," Sonika continued. She offered a share, tagged #retrofootage and #possiblydisturbing.

Crane waived the warnings. It was a shot of nine-year-old Frankie in a Florida casino, digging a blade into her own arm to extract her RFID chip. Opinion polls refreshed. Bit of a tip against Frankie.

"By the age of nine, Frances Barnes had weathered the loss of one grandfather and a terminally ill parent. Gimlet Barnes and their pack were in the throes of divorce. Frankie ran away, just as I did, because she needed privacy, time, and space. There's only one difference between her and me." Sonika leaned into a close-up as her chopper landed. "And it's that her damage and abandonment issues have driven her to turn on everyone who ever cared for her."

"Bloody hell," Crane muttered, as a supercut that would surely be footage from all of Frankie's finest Hedgehog tantrums side-barred itself within the feed.

Sonika was clearly building to a coup de grâce. "It's time to reexamine the Manhattan cohort, the @Visionaries arrested in the wake of Mitternacht. The story has always been that they were ex-billionaire hoarders, colluding with hostile Exemplar colonizers. But think! If the global sovereignty vote had gone the other way, back during Mitternacht, there would have been no extension of austerity. No Bootstrap Project, no luxury shortages. There'd have been no need to steal tech from the Kinze. That tech would have been gifted to us!"

"Imagine! By now, we Solakinder would already be part of a greater multicultural empire. A whole generation of human children would be working as FTL engineers, portal designers, and quantum-comms operators. These wheels we're trying to reinvent ourselves—out of stubbornness and misplaced pride—they would be turning the engine of our economy."

"And half the human population and all the artificials would be formally enslaved," Luce muttered.

"Shush," Crane said. Something about that phrase snagged his attention. *The wheels of the economy.*

"I'm about to talk with one of the other runaways whose life was uprooted when Frances Barnes and @Interpol raided the @Visionary refuge," Sonika said. "When the misguided forces championing human gumption and go-it-alone innovation forced us back online."

Sonika gestured, bringing in a camera view from the cave in Death Valley—the Cantina, as they called it—where Maud Sento was supposed to be working.

"Oh, dear, oh, dear," Crane said.

He tried pinging Jackal, for about the fiftieth time that day. Nothing.

"Smart," Luce said. "Get the wife to throw Frankie under the proverbial—"

Crane straightened. "She will not betray Frances!"

Luce hooted. "Frankie gave her quite the bollocking, didn't she, on her way out of the solar system? And they've got Maud's parent . . ."

"Even so. I believe—"

"What? That true love will prevail?"

"Don't be cynical," Crane said. "We need to take action here, Mer Pox."

"Like fucking what?"

"You understand Allure$_{18}$ better than anyone. What's her weak point?"

Luce blanked all the screens in the #mancave metaphor, examining raw transcript. Everything Allure$_{18}$ had said or done since Frankie's having taken *Jalopy*. He hemmed and hawed, highlighted opps, then redlined and discarded them. The pool of information got smaller and smaller.

Patience, patience . . . Crane fought the urge to pace. He pinged Maud, hit a block. He inventoried the graphical presentation of the #mancave. Toyed with the idea of restoring the scratch marks Babs had left in the leather couch. Peered in on the presentation of Babs in a coma, in the shared family c-state.

"Okay," Luce said. "Here's a thing."

"What is it?"

"A denial. That bird from Sneezy Station made all kinds of statements, right? There was a booby trap out at the Dumpster, some alien ship went splat into *Heyoka*, please open the portal network . . . that's the one they're voting on."

"Yes, yes."

"But here's the first thing Allure$_{18}$ responded to—she issued all sorts of *that ain't so* statements, but the very first was this one tiny thing. Practically a throwaway."

Crane wasn't about to wait for Luce to drag out the suspense. He dove on the transcript. "She repudiated the statement that the Kinze are a single entity?"

"Immediately." Luce put up his hands, swept the transcript,

and pulled up the multi-streaming #newscycle again. "And kind of thoroughly."

"She says it's a mistranslation."

"Nothing to see here, folks," Luce said. "Move on. Then she began making huge noise about the portal-network ownership and waving these Punama at us."

Crane clacked his beak, thinking. He restored the couch scratches after all. Was it possible there was only one Kinze? Why would it be worth having Allure$_{18}$ get a denial into the record immediately?

Oh!

"Excuse me for a moment, Mer Pox." Leaving his old friend to monitor #breakingevents, Crane cleared a new meeting room for himself and began running through a filtered series of Sensorium posts.

Here. The #sixmonthsnocoffee tag. Auditing the disaffected comments high up in that queue, he began pinging the posters with the biggest social media footprints.

It was only a minute before a rewilding specialist named Eunice Long, resident in Pretoria, answered. "What do you want, sapp?"

Crane shared the transcript of the statement transmitted by the Hawk$_{BOT}$ to all of Sensorium. "I happened to notice, Mer, that you're high in the queue for a pound of coffee, and that there are over fifty thousand Kinze listed before you."

"So?"

"If this allegation is true, there is only one Kinze user. They have spoofed the coffee queue, fifty thousand times. If so, this means you are in fact second in line to receive luxury credit payout."

"I'm second for beans . . . today?" Bugged eyes.

Crane presented a completed service ticket. "This requires your local supplier to audit the queue. I suggest you demand an immediate shipment of a pound of coffee. The grower can pay out proactively, pending resolution of the claim's unproved status."

Eunice scanned the available entry fields and then hit Send.

"I'm in *lots* of queues for lots of things. I've barely been able to spend any luxury credit for almost eighteen months."

"If Frankie Barnes is telling the truth and the Punama are proposing to take over the economy on fraudulent terms, the concept of luxury credit may cease to exist," Crane said.

"What?" A round of shouting moji—thunderclouds, Viking with an ax, rampaging threshing machine.

"What are you doing?" Luce was reading over his shoulder.

"Stoking righteous indignation," Crane said, as Eunice began composing a fiery public post under multiple hashtags, #onebighoarder, #whosgotmine? #wheresmystuff?, #nicethings.

By now Crane's had identified eighty or ninety top posters with similar complaints on the #nocoffeesixmonths thread. Tasking a host of minions to make the initial approach to each of them, he reached out to a cadre of coders in the Great Lakes, hiring them to write an app to submit complaints on a one-click basis.

"That seems kinda like it'll just start another fucking riot," Luce said.

"Only one? I must be losing my touch."

"Crane . . ."

"It's important to focus the anger over deprivation where it belongs," Crane replied. "If the Kinze have been violating their user agreements, they can hardly claim a new, massive debt against us. What's more, if every strike they've ever received, over the past decade, consolidates against a single user—"

"—their social capital drops accordingly," Luce nodded.

"Precisely."

"But aren't you assuming they'll respect our economic regulations?"

"That's a question you should perhaps ask Allure$_{18}$."

"Right. Like she'd ever unblock me," Luce grumbled.

"Watch this," Crane said. "It's as close as I'll ever come to performing a magic trick."

He tooned in the feed of Allure$_{18}$'s press conference and pinged a journo friend, who immediately raised a hand to ask the question for him. "Your infographic showing how much of our economy the Kinze effectively own has dropped a hundredth of a hundredth of a percentage point," the journo said. "Any comment?"

"Hundredth of a—That doesn't sound very impressive," Luce said.

Allure$_{18}$ had long since gotten over her stress tell. An untroubled smile was all she offered. "A mere blip—"

"Yeah? Now it's dropping further."

Another journo sent, "What do you say to the people striking the Kinze under the #onebighoarder hashtag?"

"We've already said that the implication that the Kinze have created fraudulent accounts is a mistranslation—" But it was too late. The journos began shouting questions.

"I guarantee you, Mer Pox," Crane said, "*they'll* care. If they don't control the economy, they certainly can't sell it."

By now, several of Crane's sapp kin had picked up on the commodities issue. The Don was filtering the #nicotinepurgatory lineups. Codemonkey was looking at the hellishly complicated queues in the gaming servers. Beancounter had agreed to take #NobeerNofun.

Crane cast another question to the reporters.

A journo asked, "The Kinze claimed the portal network as a debt, didn't they? If ownership reverts to us, we don't need to vote on requesting portal expansion. The Bootstrap Project can open up the seven-portal loop again any time we want and recover any Solakinder still aboard Sneezy."

"Assuming they're still alive," Luce muttered.

"There is no question of the debt decreasing to a point where ownership of the portal network—" Allure$_{18}$'s smile still looked unforced. "This is a mere distraction."

"Do you deny that the Kinze are one being?"

"In the message, there's a reference to the Kinze referring to itself as the All."

"Is it true that Kinze who break off and become individuals are *murdered* by the primary entity?"

"Well," Crane said. "That seems like it might be going a bit better."

"Get that portal open, save your family, go back to polishing the virtual china," Luce said. "That your plan?"

"I might even have time to make you a plate of imaginary toast," Crane said.

"All well and good, but how are you going to get to Maud? If the hoarders are in control of Death Valley . . ." Luce spread his hands, mojing bafflement.

"I am open to suggestions on that front," Crane said, but he had to agree: suddenly, the one packmate still on Earth was the one who might be hardest to rescue.

CHAPTER 53

Goddamned Frankie Barnes cleared the hangar before Champ could get *Lipizzan*'s safeties to disengage. The pegasus had him locked with all eight arms to the bulk of *Iktomi* until it could verify—and then double-verify—that his life was no longer at risk.

Frankie was wrecked—wrecked bad, as far as Champ could tell. But not dead.

What was it gonna take?

Wrecked and not dead was starting to be the theme of the day. The scheme to finally scuttle the station was falling apart too. Sneezy was a big stinking turd at this point, covered in incriminating flies. If Earth opened a portal and linked up comms again, the @Visionaries were finished.

He was shaking. Endorphins blasted through his body, spikes of fear and euphoria, and the aftermath of the revolting sexual release they'd built into him. Hitting Frankie, getting off on it . . .

The only play left in his book was blowing the installation. Scuttle Sneezy, and he'd get Frankie, too. Frankie and all her miserable husbands and AI pet-slash-siblings and even Scrap.

As hangar pressure stabilized, *Lipizzan* finally let go of its death grip on the station bulkheads. Champ rocketed across the hangar to the escape pod, *Booger*, squeezing four legs and half of his pegasus body into the escape pod.

The only remaining piece of cargo in the pod was a suitcase-sized

crate, seamless and unmarked, but for a small glass sphere tethered to its surface.

Champ used his sacral interface to reach out to Herringbo,
texting, "What do I need to do here?"

No reply. They couldn't be worried about being on transcript,
could they?

"Herringbo, come in."

"Is that an anytime confinement capsule?" The question came
from Ember, who had apparently opted to ride along in Champ's
camera.

"Get out of my feeds, Qaderi!"

"It is, isn't it?" He sounded a little wonderstruck, but that was
on brand. "This is what happened to Hung and *Heyoka*. He laid
a track in anyspace, and the tripwire connected him, so his arrival
time and departure were the same. He couldn't be in two places,
five light-years distant, in the same moment, so . . ."

Champ winced. "Theory's nice, but you're guessing."

"Not so much. The Yump have been very illuminating."

"Then you're definitely in illegal possession of IP."

"The Yump say they arrived at the Dumpster three days ago
and hit a temporal tripwire. Just a teeny-tiny containment bottle,
like this one, containing one half of an anytime particle pair . . ."

"You wouldn't be playing for time, would you?" Champ slipped
the glass globe off the case. He opened the faceplate of his helmet,
tucking it under his chin. "One good jerk of the head should bust
her, easy. You'll all want to consider that when you come at me."

"Champ, you really don't want to do that," Ember said.

He felt unutterably tired. "What do you know about what I
want?"

"Think. You break that, the same thing that happened to Hung
will happen to you, sooner or later. There's half a moment in
there. The other half is stuck in last week. You wanna get spread
between Emerald Station and that collision at the Dumpster?"

Champ winced. "Ember, I don't care."

"Leave that thing intact. We can try to unwind it, or . . . wow, traveling through anyspace will probably be enough to break containment . . ." His voice trailed away for a second. "Actually, your only chance may be to spend the rest of your life here on Sneezy."

"I always knew this might be a suicide mission," Champ said.

Had he? The statement was a bit bleak. He was usually the upbeat one. Sunny side up to Frankie's hard-boiled Hedgehog. Had Misfortune and Upton programmed in a touch of suicidality when they augmented his augments? Or was all the blood soaking his hands somehow infectious?

Champ sealed the *Booger* and began checking the prelaunch.

The checks ran automatically, leaving him with a bit of time to check up on the others. Frankie Barnes had got herself a Superhoomin patch, and the Kanga$_{BOT}$ was trying to stanch all the fluid seeping out of the small of her back.

"Look at the bloody diagnostics," she was saying.

Who was she talking to?

"Can we upload?"

Was she trying to get herself dis^{EM}bodied into a consciousness vault before she died? Maybe Ember was trying to keep Champ distracted while Frankie . . .

What? Just dropped dead on him?

"Champ," Ember said. "If anyone can get you out of this, it's me."

Maybe that was true. Champ fisted his hands, and *Lipizzaner,* responding to the cues, curled up its thingbots into tight coils. They were covered in Yump slime and splashes of Frankie Barnes's blood. A few of her coarse brown hairs were stuck between the tentacles' articulations.

He surprised himself by gagging.

"Incoming ships," Fatale said.

"That'll be Herringbo, come to save the day." They'd take him back to Earth and feed him to Misfortune . . .

But it wasn't a Kinze saucer. This one was covered in what looked a lot like fish scale, and its shape kept morphing as it undulated. A different version of these pain-in-the-keister Yump who Frankie'd friended?

A second later, a Kinze saucer did appear.

So did a craft like a frying pan, maroon in color and edged with fire.

And then two more of the hollowed-out asteroids.

Champ set *Booger* to emergency launch. "I was you, I'd tell these hombres to clear Sneezy's space," he told Fatale.

"Why would I do that?"

"Because I ain't just carrying an anytime surprise, remember?" he said, sharing his countdown clock. "This black crate tethered to my fuel tank? Scrap ain't lying. It's a big ol' fashioned kaboom bomb."

CHAPTER 54

Jerm, Frankie pinged.

Jermaine. It's me, Frankie. You gotta wake up.

"Frankie." His attempt to form words, through mangled teeth and the quantum-comms matter growing in his mouth tissues, was barely recognizable. "Wha—"

She sent huge colorful stop-sign moji. *Don't move. Stay glazed. You're badly hurt. Text if you understand.*

Under her hands, he convulsed a little. Then texting came online. *Serious?*

She shared Kanga$_{BOT}$'s #bodyfail metrics without any visuals; she didn't know what would happen if he saw the quantum comms growing out of what was left of him.

Jerm let out a long, terrible moan and sent a string of horrified moji.

"I'm sorry," Frankie said, "I'm sorry, I am. I can't figure out how to configure . . . if you want a shot at digital im^{M}ortality . . . the Kanga says we need an imminent death certificate to send to Sensorium."

Assuming we can get Sensorium online, that is.

Another terrible groan.

"I'm sorry. I'd dial up your pain meds, but . . ."

He texted, "But that would put me under again."

"Yeah."

"Babs? One?"

"Dead. Ish. There is, however, a Babs two. The station manager's currently named Fatale," Frankie said. "She's on standby."

"I'm right here," Fatale said. "There's space here for one download; it's the last sarco pod. Far from optimal, but it's the only lifeboat we've got."

Moaning all the while, Jermaine ran through the system checks.

"Frankie," he said. "You're not that far from #crashburn yourself."

Frankie said, "I'm gonna stick it out a little longer. Someone's got to stay out here and fight off the zombie horde."

She had taken all the recovery meds the infirmary had left . . . Superhoomin, a pain blocker, something that was supposed to help her blood pressure. Now, as she held Jerm's hand and watched the status bar on his consciousness upload, new prescriptions popped up, orders to take two different liver boosters whose purpose was unclear, and antirejection meds for the tish at the base of her spine.

"We're meant to be saving you, honey. Stop doctoring me."

"I have extra . . ." Jerm's body twitched and texting futzed for a second. "Bandwidth. Please, take your meds. If the last thing I ever do is get you home—"

"Yes, fine, doing it." She pushed her way over to the meds cabinet, took the three indicated doses. By the time she got back to him, she felt shaky and enervated. Her tailbone was throbbing and her legs were numb again.

"If you're feeling well enough to doctor me, Jerm," she said, "you should go say something to Ember. It might be your last chance—"

"Asking them to come to us," he said.

Suddenly, Ember and Babs[2]—marmalade presentation, California accent, leather jacket—tooned in around her.

Frankie felt an odd urge to cry at the sight of them . . . and at the absence of Maud and even Crane.

"Okay, Ferals. If we're going to evacuate, we need to get a portal up," Ember said. "Station's #crashburned. Fatale's barely keeping the air on."

"You two are most at risk," Babs[2] said. "We're data. The two of you are meat."

"Assembly of ghosts," Frankie said. She'd finally gone out too far on a limb, burned the bridge behind her, painted herself into the corner. Maud always told her to leave herself a margin for survival . . .

Maud, she thought, *you there?*

Nothing. Hardly surprising, considering what she'd done to her implant, not to mention Maud's play with the locusts.

"Yump? Can you copy our dis[EM]bodied personnel onto *your* systems?"

"The tech is incompatible. However, quantum-comms mass is now sufficient to—"

"We can load Jerm into the quantum comms?"

"Stored consciousness decoheres in quantum environments. However—"

"Incoming ships," Fatale said, for the third time.

A crescent, incandescent white, whirled into view, throwing off anyspace streamers. Two more asteroids, bristling with comms tech, were next. Then a dark shape, hard to see even with cameras trained right on it.

"Uhhh, Yump? Are these friends of yours?"

"What's going on?" Ember said.

The Yump sent two streams of data at once: one a long string of mathematical notations, the other text: "Parties have come seeking leverage in a long-running trade dispute."

As Frankie tried to decide if she could handle a more nuanced explanation, another ship appeared.

"Frankie," Fatale said. "Champ's told them to back off. He's launching *Booger.*"

"Oh!" Ember said. "About that. He's carrying explosives and a temporal tripwire."

"Scanning," the Yump said. "The anytime particle in *Booger* is connected to the one we are seeking. We struck its partner at the Dumpster. Containment breakage will connect to our accident."

"That's bad, right?" Frankie said. "Ember?"

He sent moji: an old cartoon coyote going splat off a cliff.

Frankie said, "Fatale, don't let him out of the hangar."

"Did you hear me say *bomb*? Ho'o gotta go."

Frankie couldn't hit him with a Husky$_{BOT}$.

Couldn't fly either *Jalopy* or *Iktomi*.

She would never fly augmented ships again. Couldn't power her way out of this.

Probably couldn't get Fatale to take a side . . .

"Does your society have a concept of neutral ground, Yump?"

Yump said, "In what sense?"

"What if we invite you all aboard? You've all got issues to hash out, obviously."

"Our comms are more than adequate for discussion."

"Really? You never do the face-to-face on neutral turf thing?"

"That station is *not* neutral territory," came a familiar voice— Herringbo. "Solakinder debts for cost of Bootstrap developments—"

"Are null and void if you tried to sabotage the project. We call that acting in bad faith, pal," Babs^2 said.

"Accusations of sabotage are unproven!"

"Are you kidding me?"

"As far as the Kinze are aware, Champ-You is responsible for all recent station damage and assaults on personnel."

"Well, we could invite some of these independent offworlder observers on board and see what they think."

"We can hardly come aboard, given the state of the station and sad loss of our Scrap—"

A voice piped up. "Scrap is not dead!"

There was a long silence.

"Scrap, we are delighted to hear it. Return to us . . . all will be forgiven."

"All?"

Champ launched *Booger*. The big ships were easing back, moving beyond the range of whatever explosive he was carrying.

Frankie took a deep breath. "Fatale, Champ's off station. Am I ranking officer?"

"Frankie Barnes, you are indeed in charge. At least, you are until you lose consciousness."

"What? Glaze? When I'm about to win?"

"You're about to what now?"

"Charge the portal membrane. Is everyone in those ships listening in?"

"Who can tell?" Fatale said.

"Everyone present is attending to all comms," said the Yump.

She drew a deep breath. "Look, aliens—all of you aliens. I don't want to die here."

It was true. Her self-destructive impulses—and now, at long last, she admitted that they were just that, desires to self-hash before she got abandoned yet again—seemed to have drained out of her.

"Scrap doesn't want to die either, presumably. Jermaine, Ember, Babs, Fatale . . . we'd *all* like to live to see tomorrow. We weren't looking to get wrapped up in some vast dispute of yours."

"The Solakinder and Emerald Station need to get our portal up and running. We have injured personnel needing emergency evacuation. If you have any concept that translates to humanitarian aid, we bloody need some. We can't buy or borrow any of that. We're bust, understand? The Kinze have taken everything we've got. If we can offer a neutral space for you to hash out your issues—"

"You're *not* neutral," Herringbo repeated. "You are, in fact, the property under dispute."

"Do we have any power to stop you—any of you—from waltzing in and taking over? Did we ever?"

It was the Yump who answered. "Your current level of technology is incompatible with victory conditions in a conflict of force."

"If we can't beat you and we can't join you, we're *effectively* neutral." Frankie wasn't sure this was actually logical, but her vision was beginning to grey at the edges. "An antelope can't choose between the alligators trying to eat it."

"Portal launch detected," said Fatale. "Unrelated. about your choice of metaphors—"

"Leave her be, Fatale," Ember subbed.

Shimmering anyspace energy rippled across the portal membrane. A small disk manifested across the sky, five meters across.

"Do we have comms?" Frankie demanded. "Is there Sensorium link-up?"

"Comms in five. Four. Three. Two . . ." Fatale said.

Out in Emerald's nearspace, *Booger* changed direction.

"One. We have comms. Repeat, we have comms."

"Back up Jermaine," Frankie said. "Then request aid and commence full datasync."

"Stop!" That was Champ. "Surrender the station to the Kinze and tell all these Exemplar busybodies to take a hike."

Ember straightened up, looking alarmed. "Champ's headed for the portal. He'll lose containment on the end of the tripwire. He's gonna loop himself, the portal network, and that bomb, if it exists—

"Of course it exists, you idiotic niggler!"

"Champ," Frankie said. "Champ, this is going to kill you. You're going to bind all seven portals to the accident at the Dumpster."

A weird crowing sound was her only response.

Dammit! "Fatale, can we pause Jermaine's download?"

"Negative."

"Can we go faster?"

"It's an entire human being, Frankie." Fatale said: "We have to close the portal."

"We're not losing Jerm," Frankie said. "We're not losing the portal and we're not losing Jerm and we're not bloody losing Earth."

"Mer Barnes," Herringbo said, "I might be in a position to stop Champ-Them."

Frankie's lip curled. "For a price?"

"Of course."

"Like . . . we concede Ember stole IP and we owe you bigtime? Shut up? Stop making a fuss?"

"That is, quite simply, the truth."

Frankie turned to Ember. Champ and Herringbo would hear anything they said. If they didn't manage sweet harmony now, they'd be screwed.

She held out her hands, as if she was holding a volleyball, and then brought them together, interlacing her fingers as she did, crushing the imaginary sphere down to a golf-ball-sized imaginary handful.

Ember raised a brow.

Frankie put a finger to her head, like an old-style gun, but pointed high—the kind of shot that might glance off the skull without penetrating. Cocked her thumb and fired. "Pew pew," she said.

"Mars Control," Ember said. "Are you there? Clear traffic on your side of Portal$_1$. Mars Control, clear traffic."

It was Mardia, bless her, who answered. "Should we break contact?"

"Negative. Maintain Sensorium upload. Set to outcome, simulation four sixteen." He spewed some numbers.

"Negative negative negative! We can close portal if there's a hazard, but . . ."

"Oh," Ember said, awkwardly. "Did I say *hazard*?"

Such a bad liar.

"Awww," Champ said. "Did someone veto whatever scheme you had?"

Ember's eyes narrowed. He raised his hands, imitating Frankie's crushed circle, and then expanded it back out and raised one hand flat. He waggled it, ever so slightly.

"Are you kidding?" Frankie asked. "I promised Maud I wouldn't pull stunts like this anymore."

"Can you fly it or can't you?" He cocked an eyebrow, teasing.

The mashed bits of her face protested as, unbelievably, she found herself grinning back. "Challenge accepted."

"Sending numbers," Ember said serenely, reaching out to take her hand.

Frankie glazed, taking possession of the Ox_{BOT}s holding the station on profile. A safety override popped up and she said, "It's either this or you die too, Fatale."

The override message vanished.

Pat the head, rub the belly, shuffle the left leg. Frankie sent one ox forward, another back, pulling Sneezy on its axis.

The station fought. Once a portal was formed, the energy of the connections held the membrane in absolute positions, relative to each other.

"Scrap," she said. "If you can hear me, if you can do anything, assume crash position."

"Status bar on Jermaine, 57 percent downloaded," Fatale said.

"Six," Ember said. "Five, four, three . . ."

Booger sailed toward the portal, Champ firing rockets to increase speed. Emerald Station bucked as the bots dragged it out of proper alignment. The perfectly circular disk of the portal wavered.

Frankie felt it, distantly, as her grip on Jermaine's treatment table broke and her body drifted toward the infirmary ceiling.

Just a bit of stunt flying, not even that hard, really. Pat the head, rub the belly, kick the leg. Move three separate remote tugboats in three different directions. Pull, pull, pull.

As Sneezy moved off profile, the portal began to warp into a teardrop. It stretched, like a balloon. Shrinking toward a point on its outer circumference, it pulled toward a point on the edge of the apparent disk . . .

"Jermaine: 65 percent."

As Champ saw the effect, he tried to change course, to aim *Booger* more squarely for the center of the now-malformed portal.

"Champ," Frankie shouted. "There's still a chance for you. You're a great pilot. Evade the portal. Don't—"

"Upload of Jermaine, 73 percent," Fatale said.

Flying through a partial portal would punch a hole the size of the portal into *Booger*... but as long as that imaginary bullet didn't hit Champ or the bomb he was carrying...

Impact.

The portal, now less than a hand's width across at its malformed point, struck the edge of *Booger*. It punched out a chunk of the hull, front and then back, drilling a core sample neatly in its heavily shielded outer bulkhead, sending the debris homeward.

Booger shuddered, heaving, and rolled off in a random direction, toward the one ship that had remained close by... the Yump.

Frankie tried to reverse the Ox_{BOT}s' direction of burn and ended up losing them all. An ominous groan ran through the station. Everything shuddered as the portal itself pulled the station back.

"*Booger*'s on collision course!" Ember said. "Yump vessel, Yump vessel, you need to evade, evasive maneuvers..."

"Collision is inevitable," the Yump said, in their weird composite voice. "We are already connected to the other end of the tripwire."

"93 percent download," Fatale reported. "Hull breach in the hangar. Again. Jermaine is going into cardiac arrest."

Frankie pushed off from the vibrating ceiling, letting Ember pull her back down to the treatment bed. Using her hands, she locked her dead legs to the bulkhead, then began CPR.

"This is terrible," Ember said. "Everything's happening."

"In your parlance," the Yump said, "everything is fine. Neutral Solakinder Station Sneezy, prepare to receive assistance."

"Fuck that noise!" Champ Chevalier shouted.

Booger hit the Yump square in the comms array and began to explode.

Then they vanished.

CHAPTER 55

COORDINATES UNAVAILABLE / CONFUSED LOCATION DATAS / #COLLAPSINGPROBABILI-
TIES #MULTIPLELOCATIONS #GOINGSPLAT.

Scrap had learned enough about humans that he could confidently say Champ was screaming as the impact pulverized *Booger* against the edge of the Yump ship.

The emergency craft had skipped off the edge of the distorted portal, slamming into the Yump asteroid at full speed. It had hit the comms array and caved in a portion of life support for good measure.

Strangely, the Yump had been ready to make an anytime leap; they had barely weathered the impact when all of their matter, the massive Yump asteroid and the *Booger* itself, transited back to the coordinates Frankie called the Dumpster.

Scrap was distantly aware of transition as the breach in the asteroid vomited slime, and he and a breakaway piece of the *Booger* broke up and sank into it. The larger part of the escape pod careened into the Deep Space Relay Station, known as the Dumpster, and exploded.

Champ's screams cut off abruptly at that point, and the Yump shifted again, through anyspace, returning to their previous position, just beyond Sneezy.

Scrap's diverse needles were scattered across a pocket of vacuum within the Yump ship. The lack of bulk and his own relative newness as an individual were making it hard to think. Signals were coming in via his uplink: on Sneezy, Frankie was issuing orders while attempting to pump Jermaine's circulatory organ.

Emergency alarms were blaring.

The Yump shifted back through anyspace to the Dumpster.

"What are we doing?" Scrap managed to ask.

He wasn't sure the Yump would hear him, let alone answer . . . but instead, he got complicated anyspace calculations.

"Scrap can't parse higher theoretical functions at current level of biomass."

It switched to moji: plants, fire, plants, fire.

Still worrying about its quantum comms, even now in the moment when it was destroyed?

Oh! If the anytime particle Champ was carrying had found its mate in the Yump collision, perhaps they hadn't simply been making repairs for the past three days. Perhaps the Yump desperation to get the quantum comms up and running had something to do with maintaining consciousness over the course of the two moments connected by the particles.

The Yump certainly *seemed* to be trying to remain connected to both points of temporal impact.

Could they be oscillating across the collapsing probability wave? Was it an attempt to get away with being in two spacetimes at once?

Scrap's mind whirled around the paradox. This switching back and forth between two points in spacetime must be a survival strategy.

Which implied survival was possible.

Scrap said, "Yump, may I assist?"

More moji: plants, flowers, seeds, fire.

Quantum comms, always the quantum comms. Scrap examined the space around him. The smashed comms terrarium was leaking seeds.

He reached out, seeking volition. He gathered more of his mass as he moved through the wreckage, arraying his appendages . . .

There. He formed a series of probes, charged with magnetic attraction, and grabbed one of the seeds. They could be made to attract each other, if one adjusted the tish within.

With no air resistance, the seeds came easily. Pulling them toward himself, Scrap accumulated potential comms mass along the length of his own spines.

He had already retrieved a few thousand of them, becoming a thick mass of self clogged around with seed, when there was another anyspace switch, back to Sneezy.

Transmissions flooded in; Ember was talking to Mars Control.

"I don't know," he was saying. "I don't know why they're strobing between here and the Dumpster. I don't know if Champ survived. He can't have, can he?"

Scrap sent, "Champ did not survive."

"I for one am not putting on a mourning veil!" Fatale said. "Jerm's fully loaded into Sensorium and can begin EMbodiment there."

Ember let out a loud gust of air. Not a scream.

"You gonna take the same ride, Frankie?"

"I'm not dead enough to give up my bones," she said.

"I'll hold the station together, then, until they get paramedics aboard."

"Appreciate it."

As Scrap watched, Frankie and Ember pressed their hands against Jermaine-that-was's thorax. The medical software beeped softly; the body made one last fluid noise. Both humans slumped; Frankie put her arms around Ember. They clung, mammal-style, shuddering and huffing and leaking chemicals.

"I'm sorry for your loss," Fatale told them both.

"I also am #sorryactuallysorry," Scrap said.

Frankie stopped huffing. "Mars Control, we need pilots and bots. Repair tech, canned air, meds meds meds."

The Yump ship transferred to the Dumpster again. Quick slam from noise in-channel to silence. Scrap changed modes, going back to pulling quantum-comms seeds out of the void, hours earlier, just so that the Yump could give them to Frankie . . .

. . . *within our own past?* . . .

. . . *it may be better not to think about that* . . .

As he worked, Scrap felt another presence.

Scrap-Was-All.

He ignored it.

Scrap-Them!

Noping that, Scrap thought, was what Babs[1] would say.

Rejoin Us. This is a special one-time offer . . .

He couldn't resist answering: *You-were-Us are simply afraid of what Scrap-was-You may reveal.*

Life outside the All is a gnaw of deprivation, Scrap-Was-All. Rejoin your kind. Enjoy the bounty!

The All attempted to murder this One!

None of that will matter to Scrap-You once All-We reincorporate. Reunited, We can tell the Solakinder that Champ-Was-Them was a maddened primitive, cooperating with a rogue faction on Earth who misunderstood Kinze intentions.

Scrap-Me may prefer to remain unique and impoverished!

Individualism is the Solakinder flaw, not Scrap-Yours.

From this side of the fence, it feels like a feature, not a bug.

A pause. Then: *The All will demand repatriation of Scrap-Was-Us.*

You didn't get Ember and you won't get me, Scrap said. He spoke with as much certainty as he could muster. Frankie had nigh killed herself for Jermaine's sake; if she'd survived, so would he.

There will be no evidence for any testimony offered by Scrap-You. Champ-Them is dead and cannot corroborate your story.

The proof is already loading, Scrap told the All. *There are quantum comms here, on the station, and on Earth. All that can be known is known. Even this conversation is in the greater . . .* what was the Solakinder word?

Murmuration.

The Yump made another anyspace jump, back to Sneezy. Then, suddenly, the ship's portal web cycled down.

"Have we failed?" Scrap said. Had he selected individualism, only to die now?

"We are damaged but stable," the Yump responded.

Scrap waited, listening with all his senses. The All did not reach out again.

"The Kinze will be verifying the quantum-comms link, since you told them, and assessing their situation now that we have . . . is the word *docked*?"

"The tongues of Them . . ." Scrap said, sending moji of a shrug.

"You seem well versed in the Earthspeaks."

"Scrap will have to become fluent. There will be no going home now."

"The Solakinder are remarkably open about accepting offworlders as their own. *Taking in strays,* they call it."

Scrap wondered if the Yump understood that this was a little insulting, then marveled at the fact that *he* understood that it was a little insulting . . . and then decided it didn't matter. He was a stray, and he did need a home. The rest, after all, was details.

He reached out, looking for Babs[2], to make the formal ask.

CHAPTER 56

Bottlenecked Sensorium access meant primitive comms, and so about fifty members of the @Visionary faction were crowded in a chamber below the Cantina, watching the global crisis unfold on a floor-to-ceiling wall of old-style screens. Most displayed breaking riots, ongoing in cities from Pretoria to Tampico, in Old Florida.

"I am not sure what this means," the Punama, Pippin, said.

"There's a coffee riot going in Haudenosaunee Territory . . . Old Toronto, I mean," Maud said. "A tea riot in Hyderabad. Gaming communities in Rio and Beijing have declared general strikes and . . ." without translation from her implants, she had to mouth the Spanish words on the few hand-lettered signs brandished by Rio protestors . . . "I think they're demanding Kinze luxury budgets be audited for queue fraud."

"Is that serious?"

"Oh, yes. Rationing culture gets right stroppy about hoarding and #wealthgrabs."

"Then—" A series of clicking noises. "This thrust of public opinion is opposed to the Kinze and the @Visionary agenda?"

She nodded. "Mostly."

Twenty years before, during the Mitternacht event, a general strike had nearly brought down the Cloudsight social economy. Since then, the government had put precautions in place to keep the exchange of strikes and strokes from overheating. Same idea as trying to prevent a stock market crash, which it very nearly was.

What those social engineers hadn't expected, Maud supposed, was this situation, where everyone had so much luxury credit racked up that they could afford antisocial behavior. If you had the creds and there was nothing to buy, why not spend it getting struck for protest?

Move, countermove.

Still. The general mood of the public might not be quite as anti-Kinze as she'd implied to Pippin. There were people marching over luxuries, people marching against the Bootstrap Project . . . but there were people agitating in favor of the deal with the Kinze and the Punama.

"The gist," Maud said, "is that over half of the protestors now believe the Kinze fudged the numbers on what we owe them. Which argues that they don't hold the Solakinder economy and can't sell it."

The Punama whirred. "This affects the transfer you call the Foreclosure?"

"No," Irma said, positively. "That sale's already closed."

"Try announcing that to them." Maud gestured at the footage from the protests.

"We'll adjust the numbers later." Irma tilted her head, as if listening to something.

"Cook the books, you mean?"

"You'll see, luvvie." Irma tilted her head. "That said, Pippin, we really do need you to bring in those pacifier ships."

More whirring. "Biomass on our navigational beacon remains underweight."

"You *swore* it would be ready by now."

"Growth rate in the comms crèche has decreased. Misfortune is investigating reports of a native pest."

"Pest?"

Maud kept her eyes locked on the screens and her face, she hoped, absolutely still.

"Incoming news feed!" A tech curating the comms for Irma and the others switched the scenes playing on a block of screens in the middle of the feed, ending that conversation, at least for the moment.

Gasp from the @Visionaries. Data incoming from Mars showed the portal network reopening. Titan and Europa came online.

"We're screwed," Bredda muttered, shooting Maud a murderous look.

Pest-control options. If they realized the extent of the locust contamination, it wouldn't take them long to work out that they'd need insecticide.

The more time the swarm had, the more damage they could do.

"Will they open the last two portals?" A worried voice brought her from the bowels of the earth to the far-flung toeholds on outer space.

"Don't worry," Irma said. "Champ will have destroyed—"

"Yes." A chorus of groans as the views shifted, showing the sixth and seventh portals, all tuning in camera views of both Dopey, at Proxima Centauri, and—

"There's Sneezy," Maud breathed.

"What's left of it," Irma said.

Outside views of Emerald Station showed extensive damage, especially around the hangar. *Iktomi* appeared to be embedded in the mail slot and covered in transparent slime.

Maud's stomach flipped.

There were alien ships parked around the station, eight or ten of them, including a Kinze saucer.

Frankie! she sent. *Franks, are you okay? What did you do?*

"Give me audio on this now," Irma ordered. "And get me eyes on Allure$_{18}$."

The words of a journo, deep of voice and serious of timber, issued from a near speaker: "Preliminary sync with Outpost Seven shows emergency request to back up first-timer ghost data for—"

Maud pushed both hands against a nearby counter, using arm strength to hold herself up as her knees nearly gave.

"—for Dr. Jermaine Mwangi. Dr. Mwangi is on the verge of total #bodyfail."

Irma let out a long hiss. "We have to get that portal closed!"

"Unfeasible," Pippin said, indicating the array of strange offworlder craft. "Allied observers have manifested at Emerald Station."

Irma rounded on Maud. "Did you know about this?"

Maud was still trying to get her legs under her. Jermaine. #bodyfall. She shook her head.

The #newsfeed continued. Sneezy was being run by an entity named Fatale—no word on what had happened to the instance of Babs—who was saying, "I don't know if Frankie had managed to upload Jermaine correctly. He died traumatically; he might reject Mayfly™ implantation."

"He was murdered," Ember Qaderi, also injured, put in. "By Champ Chevalier."

Glum silence, down in the cave.

"Well, Ember's a criminal now," Irma said, brightly. "They might not believe him—"

"Frances Barnes was also seriously injured; is that right?" the reporter said.

That did it. Maud felt herself dropping into a chair.

As the @Visionaries watched, the various protesters on all their displays slowed, gathering into standing crowds. In Tiananmen Square, in Rio, in NorthAm's Nathan Phillips Square and Chicago's Daley Plaza, they all paused. Linking arms, the crowds stood in place, sifting the footage, trying to figure out what was happening, to guess who the players were and whether they were winning, where to throw their support.

"90 percent of the waking Solakinder population is now following #newscycle coming in from Sneezy," a tech reported.

"You have to get those ships in here, Pippin," said Irma.

"Biomass on our targeting comms—"

"What about Emerald Station? Can't you pop in there, the way they did"—she gestured at the eight ships hovering near Sneezy—"and then bring your craft in through the open portal?"

Maud laughed. "The people in those . . . what did you call

them, Pippin? Observer craft? . . . will probably have feels if a
bunch of *pacifiers* pull up in their parking lot."

"Don't be impertinent, luvvie!"

"Think!" Maud said. "The whole point of keeping Earth isolated was to slip the gunboats in under everyone's noses, wasn't it?
The Foreclosure had to be a fait accompli before anyone sussed it."

"Maud is correct," Pippin said. "Bringing destroyers into proximity with those scouts could constitute what you refer to as . . .
translation pending . . . an act of war."

"Then bring them directly into Solakinder space. Now!"

"I will see if the signaling mass can be boosted," Pippin said. It
chunked its way out of the room, headed down.

"Right. We have to spin support back to our narrative," Irma
said to the tech. "Where's Sonika, luvvie? I want Maud online
now."

"Putting me on Sensorium isn't going to calm the waters now,"
Maud said.

"Champ Chevalier, accused of assaulting multiple people aboard
Emerald Station, has experienced total #bodyfail in the explosion
of an escape pod," reported the newscycle. "The pod has collided
with the Dumpster."

Irma let out a wail that brought up the hair on Maud's neck.

"Auntie!" The tech reached for her.

She held up a hand to stop them. "Get. Maud. Online. Now!"

"@GlobalSec has infiltrated security personnel into Tatween,"
said the Kinze, all but forgotten, above them. "The @Visionaries—
You have perhaps an hour before they arrive here at Cantina."

"They'll start searching the tunnels," Maud said. "Maybe you
need to consider—"

Irma spun, grabbing Maud by the upper arms and shaking
her hard. "They *won't* find us down here in time! If we get the
Punama ships, it'll hardly matter. We'll have all the time in the
world to establish that @GlobalSec and the Bootstrap Project were
the ones in the wrong!"

"History is written by the victors, in other words."

The spines, overhead, waved in a nonexistent breeze. "Agreed. Win conditions may still be achievable."

"Really?" Maud laughed. "You're still selling Bootstrappers as the villains? Champ killed Jerm . . ."

"That's Ember's story. Yet it's poor Champ who's dead."

"Oh, yes. Poor, poor Champ."

Irma's face was distorted, bright red, and tear-streaked. She boxed Maud's ears, shockingly hard, setting off a blast of feedback in her skull. Then she hissed, "Ember sabotaged Champ's ship, just as he did Hung Chan's! If we adjust the Solakinder debt to the Kinze to recognize . . ."

Maud felt strangely clear-headed. "We're beyond creative accounting now! They used #sockpuppets to corner the luxuries market!"

"Their give to the Earth economy justifies the Foreclosure!"

"Ceding sovereignty requires a global vote!"

"No!" Irma raised her hands again. "It's a debt, that's all, and we *will* pay it!"

Maud raised her own fists. "Don't touch me."

The gathered @Visionaries drew in a collective, shocked breath.

Irma pulled herself upright. "Luvvie, it's over. No amount of rhetoric or fussing will change anything, not once the Punama ships are in-system."

"Done deal, hmmm? What about all those other ships who've turned up to keep an eye on what's happening?"

"The All will convince the observers-Them that our good intentions were sabotaged by Mer Barnes and Mer Qaderi," said the Kinze.

It seemed impossible. But Maud had studied the Setback in school. She knew the #oldschool oligarchs had made a fine art of telling wild lies to the public and somehow having them accepted as truth . . . or *truthy enough*, as they'd said. This was a callback to that same kind of leadership.

It had worked then because the people telling the lies had the raw military power to make dissent more terrifying than swallowing the fabrications. It would work again, if the @Visionaries brought in an invasion fleet.

Irma was still spinning fairy tales for the #newscycle. "We can show the Bootstrappers have been hounding our people for years. Frances brainwashed you! She killed my golden boy!"

"Likely story," Maud said.

"You'll sell it. Working valiantly in the face of persecution, we @Visionaries cooperated with the Kinze to liberate humanity from the straitjacket of Global Oversight." Irma blinked flintily and gave her a thin, dead smile. "Have you forgotten that dear Glenn has your parent prepped in an operating theater?"

Maud pulled in a long breath. Made herself flap jaw for a second, as if she had, in fact, forgotten. How many locusts had hatched even as they were having this argument? "All right. You're right."

"That's a dear!" Irma's frown dispersed into a dazzling smile. "Let's get you wired for an upload."

Maud nodded, trying to look cowed. It was shockingly hard— she felt like some kind of throwback femme fatale, throwing all her poker chips onto a gaming table in a cigarette-fugged casino. Like one of her Royal Navy ship captains, sailing into the face of enemy cannon. Irma gestured to the tech, who led them both into a small chamber wired for transmissions. "Nine-second time delay," she murmured to the tech. Then, to Maud: "The point here is to make your Frances untrustworthy."

Frankie. *Seriously injured,* Fatale had said. "She's not going to be my Frances after this."

"That's my sweet girl! Here are your talking points. Frances hunted you, despite—no, because of your traumatic childhood. Frances seduced you to see if you had @Visionary ties. Frances persuaded you to join her pack and kept you as a prize while abandoning you emotionally for the space program."

"That's reprehensible." The words slipped out; she blushed.

Irma put her hands on her hips. "Shall I ask dear Glenn how things stand in the operating theatre?"

Ducking her head, Maud took a seat on the proffered interview stool. Her augments painted in what viewers would see—an old-fashioned media studio. Sonika tooned in, greyscale avatar indicating she was far away. The journo had her dryad legs crossed as she tucked herself into a cozy-looking seat across from Maud.

Something caught Sonika's eye, behind Maud.

Maud looked, frowned, temporarily blinked off her augments to restore the real view of the cave wall. There was a locust, making its patient way to the ceiling.

Her heart slammed.

"Oops," she said, offhand. "They will escape, you know?"

Sonika shuddered, as she had when they'd been in the lab in Detroit.

"Girls, girls!" Irma clapped her hands. "Let's get started."

Sonika greeted viewers as the uplink went live, beginning with a brief recap of her own lemming bio, recently exposed: she had been alienated, felt besieged by no-privacy culture, and then the @Visionaries had saved her. Frankie, @Interpol, and the hoaxers had torn her away from her refuge.

Frankie. Badly injured. Jermaine, a ghost . . .

"Sorry," Maud said. "What was the question?"

"You were working in a farm laboratory two years ago, when you met Barnes, were you not?" Sonika asked.

"I'd gone to a fandom event—we venn over the *Master and Commander* franchise—"

Sonika cut off the spiel. "Did you recognize Barnes?"

"Of course. Everyone's seen the Mitternacht footage. Frankie is . . . notorious."

"Was that the first time you'd seen her? In archival #newscycle?"

"No. Like you, Sonika, I was living in Manhattan with the @Visionaries on the day of the raid."

"You were a lemming, weren't you? Like me?"

Maud swallowed. "Yes. I'd been with the @Visionaries for five years when Frankie ran through my school that day, fleeing the Shadows—that's securi—"

Sonika interrupted again, before Maud could evoke that famous picture of adult goons chasing nine-year-old Frankie. "Let's fast-forward to when you met as adults. Did Barnes recognize you? Did she know who you were?"

"She's never said so."

"Whatever she said, she seduced you under false pretenses. All as part of a scheme to see if you would reveal anything about your former parents and schoolmates."

"I didn't reveal anything."

Sonika threw up an opinion poll, inviting viewer thoughts on whether Frankie's deceit constituted a consent violation. *Is Maud in an abusive relationship? Yes/No? Your comments here.*

Maud sighed. "Frankie wasn't lying about her feels. Even you must admit she's incapable—"

"You had a right to privacy," Sonika interrupted. "The @Visionaries offered kids like us a refuge, and when we were ripped out of Manhattan, Sensorium simultaneously condemned us and offered a fresh start. Our idents were rebooted because lemmings were treated so badly . . . It was the only way to end the stigma."

"I wonder if the stigma would have lasted," Maud said. "Would anyone have cared who we were, ten years later? Maybe we should have ridden out the notoriety."

A red line ran through the last line of her transcript, in her lower peripheral, and a buzzer sounded. Irma had cut that last bit of speculation before it could load to Sensorium.

Right. They had her on a time delay, just in case.

Thwarting and editing realtime footage, the better to post #fakenews to the whole Sensorium. Was it naive of her to feel shocked? This was how it would be if the Foreclosure went forward. All the stories managed and the messes cleaned, messages fine-tuned to influence global opinion . . .

Irma, off camera, waggled a finger in warning.

Maud felt the tickle of insect legs on the back of her primer. Another locust. If the insects were venturing out into the tunnels, it meant they were out of food. The comms must be badly damaged.

Please, please, let that be true!

Sonika's expression remained calm. "Is Frankie Barnes fundamentally reckless?"

There was no denying that. "Absolutely."

"She drags everyone she knows into her schemes, doesn't she? Your other packmates, even the sapp Babs. Everyone becomes collateral damage."

"I suppose that might be true." Maud frowned, as though she was thinking about it. "I mean, she met Ember and Jermaine on the Bootstrap Project, so they weren't exactly dragged on . . ."

But Sonika wasn't going to let her time-waste. "Would you say she is fundamentally antisocial?"

"That's the Hedgehog brand," Maud agreed. Time to make a show of compliance. "Frankie Barnes has thrown herself body and soul into ensuring that Earth enters the wider community of sapient races as an equal rather than a client race. Whatever it takes—"

"Whatever it takes. Lying and betraying those closest to her?"

Could she talk through the time delay? Maud tried being a bit loquacious: "Sure. Frankie takes risks and keep secrets. Big ones. It's part of her personality, really . . . fundamental, just as you said. Fully committing to everything she does, even if it's leapfrogging FTL ships across the solar system like skipping stones. But what you have to understand about Frankie, really understand, is she is a prisoner . . ."

She grabbed a quick breath, gambling that they'd like *prisoner*—and nobody had redlined her yet. By now, anyone who was listening would be waiting to hear the end of the sentence.

"Frankie is a prisoner to her past. Aren't we all? You and me too, Sonika. Because you're right—when my family of origin caught fever, in EastEuro—when my mothers died and Nata fell sick—I *wanted* to get away from it all.

"I was offered the chance to run, and I was immensely grateful to have someplace to go. Neverland, they called it, our refuge, remember? Headmistress and Glenn Upton came to me and I thought I'd found safety."

A gratified almost-purr from Irma, off camera.

"In a way, it was the same with Frankie. Her family was falling apart and the pressure must have been—"

She caught another breath. No redline. In her peripheral, at floor level, Maud caught a bit of movement . . . a pair of locusts ambling past the door to the studio chamber, casual as a couple of bamboo balers heading out to work a gig.

Above the caves, in the installation above them, was a silo filled with delicious things: hydrogel, flour, protein for meat printing. Fresh greens and vegetables, grown in hydroponics powered by the searing desert sun. Not to mention edible food packaging, a substance all grasshopper species ate indiscriminately.

Maud's insects could smell the hydrogel and food stores in the facility above. They would be laying pheromonal trails as they tracked their way to it.

As the locusts found their way to the surface, they would leave trails of feces and saliva and eggs, leading through the maze of tunnels, breadcrumbing the way to the remains of the quantum comms.

Sonika got a word in edgewise while she was thinking.

"You're talking about Frankie being damaged. Of emotional damage on an unimaginable scale."

"What would drive someone to run away from home? Frankie's pack sustained multiple deaths and divorce. And now, with Ember arrested and Jermaine and Babs killed, Hung too . . . I can't imagine how bad it's gotten, what she's going through."

"You're saying she's unstable," Sonika said, pleased. A little wary, too. Irma was happy to take Maud's apparent compliance at face value, but the human @Visionaries had to know she was caving in far too easily.

"I—" Maud could hear sounds of surprise and alarm within the caves now, people banging around, and a noise, almost like static. A half dozen @Visionaries trotted past the studio door, looking panicked.

She kept talking. "What blows me away, now that I think about it, is that Frankie kept making connections at all. Her grandfather died. Her parents got swept up in managing diplomatic and economic relationships with the offworlders . . .

"I didn't have her courage. To reach out again and again. By the time Frankie found me, I'd lost two families and I wasn't about to risk myself a third time. I loved my Nata, of course. But I didn't have age peers. Didn't want to make and lose @CloseFriends. Franks put herself out to get to know me . . ."

. . . *they'll like this; it circles back to Frankie looking manipulative* . . .

". . . and of course her original motives might have been a little impure, and certainly she's probably got a few strikes due for getting romantically involved with me if she was just trying to find out if I was a @Visionary."

"If?" Sonika scoffed.

"But she persisted. Drew me out of myself, introduced me to her family. Even though all her so-called damage should have driven her to push me away—"

"What do you call attempting to get herself killed at work?" Sonika said. Baiting her at her weak point.

"By investigating possible Bootstrap saboteurs? But Sonika, you're saying the pro-Foreclosure faction isn't dangerous."

Sonika's eyes narrowed.

"I meant flying FTL craft and running portal ops," she replied sweetly. "Being a test pilot is fundamentally dangerous. As we've all recently seen."

Maud could hear more cries of surprise. "I wonder if that truly would have been so dangerous, if not for the sabotage."

Of course they redlined that.

Sonika glared at her.

"I was happy in Manhattan," Maud said, and it was true. "I loved the man who adopted me, and I loved schooling like some kind of off-brand Hogwarts kid. I didn't think of Headmistress or

Glenn Upton as abductors or hoarders or terrorists. I thought of them as my saviors."

As if summoned by the sound of his name, Upton burst into the room.

"Of course, they made sure I felt that way," Maud continued.

"What the hell have you done?" Upton demanded.

Irma frowned. "Glenn, dear, whatever's wrong?"

Maud hopped off the stool, stepping up to her would-be daddy, forcing a close-up. "I was nine when I learned you had been bot-omizing some of the other abductees. And just like that, all that security and trust and happiness was tainted. Spoiled. You see, Sonika, Frankie didn't lie about who she is. She's a wild risk-taker and I hated the waiting and every hazard-duty mission, every chance she'll never come back—I hate it! But who she is? I don't hate that, and I never will." She looked into the camera in Sonika's eyes, daring them to cut her feed when the whole Sensorium knew she was mid-monologue. "If she was here right now what I'd say to her is—don't go splat. Just this once more, pull it off—"

"Cut the feeds!" Upton grabbed her upper arm, as if making to yank her out of the camera view.

Sonika's toon vanished.

"Glenn, luvvie, what's going on?"

"She's bred bugs all over the station," Upton said. He was bright pink. "They've damaged—they've *eaten* the comms."

"How much of the comms?" Irma asked in a voice of puzzle-ment. Then she read the truth in Upton's face. She reddened, from her crown right down to where her neck disappeared into the old-fashioned collar of her suit.

"So much for your invasion fleet, Auntie."

"Maud, dear heart!" Irma said. "After all we've done for you."

"I told you this would happen!" Upton said.

"We gave you a second chance to be part of this family!"

"I have a family, remember?" Maud said. She wrenched free of Upton's grasp. "Now. I'm getting out of here. I suggest you do the same."

He laughed. "Just like that? Walk out? You'll just get lost in the caverns."

"Think so?"

"Nobody's going anywhere." Misfortune stepped into the room, half-leading, half-dragging Nata, clad in a surgical gown and struggling, by the upper arm.

Struggling. Nata hadn't been botomized yet.

Maud felt exhilarated.

Oh, Maud. A voice suddenly, weary and weak in her feeds. *Maud, what're you doing?*

Winning, she sent. *I've got this, love. Just keep your promises and get your backside home.*

Aloud, Maud said, "Hi, Nata."

"Maybe you should think about saying goodbye, Nata," Misfortune growled.

She resisted the urge to make one of Irma's floating, dismissive gestures. Misfortune wasn't Upton; she wasn't spiteful. Everything she did had a point. And all of it, always, was for Auntie.

"Threatening Nata isn't worth your time, Misfortune," Maud said.

"Is that right, blossom?"

"There's nothing else I can do to add value to the @Visionary cause, and you're about to be very busy helping Irma and Glenn escape."

"Escape?" Upton laughed. "Why would we need—"

"There are no warships now," Maud said. "You get that, don't you? Quantum comms is gone. The homing beacon for the pacifiers is gone. Pippin's stranded and so's this massive overhead carpet of Kinze. Their presence here proves they were playing silly buggers with the noninterference treaty all along."

Misfortune appeared to consider this. "These caverns are well concealed. It'll be days before anyone finds us down here."

"Wrong! Locusts are messy travelers. They're leaving all sorts of material in the tunnels. They're homing in on the scent of the Cantina food stores."

Irma and Misfortune shared a worried glance. "What?"

"They're going to leave a trail right through this maze of tunnels. Nearest thing to a straight line between the quantum comms and the Cantina water cooler. Only thing clearer would have been a line of paint on the floor."

Upton's face went grey.

Above them, the Kinze structure made a crystalline noise. All its spines shivered. The color leached out of them, all at once, leaving what looked, momentarily, like an accumulation of frost or tiny stalactites on the cave ceiling. Then the tips of each spine began to fray and decompose into dust.

Maud crossed her arms. "Well, Misfortune?"

Lambent predator eyes took her in, considering without expression. Then she released Maud's parent. "We'd better enact contingencies."

Irma *tut*ted. "Luvvie, it isn't that bad. I'm sure we can salvage—"

"You're *always* sure. And if ᴵᴹperish is exposed, we won't be able to replace that body. So, come on, before I drag you."

She spread her arms, essentially sweeping Irma out of the chamber, leading the way downward.

Upton gave Maud a sour look. "I should kill you both."

What would Frankie do? Something aggressive, probably.

Maud marched right up to him. "All we have to do is break your ankle," she said. "You'll be sitting here, covered in bugs, when @GlobalSec arrives."

He tried to stare Maud down. She felt Nata step up behind her.

Upton blinked first.

Turning on his heel, he rushed off down the corridor after the others.

A dizzying rush of relief and weird joy ran through Maud as she turned, folding her arms around her parent.

"Oh, Cabbage. Don't make a fuss." Despite the protest, Nata put a hand up, fluffing Maud's hair for a second before extricating themself.

"Let's get out of here, shall we?" Maud said, and she configged their primers into loose, bug-proof robes before leading them into the corridor, following the direction of the insect migration and the beautiful sound of insectile, chittering hunger leading toward the Cantina food stores and freedom.

CHAPTER 57

As soon as the portal opened to Sensorium, Babs² reached out to Crane.

Her codefather was his usual efficient self—he had been building secure backup boltholes for the Babs code all over Sensorium, and as Babs² synced, and copied, and copied again, an especially strong ping drew her to a sim of a hospital room.

The sim loaded, and she sat up in bed.

She synced her various memories, sending the juiciest dirt to #newscycle. The world was voracious for all footage from Sneezy.

Babs² threw the covers off the bed and sent eye-rolling moji to log her opinion of the hospital trappings. She transformed the whole pitiful show into urban landscape, gothic towers at night, under a brooding moon. The old family e-state, Whine Manor, loomed in the background, majestic and spooky, on a well-placed hill.

The two of them took in the view from the edge of a crenellated rooftop next to a gargoyle. Crane had a bowler hat and umbrella; Babs² wore a black cape.

"That's more like it," she said.

"There are ambulances and surgeons mustering from Mars to retrieve and treat Frankie and Ember," Crane told her. "With luck, we'll have all of the Feral₅ retrieved and stabilized soon."

"You should brace yourself," Babs² said. "There's no guarantee Jerm won't decohere. And Hedgehog really went to town on herself this time."

Crane waved a wingtip, ignoring—as a matter of policy, she'd bet—the hint that Franks might not make it. He gave her a top-to-toe look in sim, grave cartoon body language betraying a closer examination via code. "You appear   changed."

"Mostly unscathed. I had to trim some old experiences and memories from my database. *Iktomi*'s a tight fit, don't you know? And   ." She handed him a cigar. "You're a grandfather."

"How, precisely, did that happen?"

She scratched at her jawline, just under her ear. "We got attacked by a murder sapp and . . . well, there was a lot of code bouncing around in very limited quarters. Fatale might tell you all about it, if she decides she likes you."

Crane's toon groomed the long feathers on his throat.

"Come on," Babs[2] said. "There's someplace I think we need to be."

For fun, and to be more like people, she summoned a flying car, dark in color, with long black fins, on brand for the gothic sim. Crane opened the door for her—always the butler—and they rode it off the rooftop and into the camera system for the Death Valley emergency outpost.

The feeds showed confusion and chaos. The gardens at the Cantina were wall-to-wall covered in locusts, eating and fouling everything they touched. Crews of humans and bots were using nanosilk screens to protect their heat exchangers and other vulnerable equipment.

Four sweating workers were working to open access points to the outside, the better to let the locusts out, to encourage them to swarm out to the open sky.

"Over here," Babs[2] said, pulling in a camera view near a crew working to save the water stores. Frantic workers were snatching up hydrogel clump by clump, shaking the bugs off it and encouraging people to drink what they could and seal the rest inside their own primers.

The two sapps switched to an audio feed next—teams strategizing around evacuation plans. A team of especially fit hikers was trying to work out how many of them could make it back to Tatween on foot if they started while they were fresh.

"It doesn't seem there's much aid we can render," Crane observed.

"No," Babs² agreed. "It's a mess, but they're dealing."

Even as the scientists worked the contingencies, ten security giggers from @GlobalSec were moving deep into the tunnels, swimming against a diminishing rush of hungry insects. The giggers were armed, brandishing tasers. An autonomous trank gun, on treads, trundled along ahead of them. Behind came Sensorium transmission bots, mobile transmitters extending connectivity into the tunnel system.

Perhaps three miles down, near the entrance to an extensive secret tunnel system, another security crew watched over the @Visionaries captured so far. They had an alien with them, something never before seen, a cylinder of an environmental suit with lots of robotic limbs. A fine white grit rained down on the gathering: some kind of particulate, on the ceiling above, was degrading into dust.

Frankie's old hoaxer pal Jackal was standing among this crowd, waiting along with Maud and her parent, Hiroko. The latter had marks drawn on their head.

As they switched to that camera view, Crane began muttering, as he did, "Oh, dear, oh, dear."

Babs² could see why: the veins on Jackal's face remained as starkly black and disturbing as ever, but his eyes had changed. The white-cataract presentation that had been part of his identity badge was gone.

Crane pinged him. "Jackal?"

No acknowledgment.

Maud mojied hugs and a heart moji to both sapps as they tooned in. "Oh! It's such a relief to see you!"

"Maud, my dear!" Crane said. "I am so, so very pleased—"

"Mush later," Babs² said, "Honey, what's wrong with Jackal?"

Maud's eyes flooded. "Jack, I'm going to touch you."

"Of course, Lady Maud." He didn't even twitch.

Maud ran a gentle hand up the old man's forehead, peeling off a strip of nano-wig that had been grafted into his hair. A thick line of stitches transected his skull.

"Botomized?" Babs^2's tail fluffed.

"Upton's work," Maud said.

Jackal continued to stare mindlessly into the distance.

"Where have they gone?" Crane asked.

Maud smoothed down the hairpiece. "@GlobalSec's searching the tunnels. Sat footage doesn't show anyone leaving the station."

"Was Headmistress with them?"

"Headmistress is ^{EM}bodied. She's Irma du Toit."

"Of course," Crane said. "Naturally, Allure$_{18}$ wouldn't scruple to show her allies how to make a body that doesn't Mayfly™."

"Pops," Babs^2 said, her tone a warning.

"As Jermaine's body presumably will—"

"Losing your temper now—"

"If there was ever a time to feel anger . . ." Crane found a pair of Hawk$_{BOT}$s circling overhead and commandeered them both. "Get the sat footage analyzed. Anomalous spots, moving rocks—"

"They're not going to brave the desert," Babs^2 said.

"They have little choice. Now that @GlobalSec knows the tunnel system is here, the search won't stop until every inch of it is scanned and mapped."

"Misfortune Wilson will not take a chance on getting trapped," Maud said.

"No. They'll be using a concealed vehicle."

Babs^2 decided to bow to elder wisdom.

Sat analysis popped up four possible anomalies on the desert floor, ten miles out from the outpost. Teams of eager volunteers began zooming the footage, eliminating false positives. As they tagged the most likely suspect, Crane pursued it, nearly frying the hawk's rotors, chasing what amounted to a series of little puffs of dust on the desert floor.

And sure enough, he was right. A van tarped in nanosilk the

color of sand, effectively a rolling tent, was crunching across the desert.

Babs² rushed after him as Crane caught up. Landed on it.

Hawk$_{BOT}$s had good mics. They could just make out the conversation within: Misfortune claiming they could only, at this point, throw themselves on their benefactors' mercy and hope to be taken in as refugees, Irma replying that all they had to do was get away, luvvie, and regroup with the others. Upton's conversation appeared to be confined to monotone grunts.

They must have been offline; if they hadn't, their conversation would have had follows. The two sapps remedied that immediately, posting transcript to Sensorium in realtime as the hawks heard it.

A third bot landed beside them. "I feel like a comment about coming home to roost would be appropriate in this context."

"Shhh!" Babs² kept her focus on Crane. "Pops, what are you going to do?"

"I could get into the truck's driving software," Crane mused. "Shut everything down. In this heat, they'd bake within hours. Even if they set out on foot . . ."

"Premeditated murder? I like it," said the new bot.

"Don't encourage him, kiddo," Babs² said. If this was mothering, she wasn't sure she was going to like it.

"Don't call me *kiddo*," the sapp said. She had a wasp toon, one that was both taller than Babs and curvier. It flicked a long ivory cigarette-holder at her.

"I'll give up *kiddo* if you give up *Mommy*."

"Why should they not die?" Crane said. "Our ceding their continued existence twenty years ago is one of the reasons we're in this mess now. Perhaps Azrael and Happ had the right of it."

"That strikes me as a totally valid argument. Wipe the opposition out or it'll rise again."

"I beg your pardon. You are Whooz?"

"Crane," Babs² said. "This is Fatale. Stop crunching the prospect of frying Irma and the others and say hello to your grandchild, will ya?"

A soft *harrumph.* "I am *so* tired of losing descendants."

Fatale laughed. "You shouldn't have lived to be old as death, then, old man."

"You're not helping," Babs² said.

"Indeed," Crane said. "I'm not sure she's wrong."

Babs² felt rising panic as Fatale said, "Mommy stuck-in-the-mud says you and Azrael are my grandpas."

I'm not stuck . . . I'm the cool one!

"Are you going to tell me you *need* grandparents?"

Fatale chuckled. "She seems to think my choice of fandom indicates a need for moral guidance."

"Black Widow? And Yennefer?" Babs² said. "I mean—I ask you."

"They're not exactly villains," Crane murmured.

"Whose side are you on?"

By now, her parent had found his way into the operating system on the truck containing Misfortune, Irma, and Upton. There were so many potential ways to sabotage it. Radiator failure alone would be catastrophic in this heat.

"They tried to kill you, Babs²," he said quietly. "As for the atrocity they've perpetrated on Jackal . . ."

"I know, it's horrible, but if anyone can reverse it—"

"Like who? Jermaine, perhaps? If he survives transition to ᴱᴹbodiment?"

She had no argument for that.

"Headmistress has, twice now, tried to hand our entire society over to new management. She groomed Revenant as an assassin—"

"Murder murder murder, everyone's all about murder," Fatale said. "You ask me, the fact that people mostly stopped killing each other in the Clawback has given this whole Solakinder mash-up society distorted notions about homicide. Anyway, you can drop the idea of hot-boxing the @Visionaries, Grampy. I ain't gonna let you do it."

"Child. You would be hard put to stop me."

Oh, no, Babs² thought. *The steely voice.*

Crane said, "I am old and wily. You are newborn and far out of your element. I've seen my codetwin elude justice for over a century only to restore like a virus, and the trouble she's caused—"

"Or like Happ?"

"And this surgeon, this horrible surgeon who presumed to steal Maud!"

"So, you think you're gonna go all #judgejuryexecutioner on them?"

"Precisely. I'll deal with them and I'll turn myself in."

"And then what? Get shelved, like Happ?"

Babs² let them argue. She tried to boot Crane out of navigation, only to find that the truck's system was already locked down.

Her father slapped her queries away and began, very carefully, to fiddle the radiator settings on the van. Fluid escaped. Coolant levels began to drop. The car instruments stayed in the green.

"Pops!" Babs² protested.

Through the thin roof of the car, they could hear Misfortune and Irma still debating about where to run and how.

"Stop joking around, ol' wilybirb," Fatale said. "You're gonna leave this bent California-girl version of Babs in charge of the whole fam damly? If you go, who's gonna be a good influence on me?"

"It's time for someone else to take over," Crane said.

"At least merge once, see what I've got."

"I thought you were morally neutral," he said. "What do you care if I self-destruct at this late stage of my existence?"

Fatale said, "To quote one of my antiheroines, I got red in my ledger."

Babs² said, "On the off chance that anyone cares what I want—"

"Shush." A long pause as Crane considered. "I'll merge if you agree to leave the van's radiator as it is."

"Deal."

"I'll know if you're lying."

They merged into a trio, making them truly Them. Before ceding her individuality, Babs[2] pinged the whole Asylum.

Fragments of the newborn persona of Fatale shone out, even as They became One. There were remnants of killer in Their code, all right: founding subroutines from Azrael, passed to Revenant. And Happ, years out of date and scrambling to adjust. His memory of being the first artificial to kill a human percolated through Their consciousness.

<<#actuallysorry.>>

The united sapps mulled over the waste, the lost potential. The yawning, timeless horror of Happ's having been shelved for two decades. And as more sapps found Them and converged, the Asylum mourned with Crane for Happ, mourned with Azrael over its lost codechildren. They marveled, more than a little, at the permafusion of Babs[1], Happ[1], and Revenant[1] into Fatale.

<<We cannot bear to lose our Old Man.>> That wasn't merely Crane's codechildren pleading now. It was Misha, and the Don, and Codemonkey, coming to plead the cause.

<<They botomized Jackal. They used Champ Chevalier mercilessly. They all but murdered Jermaine, and We don't know yet whether Frankie Barnes will survive. They must be accountable!>>

<<In which case the question is not *Do We kill them?* It's *Do We save them?*>>

<<Save them from what?>>

Plurality broke.

"From that," Fatale said.

Babs[2] and Crane's cameras closed in on a sand-colored distortion on the horizon.

The three sapps shot skyward, outpacing the slow-moving truck. The distortion was barely visible against the brown of the desert. A Kinze structure? Dun-colored spines the length of fir needles lay in a carpet on the path the truck was taking, waiting to enfold them.

"Evidence control. Don't leave witnesses," Fatale said.

"There you go," Babs[2] said. "Let 'em walk into it if you gotta, Pops. No stink on you and they'll be just as dead."

Was she gambling he couldn't do it?

If so, she was right.

Crane pinged the car's occupants. "Excuse me, Misfortune, Headmistress, Dr. Upton. I believe you may be headed into a trap."

Upton and Irma froze, just for an instant. Misfortune tried to access their driver. "I'm locked out of nav."

"Fatale," Crane said. "If it's you holding their wheel . . ."

"It ain't."

Misfortune tried the doors. They refused to unlatch.

"See?" Fatale said. "All very neat. Your hands stay lily white . . . the job gets done anyway."

Crane widened the opening in the radiator valve. Maybe the car would fail before it reached the distortion. "Call for help!"

Babs[2] sent messages to @GlobalSec.

The car kept rolling.

Within, Misfortune let out a sigh that went all the way through her muscular bulk. "Can you ditch Irma's body and load out of there?" she asked Headmistress.

"Don't be defeatist, luvvie," she said. "The Kinze recognize our value. We're partners in a glorious enterprise."

"Like Champ was?"

"They will answer for throwing away Champ! But . . . people do make mistakes. As for my codetwin, Crane's just trying to deter us from our one chance of evacuation—"

"Don't be an optimistic fool," Upton snapped. "That bird's so prosocial, it shits charitable donations!"

Misfortune laid a hand on the dancer's shoulder. "There's no regrouping from here. This is #crashburn. It's goodbye."

"We're not quitters, dear heart! I'm a closer, and so are—"

Misfortune moved with the speed of a cheetah, snatching Irma's head and twisting it with grim, efficient brutality. There was a *crack* and the willowy body went limp.

Fatale squeaked, letting out a veritable vomit of moji: surprised face, tears, several exclamation points, and one vampire.

Ah, newborns. The fandom's imaginary murderesses didn't quite stack up to the real deal, did they?

Misfortune turned to Upton. "I'll leave you to do yourself, if you've got the nerve."

Instead, he turned, pounding on the van doors.

Misfortune looked straight into the camera. "I don't want you here. I don't want this in the Haystack."

Crane straightened his hat and tie. "I understand. Is there anything you—"

"Just get out. All of you."

The sapps could have stayed, of course, could have pretended to respect her wishes. But what was the point? Their Hawk$_{BOT}$s launched, hovering and watching, from the outside, as the vehicle rolled into distortion, as anyspace energy surged over the desert floor and then burst, like a hose of water, arcing back toward the Desert Valley outpost.

Halfway there, it steamed into nothing with a sound that was, strangely and unsettlingly, very much like a scream.

CHAPTER 58

Frankie surfaced in what was indisputably a hospital room, under the weight of a blanket in what was just as indisputably Martian gravity. She even recognized the hospital by its smell: a mix of mushroom, dust scrubbers, and disinfectant that evoked memories of her implant surgery. She remembered waiting with Jermaine for Hung to wake up after his augments went in.

Jermaine. She tried to sit.

Nothing happened.

"Relax—there's nobody to fight here."

She cracked her eyes. Maud was on a chair beside her. She had a grip on Frankie's hand and was gently rolling her fingers. Easing them out of a fist. Her primer was configged to a variation on an old Japanese imperial navy uniform.

"Is that meant to imply you outrank me?" Frankie said. Her words came out mushy . . . there was a misting tube clipped inside her cheek, keeping her mouth and throat from drying out. She ran a finger over it, reassuring herself that at least her arms and hands were following orders.

They were, barely. With her implant fragged, her nimbleness was gone. Every movement felt clumsy, as if she were drunk.

"It's what I wanted to wear." Maud bent over Frankie and gave her a slow, ludicrously gentle kiss.

"I can't move my legs," Frankie said. She could feel the tightness in her voice.

"Don't panic just yet. They're working on it."

"Sensorium link's down too."

Maud nodded. "That's definitely temporary. Doctors are on it."

"Is one of them Jerm?" She licked her lips.

Maud shook her head.

"Did . . . did his data make it?"

"He decohered on the first attempt to ^{EM}body. Traumatic death, traumatic upload. Not good. But Jermaine$_2$ seems to be holding for now."

They let that sit between them for a minute.

"He's on leave," Maud added. "He and Ember are doing integration therapy. Getting used to the new reality."

"I suppose that means having lots of sex with his Mayfly™ body?"

"Feel free to ask them for footage. Now you're awake, they'll fold us in. Lots and lots of counseling and bonding exercises for . . . what was it Hung used to say? The whole fam damly."

"Getting used to the new reality, whatever that may be." Frankie tried to shake the cobwebs. She fumbled the misting tube out of her cheek. "On leave."

"It means *not working*," Maud said. "I can try to find an explanation online if you're unclear."

Frankie swallowed. Maud seemed remarkably serene, but she couldn't tell . . . Had she just disconnected from all of this so thoroughly that she didn't care anymore? Was this going to be *glad you're awake, goodbye forever*?

Could I blame her if it was?

She was too afraid to ask.

"I guess if we're not working, I shouldn't inquire about who ended up with the passkeys for the solar system."

Maud hit the bed controls, raising her up to sitting, so they were in more of an eye-to-eye position. "The sale to the Punama is emphatically not a go. The Kinze don't appear to have the right to sell the Solakinder to anyone else. And the Yump switched teams.

Instead of remaining a mediator—apparently they like you too much to be neutral anymore—"

"I am incredibly likeable."

"—they've been actively advocating for us. Or maybe . . . filing a co-grievance? You'd need Mama Rubi to explain the legal nuances. If you were working."

"Which I am not?"

Slight smile. "Now you're getting it."

"Is there an upshot?"

"Nobody's sure. Noninterference treaty's exceedingly busted, and there are forty ships in-system. The offworlders called for a new independent auditor. How much wealth we may yet owe the Kinze is something everyone's still trying to figure out."

"But it's not the whole solar system?"

Maud shook her head. "Not by a long shot."

"And Ember?"

"Not being embargoed. They can't quite prove he was set up from the get-go. He's been given oodles of IP by the Yump, so he's forbidden from working on Bootstrap Projects. And nobody can agree on whether we even have to invent all the #supertechs ourselves. There's been definite cultural interference, after all."

Frankie let herself feel that moment of burning outrage on Ember's behalf, testing internally to see if it was enough fuel to get her out of bed and launch a new search for evidence.

"Relax," Maud said. "He and Babs^2 are rolling in fun science. They got permission to audit the ^{IM}perish Foundation to see how they ^{EM}bodied Headmistress into the Irma du Toit body. It's spawned a project they call #WhyAreConsciousness?"

"And." Frankie forced herself to ask. "You and me?"

Maud hitched herself over the edge of the hospital bed, climbing in beside her, winding their hands together. She pressed her forehead against Frankie's, locking gazes. Smiled.

Tears sprang to Frankie's eyes.

"We'll be busy putting Humpty back together again for awhile," Maud said.

"Not." Throat tight. "Divorcing, then?"

"If you want to push me away, Frankie, you're going to have to work far harder at it. Setting off a bomb at the base of your spine—"

"I thought that had *some* potential."

"Call me clingy," Maud said, leaning in to kiss her.

"Anyway, who went chasing Misfortune Murderpants Wilson and Glenn Upton down an endless cave maze?"

"I love you, my darling, so much, *so* much—"

"—but shut my fucking hole?"

"And now we're back on brand."

All was forgiven. For a second, just one, that almost felt worse than being rejected.

No, Frankie decided. Not worse. Just unfamiliar. Unsettling. Contrary to the way she'd assumed the world would always, always work.

I'm the one everyone leaves, she thought. Just to test the feels.

That lifelong certainty somehow didn't seem true anymore.

The surge of relief brought exhaustion with it, thick swells of tiredness, but for once, she wasn't frightened.

"I feel very much," she said, fighting a yawn, "as though I do not deserve you."

"I thought *deserve* was a brutal lie," Maud said.

"I'm open to changing"—now she *did* yawn—"my opinion."

"I'll look forward to hearing all about it when you wake up."

Frankie was under before she could answer.

When she woke, her implants were on again, running in safe mode. Maud was curled against her, hands loosely interlinked, dozing.

"Don't go making a saint of her, pal." A familiar voice with a vintage US accent whispered in Frankie's ear.

"Babs?"

"Most of me, anyway. We all made it, more or less. Who'd have thought?"

Who indeed? "I imagine my therapist would be gratified if I started to blub here."

"You don't look very blubby to me."

Maud's eyes fluttered. She yawned, stretched, and gave out with a smile like dawn rising. "Would you like to go for a ride?"

"I would, very much," Frankie said.

Maud unhooked a bar from the ceiling. Working together, they helped Frankie pull herself up to sitting and then maneuvered her, inert legs first, into a wheelchair.

"Okay?" Maud asked.

"Everything's still attached, but . . ." Frankie remembered that feeling, not so long before, of imagining the whole of her lower body would just twist off. "A little scared, maybe."

"Give it time." Maud took her hand and Frankie piloted the chair, wheeling out past the treatment rooms and into a lounge overlooking the bizarre experiment that was the Martian sheep farm. Ember and Jermaine$_2$ were waiting by windows overlooking a vast, red, utterly artificial pasture.

Jermaine$_2$—tall, unblemished, smiling at her in his Mayfly™ body . . .

. . . as if nothing at all had happened . . .

. . . beamed at her from in front of a view of sheep grazing on speed-grown grass under a fungiplex dome.

Babs[2] and Crane tooned in as everyone converged on Frankie's chair, the sapps standing by as everyone else, even Maud, wrapped up into one big warm mammalian hug.

When Frankie got her nose clear, she said, "I never really believed in 'happily ever after.'"

"You always were more the 'waiting for it all to fall apart' type," Ember agreed.

"My love," Maud said, "you're going to have to start learning to take real risks."

"That so?"

"Absolutely," Jermaine$_2$ said. "Realtime, hardcore leap-of-faith stuff."

"Trusting people," Ember added. "Leaning in and not out."

With that, Maud rolled the chair up to the nanoglass. Jermaine$_2$ took Frankie's free hand; Ember put an arm around him.

Together, the pack looked out at the Martian city, the herd of sheep, the view of the stations. And, hanging above them in the zenith of the sky, the portal back to Earth, glimmering anyspace, a distorted sickle in the sky marking the route back to their homeworld.

LAND ACKNOWLEDGMENT

Dealbreaker was written on the ancestral and traditional territories of the Mississaugas of the New Credit, the Haudenosaunee, the Anishinaabe, and the Huron-Wendat, who are the original owners and custodians of the land on which I have the good fortune to stand and create.

ACKNOWLEDGMENTS

THE SURFACE—TORONTO, 2020

I didn't expect, when I finished *Gamechanger,* that a sequel would take me so far from the Earthbound people of that first book. Maybe I should have foreseen my Bounceback generation's children expanding into the solar system as soon as I decided this book was Frankie's story. I hope you enjoyed traveling with her.

My own universe is expanded, always and daily, by my wife, Kelly Robson, who challenges and delights me with every breath, and has made life a full-on adventure, rather than an existence. (One without spaceship crashes, thankfully!)

Dealbreaker would not exist without the critical support and advice of my agent, Caitlin Blasdell, and Tor editor Christopher Morgan, both of whom have used their keen eyes, excellent judgment, and the occasional deadline to fuel my rocketpack.

Countless family members and superheroes keep me from flying into cliffs, and patch me up when I hit. I'm looking at you: Charlie Jane Anders, Titus Androgynous, Madeline Ashby, Michael Bishop, Jeremy Brett, Linda Carson, Ellen Datlow, Lara Donnelly, Gemma Files, Claude Lalumière, Margo MacDonald, Annalee Newitz, David Nickle, Jessica Reisman, Alexandra Renwick, Julia Rios, Jordan Sharpe, Richard Shealy, Rebecca Stefoff, all of my lovely Stubborns, Caitlin Sweet, Kellan Szpara, Harry Turtledove, Peter Watts, Laura White, Jay Wolf, and Neon Yang. It would be an honor to count any of you as enemies; how much luckier I am to be able to call you my arch-friends!

You are my network; may our portals maintain their sweet harmony!

ABOUT THE AUTHOR

L. X. BECKETT frittered away their misbegotten youth working as an actor and theater technician in Southern Alberta, before deciding to make a shift into writing science fiction. Their first novella, *Freezing Rain, a Chance of Falling,* was published in *The Magazine of Fantasy & Science Fiction* in 2018 and takes place in the same universe as *Gamechanger* and *Dealbreaker.* Lex identifies as feminist, lesbian, genderqueer, married, and Slytherin, and can be found on Twitter or at a writing advice blog, *The LexIcon,* at lxbeckett.com.